DEMON FLIGHT—

He had braved the Hounds of Night, Lord Azhrarn's deadly hunters that harried unfortunate souls to horrifying dooms. He had found the isle of mist where the Lord of Night's daughter languished, bespelled.

Now, awaking her to the knowledge of her power, he cast himself upon her mercy. For only the Daughter of Night could summon the demon steed to carry both the lady and her rescuer to freedom and safety in the world of men.

Yet quickly and secretly as they fled, the hunters still pursued them. Time was running out for the Daughter of Night and her Master of Delusion. Before them stood the gates dividing Underearth from the lands of men—gates that opened for none but Azhrarn, Lord of Night. Behind them raced the vengeful demon hordes. Now was the time for Azhrarn's daughter to prove the strength of her power—or face a truly demonic doom!

DELIRIUM'S MISTRESS

A Novel of the Flat Earth

Tanith Lee

DAW BOOKS, INC.

DONALD A. WOLLHEIM, PUBLISHER

1633 Broadway, New York, NY 10019

Illustrations by Tanith Lee.
Cover art by Michael R. Whelan.
For color prints of Michael Whelan paintings, please contact:

Glass Onion Graphics
P.O. Box 88
Brookfield, CT 06804

DAW Collectors Book No. 674.

First Printing, June 1986
1 2 3 4 5 6 7 8 9
Printed in the U.S.A.

AUTHOR'S NOTE

Concerning those other histories referred to in *Delirium's Mistress:*

The stories of Zhirek the Magician, and of Simmu who stole Immortality from the gods, and of the city Simmurad, are to be found in *Death's Master*. As are the stories of Narasen and her pact with Death, and of Kassafeh and hers. And of the dealings of Lylas, too.

The stories of Shezael the Half-Souled, of the poet Kazir and Ferazhin Flower-Born, of Sivesh, of Zorayas the witch-queen, and of Bakvi the Drin (and, too, of Azhrarn's first meeting with the sun) are told in *Night's Master*.

Dunizel's story, and that of her mother, are contained in *Delusion's Master*, along with the account of the building— and fall—of the great Tower, Baybhelu.

FOREWORD

IT HAS BEEN recounted* how, in the days of the earth's flatness, Azhrarn, the Prince of Demons, Night's Master, one of the Lords of Darkness, loved the maiden Doonis-Ezael or Dunizel (Moon's Soul), a priestess of the holy city Bhelsheved. And that because of the value he set on her (but mostly, let it be said, to make mischief in those lands, which had angered him), he got her sorcerously with child.

When this child, a daughter, was born, Dunizel was condemned by her people, who greatly feared, yet did not fully comprehend, the powers of Azhrarn. And despite the safeguards her demon lover had left her, she perished.

Now, her death seemed due to a trick played by another of the Lords of Darkness, Prince Chuz, whose other name is Madness, Delusion's Master. Therefore Azhrarn, meeting with Chuz, swore they should thenceforth be enemies, and that, no matter where he might hide himself, Chuz should be hunted down and the vengeance of the Demon completed on him. Such a thing was very terrible indeed, that any of the immortal and mighty Lords of Darkness should wage war with each other. ''Do you think I shake at you?'' inquired Chuz. Yet it is possible he was not quite sanguine at the development, for all that.

Dunizel alone had Azhrarn loved; for the child, she had never been more than a game piece to him. However, he had noted the speculative eye of Chuz upon her. In anguish and fury, then, Azhrarn bore her to his city of Druhim Vanashta, underground.

*Delusion's Master.

CONTENTS

BOOK ONE

Sovaz:
Mistress of Madness

1

IT WAS DUSK, and for a while the young man seated on the high roof gazed up into the great sloping dome of sky. Then he read aloud from his book: "Blue as the dark blue eyes of my beloved, the twilight fills all heaven. The stars put on their silver dresses and they are fair, but none as fair as she." His companions lay on their elbows and looked at him, quizzically. He shut the book and said, "Love, too, is simple madness."

At which they made wild gestures of dismissal.

"Love does not exist. 'Love' is the name women, and their wretched old fathers, put on the trap of a ring."

"Love is lust. Why make songs about an itch?"

The first young man smiled. He was unusually handsome, pale, very fair, with beautiful eyes the color of low-burning lampshine. In repose, there was a sweetness to him. With sweet melancholy, he sighed.

"Ah, poor thing," they said. "What troubles him this evening, our Oloru?"

Oloru said, "An answer, which has no question."

"A riddle!" cried the other young men. They grinned and shouted: "Make us laugh, Oloru."

And all at once the eyes of Oloru glittered like the eyes of a night-hunting fox. He sprang to his feet, curled over, next dropped in a ball, next lifted his whole body straight in the air, supporting himself by one hand, palm down, on the roof. Then he began, on this one hand, to hop about, crying out all the while in a raucous irritated voice: "Oh, how tiresome this is. You would think by now the gods could have invented a better way for a man to travel."

13

The companions, duly diverted, laughed, applauded, and called the entertainer names. Oloru went on hopping, though one of his fine silk gloves was by now probably quite ruined. He hopped to the western parapet, and here his slim upside-down body wavered, so the stars seemed juggled between his feet. "Behold," said Oloru, "here the sun fell over." And he toppled sideways through blue dusk and stars, and right across the parapet, and vanished.

The remaining young men on the tavern roof leapt to their feet with yells of horror, upsetting wine jars and other paraphernalia. Oloru was a favorite of their lord, one of the magician-princes of this city. To take this powerful man the tale of said Oloru, smashed on the cobbles seven stories below, was not a charming notion.

But rushing to the parapet and leaning over, they could be sure of nothing in the narrow alley but the gathering of darkness.

Elsewhere, the city spread around them under the sky, its terraces pearl-strung with lamps, its towers bright-eyed with lit windows. Nowhere in that city could they be safe if they once angered their prince, Lak Hezoor. While close at hand rose the palace of this very lord, each of its spires made into a somber candle by the cresset ablaze on its roof, and each cresset seeming now to glare over at them intently.

Consternation. Some ran onto the stair, meaning to descend and search the street on foot. Others were already making up excuses for a violent death that had nothing whatever to do with them. In the midst of this, suddenly Oloru stepped out of a climbing fruit tree that spread its branches along the eastern parapet.

"Yes, love is madness," said Oloru. "As all things are madness. Piety, wickedness, pleasure, sorrow—every one an insanity. Indeed, to live at all—"

"*Oloru!*" cried the young men. Two of them ran forward as if to thrash him.

Oloru shrank back against the tree. He lifted both hands in their gemmed gloves, to shield himself. "No—forgive me, my friends—what have I done to anger you?"

The friends gathered menacingly. Oloru was at all times the veriest coward. They knew he would be terrified by a threat or a raised fist. So they berated him, and he grew paler and paler and shrank back into the slender arms of the fruit tree. He explained, stammering somewhat, that he had caught the stonework under the parapet and thus eased himself along the side of the building, unseen, to the tree. Here he had clambered once more to safety. He had not meant to annoy them, only to amuse. They allowed him to go on and on, enjoying his faltering musical voice, his eyes swimming and full of tears of anxiety. In the end, when they had squeezed him sufficiently, and it seemed only the fragile tree kept him on his feet, they relented, flung their arms around him, kissed him and smoothed his golden hair, swearing they forgave him anything, he was so dear to them. Then he tremblingly laughed. He thanked them. When they asked, he took up a lyre of gilded wood and sang for them exquisitely. His voice was so beautiful, in fact, that here and there round about shutters opened quietly. Lovers and losers together leaned into the night, to catch the flavor of Oloru's song.

> *"In the lyre-land, string and chord,*
> *Bring me music in a word.*
> *Bring me magic in a look;*
> *For your eyes are like a sword,*
> *And your smile is like a bird*
> *Singing from an ancient book. . . ."*

And "How you flatter me, Oloru," someone said. "But you always do flatter better than any other, and perfectly in key."

Lak Hezoor the magician-prince, clad in dark finery, and with two guards behind him, had come up on the roof very silently. He and his minions could move most quietly, when they wished, and such noiseless arrivals were a habit of his. In this way he often happened on his courtiers at their various and more intimate games. All had grown careful, even in the most frenzied acts of the flesh, to think, and if necessary to speak, well of their lord. Shadowy as his raiment was his long curled hair, and on the gloved hands of Lak Hezoor jewels burned dark as the night had now become. Two great leashed hounds, by contrast blond as Oloru, stared about them, quivering with abstract eagerness for things to chase and rend.

The young men had all obeised themselves. But it was Oloru the magician-prince raised in his arms and kissed on the lips, without haste.

"We are going hunting tonight," said Lak Hezoor.

Those on the roof who had had other plans for the evening quickly dismissed them from their minds. Only Oloru was heard to say plaintively, "My lord, I hate to see anything killed—"

"Then, sweetheart," said Lak Hezoor, "at the supreme moments of the death you may hide your face in my mantle, and not look."

The moon was rising in the hour the hunt set out. It was a full moon that night, and certain exhalations and smokes of the sorcerously tempered city made her appear unusually large, so she dwarfed the towers as she hung above them. She blushed, too, standing there over that place, and drew a cloud around herself. But her feverish light burned through, and laved the black horses and the black or white hounds of Lak Hezoor, and flashed on the loudly blowing horns, the knives and jewels, and in all the host of eyes.

The city disgorged the hunt, its gates flying wide before it without a command needing to be given. Beyond, a long paved road opened through the plain. To either side of the road ran lush fields and groves and vineyards, but off to the west was hill country and a forest many centuries older. Strange stories were told of the forest. Men wandered in there and were never seen again, or other things, not men at all, wandered out of it, sometimes having human shape, and sometimes not. But the magician-masters of the city found the forest tempted them from time to time. Particularly it tempted Lak Hezoor, who was intellectually obsessed by night and all dark things, just as his flesh was inflamed equally by examples of exceptional paleness.

It was a time of harvesting, and now and then the hunt, riding hard and savagely as if already in pursuit of the quarry, passed by some firelit camp of people, or some village set near the road. Then all the lowly folk gathered there would rush forward to the road's edge, calling aloud praises on the magician-princes, and on Lak Hezoor in person if they recognized him. It would not have been sensible to do otherwise. Seldom, however, did Lak Hezoor pay any attention. It happened, though, when the upswept black walls of the forest were less than a mile ahead, that the sorcerer lord did spy something that checked him. There in a meadow a tallow lamp had been hung from a pole, with a kneeling man under it. Close by a girl was tied to a tree. In the faint lamplight, she shone pale as a pearl, and her long ash-brown hair, woven with white flowers, was her only garment.

When Lak Hezoor drew rein, his company with him, the man ran up and kneeled again on the road.

"Speak," said Lak Hezoor.

"She is my sister's daughter, just fifteen years of age, a virgin."

Lak Hezoor sat his horse and looked over at the girl, while his courtiers slyly and fawningly smiled at him and at each other.

"Once," said the lord Lak, "maidens were left in this way to entice dragons. Are you expecting any dragons?"

"No—oh, *no*, mighty Hezoor. It is just the wish of the girl's heart to give you a moment's diversion, that is all."

Lak Hezoor dismounted. He walked away over the meadow to the tree where the girl hung as if half-dead of terror. For a second more the magician was visible, leaning to his dragon's prey. Then a fan of blackness spread there, occluding both of them. While in the blackness a dull reddish snake of fire seemed to twist, and sparks burst, hurting the eyes of any who still peered in that direction. Once, twice, a sharp scream pierced the sorcerous veil, but nothing else of sight or sound.

The man who had brought the lord his niece waited patiently, eyes lowered. The courtiers sipped wine from golden flasks, petted their horses, discussed fashions and gambling.

Lak was not long over his transaction. Quite abruptly he returned through the black screen, calm and undisheveled as if he had paused to taste some fruit from a wayside bush. The sorcerous screen began to die at once behind

him. There showed now something pallid flung on the
ground, motionless, amid torn hair and broken flowers.

"What did you hope from me?" asked Lak Hezoor of
the patiently waiting uncle. "Not anything much, I trust,
for she was very disappointing."

"No—oh, *no*. Nothing but to please you, lord."

"Well, I was not greatly pleased. But you meant for the
best. I will not chastise you. Are you content with that?"

"Mighty lord, I am your generosity's slave."

As they galloped away, a backward glance revealed the
man bending over the paleness in the grass, which did not
answer him even when he gave it blows.

"Now, my Oloru," said the magician-prince as they
rode up to the tall gates of the forest, "you seem downcast."

"I?" said Oloru. "I was only devising a poem to honor
you."

"Ah," said Lak Hezoor. "That is well. Later you shall
tell it me."

The depths of the forest, then. Not its heart; it was so
old, so labyrinthine, the forest—who could enter the heart
of it, save some lost traveler in one of the sinister tales? Or
else, perhaps, the forest had many hearts, each slowly and
mesmerically beating, its rhythm growing a fraction slower
and an iota more strong for every passing century.

Certainly, there were portions of the forest where its
atmosphere seemed especially and profoundly charged. In
one of these spots there was a pool of unknown deepness
where the animals of the forest, whatever they might be,
would steal to drink. Although it was said that any man
who drank the waters of the forest would be changed at
once into just such an animal himself—a deer, a wolf, a
sprite, or some monstrous creature that had no name.

All about the pool was blackness, but through the colossal roofbeams of the trees there showed the rim of the
moon. She was no longer blushing but cold now, and her
snowy fire turned the mysterious water to a solid white
mirror one might think to walk on.

Thrice, Lak Hezoor's men had started deer. Pale as
ghosts they sprang away, and the hunt madly pursued
them. Torchlight crackled through the boughs. Shouting

and whooping tore the curtains of leafy air. Sometimes the noise and tumbling speed and spilling lights disturbed curious birds—or winged things of some sort—which rose away into the higher tiers of the branches. On occasion disembodied eyes were lit, and as quickly extinguished. As for the quarry, twice it vanished without trace. But when the third deer broke from cover, Lak Hezoor cast a shining ray about it like a net. Try as it would then, bolt and swerve and seem to fly, the deer could not break free of his magic. Loudly it panted, and groaned like a woman in childbirth, so the hair of the magician's courtiers bristled on their necks. But at length the deer stumbled and the torrent of the hounds swept over it.

Though a female, it was a huge beast, this deer. So the hunting party was satisfied, for the moment, and made their way into the clearing, to the pool like solid mirror, and dared each other to taste of the water, but none of them did. Instead they lolled on the rugs and bolsters the servants of Lak Hezoor put down for them, and drank wine in glass goblets that the fires turned to golden tears.

Lak Hezoor himself oversaw the gutting of the deer, and now and then himself threw portions of its entrails to his favorites among the shivering dogs. Nearby, Oloru leaned on a tree, his face averted, and his gloved hand lightly over his nose and mouth.

"Come, be my hound, beloved, and I will throw you a piece of its liver," said Lak Hezoor.

Oloru shuddered, looked at his lord under long lashes, and away.

When Lak Hezoor lost interest in the bloody work, he went to sit among the cushions and fires. He beckoned Oloru to follow him.

"Now sing for me the song you were making in my honor," said Lak Hezoor.

"It is not finished," said Oloru, in an offhand way.

Lak Hezoor turned one of the rings on his left hand. It dazzled a searing ray—it was this very ring which had cast the net about the deer and so weakened and killed it. The ring had done as much for men.

"I give Oloru," said Lak Hezoor, "three of his own

heartbeats to complete the song. And since his heart now beats very fast, I think the time is already up.''

Oloru lowered his eyes that were like smoky amber. He sang, sweetly, swiftly, and with utmost clarity:

> *"Our lord found a girl in a field,*
> *Not with cash but with malice he bought her.*
> *He took her behind a black shield,*
> *But one fact he has surely revealed:*
> *He makes love as another makes water."*

For a troupe so loud, the assemblage now proved itself capable of a vast silence. With their eyes and mouths open, men stared at Oloru, goblets halfway to their lips and frozen. By the pavilion of sable satin, the servitors of the magician-prince, which some said were themselves not quite human, stood blank-visaged as ever, yet every hand now rested on the hilt of a long knife.

Having recited, Oloru looked into the face of his lord, smiling a little, and Lak Hezoor looked back at him with the same smile exactly. Then Lak Hezoor stood up, and Oloru also arose. Lak Hezoor snapped his fingers, and out of the air itself appeared his sword, and slid into his grasp. Lak Hezoor extended the cruel bright blade until the tip of it touched Oloru on the breast.

"Now I shall kill you," said Lak Hezoor. "It will be thorough but slow. Indeed, you shall fight me for your death. You will have to earn it."

And Lak Hezoor spoke a sorcerous word and a second blazing sword fell into the hand of Oloru, who, whiter than the moon in the pool now, dropped the weapon at once.

"Pick it up," said Lak Hezoor. "Pick up the sword, my child, and we will dally a while. Then I will cut you up for chops for my dogs, an inch at a time."

"My—lord—" whispered Oloru, standing shaking above the fallen sword, "it was a jest, and I—"

"And you shall die for your jest. For it did not make me laugh, my Oloru, so something else is needed to entertain me."

"Oh gracious lord—"

"Pick up the sword, dear heart. Pick it up."

"I beg you—"

"Pick it up. Why should it be said I kill my friends unarmed?"

"Then I will leave it lying—"

"Then I will kill you defenseless after all."

Oloru covered his face with his hands. Under the torches he, like the glassware, seemed made of pale precious gold, and of tears, too.

"Forgive me, oh forgive me—" he cried.

Lak Hezoor grinned, pulled down Oloru's hands, and pointed to the sword lying in the grass.

"Look at that, pick up that, and die with it."

Oloru looked one long last minute at the sword, and then he dropped down in the grass beside it and lay there, in a dead faint, at the feet of Lak Hezoor.

At this, the magician did laugh. He flung one glance across his silent court. It cut them with such contempt and indifference, and under that with such implicit threat, it was as if he had sliced at each of them with the blade he held. Then the blade vanished, and with it the other in the grass; all about the hands of the prince's minions left their knives. Lak Hezoor lifted Oloru in his arms and walked away with him and into the sable pavilion, out of their sight.

Out of sight of any but his prince then, Oloru the jester and poet presently revived. He came to himself on the magician's silks, his face turned on the magician's embroidered pillows, the weight of Lak Hezoor already upon him.

"You, my treasure, who dare insult me as no other does," murmured Lak Hezoor, resting his face also down on the pillow, so his black eyes glared into the amber eyes of Oloru and their lips almost met at each word. "But I forgive you. For you know you lied."

"O my soul, my body's watchman, you were absent when this citadel was invaded," said Oloru. Lak Hezoor smiled cruelly at him, for this was very true.

"Tell me of demons," said Lak Hezoor, as his sinuous body stirred and curved, heavy as a python, upon and within his third prey of the night. "Tell me of Azhrarn, Night's Master, the Bringer of Anguish."

Oloru spoke softly, sometimes without breath.

"They saw a king's daughter, a sorceress, called to him by means of a token Azhrarn once gave his lover, a beautiful boy, Sivesh, or as some say, Simmu. And when the Demon came to her, this sorceress, it was in a pavilion with a ceiling of blackness and jeweled stars, where winds and clouds moved, but only by mage-craft. Azhrarn mistook the pavilion's roof for the sky, as he was intended to, and thought he should gain fair warning of sunrise, for the sun slays demons, they say. They saw—" (Here Oloru broke off. But: "Say on, my Sivesh, my Simmu," insisted Lak Hezoor.) "Then—trapped by the witch, the sun having risen unseen beyond the pavilion's false night, Azhrarn must deal with her and grant her all she wished: power, riches, beauty beyond all beauty—*beauty*—" (And here Oloru could say no more, only cling to the pillows, his spine arched, and his throat, and through his golden lashes the tears running like silver ribbons.)

But when the python lay quiet on him and the heavy silken darkness of the tent returned from out of blood-red thunder, Oloru said, "Yet, if she was so great a sorceress, why did she not grant herself these things, why did she not make herself so beautiful? Ah, then, because the genius of her sorcery was built on rage, and rage does not make beauty. And her yearning was for love, so that only love could work miracles upon her, even his love, Azhrarn, that Prince of Demons. And besides, it is not certain any such token could summon him if truly he would not be summoned. Nor must he definitely grant wishes at the summons. Nor could such as he be made a fool of by a ceiling of jewel stars and illusory winds. Unless he had desired the novelty, desired dangers and a snare to befall him. Madness, Lak Hezoor," said Oloru, "is no respecter of persons. We perceive even the mighty Prince Azhrarn has been its gull. But a short while since, he was mad of love, for love is simple madness. A girl with moon hair and twilight eyes. Love and death and time sweep over all events. And madness sings on top of the dunghill, to the accompanying music of an ass's jawbones."

But Lak Hezoor slept. He lay deep in sleep as if drowning in a muddy river. So he did not see, nor feel, Oloru begin to ease from under him. Nor did he witness, the mighty magician-prince, what finally emerged from the couch, jumped to the floor, and paused there an instant, in the murk of the dying candles.

Men who drank from the waters of the forest might be altered—to animal or elemental, or to monster. But Oloru had drunk only the best wine. It was not the crystal ichor of the forest, then, which worked this change in him.

Outside, the magician's courtiers slept. The servants slept or stood tranced, lacking his bidding. So none started when there stole out from the tent a yellow jackal with dry embers for eyes. It looked about, its mouth agape as if it laughed, then turned and trotted away among the black robes of the trees.

2

NIGHT ON the earth, every inch of it, for the earth was flat and up in that domed ceiling of heaven the lamp of day was out. Not a forest of earth then that was not black, not a sea that was not black and ribbed with silver by the moon; not a mountain that was not crowned by stars. But down below, held in the inverted underdome beneath the earth, it was not night, nor was it ever night, there.

Underearth, the demon country, bloomed in the endless changeless glow that exhaled from its very air. That light, they say, radiant as the sun, subtle as the moon, lovelier than either. And in that light, stretched the landscape of a dark impassioned dream. And, seemingly made of that light, a city rose into the lambency of an indescribable and nonexistent sky.

The city of the demons was ultimately also changeless. There it glimmered and gleamed and sparkled, putting the marvels of the world to shame. And yet, Druhim Vanashta (whose very name means, if approximately, Who Shines Without the Sun, and More Brightly), Druhim Vanashta had about it a strange shadow, which had nothing to do with the glowing shade of Underearth. It was rather the pall of a desolate and grinding and relentless—and *silent*— lament: the mourning of Azhrarn.

Some time had passed on the earth. Years, perhaps. And under it, too, time had passed, the time of demonkind which was not of the same order, though time still. But it was the curse and glory of the Vazdru, that highest caste of the demons, of whom Azhrarn was one, that in time or out of it nothing might ever be forgotten. Not the greatest sweetness. Not the most tearing agony or grief. And the adage ran that the wounded hearts of demon could be salved only by human blood.

However, he had taken no revenge, Azhrarn, exacted no penalty.

It is seldom disputed that, of all his many and various loves, he had loved her best, Dunizel, Soul of the Moon. White-haired, blue-eyed as early evening, in whose body he had grown, like a wondrous flower, his child. It is suggested there should be no surprise in the delay or absence of retribution. She had been so gentle, so compassionate. She had taken even that means away from him, for a little while. To think of her and plan deeds of blood was not easy, maybe. No, it was his heart which bled. And his pain which clouded the city.

Nor did he seek solace in his daughter. It had been his contention from the start, forming the child for wickedness as he had meant to do, that this offspring—though carried in Dunizel's womb—was all his and only his, the female principle of Azhrarn, whose role and aims were cruelty and maleficence and lies. Therefore it seems he could not bear to look at her now. Could not bear also, conceivably, to look in her eyes, blue as blueness, that were the eyes of her mother.

Thus he had brought her to his country but sent her far off from his haunts. And left her there, far off.

There was a vast tidal lake, or a small inland sea—either or both. It lay, in a man's reckoning, three days' journey from the demon city, yet of course in demonic parlance three days have no meaning at all. It was as near, or as distant, as will could make it.

In the crystal air of the Underearth, the waters of the lake, too, were like crystal. So clear they were, it was possible to see right to their floor, which looked to be a long way down. Here shapes moved, seeming weeds and sands, and winged fish flying. But though the water was transparent, the passage of the tide made vision uncertain. How there came to be a tide was itself unsure. The water obeyed, perhaps, the drag of the hidden moon of earth so many miles overhead; or else the drag of some other hidden moon *beneath*, in the substance of chaos which flowed beyond and about all things, earth or Upperearth, or the subterrain.

From the crystal sea-lake rose islands. Many were slender, of a circumference only big enough a bird might try to perch there, had there been birds. Several were the size of earthly ships, and masted and sailed with heavy midnight trees that drooped down into the water, but not reflecting in it, since it was so clear. Then again, in places smooth tall pillars of rock went up, thousands of feet high, like windowless towers. In all of them, the little rocks and the great, burning colors pulsed and faded, swelled and went out and ignited again. And the sea-lake did mirror these colors, so it seemed stained here with wine, and here with a flickering dark lamplight, and there with translucent heliotrope, like the blood of the gods themselves.

Somewhere in the midst of the water and the fantastic rocks, one island lay which was of larger horizontal scope and different appearance. It did not throb with colors; only a mist normally surrounded it, so it seemed like a phantom, not entirely present in the lake, as, indeed, maybe it was not.

To view this island, one must pass within the mist, which had never been done. Those that dwelled there had

preceded the fashioning of the mist. No one had visited the
island, or come away from it, since then.

She lived inside a hollow stone, the daughter of Azhrarn.
That the stone was beautiful in its cold pure way did not
much concern her, if at all. It was a cliff of quartz galler-
ied and windowed and staired apparently by random ero-
sions, pierced by a hundred caves. The light which never
altered gamboled and slid about the cliff, and winked from
each of its facets. The pearly mist stole in from the sea and
threaded through the openings, so the whole edifice seemed
to float. And sometimes a wind fluttered in and out, and
then the cliff played weird chiming, thrumming notes, as if
the structure were one huge instrument of strings and
pipes.

Two of the greater caves had become rooms. They were
furnished—at the order of Azhrarn, probably, how else?
Yet if it was his doing, he had not come to look at the
results. Draperies hung there and carpets, and silks lay
thick on the ground, and lamps rested in the air which
would light themselves at a whim, not to give illumination, but to tint and highlight something or other. These
rooms had windowpanes of painted glass that showed
pictures which occasionally altered, telling stories, if any
had observed them.

In an annex there was a crimson bed with columns of
deep-red jade, and filmy curtains.

Here lay a doll on its back, all white in a dress of white
tissue, save the black hair blacker than blackness, that
curled around her and down onto the floor, and the open
eyes so blue they seemed half blinded by their own color.
Did she, looking through those sapphire lenses, see a
world shaded by them also to blue? Who could tell? Who
would ask? Certainly she would not say. For she had never
spoken, no, not even when in the world with her mother.
Vazdru child, yet she had had that way of the demon
Eshva, the servants, the handmaidens of the Vazdru. The
Eshva did not communicate save with eyes, with touch,
with the rhythm of their breathing—yet having such intensity in this mode that they might be said to have spoken.
Those few mortals who spent childhood in their company

(Sivesh, the lover of Azhrarn, for example; Simmu, who once mastered Death) were heard after to refer to Eshva *voices*. . . . But it was a figure of speech, it seems. For the daughter of Azhrarn, she too had known Eshva. They had attended her birth. They had given her demon blood to drink, and steeped her in an enchanted smoke. Brought here to the island and the hollow cliff, a band of Eshva had come with her, to serve and tend her. But these Eshva pined. Far from Azhrarn, whom they loved beyond all things, far from the burning dream of the world that was their dancing floor, they moved like shadows, and their tears fell. Their tears which said: *I despair*. They entered a sort of living death, these immortal beings. The singing cliff seemed full of sad songs.

Sometimes the girl looked at them as if she pitied them. She did not want slaves by her, yet they might not leave. But who would guess if she pitied them? And she would not say.

She entered Underearth as a tiny child, though seeming already older and more formed than a human infant. Exposed to the aura of Azhrarn's kingdom, she fell for a while into a kind of daze, and then years came upon her like whirlwinds, twisting and pulling at her, speeding her growth so rapidly that sometimes her skin itself was torn by her bones, and her dark blood—*demon's blood*—ran and gushed on the ground. When it happened, she cried out, she screamed, for she had a voice to use for this. In the length of seventeen mortal days—hours, moments, in the Underearth—she grew to be some seventeen years.

At this time, the Eshva had attempted to console her. They had soothed her, caressed her, brushing her with their hair, drugging her with their perfumed sighs. When the terrible process stopped, accomplished, and did not resume, still for a while they seemed to wish to divert her. But she became an icon then, awake yet sleeping. A closed door. And gradually the Eshva dropped away from her like moths with broken wings.

They wandered the island, her servitors, her fellow prisoners and exiles. Their noiseless ennui and wretchedness soon embued every valley and height of it. She was, after all, Vazdru, a princess. The leaden nothingness she had succumbed to bruised and damaged them. They paled, they faded.

She, too, sometimes traversed the island. But even as she walked, she slept. Somnambulist, she would hesitate on the brink of some precipice, from which, being what she was, no doubt in any case she could not fall. Or, hearing the music of her cliff in the distance, she might turn her head. But when the mist about the island thinned a little, and the Eshva would creep gracefully down to the shore and stand there, gazing to the sea beyond, she did not stir.

No doubt, too, she had learned many things without any tutor, had been born, even, with knowledge denied to humankind. No doubt too and too, she did not know what knowledge was, or its value. Nor what she herself was or might be. That she remembered her beginning, the mother who had told stories to her while she was yet in the womb, the awful death of that mother, her own first abandonment to men, her second to the island, so much is unarguable. Yet even these memories did not seem to move her to any expression. Even if she was aware of it, she did not *know* what she was. How then could she express anything?

She lay on her royal bed in the Underearth, three days away, or three thousand years away, from Druhim Vanashta. Perhaps she even felt, like the dim echo of some gigantic exploding star, the resonance of Azhrarn's mourning. But if she did, it gave her nothing, it asked nothing, it turned its face from her.

And so she was—or so she was not.

3

"HE IS NOT a bad son," said the widow. She
wrung her hands and paced up and down. "Those that
speak of him, speak well. But then they were afraid of the
master he serves. They will not speak ill of my son for fear
it should seem they speak ill of Prince Lak. But they look
askance. Do you hear much from your Oloru, they say,
and their eyes say, He is a cheat and a deceiver, a buffoon
of the court who practices all its vices." She sat down in a
chair. Her elder daughter, who had heard her mother
pacing and come in to comfort her, now took the widow's
hand. "But I say this," said the widow, "it is a weakness
in him. Only a weakness. Do we blame a man who is born
without sight, or a man whose leg is broken and who
walks crookedly thereafter? Why then blame a boy whose
spirit is unable to see and whose nature has been warped?
Can he help it any more than the poor blind man or the
unlucky cripple?"

"There, there, Mother," said the daughter, who was
young and fair and golden, somewhat like Oloru himself.

"You are a good girl," said the mother. "Both good
girls. But oh, my son."

In the window the sky was black and many-starred
though the moon had gone down. It would not be dawn for
two hours or more. Away beyond the walls of the old
house, the ancient forest (the same in which Prince Lak
now hunted) could be seen raising its spears and plumes to
the sky. Nearby, a ribbon of road turned against the trees
toward the city. Along that very road a year since, Oloru
had traveled. Wellborn though poor, he meant, he said, to

29

find some great lord who would be his patron. And he had found one. He had found Lak, whose vile hungers and bestial unkindnesses overtopped the misdeeds of all his fellow princes put together.

"Oloru should have stayed at home with us," said the mother. "He was happy with us."

"Perhaps he is also happy now," said the elder daughter, sadly.

His letters had given them to think so. He did not mention what he did at the court of the magician, but only the rich food and fine clothes, and always he sent extravagant presents.

"It was the forest," said the mother in a whisper now. "The forest is to blame."

The elder daughter glanced at the window and made a little sign against evil enchantment.

It was a fact, a month before Oloru had undertaken to seek his fortune in the city, there had been a strange incident, though not a rare one for those who lived in the periphery of the forest. Even by day, the wise did not venture there, but Oloru, the widow's only son, had always scorned such superstition. Now and then he would hunt these woods himself, and bring back game, for which the house was grateful enough. Then came an afternoon when their servant, the only retainer left to them, hastened home alone. Oloru had gone out with him at sunrise, but somehow they had been separated in the trees. Then the servant had searched all morning, and long past noon, but could not discover the young man or any trace of him. At last the servant returned to his mistress the widow, in trepidation.

A few terrible hours then passed in the worst perplexity and distress. Though she dared not venture into the forest, the mother stood at her gate, and the two fair daughters and the servant with her. There they stayed, praying or weeping or silent, or trying to reassure each other, or calling Oloru's name vainly, shading their eyes against the westering sun and gazing at the trees as if by desperation alone they could draw him forth again. The sun began to go down in a curdle of fire, the road, the house, the waiting figures, all were dyed red, and the trees all black with their tops seeming to burn. Suddenly something moved out from the blackness into the redness. There on the road, walking toward them, was a fifth figure, that of a young man. Oloru.

The household flew toward him, laughing and crying at once. And he too began to run toward them, his arms outstretched.

Then, there seemed to come a curious check. The widow and her daughters faltered and stopped still; the servant drew up with a muttered oath. For himself, Oloru also halted. He lowered his eyes and next his head with a modest shyness.

The mother stared at him. What was it? Was this her son?—yes, yes, who else but he? Her own Oloru that she had thought lost to her. Although— She looked and looked, and her heart beat loudly enough to deafen her and to muddy her eyes, so in the end she thought it was only that. Then she ran forward again and embraced him and he in turn embraced her, and said, "Mother, pardon me for alarming you so. I mistook my way. But as you see, I regained a path and have come back to you." And while he spoke his bright hair brushed her cheek and it seemed to her she knew him, of course she did, he was her son.

Yet to the sisters also, and to the servant, there had at first seemed something not right, something bizarre. Later, the elder girl had a dream, and in the dream the left side of her brother's face, as he returned out of the forest, was covered by a half-mask of enamel, and when he drew it off, his own face under it had changed to that of a decaying and horrific male devil. The younger sister also had a dream in which the eyes of her brother had become like the sunset, black and red, and she woke up shrieking. But these dreams were soon forgotten, for there was nothing amiss with Oloru, it was only their troubled fancy. He was as he had always been, golden and handsome, and full of jokes and poetic reveries.

It seemed to them they loved him more than ever in that month, after thinking they had lost him. And then he left them for the city and the magician-lords, and was lost to them in truth.

Presently it was the mother's turn for nightmares, and

often she would rise and pace about, and if her daughters heard her they would come in to comfort her. And she would say, "He is not bad." She would say, "It is a weakness." And she would say, "It is the forest's fault. The forest is to blame."

Now the elder daughter rose and said, "I will light another candle; this one is almost out. Let us be as cheerful as we can. Who knows, he may tire of that other life."

The mother sighed deeply.

Oloru's elder sister went to fetch a second candle. As she did so she passed the window, and happening to look out she gave a sharp cry

"What is it?" exclaimed the mother.

"There—by the well—a great pale animal with ghastly eyes—"

The mother hastened to look. Huddled in the window, the two women stared down at the courtyard. The gate was locked at night, and surely nothing could get in. Nevertheless, there beyond the stone curb of the well, something moved.

"Even by starshine I saw it," said the girl. "As if it glowed of itself."

"Lift up the candle," said the mother. "Let us see this thing and be sure."

So the feeble candle was lifted, and a little more light fell into the yard. Around the well at once and out of the shadow of a tree which grew there something swiftly came, and the girl parted her lips to scream.

But, "Oh, the blessed gods," the widow said. "What were you thinking of? It is your brother."

And there under their window stood Oloru, looking himself like a prince, his eyes fixed on them, more beautiful than all the jewels with which he was dressed.

Soon the whole house was roused and down in the antique pillared hall with Oloru. It was a sad place, this hall, for there were not enough servants now to keep it as it should be kept, and all the best things had been sold years since. But a good wine was lugged up from the cellar, and a host of candles fired.

"I cannot stay with you long," said Oloru. "But I will return shortly. Then *he* will be with me."

"What can you mean?" cried the widow in horror.

"What you think I mean. I intend to bring Lak Hezoor the magician home with me, to be our guest. He will sit here and we will dance attendance on him. He will see my two sisters and lust after both of them."

The sisters shrank. The elder said, uncertainly, "Do you jest with us, brother?" But the widow cried, "He has gone mad!"

Oloru laughed at that. He flung up his arms, and looked some while at the spiders' webs in the rafters. "Do you not trust me, dear Mother? I, your only son?"

A cold breath seemed then to blow through the hall. The candles felt it and sank. The women felt it and they trembled. But then Oloru brought his gaze down from the rafters and he said gently, "It is perilous, this enterprise, but I must do it. Once it might have been done another way, easier, and more gaudy. But as things are now, I require such means as you."

"What are you saying?" asked the widow.

Oloru seemed puzzled. "I hardly know. But this I will promise—no harm shall come to any of you, I swear. What shall I swear on?"

The three women eyed him in dismay and fascination.

At last the mother said, "Swear on your life."

"My life? No, on something better than that. I will swear it by the power of love."

The candles straightened up. The coldness went away as if it had heard enough.

"What are we saying?" asked the mother. "This is all nonsense."

"No, Mother. Never was a fact more sure." And he sprang to his feet. "Now I leave you. By midmorning we shall be here, I with that monster, and all the parasites who cling about the monster, and the dangerous fiends that wait on him. Be ready." And he darted out of the hall through the door into the courtyard. When they hurried after him he was nowhere to be seen. The elder sister stole to the opened gate. "What is that creature which runs into the trees?" But the night and the forest were very black. It might have been nothing at all.

*   *   *

Lak Hezoor the magician-prince woke from his stupor and turned about on the cushions. There in the entry to the tent stood a shape, pale and dark, whose eyes seemed cast from far millennia of nights and stars. Lak Hezoor spoke at once a word of power, to detain this visitor, for he sensed a supernatural quality. But even in that instant it was gone.

"A demon," said Lak Hezoor. "One of Azhrarn's tribe. Or did I dream it?"

"A dream," said a charming voice. "What would demons be doing here?"

"Sorcery attracts them. It is well known."

"But there has been no sorcery."

"The forest stinks of it. Besides, tell me what *I* am, Oloru."

"My master," said Oloru, who was seated by him on the cushions. "Sun of my life. And a mighty magician. I perceive my error, glamorous lord. Of course the demons follow you as sheep the shepherd."

Lak Hezoor only grinned at this banter. Plainly Oloru had not seen the demon, lacking the ability or else asleep . . . or only intent on playing with a curious brass toy he seemed now to have about him, a sort of rattle, which he shook up and down.

"Where did you come by that?"

"In the forest, master of masters."

"What were you doing there, my child?"

"Giving back to the earth what the earth had earlier given me. How changed was the wine I returned her!"

"Well, it will soon be daylight," said Lak Hezoor, and he began to fondle the hair and body of his companion.

"I wonder," said Oloru, "how my kindred do at home. I wonder how it is with them." And then he said, "Imagine I am prostrate on the road at your feet. Imagine I say: She, and she, are my sisters. One is fifteen and one thirteen years of age. Both are virgin."

"And is that true?" said Lak Hezoor with lazy interest.

"Quite true. And the house is an hour's journey from this spot."

"And do they resemble you, your sisters?"

"We are mirrors to each other. Except, I think the younger girl is palest and fairest of the three."

"Why tell me of it?"

"To give you a moment's diversion."

"You have done so."

The brass rattle, set aside, went rolling across the gorgeous tent, and it made an uncanny, unpleasing noise as it did so, as if it were full of the crumbs of smashed wits.

Oloru's mother and sisters may also partly have believed they had suffered some communal dream. The emanations of the forest might facilitate such things. Nevertheless, in haste and some fear, they prepared as best they could for the influx of unwanted guests.

The sun was halfway toward the zenith when, as Oloru had warned them would happen, the trees spilled over in a great cavalcade. A few minutes more, and the hunting party of Lak Hezoor was hammering on the gate.

The mother and her two daughters kneeled in the courtyard as Lak Hezoor looked down at them from the height of his horse and his omniscience.

"He speaks well of you," said the prince to Oloru's sisters. "He says you are virtuous and have never known a man. Are the men in these parts eyeless, or eunuchs?" This was his supreme courtesy to them, since Oloru was his favored one.

They went into the house, and the women trembled so they could hardly walk.

"My lord," whispered Oloru, "if it were possible to leave your attendants, and the rest, outside . . . You see how my sisters shake."

"I thought that was for me."

"No, my lord. They are distracted by their terror of your slaves. Remove this distraction, then they will palpitate in terror of you alone."

Lak Hezoor was much amused by this. In the stone house with only an old servant, an old widow, two maidens, and maidenly Oloru who swooned at the sight of a sword, what need for devilish guards? So he packed his servitors out again, and his distempered court, which had wanted to come in and work havoc. The doors of the house were shut upon the intimate party of six.

For some reason, probably its novelty, it had come to

the prince that it joyed him to be civil. So he sprawled on a couch and made idle chat with the widow and her daughters. (He treated with them as if with a brothel keeper and two of her whores.) Food there was in plenty, for the hunt had been well provisioned. The splendid wine, the only wealth of the house, was added, and Lak drained it like water. Oloru too set himself to please. His jokes were wholesome but most droll, and his verse sharp as vinegar. Even his anxious sisters found they had an appetite for the good dinner, and sometimes laughed, though they looked sidelong at their brother, too, seeing how well he understood his master. As the afternoon lengthened, and the sun began to turn its face toward the horizon, Oloru took up his lyre and sang to them. The songs were not ribald, they were all of love. And once he sang of the blind poet Kazir, of his journey through the River of Sleep into the Underearth, where he won Ferazhin Born-of-a-Flower, by matching his heart with the malign intellect of Azhrarn.

"This one is my shining jewel," said Lak presently to the mother of Oloru, and he stroked Oloru's thigh, so the widow could have no doubt that not only did the jewel shine in mirth and song, but between the sheets, too.

"How a palace dulls one," said Lak Hezoor. "What a delight is this simple life." And he shouted for another jar of wine.

Outside, the courtiers held their own revel, not in any way restrained by the pretense of civility. They encouraged their horses to foul the courtyard, and so did they. Household items, when come on, were broken from sheer bad-fellowship. They had pilfered the yard tree for a fire, and eased nature in the well.

Above it all, even in decline, the sun went down into the forest, leaving behind it only one rose-red cloud. The evening star lifted in the east like a frozen silver firework.

"Well, madam," said Lak Hezoor to the widow, "I am very weary. Where is my sleeping chamber?"

The widow told him meekly.

"I hope," said the prince, "I shall not be left lonely there for very long."

The widow put her hands to her mouth. Lak removed himself with a flourish; at the sisters he did not glance.

"The passages are gloomy," said Oloru. "I will guide you, dear lord."

So they went up through the house together, Lak walking, as ever, lighter than dark dust, and—let it be said—Oloru no more heavily. They reached a door, which Oloru opened. It was the great bedchamber of the house. The tall-posted bed nearly touched the ceiling.

"Now," said Lak Hezoor, "you know that if your sisters do not come to me inside the hour, I will go to find them. Or I will work a spell to bring them here, mindless, and unable to object."

"Oh, indeed," said Oloru. "But where is the sport in that? Is it not greater fun to force, to rape, to the accompaniment of screams of agony? Or on the other hand, to have one who is willing and screams in her delight? Both so loud, their mother hears in an adjacent room?"

"He knows me," said Lak. "Well, then?"

"My lord, I can persuade the elder to lascivious compliance, for she is hot under her coldness. And the younger I can assist you with so no sorcery is needed that will take off her edge and leave her only a limp doll. She shall struggle and wail. You will have a feast of desire and a feast of terror."

"And in return, what do you want? What have you been wanting all along, sweetheart, that you brought me here and tempted me with such alluring relatives?"

"He knows me," said Oloru. "Well, then." And he told Lak Hezoor what he wanted.

Lak Hezoor considered. He seemed not to think it any enormous thing, this notion of Oloru's, picking over it only as a man does a meat bone, to be sure nothing tasty is missed.

"And so you sang of Kazir," he said. "What put such a stroke in your mind?"

"The demon by your tent. Talking of demons, as we have done."

"But you are not brave, my love. Do you not quake at such an adventure?"

"How should I fear? I shall have your lordship's protection."

"You suppose me a match for Azhrarn?"

Oloru smiled most demurely. "*Someone* may be listening," he said. Then he went to Lake Hezoor and whispered in his ear, "*Yes*."

The magician was well pleased. It was his weakness to suppose himself a sort of earthly Azhrarn, a demon prince as well as a temporal one. Dark of hair and eye and cat-footed, with abnormal powers, and surrounded on all sides by those who feared them, and addicted, moreover, to artistic sadisms . . . it seemed to Lak his credentials were sound. And how frequently he had called this pretty plaything of his Sivesh or Simmu or by some other name belonging to one of Azhrarn's male or ambigendered consorts. Now, full of wine, and of himself, as ever, and slow and eager both with anticipation, Lak was disposed to try this perilous scheme. Perhaps he would, one day or night, have thought of it himself. He might then have rejected it, too. For something in the winsome whispering of Oloru drove him on. Thus Lak, imagining himself seduced, not driven, into granting a crazy boon, complied.

"Do as you promised with the women, and I will undertake your venture. Only I believe you will faint away with fright and miss all the marvels. Do not reproach me after, if that is so. Nor must you regret the fate of your sisters. It may be," and here he stretched himself and yawned, "a stormy time for them."

"Oh," said Oloru, "they are due for that."

He left the room as his lord was reclining himself upon the great bed.

No, Oloru did not walk heavily. He blew like a blond paper through the house, by the windows from which he might look out and see—and hear—the drunken wretches of the magician's court involved in nasty play about the widow's yard, and on through a passage where the widow's servant sat with a stick grasped in his hand, prepared for the defense of his mistresses—the whole might of his old worn body and a length of wood against Lak's power and sorcery. (He regarded Oloru as the young man silently passed, and gave a kind of snarl, but did not otherwise move.) And so Oloru arrived at the doorway of the pillared, spidered hall. It was full night now, and only three poor candles burned there. It was not therefore surprising the widow and her daughters did not see him as he stood on the threshold before them. They sat in their places, white-faced but immobile, with all the dignity of the condemned who will not remonstrate.

Then Oloru spoke. It was only a word or two. He had learned them from the magician's books. These words took effect instantly.

A composite soft sighing winged over the hall. Along the passage, there came the clatter of a dropped stick.

Soon, Oloru scratched on the door of his guest's bedchamber. "What shall be first, my lord, to rape or to roister?"

"Bring in all there is," said Lak.

Then through the door, and into the low-lit room, came three shadows, one urging the other two before him. And there was the glimmer of pale hair and white flesh, and a sable stirring and a flicker of flame on eyes and teeth, and some sobbing and pleas, and next some wild screaming that seared through the house, but whether the outcry of agony or ecstasy there was no telling at all.

The three candles were almost consumed when the sisters and the mother of Oloru opened their eyes, and looked about them. It seemed they had sunk deep asleep. That was strange in itself, for they had been in nervous dread. Stranger still it was that none had come rudely and violently to waken them. And it was very late. Even the rioters outside had fallen quiet.

At length the mother said, "What can have happened? Can Oloru have persuaded him to clemency?"

"I do not suppose so," said the elder girl. "Nor do I suppose Oloru would attempt it."

"Hush," said the mother. She got up from her chair and lit three new candles. The meager light revived and touched fresh pallor into their faces. And then the younger sister cried in a wild broken voice: "Mother—look there by your feet—and here, by mine!"

"Oh, what is it?" asked the mother, and she looked with her heart in her mouth. But all she saw on the floor by her feet was her own shadow cast away from the candles. Then, looking down at the feet of her younger

daughter, she saw there was no shadow there at all, the
floor stretched empty.

"Merciful gods protect you," gasped the widow.

"Then let them protect me also," said the elder girl,
"for my shadow too has left me."

And it was so. Turn about and about as the two sisters
would, however the candles described them, the light made
no shadows for them anywhere.

Now a shadow was and is only this, a portion cut from
the passage of a light by that which stands between the
light and all else it would shine on. In some lands of the
flat earth, it is true, a shadow stood as cipher for the soul,
or at least for the physical soul which resembled, so
exactly, the body which had spawned it. Elsewhere, a
shadow was just a shadow. Yet, there is this to be considered. One who can no longer cast shade has surely lost
some part of herself, some element which makes for opacity and substance—or else how does the light pass directly
through her? To lose one's shadow, then or now, was and
would be cause for some concern.

The sisters ran to their mother for solace, and she tended
them as best she might.

Eventually it was the elder sister who drew away, and
said, "This is our brother's doing. Some new treat he has
devised for his lord." She dried her eyes and put back her
hair. She said, "Sorrow gives way to anger. I will go up
and ask them what they mean by it."

"Oh no—do not, for all our sakes."

"Yes but I will. To damage and debase the flesh is
wicked enough. But to meddle with the psychic parts is
beyond enduring. The gods will take note, Mother, of our
righteous distress, and come to my assistance." In this
pious belief she was, of course, quite mistaken (since in
those days the gods cared nothing for mankind). But the
mistake sustained her and she rushed from the hall. Along
the passage she went, where the servant was snoring still,
and up through the house to the room they had allotted the
magician. Here she rapped on the door before her valor
should desert her, and called out: "Let me enter at once!"

No one replied.

"I will come in!" exclaimed the girl. And she thrust wide the door and ran through.

How odd the familiar room looked in its guttering prodigality of candles. But more than light, it was a darkness there that had changed it. For the space seemed full of a living dimness, an invisible, swirling, murmuring something—she did not know it for what it was, the ambience of a weighty spell, but it turned her cold, so she would soon have run out again. Then she beheld, through the fog of the sorcery, the magician lying there on the quilts, heavy as lead, seeming not to breathe, locked up in such a closed prison of sleep that it instantly suggested death. And this sight, though it was more terrifying than anything else, also stayed her.

Just then, a whiteness that had seemed to hang like steam over the cushions on the floor rose up.

Now the elder sister was surely transfixed. She stood in horrified wonder, all eyes. Two pale and ghostly girls poised before her, their long bright hair spilling around them. Both were naked, both were known. One was the younger sister, the other the elder sister—herself. Neither did these two possess, either of them, a shadow, and it was clearly to be seen how the candlelight passed straight through each.

"Do not be afraid," said the ghost of the elder sister to the reality. "Oloru brought me forth from you and Oloru left me power to tell you of it."

"Say what you are," trembled the girl.

"Your shadow, or that which enables you to cast one—some of your substance, yet not your self. With me, and with this other"—here the ghost indicated the ghost of the younger sister—"the monster Lak had his wishes. To him it seemed he ravished and rent and mastered flesh, but he did not. Nor is it anything to us what he did with us. Neither, when we presently return to you, will you think anything more of it than we."

"But you are my immortal essence," cried the girl in a worse dismay than ever. "He has done all these things to my soul and the soul of my sister."

"No, we are not your souls. Your souls are not of this fashion. Only colored air are we. Let me come back to you, and you will know at once all is well with you."

"Come back then," said the girl, and she braced herself for pain or lunacy. But the ghost drifted to her like a moonbeam and glided over and through her, and was one with her. And with great happiness the girl saw her shadow appear immediately on the wall, like an omen of perfect good.

"Now go, and bring here to me the one to whom *I* belong," said the second ghost in a petulant susurrus of the second sister's voice.

"But he—" said the girl, recalling Lak slumbering like the dead not ten paces from her.

"He has other business."

"Where then is Oloru my brother?" demanded the elder sister; relief had made her bold. But the ghost did not respond, merely folded its hands patiently, just as the younger girl did when she was exasperated.

The elder sister felt she had no choice but to hurry below and tell the glad tidings. As for Oloru, she blessed him, and her tears fell warmly, for she knew herself whole, as the ghost had assured her she would, and her rescue was all his doing. And in that way she forgot he had also been the cause of her peril.

4

AND FOR WHAT curious reward had Oloru gone to so much trouble? What had he bought from the magician-prince with a delusion of white bodies and screaming? What indeed, Oloru having proved *himself* such a competent mage, did he require from Lak Hezoor that he himself could not manage alone?

Down, down, down; miles down beneath the country of

men and the comprehension of men: the Underearth, the demons' kingdom.

At the kingdom's very boundary wandered Sleep River, sluggish as a blackish treacle, between the high tasseled heads of the white flax that grew there. Here on the river's flaxy shores, with blood-red hounds, the Vazdru hunted, not lion or deer, but the souls of men asleep, which ran shrieking before them. Though it was only the souls of those near death, or the insane, which the dogs were able to catch and tear. Even these were allowed to escape in the end—it was merely a sport to the demons. Besides, there had been no hunting a long while now, as there had been little of anything—music, gaming, intrigue, love, the immemorial pastimes of Druhim Vanashta and its lords. Nor did the hammers of the Drin, the demon metalsmiths, often sound. Nor did the creatures of that underworld frequently fly or sing, or the flowers extravagantly bloom, or the waters magnetically glitter, as once they had. That pall of Azhrarn's rage and grief hung over everything.

Nevertheless, it might be considered still a place of wonders worth seeing. Centuries before, Kazir had come there by witchcraft, passing through the River of Sleep, as generally men did solely inadvertently. Kazir had had a mission to perform. But Lak's poet, Oloru, had begged that he too might go sightseeing through the treacherous underland, in the protective company of Lak. What songs, opined Oloru, should be made of this excursion after! (And of the bravura and cunning of the magician.)

Now, in order to go down into Underearth, without invitation and the spells of the demons themselves to free the way, the one means was to travel incorporeally—as Kazir did in the story.

It was therefore the soul which must be the traveler, that is to say, the physical or astral soul, that elemental greater than mere shadowplay, though formed in the likeness of the body; equipped also with that body's talents and learning, whatever they might be.

There were in that era several towering sorcerers abroad on the earth. Interesting, perhaps, so few of them made this trip below. It would seem to indicate some excellent reason for even the most wily to keep out. . . . However,

Oloru had inspired his lord to the knowledge that he need have no qualms. That he, Lak, was a match for the Vazdru, eons ripe in all things uncanny. In fact, no less than a rival of Azhrarn. Madness.

So, the orgy completed, the women left lying like thrown-off clothes, Lak—with scarcely any preparation, full of drink and meat, lethargic and satisfied—set about the business of astral descent. "But," had said Oloru encouragingly, "do not expose *me* to them, *my* poor shivering soul. Carry me with you as Azhrarn carried Sivesh—he an eagle, and Sivesh one feather on his breast. You a lord of lords, and I . . . some small ornament upon your person."

It is not recorded, the actual caliber of Lak's magery, but he was mage enough for this, it seems.

In a space, the breath of magic filled the chamber and the magician's body slumped in its trance—the soul had gone. While of Oloru, surprisingly, nothing at all remained. No, not so much as an eyelash on the pillow.

The tide of Sleep River swarmed with faces and forms and mental wanderings. It took some guile and cerebral purpose to get through the wash without succumbing. Through it they got, nevertheless, Lak and his loving friend, and arrived on the shore.

Here they stood, gazing out across the ebony landscape, in the sheen of the mystic jewelry light.

Lak seemed only himself, a dark soul princely dressed. Of the soul of Oloru there was no sign, no trace. Not one? Yes, after all, one trace. On the breast of Lak Hezoor there hung a little nugget of polished topaz, somewhat reminiscent of an unmarked die. Oloru? Oloru.

It was said to be possible to glimpse the demon city from the banks of the River, on a clear day. But no days were ever unclear in the Underearth, nor were they "days." It would seem then that something, perhaps only the vision of the arrival, hid or revealed Druhim Vanashta. If Lak made out the distant architecture is debatable. But be sure the yellow gem upon his breast, common example of the dice species though it was, saw everything.

Maybe it communicated also with the magician, urging and cajoling. For certain, Prince Lak began to walk in a definite direction, through the fragile groves of ivory and silver and between the black willows that trailed down their tendrils like unstrung harps. There was no hesitation in his step. Once or twice, when some vaporous thing seemed to flutter at him out of the air (such emanations abounded here), he brushed it aside with a potent phrase or mantra, as a man waves away a gnat.

They, the lord and his topaz, reached in a while a wide road. It was paved with marble, lined by columns. This was the path to the city, and conceivably Lak paused a moment on the brink of it. But there must have been rendered then more persuasion and praise. In a moment, Lak Hezoor stepped upon the marble road.

Almost at once a peculiar feeling fixed on him. It was not a feeling he was intimate with, though he had often been its author in others: fear. Now it might be supposed even Lak should experience some misgiving simply at getting quiddity in this place, yet so far, patently, he had not. Nor did there seem any pronounced cause for the emotion to strike at him this instant. The air was still, no threatening noise disturbed it, and no agitation was visible anywhere—except the glint of the city at the road's end, if he even saw it. So Lak resumed his walk boldly, and the clutch of fear grew stronger, nor could he control it. With every stride it grew worse, until he halted again. This time, having looked carefully ahead, and all around, Lak looked over his shoulder. So he noticed an oddity. The marble road, of which he had only traversed a brief length, extended for a mile or more behind him. Such elongation did not console Lak Hezoor.

As a man sometimes will, when unnerved, the prince spoke aloud to his companion.

"This highway is unorthodox. No doubt some weird plan of demonkind to discommode the pilgrim. I think we shall return to the road's beginning and take our bearings." And when there came no speechless answer, Lak grinned and said, "What? Already swooning, dearest?" And he put up his hand to pet the die. His fingers found nothing.

Many conclusions might have gone through the brain of Lak Hezoor at this discovery. He might have thought the gem had somehow loosened and fallen and been lost, or that one of the wafting emanations had stolen it, or even that its own fright had pushed it back into the world above. But actually, the magician thought none of these things. One may conclude, then, he was at least sage enough to know he had been duped.

He had less than a minute to revel in the knowledge.

At last the chaste and windless air began to convey to him a sound. No sooner did Lak hear it than he understood it. It held every motive for his mounting fear. It was composed of a succession of belling notes, decipherable to one who had hunted, the noise of dogs that have the scent of their quarry in their nostrils. However, those that tell of it remark that it was more like the baying of starving wolves—yet worse, much worse. The fortunate would wake from sleep at its echo, screeching. The unfortunate did not wake, but turned and ran, and the sound ran with them, growing always louder and more near. It was the cry of the hounds of the Vazdru.

Lak Hezoor, magician-prince of a city of earth, stood on the road and spoke swiftly but faultlessly the charm which would remove him from that spot. And the charm failed him. It failed him totally. Not a fraction of his plight was altered. Here he still lingered in the Underearth, the belling of the hounds ringing on every column around, and within the hollow of his soul's own psychic skull. And peering along the forward vista of the road, it appeared to him now there was a cloud there, black and winking silver at its apex, brilliant and bloody below, and the cloud raced to reach him.

Then Lak Hezoor the magician also turned and ran. He fled along the road toward the groves and the flax-framed river. He fled howling, emptied of sorcery, filled to the brim with horror and despair. And fly as he would, the road was endless. It went on and on before him, as at his back. He could not, would not reach the river. And the cry of the hounds was so loud now it seemed already ahead of him and to both sides, and though he dared not turn to see, he felt a blast like fire on his heels—the panting of glad murderers.

But finally, the road did come to its beginning, and Lak

beheld the River of Sleep, his nightmare's border, on the edge of distance. He flung himself forward, but as his feet touched the sweet sooty grasses, warm weights slammed hard against his shoulders, and long bodies, curiously textured as if smoothly scaled, tumbled and flowed over him.

The red dogs pulled him down among the willows. There they rolled him and tore at him, and through the abstract blindness of his suffering and screaming, he saw their scarlet eyes and teeth scarlet with his astral blood. The color of blood they were, and soon they dripped with their color. The torment did not abate. Over and over the unbearable was borne, the mawling of a death which did not kill.

Eventually only a demented bundle of rags flopped back and forth shrieking among the hounds. Till some signal was given and they were called, and slunk aside, like sinuous shadows, to the caressing hands of their masters.

One came forward then, and stood over the physical soul of Lak Hezoor, or all that was left of it (it was not very much). The deranged vision of the hunted creature could discern but little, yet this single object it did see with utter clarity. A man, slim and tall, clad in night itself, with hair that was night, and night in his eyes. And the dreadful beauty of him was like another torture added to what had gone before, like acid sprinkled into gaping wounds. Lak screamed with greater wildness at it, at the piercing embrace of the acid, but Azhrarn the Prince of Demons raised his hand, and Lak could scream no more.

"What thing is this?" said Azhrarn. There was no cruelty in his voice which was in its contrasting turn so beautiful it even soothed the victim, momentarily. "This is only a man. I was deceived." And yet, the voice which had no cruelty in it was all cruelty. It smote against the soul's broken core and the soul longed for death. "You may inform your brothers," said Azhrarn, "you met with the Vazdru under the earth." And that said, he moved away; he vanished.

With him, restraint vanished. The mawled soul began to scream more terribly, and in the midst of its screaming it was hurled down into the River of Sleep.

*   *   *

And where was Oloru, instigator of this? And *what* was Oloru, that he had been able to escape it? It would seem that, like Kazir in the story, this poet also had a mission in the Underearth. For some bizarre reason he could not enter by himself, so Lak must bring him, but being in, Oloru was at liberty to journey and to busy himself as he desired.

Oloru had no soul, astral or otherwise. He had that within him which passed for and was the equivalent of a soul. It is possible, if not certain, he might under slightly dissimilar circumstances have penetrated the kingdom of the demons, but then he must have done so in his actual form. And in such guise, the whole place would have felt him as an oyster feels the twinge of grit. Decidedly it was the hint of Oloru's presence that had disrupted and alerted the brooding inactivity of Azhrarn, and brought him forth pitiless, a hunter on the road. Which carnage had provided an opportune diversion.

Once the topaz die removed itself from Lak Hezoor, it had spun away in an opposite direction to that towered pile of steel and shattered stars, Druhim Vanashta. The demon city was not its destination. As it went, the image of a die went, too. The article which was the atypical essence of Oloru turned to a slender rod of yellow radiation, vaguely purplishly limned.

Hours it ran, months, years, or half a minute. By which unabsolute time it was dashing over a transparent land-locked sea. In the sea were islands, some small, some treed, some high as the sky-which-was-not-a-sky, and all throbbing stained-glass reflections in the water. And then there was another isle, in a fog.

The rod of amber and amethyst jumped into the fog and out the other side of it. Where, a mite disheveled, it dropped at the feet of an Eshva handmaiden who had been waiting—though for what?—on the shore.

Something oblique had befallen the collective Eshva exiled on this island. Demons, they had as a rule a preference for beauteous mortal form, in which garb they took to the earth and overwhelmed humanity. But, precisely because both Vazdru and Eshva were capable of a multitude of shapes, their intrinsic nature was obviously not any one of them. The Eshva on the island, who had started as pale-skinned exquisite males and females, with eyes of darkness and long black hair that domiciled silver snakes, had pined and faded away to basics. She—or it—at the feet (they were not feet) of whom or which Oloru had thrown himself was now only a slim vertical of effulgent lapis lazuli.

Nevertheless, when the radiant rod brushed against this effulgent vertical, a reaction occurred.

Firstly, the vertical swayed, bending down. Secondly, the rod was raised in what became, gradually, two slender hands. Lastly, from the gaseousness an alabaster face emerged, with eyes.

"It lives," said the Eshva, of the rod. She did not speak in any way recognizably. Her eyes and a motion of her fingers said the words. But Oloru heard her. In her almost existent hands he shone, and shivered. So she clasped him to her, enthralled at the sensations he imparted.

Anything out of the ordinary was a novelty on the island. No wonder the Eshva was quickened. No astonishment either that, handmaiden as she was, she next, her find most lovingly clasped, began to make her way toward the hollow cliff where dwelled her Vazdru mistress.

Azhrarn's daughter was lying, as so often, in her sleep of negative unbeing, on the bed with pillars of red jade. And as she did this, let it be stressed, she looked most fabulously and startlingly beautiful. So much ran in the family, you could say.

The worldly version of what then took place, goes as follows: A delicious waiting-woman bursts into the mansion of her gorgeous lady and cries: "See, princess. I found this fascinating artifact on the beach. Do pray examine it for yourself." But, contrary to anticipation, the lady does not stir. She lies prone on crimson, her eyes fast shut. And in a little while the delicious maid droops, losing her own interest in all things.

There the Eshva hovered then, once more an upright translucency, before she disappeared altogether, to resume a melancholy vigil for nothing on the shore. The radiant rod was left lying by the bed.

He is alone now, alone with the one he came seeking.

No other is near. No demon dreams mischief is running amok here in the land's very womb. Even Azhrarn does not dream it, as he rides in chase, his hounds and court around him, after the illusory wraith of Lak Hezoor—mistaken for another's taint, or burnish.

So then.

Shortly there begins to be a rearrangement of molecules. The amber and amethyst blaze up and go out, and from the void of extinguishment springs a young man, expensively dressed and with silk gloves; with silk gold hair, low-burning *burning* eyes, and handsome, oh indeed, enough to scorch the island. And this glamorous gentleman stares a long moment at the loveliness asleep, or negated, on the coverlet. (He saw her last when she was a child. The promise of her infancy now fulfilled seems to take his breath away.) Then he leans down to her and his beautiful hair brushes her beautiful throat. He sets his lips gently to the lids of her eyes, through which, even closed, the irises reveal themselves in a glaze of rapturous blue. But then he places his lips more gently and more firmly upon her own. He kisses her. At his kiss, the whole tuned cliff lets forth a strain of melody, as if the pent-up singing of years has passed through it.

And she, of course, opens her eyes.

"Pretty and beauteous and amazing maiden," said Oloru, in a voice so low he might hardly be said to speak, "your father hates you and neglects you. But I am your guardian, and maybe you remember me."

The blue eyes (what a foolish word is "blue"—oh for an adjective of the old first earth to describe them) looked back and through and deeply into the amber eyes of Oloru. She said nothing. But as with an Eshva, her eyes said, "No, I do not remember. But you may attempt to remind me."

"Yes. But not here or now. Here or now I am at risk. I leapt most happily into danger for your sake. Pity me. Make me safe."

He had taken both her hands in his gloved ones. She did not resist. She lay there looking at him. She, that her mother had named Soveh (Flame), and her father, in an instant's mocking unkind correspondence, Azhriaz.

Then she did speak. One word. "How?"

Oloru now kissed both her hands. And she, very quietly as he did so, brushed his hair with her mouth. To be abandoned, then to be claimed—what other explanation is required?

Oloru felt that lightest butterfly kiss, and raised his head to gaze at her again. He told her how easy it was for her, and for himself if with her, to escape—not just the island, but from Underearth. And when she smiled, *No, not so*, he said, "Only think. He is Azhrarn. But what are you? *Azhrarn's daughter*." And it seems this caused her to think in truth.

She left the crimson bed. Her hair swept the earth. She looked up at Oloru where he stood beside her. She kept one of his hands, the right, relinquished the other. Like children they ran down the stairways of the lacework cliff, down the slopes of the island, and came to the shore.

There, some way off, the debodied Eshva still waited. Azhrarn's daughter murmured something, and the Eshva drifted obediently, listlessly away.

Seaward of the shore, only mist was visible. Azhrarn's daughter, Oloru's ward, cupped her hands about her mouth, and she whistled. It was not a human, nor even a fleshly demoniac note. It was the shrill of a silver pipe shaped like the thighbone of a hare. She had heard it once, when first her father brought her underground, and could mimic it exactly. It summoned transport.

Sure enough, in seven heartbeats, a darkness hurtled through the mist, bringing with it the spray of the sea-lake over which it had run. A demon horse, black, and azure-maned, which stopped beside them but yet pawed the ground to be off again.

The daughter of Azhrarn looked at Oloru. "I am equipped to leave. You?"

"You are able, if you will, to picture how I came here. The rest is yours to decide. I am at your mercy, but there is no other state in which I could wish to be."

"O flatterer of demons," said she aloud. Then she snapped her fingers. Doubtless she felt intimations of her power in that moment. For he, and he was someone to be reckoned with, was gone, came back otherwise, and fell into her hand a topaz die. Flirtatiously then she placed the die in her mouth, under her tongue for safekeeping.

She mounted the demon horse. Her impulse told it where it should go.

It broke out again through the island's mist, trailing streamers of that veil, and sped over the water to the farther shore.

All this time, and she had never thought to do such a thing, or that she could. To be abandoned, to be claimed, what other explanation is required?

Across demon lands, then, past the shining city, grazing its walls with the winged wind of their passage. None knew her, or what she did. But *everything* knew it. As she rode, black lightning under her and a jewel in her mouth, Azhrarn's daughter felt the soul of that wicked kingdom gather itself in incoherent outrage. Through the diamond air came spoor of hatching storms. The waters of pools and fountains ruffled and roared. Forests of trees like spangled bones stretched out their hands to catch her flying hair, but she struck them aside.

The entrance-exit of Underearth she recollected. Three gates, the innermost of black fire, the secondmost of blue steel, the outermost of agate. Beyond these, the scoured vein of a dead volcano opening to a country of lit volcanoes—the earth's magmatic center.

She came to the first inner gate.

Before her father, the ruler there, all three gates had flung themselves wide. But before Azhrarn's daughter they did nothing. And the horse, reined in, snorted, and raked the ground, now with one forefoot, now with the other. She sensed too, this fleeing girl who was so much more than any fleeing girl, the gathering of the thunder at her back. What now?

Under her tongue, the die tickled her like juice from a lemon.

It reminded her of something so obvious that she shook her hair, being unable to open her mouth and laugh. For though the Demon was her father, her mother had been mortal, and something besides, the child of a solar comet.

The sun.

She said it, the fleeing girl, with her brain only. But the

authority of this inimical symbol, to which she had such
rights, and which no other here would ever seemingly
conjure, was like a blow. It crashed against the gate of
black fire, searing a hole in it, and through this hole she
forced the horse to go, though it did not like to. The gate
of steel was next, and to this gate also Azhrarn's daughter
displayed the image in her mind, and the gate recoiled,
withered, and she plunged through it. The gate of agate, a
diplomat, had already prudently unlocked itself and let her
ride by without fuss.

Above her now the funnel of the volcano, showing no
light, nor suspicion of anything.

The horse was spent. She slipped from it and let it trot
away, head hanging, back through the gates before they
could heal themselves.

No longer needing to ask questions, Azhrarn's daughter
lifted her arms and touched the cool air in the volcanic
chimney. And into it she summoned a volcanic wind, a
smoldering sail fringed with great embers. It whirled down
about her and bore her aloft, up and up and up, through
the funnel, up and up and out into the sky of earth.

Earth's was a sky of darkness, too, underlit by the
furnaces of the burning mountains. Yet in the east miles
off one mountain burned that was not a mountain. (Dawn.)

The wind, her slave, carried her some way before,
robbed of its fire-born impetus, it sank. On the hillside
where it left her, she stood and watched the dawn, Azhrarn's
daughter. She watched alone and jealously, for she had
been, it seemed to her, a thousand years denied this sight.

The glory of a thousand mornings in that sunrise for her,
then. And the colors of the earth blinded her and made her
weep. She could endure the day as could no other demon
thing. Yet half her atoms shrank from the view that the
other half of her atoms loved, and were kindred of. She
was doomed equally to search out and to eschew the sun.

She had taken the topaz from her mouth and left it lying
on a boulder. She sought the shadow of a rock.

They say the waters of her blue eyes turned to sapphires
as they met the soil of earth; she wept corundum. But
perhaps after all she only wept tears.

Oloru came to her then, and now he wore a damson

mantle, into which he gathered her. He kissed her eyes again, wet with tears or sapphires.

"Here in the world, my own gifts are rapidly leaving me," he said. "But for now—"

The mantle flared its wings with the sun caught in one of them, and, as it seemed, a horde of stars.

And the hillside was vacant.

5

THE SAME SUN it was which rose behind the widow's house. The scene it gilded there was less impassioned, to begin with.

Out in the courtyard lay the rioters, in all the attitudes of riot's aftermath. In the forest over the way, the birds woke and sang, but those who woke in the yard were not inclined to copy them. They held their heads or their bellies, called for medicine or for more drink. Some had the temerity to call also for their lord, Lak Hezoor. When none vouchesafed a reply, these noble courtiers began to beat on the house doors and windows. They croaked or bellowed that they feared their patron had come to some harm, injuring himself in scaling, maybe, the obdurate icy breast of a virgin.

Now it seemed to them that they had every excuse—the security of their prince—for breaking into the house. Already they were cheered by the prospect. Then came a new burst of singing.

The song was alien to the morning, yet age-old as the tribulations of men.

The courtiers dropped back when they heard it. They clutched each other and asked: "What can that be?" Though they knew very surely it was one demented, who shrieked and moaned. So accordingly they said, "It is just that Oloru, trying to unsettle us."

Just then the shutters of an upper room flew open.

A man appeared there in the window. For some seconds they did not, any of them, know him. His countenance was twisted, his eyes showed only the white balls, his mouth gaped and blood ran from it where the tongue had been bitten. His whole body seemed streaked by bloody hurts, and as they watched appalled, he clawed and scrabbled at himself, causing fresh injuries with his nails, or turning to bite himself on the shoulders or arms. They were loath to recognize this beast. It was only the sable hair, though he tore it out in handfuls, that told them this was Lak Hezoor.

Gray-faced, the men in the courtyard one by one took note, and stepped away backward. Some ran to their horses and bolted almost at once. The others shook in their shoes and stuttered. One dared to call again his master's name—at which the apparition in the window screeched more raucously, and, hauling and wrenching itself through, commenced to crawl toward the courtyard down the stones of the wall.

At this every man there turned tail. Lak had gone mad, and plainly, if he caught hold of any one of them, he would pull him in bits.

Cacophonously as they had arrived, therefore, Lak's court departed, trampling each other underhoof.

Somewhere along the city road, though it is not recounted where, those that could held conference together, and decided what story to offer in the city. They had determined by then that Oloru and his family were mighty sorcerers, mightier far than Lak, demonstrably, since they had dealt with him as had been witnessed. It would thus be preferable not to refer to Oloru's house, to Oloru, or to Oloru's relations. What could mere mortals do against them? (For there was another thing, which they had not properly grasped in the panic, but recollected now—those especial servitors and guards that Lak had kept about him, not one had gone to his aid. Rather, they had stayed

like statues. . . .) If such as these had not been able to
assist, it was best for ordinary men to leave well alone.

For Lak himself, one last rider swore he had seen his
erstwhile prince, foaming at the lips and tearing himself,
proceed into the forest at a lurching run. What else should
they say, then, in the city, than that they had lost their lord
in the woods where fearsome things were known to reside,
and whose numbers it seemed he had gone to swell?

"What can we do?" said they, limping home. "We are
only ordinary men."

By which they meant they thought themselves extraordinary enough that their skins must be saved at all costs.

In the stone house, alarmed by the besieging courtiers,
the women and their servant had run down to one of the
smaller rooms, an old cellar under the hall, and bolted the
door. There they remained, and when the awful awakening
cries of Lak Hezoor penetrated their sanctuary, they were
very thankful to have chosen it.

In the end, all grew peaceful. Presently, the elder sister
and the servant, with a stick apiece, went up to see.

A great deal of mess lay about. But of the visitors—not
a whisker.

They searched the house then, and even inquired aloud.
But the place had been vacated. Only the sun came in, and
set a bright marigold on every edge and rim. Beyond the
wall, the birds sang. The forest and its inhabitants doubtless understood how a man, already some quarters insane
with his own vanity and sadistic designs, could meet the
Vazdru under the earth one night, and give up to them what
sense he had.

Only in the courtyard was there something a touch
worrying. Some little hard stony lumps, for all the world
like tall men of granite, who had melted. (Lak's blank-
faced servants?)

"So he has deserted us again," said the widow, dabbing
her eyes. "My son, my Oloru. Ridden off with his lord,
and not a word of farewell."

"Yet he saved us from Lak's cruelties," said the elder
sister. "I will never speak slightingly of my brother again."

"He is not a bad son," said the widow. "Look at these
jewels and rich garments Prince Lak left us in payment.

We shall live well again, as we have not done for years. That would be Oloru's doing. The rest is just his weakness. Oh, but I wish he had stayed here with us. I would have forgone the jewels and the comfort they will buy, just to have him at our fireside. That life is not for him.''

''Who knows,'' said the younger sister wistfully.''He may one day tire of that life.''

6

IT MAY have been the forest of Lak's hunting, or quite another forest, wherein the glade was situate. Certainly the place was ancient and somewhat sorcerous, and very dark. By day, the sunlight hung there in rare tinted drifts, or broke and scattered everywhere like golden rain. By night, at moonrise, there fell a rain of opals.

For the creature of dawn and dusk, seeking and turning from the sun, an ideal habitat.

Sunset: and a rain of coral.

The blue-eyed demoness was seated on a bank where swarthy lilies grew, staring down at her reflection, as the lilies did at reflections of lilies, in a pool. A spring fed the pool, and made it always unstill. She could not be sure of herself in this unsettled mirror. Only those eyes of hers shone out at her. It came to the demoness they had been paler and harder in her childhood, and cooler. *Bathos, then, has deepened them.* ''Bathos''—for she was almost shamed now by her quiescence in exile.

Across the pool, he lay on one elbow, her guardian, the prince who had kissed her awake, and carried her on the last stage of their journey over earth and air, folded in his mantle. But the mantle was absent now, and some of his presence with the mantle. It was just an exceptionally toothsome young man who reclined there. Her child's memory, her intuitive knowledge, both were well honed, or she too might have doubted, or forgotten.

They had not conferred for hours, or even days, these two escapees of Underearth. Until she said to him, carelessly: "Dear guardian, grant me a name."

But he only bowed, charming eccentric Oloru, and replied, "Who *are* you that I should know how to name you?"

"You knew me, and told me of it."

"Did I? In some dream—"

"And now you do not know me."

"Only that I found you as Kazir found Ferazhin, a flower grown in the shade. The rest—I unremember."

"Why?" said she, and now her eyes *were* paler, harder and more cold. Like spearpoints of turquoise, as he should have recalled them, having seen them so previously, in the temple of holy Bhelsheved, the day after her mother's death. But Oloru did not recall. He shrugged most gracefully. "Why?" he said. "Why not? Pardon me, I am partly mad. Everyone says so."

"Yes," she said, "it is politic to forget yourself. You who destroyed my mother by your trickery. Should I not detest and be revenged on you for that, as my father means to be? He will hunt you over the edges of the earth. I heard him promise as much to your face. That two-faced face which once was yours and will be yours again. One promise of Azhrarn given you, and then a promise to me, and he took me below with him. But he put me aside and forgot me, I was of such little worth there. Or here." The demoness who was also a human girl put out her hand and touched one of the lilies. "My loving parents," said she, and the lily shriveled and rotted from its stalk. "That night Dunizel died and left me comfortless, she sought out Azhrarn. Her spirit came to *him*, and put on flesh for *him*, and they were lovers together. What was I to either of them in those long moments? Nothing. He made me for that promised complex game he planned, but has since discarded. And she—she held me in her belly and brought me forth only to gratify him. When I was a child," said the girl who was also a demon, "Dunizel told me stories. In the womb I heard her voice, my mother's, sweeter than the songs of the stars. But I was nothing to her but something of *his*, while he hated me always."

"Your eyes, they scald me," whispered Oloru.

"Be scalded then, court jester," she answered angrily. "Play your silly part and see if I do not betray you." But then she went on softly, dangerously, with her former theme. "*He* named me *Azhriaz*, to mark me as his. But I am not his. *She* named me by her own first-given name, Moon's Fire—*Soveh*. Though I disown my mother, I would rather be hers than his. I will resume that name."

"Your eyes," whispered the young man, "are burning the marrow from my bones. Are killing me."

"Die then, as if you could."

"When I am dead ashes at your feet, consider only this. You are a sorceress, and whatever name you take, it must bear the symbol of your calling."

She looked at him. She said, "Good. Her name is better altered. Not, then, Soveh, but Sovaz the witch. I will be Sovaz."*

"Sovaz, you are fair," said Oloru. "You are the evening star, the hyacinth that shades all heaven with its dye, the silver taper that lights the moon."

"Is she so, this Sovaz," said Sovaz, unsmiling. "But I see now what you play at being."

After that she fell silent. Silence was yet her métier, speech only a new fad that might be relinquished at any moment.

Merely, she let down her hyacinthine hair into the pool. The lilies rustled, stretching their stems like thirsty swans, to dip their petals in the water her hair had spiced.

A short while later, perhaps only six or seven hours, the lilies and the hyacinth lifted their heads from their reflections at a sudden sound. It was a noise which has already been described in some detail. A belling of hounds, but not mortal, nor far off.

---

*As with the K that concludes a masculine name to denote the magician, so the symbols which translate as AS or AZ in the female—at the end, or very occasionally within, the name—denote a sorceress.

She who was now Sovaz glanced first at her traveling companion. Innocently, beautifully, Oloru slept. Neither did the uproar rouse him, though psychic and horrible and limitless, it seemed to rape the forest, to rip down branches and uproot the grass. Not one live thing, natural or un, could ignore the cry. That Oloru slept on was his great wisdom. She despised and respected him for it. Also, she thought, *It is not for me Azhrarn comes hunting. Even to hunt me has no value for Azhrarn. Can it be he even guesses I am gone from prison? What loss if I am? No. It is this other he seeks.*

And she spurned the "other" lightly with her foot as she went to the brink of the glade, to see.

Now, she was Vazdru, Sovaz, the Demon's child, and she had drawn her genius about her. As the wild hunt dazzled along the avenue of trees, the glade winked out like a flame in water, because she willed it to. How strong, how confident her sorcery. Azhrarn himself, riding with his folk about him, did not spy what she had hidden, though he turned his dark head as they pelted by, maybe unsure, considering—but even the blaze of her eyes she sheathed from him. *I am not here, Azhrarn, Prince of Princes. And he is not, that other prince you seek.*

Then, like storm-wrack, they were gone, and the wail of the dogs died like the sting of a numbing blow, away through the forest, away through the world, and out of it.

Soon Sovaz returned to the pool. She stood looking down at Oloru, who had called her Evening Star.

"Yes, just as he promised, he is hunting you. He knows you have dared his lands, idiot and mad thing that you are. He came very close to you. Do you fear him then, this demon unbrother of yours? Well. I did not betray you. It seems we are to be friends." And she kneeled by him.

"What?" said Oloru, opening his amber eyes slowly.

"Fool," said Sovaz. "Yes, it is a canny disguise, not to know yourself. Maybe he will never find you in it. But now, gentle guardian—" And before Oloru could prevent it, she seized both his gloved hands, and tore from them the jeweled silken gloves, and flung them away.

Oloru stared at his hands.

The left was well shaped but gray as river clay; it

trembled, and he saw the long nails were red like lacquer, and its palm was black. He let it down hastily in the grass and would not look at it. There remained the right hand, then. The right hand of Oloru was constructed of brass, but the four fingers of it were four brazen serpents that snapped and hissed. The thumb was a fly of dark-blue stone, which, released from the glove, quickly spread its wings of wire and clicked its mandibles frantically together.

Oloru screamed. He erupted to his feet and fled, trying to elude the monstrous hand. But of course the hand ran with him, irrevocably attached, and the snakes waking and fuming and spitting, and the fly rattling its wings and jaws and feelers irritably.

Away through the forest, insane with terror and shock, Oloru sprang.

Sovaz did not wait, she went after him, running as lightly as he, and as fast. In less than a minute, perhaps, she caught him, by his sleeve and by his shining hair. Oloru slumped against a tree, shivering and shedding tears, white as death, calling to the gods piteously.

"The gods?" inquired Sovaz. "You know they have no care for men. For yourself, what do you need with gods?"

"Is this some bane you have thrown on me?" asked Oloru. "Oh, let me free of it."

"Bane? Look at this *bane*. Do you not, even for the moment of a moment, remember its inventor?"

Oloru looked. He looked at the lively snakes and the blue fly. Then he closed his long-lashed eyes and sank, senses vanquished (ever Oloru), to the earth.

She laughed a whole instant, did Sovaz. But then her laughter was done. Some other emotion rushed now over the first. Unlike herself, it had no name for her. It filled her with inexplicable excitement and hurt.

Again, she knelt beside him. She held him to her so her supernatural warmth should come between him and the skin of the world that was to all supernatural things, always, a lure, a lover's embrace, the snare of an enemy. In that second of confusion, she nearly understood her father. But this passed.

Once, then, there was a young aristocrat, most handsome but most poor, who lived with his widowed mother and his virgin sisters beside a fey black forest. And here he went hunting, scorning superstition, taking with him the only servant left to the house. And here too, one day, he was lost by this servant, who spent many hours in trying to refind him. But he was not found. No, not till he returned himself at sunset, out of the depths of a wood which was famed for the egress of things irregular.

The young hunter's name had been Oloru. Had been, for he claimed it no more. Another claimed it. Another became it, growing over and through it like a vine.

It was this way.

He was not cruel, the first Oloru, to the beasts of the forest. He hunted only for food, and that since his family had always one extra at their table, Lady Hunger, who sat there with them and gnawed her own knuckles, glaring at their plates the while from under her famished eyebrows.

Nevertheless, in the way of hunting, Oloru brought down the youthful deer with spears, laid traps for the cinnamon hares, overfeathered the wings of wild ducks with arrows.

The forest was bewitched. Who did not agree? Only Oloru paid no heed to the rumors. And he was there so often, and his dwelling so close. How could the composite entity of the forest fail to learn his name and his person by rote?

So one morning the first Oloru rose early and went with her servant into the forest after game. The young man walked singing, for he saw no wrong in what he did, nor thought any other would see wrong in it. Turning then under an arch of trees, Oloru felt an unexpected chill, as if the dew had changed to snow. Looking around to comment on this phenomenon to his servant, he found the servant gone. And then the whole of the forest seemed to run together in a wall. Oloru was in a little space, no bigger than he could pace around in three circling steps. The rest was a black towering—trees—or something older, more intense, of which the growths of the forest had been only a residue, till some arcane magic called it forth again.

Oloru was afraid, but, unlike the later model of himself, no blissful coward; ready to fight. He shouted at the forest, for justice. Justice came.

It began with a raging thirst that fastened on him abruptly, without warning. And it continued with a stream of water plashing at his feet. He had never drunk the waters of the forest, never needed to. But this water he must have, and though some instinct, against his own skepticism, called to him to beware, he did not heed, nor could not. He lay on the ground and lapped the stream. There was no pang, not even a discomfort. None of the fruitless battle he had thought to offer. He lay down to drink a man. He rose up a yellow jackal, which feinted and danced with its shadow, barked and howled at nothing at all, and ran away into the wood. All human rites of intellect or body were null, gone between one sip of water and the next. To Oloru, no longer Oloru, there was no punishment. He dawdled and bounded deep into the trees, he sought his own current kind, who accepted and were fond of him. He lived as a good jackal should, until in the fullness of years he died one. And then his soul recovered itself with some startlement.

Yet, unpunished, he hunted no more. And unpunished was he punished, Oloru, who had been born a human man.

Now. In those days, or in these, when the smallest pebble was or is dug up from the soil, it leaves an impression behind itself, the size and shape of itself, though empty. And in those days, so too with all things of being. There had been a young man in the forest, but the forest had changed him to a yellow jackal. That digging up from the soil of existence left an impression behind it surely enough, a kind of cast or mold, into which some other, if he were sufficiently vital, could pour his fluid form and *set*, flesh-hard, to an exact replicate of Oloru the mortal and the no more.

One was by, and vital enough.

Chuz, Prince Madness, had been some while wandering the earth. His last meeting with Azhrarn may or may not have discomposed him, but doubtless it gave him to think, in his own obscure fashion. Dunizel, beloved of the Prince of Demons, had died through Chuz's fault; the evidence of the matter could show nothing else. But whether it had been a deliberate fault, an error in judgment, or a mad impulse—who was absolutely sure? For the mind of such as Chuz inclined to be unfathomable. Notwithstanding that, he had incurred the wrath of Azhrarn, who spoke of retribution. Would Chuz fear that? He had powers and to spare, there was not a Lord of Darkness who was without powers of many and awe-inspiring sort. And by very reason of this, such a duel could hardly be taken lightly. There was once an occasion when Azhrarn himself, finding he was on the borders of an ultimate disagreement with another of his peers, Uhlume, King Death, had approached Uhlume and placated him, giving him even a tactful clue as to how their game might be won. It is to be concluded Chuz now sought some tactful means of appeasement.

At one time it had been supposed all Lords of Darkness avoided the earthly sun, which would scorch them, or reduce them to ashes. This, however, was only true of one—Azhrarn, by virtue of his demon origins. Nevertheless, every one of those other four Dark Lords had a definite penchant for the night, and for night games and shadowplay, and shadowy places. In this way it came about that Chuz was at large in the somber forest, enjoying the feel of its sorcerousness, no doubt, as another would enjoy the scent of flowers, at the moment of the first Oloru's transformation. Doubtless too, Chuz was instantly drawn to the spot, the surge of magic like the call of some fascinating bird. Once there, he made his decision, having perceived what had occurred. Having also formed some attendant plans, he poured his fluid unconscionable self suddenly into the metaphysical mold, settled, hardened within it invisibly, and at last stepped forth, stunned, into the day's ending.

As a disguise, it was a unique one. In the way of transforming the humanoid aspect of Chuz, Chuz being yet Chuz, it did not utterly succeed. Prince Madness, or most of one side of him, had always been fair to look on. And he was besides apt at that time to be translated to overall good looks; had been practicing them in Bhelsheved. Thus, where the form of Oloru was fair enough, never had it been as fair as the influx of Chuz now made it. Nor had the first Oloru been as poetical, or as lunatic, as the second Oloru, which was of course only fitting. So, in the effect of appearance, the ruse was no more than theater, and

easily undermined. However. The steely root of the disguise lay in another direction. Chuz, reborn Oloru, *became*
Oloru. Chuz forgot he was Chuz.

Before, the passage of Chuz's footstep two thousand
miles off might have tingled the perceptions of Azhrarn,
for each Lord of Darkness exuded the glamour of his ego
from every nonearthly pore. But now, only Oloru was
there, who knew he was only Oloru.

It was a fact, time and again the second Oloru had
brushed by demonkind in the dark of the world's nights.
Sometimes they had even been attracted to him, sensing
something. But when they came close, there was only a
handsome crack-wit larking or jeering or shaking with
frayed nerves. Oloru's essence cried loudly: Youth, male-
ness, self-conscious sexual ambiguity, charm, brinkman-
ship, neurasthenia. And such were the notices of mortals.
And the demons, maybe briefly puzzled, withdrew again
and left him alone.

This then, the gracious obeisance Chuz extended to
Azhrarn: See how I honor you and value your wrath,
unbrother. I am hiding in earnest.

Azhrarn's anguished lethargy had had its uses, too. It
had provided the margin for Chuz to indulge in wandering
experiment, and, once the second Oloru came from the
wood, the space to explore and develop his role.

Not until Chuz's invasion of Underearth had Azhrarn
turned his head to listen, and his inclination again to the
format of revenge. Even there, the pursuers were mistaken. Hapless Prince Lak, with all his long life of wrong-
doing bright before him, took the brunt as ingenuous
decoy. The razor-bite perfume of Chuz had been all over
him, while Chuz himself, die and rod, was singularly
lacking in it. For even in such guise, he still believed
himself only Oloru, to begin with.

Chuz, as himself, could have worked Lak's magic of
astral descent, and magics far superior, with scarcely a
thought. But as Oloru, he was not able. Chuz as himself
would never have dared (probably) to enter the Underearth;
it was an act of unnegotiable hostility. But Oloru was
simply a poet seeking forbidden thrills.

When the spell took hold, the entire package, Chuz-

Oloru, life force and flesh, went down below ground in the topaz. An immortal, Chuz had no soul, or else he was completely a sort of soul, pure demonic energy, if no demon.

All the actions of Oloru, to the very point of crossing the sea-lake and alighting on the island, had been apparently random insane high jinks. Naturally, they were not. More than a year before, in the seconds of his decision to become Oloru, Chuz had implanted certain impulses in his own secret brain that would come not to know itself. To seek a magician master from whom he could steal handy provisional magics, next to entice and wheedle him into a trek below. There to fly off at a tangent, and happen by intuition on the being last seen, though not recalled, as a tiny child; Azhrarn's progeny. Dunizel's daughter.

In truth, though he had not realized it, she was all the goal of Oloru's second life. To find her out, to steal her away.

She captured Chuz's attention from the first. He had looked in at her even as she lay in Dunizel's womb, and he had said to Dunizel and her demon lover, "I come to stand uncle to your unborn child." Which suggestion, suspicious in itself, had been so hedged about with admiring taunts and loving insults offered Azhrarn, it had as much hope of success as ice in fire. Perverse, Chuz knew as much. He wanted, did not want, did not know what he wanted, took care as Oloru to forget what he wanted—and then set off to fetch it to him, through levinbolts and brimstone.

And, sorcerous thing which unavoidably still he was, the proximity of other sorcerous things galvanized him, even in amnesia. Thus the forest had tickled him into employing the shape of Oloru's own jackal, in the interest of a speedy gallop. Thus Chuz's own fearsome strength of persuasion came to him to allow him to drive Lak Hezoor to the last organized folly of his life. While the quintessence of Underearth worked on Oloru like a fine chisel, and chipped away the armoring.

By the moment he stood over her, the mistress of his quest, he had begun to remember himself. His kiss was vibrant with that remembrance, and how could it help but wake her, too?

The successive escape from exquisite hell, the damson-winged flight across the sunrise, these were the exploits of Chuz. But here in the glade, on the breast of the world again, the inner Chuz ebbed away. Oloru was Oloru once more. Although even that not totally. As smoke cannot be kept in a box, all Chuz could not be kept in human skin. Something was bound to get loose. It turned out to be those worst of all Chuzian attributes, the hands.

Therefore he lay, a Lord of Darkness brought low by his own intrinsic terror. And who, indeed, has never looked deep within himself but once, and been afraid?

Now he rested, in her arms, the arms of the demon-child-woman who had been, since her conception, his madman's goal. She had read the whole history from his unconscious unhuman mind. Aggrieved at desertion by others, she warmed herself now at his psychotic constancy.

7

MIDNIGHT: And a rain fell that was merely rain. But the forest dressed itself in the raindrops as if in clusters of zircons.

Rain bathed the eyelids of Sovaz. She raised them, and saw the eyes of Oloru were also open wide.

"I have, after all, been dead a little while," he murmured. He looked very long at her. There was a curious luminescence abroad in the forest; the rain had washed it out from the trunks of the trees, the grasses, and the lilies shone like tongues of shady flame. In this gleam, Sovaz, too, seemed lit by her own soft light. Oloru glanced at himself under the lamp of it. "I dreamed—" said Oloru. He flexed his elegant poet's hands. They were no other than the hands of a poet should be. (Somehow, by her own occult methods, she had overridden his, and made them whole for him.) "I am glad then Lord Death did not keep me as his guest. I ran to him for sanctuary, but had no hope to stay. There are many he does keep, blue-eyed Sovaz, down there in the Innerearth. But they have sold their souls to him for a thousand years. Death," said Oloru, "may not walk where nothing has died. There are such places. He may not walk the gods' country. Or in the country of the demons. For even those creatures that seem to die in Azhrarn's lands undergo only the facsimile of death. Stories that say otherwise are told by liars."

"And are you not, then, a liar?" inquired Sovaz, although as softly as the soft light that hung on her.

"A liar? I?"

"I think you must be something of the sort," she said, "for you speak of the demons' kingdom as if neither of us had ever seen it."

Oloru shut his eyes at once. His fingers clenched on the grasses.

"Do not," he said, "say these words. They remind me of my dream of fear." So she beheld that even her own beginnings were now wilfully expunged from his awareness. She did not really mind that, Sovaz. What happiness had there been in her beginnings, after all, that she should wish them celebrated?

"I concede," she said. "We will discuss only how we found each other, wandering in this forest. Myself an orphan. You mysteriously bereft of your patron, the magician-prince."

"Yes," said Oloru. And just then his eyes caught fire from an inner glare and were for a moment like the eyes of some cruel rare beast of prey. See, said these wicked molten eyes, how entertaining it will be to play this game together.

At which her eyes grew darker than the forest's shimmering dark, so starry space itself might be glimpsed in them. I wonder, said these other eyes, if it will.

And then she lay down upon him, clasping him under the arms with her slender hands, and clasping the strong calves of his legs with her slender bare feet, and his mouth with her mouth.

As unlike their first kiss, this second kiss, as earth to air. Not less potent for all that, nor less of a summoning.

"Most beautiful of mortal women," lied Oloru.

"Most beautiful of *mortal* men," lied Sovaz.

And they laughed, shedding their garments like snakes, and brought their bodies together like two clasping hands.

But it was she who lay still above him, and soon the black fleece of her tresses seemed to become one with the black foliage of the forest, so he was stretched out under a maiden whose hair itself was all the nighttime earth and the midnight sky. And her touches and her skin and her moving upon him, these were like the ambience of the world, as if the world lay on him and caressed and found him out, and drew him into itself. Virgin, yet lacking any need to be broken, knowing everything yet innocent of all. And as he pierced to the core of her, her hair and the night and the trees and the sky, her caresses, the air and the world, the very ground under his back seemed to begin making love to him.

"No," Oloru whispered then.

"No?" she whispered in return, inside his very mouth, her tongue a flame, one of the lily flames that burned in the grass.

"No, Sovaz, Sovaz, for surely then I will be there before you, and our journey ended."

But her eyes held all the oceans and the seas and the rivers, her hands or the hands of the earth stole beneath him and found a fire there, a serpent that dwelled there under the spine, a dragon waking.

"When you reach the gate," she said, or her eyes or her rushing body said it, "cry out. And I will come to you at once."

At this the dragon woke. The whole forest burst up in a swarm of lights and he with it so that in the strength and vehemence of that arching bow she too was lifted as if on a wave's high crest. As he did indeed cry out aloud to her, and hearing him she came to him at once as she had told him, her head thrown back, her throat curved like the crescent moon. And her cries, wild as those of a bird that flies a whirlwind, and three in number, split the ceiling of rain and leaves, and struck maybe the floor of very heaven above, the denizens of which abode did not comprehend such crying and were incapable of it.

But presently, in the stillness, she said to him, "There, too, is death. And there is my omen. One day I shall die. I know it now."

"Our kind does not die," said Oloru, forgetting an instant to forget.

But she did not answer him.

PART TWO

Lovers

1

AZHRARN—*Azhrarn*—sang various voices which had no sound, but were so beautiful they made the air seem filled by perfume, melody. *Azhrarn!*

It might have been the voiceless all-speaking Eshva, or some spiritual cry of his kingdom, the roots and rocks of it, the scintillant stones of his city, the jewel windows of his house. Or yet some cry from within himself, some part of him he did not recognize, for even with human men, several persons may live together under one name and inside one skin.

Whatever it was, it had haunted his palace all the dayless days and unnight nights of a mortal year. It was plain to any who had, for a moment, glimpsed him, that this sound offended him. He paced the long rooms up and down, and the tall roofs. He stood and looked away into nothing and everything, and the flying things of the Underearth, sorcerous or mechanical, meeting his sightless gaze, fell down on the black grass of the lawns.

Azhrarn—

"I hear you," he said. "But be still."

There was a silence. It was so profound, the whole land seemed to have gone deaf and dumb at once.

He walked out, in this silence, disdainful of it, into the gardens beyond his palace. In the midnight trees the golden furnaces of burning-colored fish, clustered all together, their wings closed fast. By a pool, a princess of the Vazdru had been plucking green irises. She had become still as a statue; the water drops did not run off her fingers' ends or from the flowers or from the gems of her bracelets— the water drops did not dare, for in doing it, they might make a noise. No one else had, for a great while, risked venturing so close to Azhrarn's halls. The Vazdru woman stood and stared at her lord. She was superlatively beautiful, but there was nothing in that; all her caste were so.

Azhrarn looked at her. She bowed.

"Why are you here," he said, "stealing plants from this garden?"

"Green iris, the flower of pain," said she. "A large number grow in your park now, illimitable prince. The blooms I shall weave into a garland, and wear until they fade. The stems I shall plait finely and string a lyre with them. They will make a miserable, lovely music."

Azhrarn seemed about to leave her.

"You have cast down your kingdom," said the Vazdru. "Pain is your lover, my lord. We must share your agony. The Eshva lament in the living death of ceaseless mourning. But the Vazdru are different. The Vazdru must have artifacts. And all this for a mortal woman, a child of that thing, the sun."

"Remind me," said Azhrarn, "of your name."

"Vasht," said the demoness. And she shook the water drops from her hands and from the flowers. Each drop fell into the pool with a loud crack.

"Do you hope to be punished, Vasht," said Azhrarn, "that you dare to chide me, with whom I have loved, and with how I have loved?"

"You kill us with your grief," she said. "And since we cannot die, it is a murder and a death that never end. What is one more punishment beside that?"

"You will anger me," said Azhrarn. "Do not do it."

"Is it possible to anger you? You who vowed war on

Chuz Mischief-Maker, and hunted him twice, and returned twice, while he roams the world of men by night and day, laughing at you. And when he wishes other amusement, he lies down with your daughter, that child you made in the womb of your moon-sun girl, your *Dunizel*. I was your chosen love, once, eons ago by the reckoning of those little crawling worms called *men*. You caught for me a piece of the starlit earth sky, and gave it me in a ring. You were my beloved, Azhrarn, three hundred mortal years. But then mankind grew precious to you, and you adored their foul flesh, liked it better for its very uncleanness. Now, you unremember even my name. You, who gave me the sky.'' And she flung the green flowers at his feet. They fell with a crash like swords.

But Azhrarn only said, "So Chuz and she travel together.''

"Did you not know it? Has not every reed and blade of grass in the world whispered the story to you? Every cloud scribbled the message over the moon? How he came here by a trick and rescued her from your care. Even the tides sang the song. I have heard it baldly enough.''

"I knew then. But, as with your name, you have reminded me.''

He walked on. The demoness followed, her long and lustrous black hair trailing over the black lawns, where it struck sudden sparks.

"Then,'' she said, "what will you do, Azhrarn, Prince of Princes—go back in your dark tower and weep tearless tears of blood?''

Azhrarn stopped; he turned and beckoned her. She came up to him, apparently without any fear.

"What do you want from me, Vasht?''

"To make you again what you were. Though, *she* has changed you.''

"Beautiful Vasht,'' he said. "I remember you. You were the pleasure of dawn and first light. But the day has advanced.''

"These terms in your mouth—you hate the sun, the dawn, the day. She taught you such words. And what pleasure then was *she*, your Dunizel?''

"I will show you," he said, "since you are fool enough to ask me."

And he kissed Vasht on the lips, and stepped away. Only a moment did she stand before him, the beautiful lover of the forgotten long-ago. In a moment more, she melted into flame paler and less substantial than a mist. The flame itself crumbled, and went out. The dark lawn was burned blond. But out of the ashes, a tiny thing emerged. A butterfly, with wings like green iris. It fluttered for a little space over the burned lawn, then darted into the shade of the great trees, where it vanished. But Azhrarn looked across the architecture of his city, thinking.

He had always known, or been always capable of knowing. Two abortive hunts, in Underearth and out of it, had yielded no "kill." Yet he let the matter of vengeance rest. Let the matter of escape slip. . . . Now, though he cared no more for her, Vasht it would seem had had some power to wake in him the old true rages, spites, lusts, certainties, *schemes*, of his beginning, that somber primeval "dawn" he had mentioned, shadowy sunrise lacking a sun. So Azhrarn thought now of Chuz, and of a child which was his, whose face he did not or could not recall, only the eyes. And presently three of the Eshva were summoned to him in the shapes of three smoky doves. "Go," said Azhrarn, "and find me *that*."

Far and wide, the Eshva flew.

They may have been some of those formerly sent to serve Azhriaz-Sovaz on the island of the hollow stone, and this a form of expiation—since they had allowed her to leave that place without so much as a sigh of warning, so intellectually recumbent had they grown there. (Catching his sickness?) It is not recorded that Azhrarn punished any one of them. But they, leaving that sphere of uselessness, altering, may have wished to be punished, or simply to atone.

Far and wide—

Well then, for some while, many a blue-eyed dark-haired girl was scared or lured away into the night, lost there, later found, or not found. . . . "Oh where is my daughter—sister—bride? Have the demons stolen her?" It must have been an emblem of theirs, this faulty diligence in searching. Surely they grasped, even if they had not themselves attended her before, that only one could be the daughter of Azhrarn, and they would know her at once.

She was well hidden. They would not find *her* out. Even *they*. For what was she but archsorceress, their mistress as Azhrarn was their master. As for that other, crazy Chuz, lord of craziness—for a great while he had kept out of sight behind his own immaculate blind.

Search then, on and on, they must and did, and chased the black-haired maidens in the woods, and the handsome lackwits, or men having discrepancies in their looks, one side of the face beautiful and one deformed. The Eshva were saying by all this, See, we are searching. Leaving no stone right side up.

In Underearth, Azhrarn stood by a window of emerald, and through it saw a green-winged thing fluttering. But all winged things—all things—were green, seen through that window. Azhrarn did not waste much time upon the sight.

On a stand in that room there was, or came to be, a book, in size one quarter of the height of a tall man. Its covers and papers were of thin pure bronze, and decorated with strange gems whose names are no longer recollected. Azhrarn approached and spoke to this book. At the words, the pages strayed apart, and turned themselves, and stopped. Azhrarn glanced into the book, where it now lay open. The images that were shown there could mean nothing to one unversed in them. Yet Azhrarn instantly turned from the view, disgusted, apparently, by the ease of divination.

While to three shadowy doves, flying high up under the moon, there must have come some special instruction. For they dived suddenly, as do hunting gulls upon their prey, down into the well of the world.

2

MANY TALES were told of that return of the Demon's child onto the earth. These tales bear all a similarity. It is like a snake's dancing, or a beautiful sword which knows it was made not for beauty, but to harm. Also, it is like a baby playing with her toys, and each toy a man's life, or a town burning. And the teasing malign mischiefs have too a sort of immature hurt and anger in them. It is to be remembered, though she was seventeen years old in her form, her cunning and her learning were surely older, and over all, the blossom had been forced. Within herself, she was still a child that had yet to grow. Or had she ever been such a thing as a child? She was never positively ovum and seed, only dark light, magic and will—and the fierce love of two others, which had seemed to exclude her consistently.

So stories gathered like flocks of birds about her.

But there is another tale, which says she did not do so much, not then; that in her own way she lived quietly. And perhaps there is some truth, too, in that, or why had she been so difficult for the Eshva to find?

"There are supernatural creatures in our woods," they said, in the surrounding villages and towns. Why? How do you know it? "Travelers have been set on. One came here in a lather, he had seen starry lights which followed him." "And another woke up from a noon sleep in a glade, to find he had the ears of an ass!"

Sometimes, when the wind blew, exotic aromas flowed on it out of the wood, or the sound of music or bells.

Animals avoided certain parts of the wood, or else will-fully ran off to them. Seven merchants, riding hard for a town just before nightfall, declared an *object*—which might have been a velvet carpet some fifteen feet up in the air, with two dim shining figures seated on it—had whizzed over their heads. Some girls who went out one dawn to gather edible fungi, arrived at a break in the trees and saw suddenly, as if it broke through the sky with the sun, a high magnificent house of white marble and flashing gold. But even as they stood astonished, the mansion disap-peared, and all they could make out was a little old ruined cottage on a slope half a mile away.

Supposedly then sometimes a cottage, sometimes a man-sion, the dwelling place of Oloru and Sovaz. On cold nights, a fire on a rough hearth with a copper pot sus-pended over it, crooked shutters fastened closed, a straw pallet under fleeces—or a towering hearth with stone pil-lars, scented braziers and swinging lamps, magic food con-jured to an inlaid table, a bed five yards across and canopied with silver tissue. And in summer, a herb garden with wild roses, a park with fountains springing at the skies.

One afternoon, late in the day, when the sun had entered the western quarter and the air was plum yellow, a traveler came up through the woods and paused to look at the cottage on the slope. The trees fell away around the in-cline, so the old tipsy cottage roof showed plainly. Still, something in the yellow air deceived, for there would appear to be a second outline behind the first, several roofs where there was one, each taller, and all glittering.

Now seldom did travelers take this track, since it lay in the wrong direction for the nearest towns of the region. But those who might have ventured here, seeing the mi-rage, would have rubbed their eyes, sworn, and hurried off. This traveler, seeing it, laughed.

Sounds carried in those parts.

Far up in an arbor of ivory, on a flat roof girded by golden railings, a young man and a young woman raised their blond and sable heads.

"What strange bird is that?"

"Not a bird," said Oloru, "an orange beetle, which is crawling up from the trees toward the house."

Sovaz gazed from her roof's pinnacle. She frowned.

Presently she descended three marble stairways in her silks and came to open a warped wooden door in a home-spun dress.

There on the sunken doorstep sat a man. He was clad in a beggar's garment of dull reddish orange, much stained and rent, a fold of which he had drawn over his bowed head. Beside him lay a beggar's bowl, curiously gilded, and in his hand he held a staff of greatly rotted wood.

Sovaz did not speak, she waited. After a moment the man murmured, "Alms, kindness, succor." His voice was beautiful, yet unknown. Sovaz said nothing, though she stood as still as the hidden marble. "Be charitable to me," said the beggar. "Who knows but one day your lot may be mine and you too must go entreating pity through the world. Once I was a king. Now regard me. Alms, succor, kindness." And then, very low, he laughed again his startling laugh, which was like the cry of some wild bird. "Who, after all," said he, "can escape cruel fate?"

Then Sovaz grimaced—had she been a cat, you would have said she laid flat her ears and hissed at him. She stood aside and flung open the wooden door, which almost fell off at the impact, and which altered to a silver door set with golden images.

"Poor destitute," said Sovaz mockingly, "enter my modest abode."

Then the man got up and passed into the house.

It was all grandeur again, with glassy floors, and pierced by rays of light daggering through it from the large win-dows. On a stair of marble sat Oloru, idly striking chords on a lyre. When he had regarded the traveling beggar, these chords came very sour. Oloru said, "Can one go nowhere to evade one's wretched relations?"

At this the visitor raised his head and the fold of cloth fell back from it. He was altogether a strange sight. Tanned, as if in a vat, from much journeying in various weathers, his head was like a bronze icon, for it was shaved of all hair. The bizarre robe he wore now seemed the rich color of the blood orange, and you saw that every stain upon it formed a most intricate and pleasing pattern, just as did every tear in it, as though each had been skilfully painted on or cut out. The begging bowl was not merely gilded, it was evidently gold, and dappled with somber jewels. His staff of rotten driftwood, too, was elaborately carved and had budded dark gems, and up it ran a slender ginger lizard, to perch on his shoulder, and look about with eyes of fiery jasper. The eyes of the man were rimmed with gold, blazed with it; their hue was not to be seen, nor was it easy to meet his gaze—indeed, more trouble than it was worth.

Oloru sighed, and lowered his lashes. *Chuz* said, "Unwelcome, uncousin. Or are you an unbrother to me? I am inclined to forget."

"Our relationship is often deemed a close one," conceded the traveler.

"Why are you here?" said Chuz by means of Oloru, and he threw a golden die at the lizard, which caught it in its mouth.

"Do not feed my pet," said the traveler, and extracted the die, which, in his grasp, turned to ash and sifted to the floor. His nails were golden also, and very long. The lizard rumbled like a tiny lion, balefully, at Chuz. "Why am I here? Why not? I must pass everywhere at all times. You see me in this place. Others concurrently perceive me elsewhere. And even you have not left the earth particularly sane by your apparent retreat. Some essence of you, too, mad Prince Chuz, roves and roars the world about."

During this exchange, Sovaz had stood to one side, watching and listening. Now she spoke again.

"I know you," she said, "and do not know you. A beggar king? You named yourself, did you not, at the door?"

The man turned and inclined his head to her, smiling. A golden diadem evolved upon his hairless burnished skull. The lizard looked up at it and purred like a kitten.

"Which name did I use?"

"Fate."

"Then I am Fate."

"King Fate, one of the Lords of Darkness," said Sovaz, and she swept him a scornful bow such as some young warrior might have made him, though every line of her was woman. "A gentle reminder that even I will not elude you?"

"Oh, come. Have you spent so long with *him*, and learned nothing? I am only the symbol of the name. Like poor exhausted Death, tramping about the earth with his carrion baskets, longing to get back to the quiet soft arms of his handmaiden, Kassafeh. Or like that very one, there, who has gone mad himself to prove he exists and is real, *not* only a symbol. While under our feet this instant there prowls another, your own father, Wickedness. But he was always different. He firstly existed, and then took on the rôle. We humble others the rôle itself has created."

"What nonsense is this peculiar fellow talking?" inquired not Chuz, but Oloru, languidly. "It seems he presumes on the maxim 'Enough is never enough.' "

But Fate, if so he was (and so he would seem to be), looked at Sovaz and said, "He is close behind you."

"Who is that?"

"Azhrarn. Who else."

"Fate warns me of my fate. Does unhumbly rôle-playing Prince Wickedness wish to kill me?"

"How could he? How could he wish it?"

"You are mistaken," said Sovaz. "He has no interest in me."

Fate looked about. Politely, he examined the hall of the wondrous mansion, touching the tapestries and crystal cups. The tiny lizard mewed and jumped down to chase sunbeams on the floor. And here, leaving the aura of its master, it took on the tints of sun and floor, becoming nearly transparent, for it was changeable, too, a chameleon.

"Are you then," said Sovaz to Fate, "Azhrarn's messenger?"

"Do I, a king, with my own kingly business to attend to, seem likely to perform duties for another?"

"Discuss your own business with me, then."

"I am here," said Fate simply and not unkindly. "You have glimpsed me. And that is all which is needed."

And so saying, he summoned the lizard again to his staff, and moving into a dagger of westering light, he became one with it, and vanished.

After the sun had gone, and nightingales sang in the walnut grove which stood always, cot or palace, beneath the house wall, Sovaz left the arms of her lover. She paced about in a gallery of columns open on one side to the night. How intently the stars gazed at her over the tree-tops. How wildly the nightingales sang, as if something had disquieted them, with ecstasy or fear. Presently, silently, Sovaz called her lover back to her. She put her hand on his shoulder. Her eyes said, There is no rest for me. Let us walk out in the darkness.

So they wandered through the woods, where the black foxes came to play about them, and the night flowers glowed and sent up their perfume. And sometimes, by starlight, the two wanderers cast five shadows. But later, three of the shadows vanished, though there went a faint sound through the branches, like wings.

Coming at length into an avenue of ancient trees, Sovaz and Oloru saw a town spread below and before them, out of the wood.

"We will go down. We will see what humankind does with itself in the last hours before dawn."

Oloru smiled chidingly. (*Humankind?*) But then there was only a ghostly jackal which ran at her heels, grinning. Sovaz paid no heed, nor did she assume herself any feral form. Her own skin was too unfamiliar to exchange itself for others.

The barricades of the town were shut, but there was a herders' gate which Sovaz breathed upon, and it opened itself.

Down the streets, then, the woman walked, with a jackal loping after her. She had sorcerously re-formed her apparel—or maybe she had only put on fresh apparel in the ordinary way—to the garb of a young man, soft boots on her feet, her hair wound in a cloth, a long knife at her belt. It was Oloru who, when he should choose to resume human shape, would be found in an embroidered robe and pearl-fringed slippers.

The lamps burned low in the town or were put out. Here and there a sleepless window, or the inflamed eye of a tavern.

I might, Sovaz considered, *float upward like a leaf and look in at all these sleepers. I might slip in under doors, between the narrowest lattices, revel in their sins, virtues, absurdities—and be gone like the night breeze. Or I might*

*take the being of a nightmare, and cause them to wake
screaming. Or seduce, or thieve, or kill. More, the whole
town I might stir to havoc and panic, to madness—and
then he would forget himself, my beloved, and remember
himself, and help me at the work.*

Overhead the stars massed thickly. So many had come
out tonight to look on Sovaz, the Demon's daughter, with
their concentrated stare.

But why, thought she, *why do it? Is the only challenge
in the world to be greed and viciousness? Is the only
satisfying power the power of the ascent over men, the
only dream, ambition? And must the alternative to greed,
evil, ambition—be only sluggishness?*

At which she felt a gloved hand smooth her cheek.

"Sluggishness? Is that the name you call our love?"

"Our love," she said aloud to Chuz, who for a second
in the person of Oloru walked at her side, "our love rocks
the world. Yet what a little event is our love."

Chuz laughed, like a jackal barking. Oloru said plaintively, "You will smash my heart in fragments."

"You shall be shaken then, and what a pretty sound you
will make, like a temple sistrum."

And at this point they reached a wineshop door and
Sovaz walked in there, as if it had been all along their
destination.

The guests who remained were mostly sleeping, their
heads on their arms, or their feet on the tables.

Sovaz seated herself in a dark corner, and Oloru with
her. A wine server approached them sullenly. "Wine,
young . . . sir?" he asked Sovaz.

"The wine here," said Oloru melodiously, and loudly,
"is fit only as a purgative for pigs."

"True," said the server. "But do you wish it or not?"

"However," continued Oloru, more loudly still, "there
is logic to that. Since all these slobbering swine in here
seem due a spewing."

This caused some reaction throughout the room. The
server backed away and scurried out of an inner door.

"Who calls me slobbering swine?" demanded a burly
villain.

"Not I," said Oloru, with winning grace. "I doubt I

should dare. But someone more truthful than I is sure to have done it."

And standing up again he drew from his sleeve the lyre, and strummed it lightly.

> *"Lovesome pig,*
> *Bold and big,*
> *All the poets will vie*
> *In creating a shy*
> *Little ode, by and by,*
> *To your charms in the sty—*
> *So be patient, since I*
> *Think it wrong*
> *To make song*
> *To a pig."*

Drawing out a notched cleaver, the subject of this fancy now rolled from his table toward Oloru, who, naturally, shrank away.

It was Sovaz who stepped between them and said:

"What is your quarrel?"

"Off the path, stripling. The other stripling has earned himself a taste of my instrument here."

"Why? Because he called you 'pig'? Are you not then," said Sovaz, in a silver voice, "exactly what he called you?"

At this the villain shouted and raised his murder weapon in the air—but the shout became a mysterious grunt before it finished, and the knife clattered on the floor. There, standing upright on its back legs and waving its fore trotters madly, was a bristling and most angry male pig— nor, alas, was it even a boar, but of the farmyard sort, lacking now the use not only of one weapon, but of two.

Upon this cue, even the weariest sleepers in the tavern awoke or were awakened.

"*Sorcery!*" came the cry on all sides, and over went the jars and cups and down rained the candles, and every man stampeded from the place. With no surprise, let it be added, only with a kind of smug fright. Had it not said for months, this area, that there were supernatural creatures in its woods?

Only the pig remained stamping about the wineshop, furious but already forgetting why, and questing for something to eat among the spillages of exodus.

"Too apt," said Oloru with some pleasure, admiring the pig. "Let it go home now, and donate its bacon to its doxy."

"Better than that," said Sovaz, "let it go home and get into bed with the doxy, and see how they both like it." And she pointed at the pig, which gave her an unwilling glance. "Do then as I bid it, you. And when the sun rises, be a man again, if you ever knew how."

The pig ran out, looking irate.

Oloru sighed. "Too lenient. Wait. I know a jackal who will chase that pig all through the town—"

Yet, "Hush," said Sovaz suddenly. "Look there. One who did not run away. Now why is that?"

Then Oloru was hushed, pale as ice. He looked, as she looked, into another deep corner of the tavern. For it seemed indeed one sat there, all muffled up in smoke and shade. Cloaked and cowled in black, only a hand showing white on the table, toying idly with some little figurines that glimmered in the upset light. And on his fingers many rings smoldered.

"Now," said Oloru, "if I were a man, I would howl to the gods to protect me."

"But you are not a man," said the voice from the corner. "And you know better."

Oloru gazed at Sovaz. His eyes enlarged with tears. He said softly, "Let us fly to some other spot."

"Do it," said the voice from the corner. "I will be there to greet you."

It was a voice so fine the atmosphere was already charged by it and grew electric, as if before a storm. It was so fine, even the mice who lived in the walls, and the spiders who wove in the rafter boughs above, crept out to listen and to see, then froze there, between dream and dread.

Then Sovaz remarked, "The night has found the power of speech."

The voice did not answer her. But one of the little game pieces the hand had toyed with fell abruptly to the floor and broke in bits. It had been the figure of a fair-haired damsel robed in white.

Sovaz laid her hand against Oloru's breast. "My companion," she said to the corner, "is not alone."

But at that moment, an ass brayed rackingly, once, twice, thrice, so all the mice and spiders fled swooning and squeaking and trailing droppings and gossamer.

"Oh, are you there then, after all," said Sovaz.

And she left Oloru where he stood, and kicking aside the shattered winecups, she walked to the corner and sat down on a bench facing the one in black, only the trestle between them.

He raised his head. At first there came only the black flame of two eyes, until he put back the cowl. Then there was the face of her father, Azhrarn, sculpted and pitiless and immeasurable, and empty. She had not properly seen him some while. Perhaps not since that hour he had first taken her to his kingdom and abandoned her. She had sighted him since only once, in a forest, hunting, but far off, and not for her. Always it seemed to have been this way, distance and uninterest. He was no father, no prince, no friend to her. She owed him nothing save the inspiration of life, if she should even be grateful for such a gift.

They looked at each other, and finally she said, in a small voice no longer silver but iron, "And do you behold in me my mother?"

He said, "She would not have looked at me with such impertinence, or such hate."

"She had no cause, it seems."

"Every cause. But she was the honeycomb. You, conversely, are my child, through and through. Unforgiving, arrogant, and proud; the wicked callousness men worship when they say my name, all is in you. But your wings of malice are not yet hardened. When you are able to take the skies with them, then we shall see what you can do. Dunizel's daughter? No, you are only mine." And he smiled most gorgeously upon her.

When he did so, Sovaz spat at him like a snake. But the spark of demon spit altered instantly to a silver flower. He caught it in his hand and held it out to her, still smiling. Sovaz rose to her feet and turned and walked three paces away. No longer looking at him, she said, "Women you may woo, but not this one. You have told me, I am yourself. In vain then your blandishments or threats."

"Do you suppose I could not destroy you in a second?"

Sovaz looked over her shoulder at him.

"Do it."

Azhrarn let the flower fall on the table. It was gone.

"You forget," he said, "you are my puppet that I made and mean to use. I have said, Let us wait until you harden in the mold. When the paint is dry on you, you will come to me, and show me the virtuous respect a daughter should."

"Then," said Sovaz, "may all the seas be fires."

Seated cross-legged on a nearby table, a handsome young man in a purple robe observed, "Alas, I am forgotten."

"Not so," said Azhrarn. "Be flattered, Chuz, I came seeking you. The woman is not much to me, which she sees, as we note from her rage. You, I have taken trouble to close upon. You I have pursued like your lover."

"Yes," admitted Chuz-Oloru from the adjacent table, "I am distinguished enough now to tempt even your palate. But it would not be politic, Azhrarn, for two Lords of Darkness to couple, as it would not be sensible for them to engage in enmity. These are joys we must forgo."

"Must we. I promised you war, Chuz. My promises I keep."

Chuz said indolently, "One blow shared between us will obliterate the town. If we duel, how much of the earth may be damaged before one of us bests the other? And the earth is dear to you, I believe. Besides, can you slaughter me? I, too, must be reborn. While there is madness, there *I* am."

Azhrarn in turn rose. As he moved from the corner, all the blackness of it seemed to come out with him and to leap simultaneously into lights. Firmaments and whirlwinds were caught about him, in his black hair, the wings of the cloak which restlessly beat. Stars crashed in every ring on his hands, and in his eyes worlds ended and began and ended. To this apocalyptic background, he gently said, "I mean to pay you out. It will be done. You harmed what was dear to me and under my protection."

"I have said before," said Chuz, yet perched on his

table, yet almost like a man, "it was no fault of mine. Blame that other one, he whose murmurings seem to have driven us here, Lord Fate. Blame yourself. Blame Dunizel for her destiny as a sacrifice. Blame everyone but me. What am I? Only the world's servant." Then Chuz himself raised his golden head. The face was still flawless, still Oloru's. But no longer Oloru's at all. And out of the eyes looked some appalling red-black thing. "But I lie," said Chuz. "You know I lie. It is my homage to you, as was my careful disguise, and my frantic running away all this time. Yes, conceivably her death may be seen as my fault. If so, I do not know why I should have wanted it, for she was lovely, innocent, and wise. But insanity does nothing by the book. Guilty then, unbrother, as you wish." And Chuz came from the table and went to Azhrarn. And standing there, meeting his terrible eyes with eyes equally as terrible, Chuz said this: "You may not eradicate me. You would be as foolish to fight with me as I would be fighting with you. But see, I offer myself before you and will accept any penance you decree, provided it may be compassed. Such an offer is madness, therefore fitting. Take your vengeance then, chastise me. But, Azhrarn, you do it by my agreement only."

At these words, Azhrarn cursed Chuz. Every flickering candle in the tavern died at once. Outside, the last lamps of the town perished. The very stars seemed to falter overhead, though probably they did not.

"You are clever, Madness. Yes, there is no other means," said Azhrarn in that black quiet. "I accept your terms. We will so conclude our quarrel. This the first night, tomorrow the second; at the third expect my answer, and your punishment. It shall not be nothing, Chuz. You are warned."

Then, where the Prince of Demons had stood was only a column of scarlet searing lightless flame, which, going out, left a cold-hot wound in the dark, that faded slowly.

While in all the land about, dogs wailed, and winds howled, and leaves rotted from trees, and a brief rain fell that stained the walls of the dwellings of men like diluted blood.

"If I were a woman I would say, What now will

become of you? And I would weep. You will be ripped
from me for some living death he will devise. I cannot
think what. But so it will be."

"If I were a man, I would hold you in my arms, as I do,
and kiss your hair, as I do, and the blue tears of your blue,
blue eyes would spring into *my* eyes, as they do. And I
would say, What else is to be done?"

"Why did you kill my mother?"

"Did I kill your mother?"

"Why did you kneel to my father?"

"Did I kneel to him?"

"Liar and fool."

"What is any of this to us? Time is endless and ours.
Love and death are only the games we play in it."

"You have been my father, you have been my brother,
and my beloved. If I were a woman, if I were a child, I
would weep. Oh, let me weep."

3.

TWO DAYS and a night between them. What to do
then, with these last seconds before the ending of the
world? Unhuman beings, they made the time seem to
stretch for them, yet, such vistas before them, eternity,
how swiftly this small ration ran away.

The cottage was a mansion. They lured to it by sorcerous means a host of people, feasted them, created for them
an orgy of pleasures, and lorded it, prince and princess,
and loaded with presents the ensorceled guests. And some
of the donations were sumptuous and goodly; some turned
to frogs and owl pellets on the route home.

The mansion was a cottage. They spent a day as peasants. Sovaz baked black bread and cooked a broth of herbs and roots. Chuz (you could not call him Oloru now, though still he wore Oloru's shape) cut grass for hay and logs for the fire. With garlands of wild flowers in their hair they ate the impoverished meal, where, garlanded with rubies, they had just previously supped on transparent wines and magic meats.

In the second night, those two days' center, they roamed about the trees. The pools of the wood sprang to diamond, the foliage spangled, and breathed disembodied music. Birds which sang by day stirred and sang for them by night. They lay down there, the lovers, and loved. Remember me by this, they said, as lovers then, now, have always said, who must part.

But the third night, after their humble peasants' day, they arrayed themselves like kings and left the cottage deserted. They went deep into the wood, to a place that was so dense and black nothing came there ever, not bird or beast, not man, nor even demon, probably, till then. And here they waited for Azhrarn.

A long while, too, they waited, or a long while Azhrarn, the Prince of Demons, made them wait. The moon passed over the black place, and one thin wire of light probed through, and then was drawn away again.

She said at last, all pretense over, "Do you guess what he will demand of you?"

"I think I guess. I believe in a manner I have been foretold of it by him."

"It is fearful?"

"Perhaps. And just, in its way."

"Cease speaking as a man. Speak as Prince Chuz now, my guardian, my lord."

"Oh, beloved," he said, "my lady, my soulless soul's dream of night and sunrise."

"*No*," said Sovaz, "unless you will refuse him."

"Impossible. It must be done."

"What will the legends say of you?" inquired Sovaz bitterly. "*You*, a Lord of Darkness, to accept the bane of a Vazdru who only hated you for slaying his mistress."

"Once it was, 'Why did you kill my mother?' "

"Once. But she was only his. Does the wine call the jar

'Mother,' when the wine is spilled? So I was for her, wine for his use.''

But then the moon came back into the dark. Not one dull wire now, but a vast iridescence, as if dry water poured through the trees, or a heatless conflagration.

He had announced himself, knocked upon the door. It was not politeness, only a threat; they should notice and be careful.

Azhrarn walked after the light, entered the glade, and stood in it with them.

And as she had said to Chuz, so the Demon said to him instantly: "Do you guess?"

"It would seem I do."

"Do you consent?" said Azhrarn.

"I admire you too well," said Chuz, "to wrangle."

"Azhriaz," said the Demon.

But she answered, "That is not my name."

"It is your name," said Azhrarn. "Azhriaz, what will you do, when he is lost to you? You are nothing to me as yet, but I am curious."

"Stay so," she said. "I shall only follow him."

"Thus let it be," said Azhrarn. "Now I shall tell you what you will follow. He has been a man, and fair, and he has been pleased to claim all such deeds are his madness. But by our agreement now, to give me some recompense he must relinquish his state and his powers, and even the evidently charming mortal guise that he put on for you. Mad now Chuz shall be. Truly mad, as a mortal knows it. Mindless, screaming, foaming, and tearing himself. More beast than any ass or jackal. Less a man than any man he has artistically dressed himself to imitate. A shunned outcast of the tribes of the earth, a mock for every unearthly thing. To demons, a new joke they will indulge and disdain. No longer a lord, a prince, or a magician. Foul and disfigured, each side of him—allow that I miss no quintessence of the irony—matted and maimed, and so to go scrabbling over the world. That the world may see, if it is able, that even his day-playing peers must be courteous to the Master of Night. And all this, for a mortal lifetime, he must and will endure, till some gross mortal death rids him of the vile disease that is himself. Only then, Chuz, may

Chuz be Chuz again. The whole sentence you will serve. Or serve none of it, and we will find another way."

"My dear," said Chuz, languidly, "what greater happiness can there be for me than to experience—if for such a little, *little* while—the life-style of my own subjects?"

"Go then," said Azhrarn. "Be happy."

"No," said Sovaz. She spoke coldly and she seized the wrist of her lover. "You were Oloru. You are mine. You may not leave me at his whim, to suffer for his disgusting sport."

"He will leave you," said Azhrarn. "He will suffer."

"Then he too betrays and deserts me," said Sovaz. "Chuz, do you hear what I say? If you obey him, I conclude it must be your will and your wish."

But the face of Chuz had subtly altered. He said to her, "As men die in the flesh, so the undying, too, have their deaths. This it would appear is to be a death of mine. And he, he has died often. One night, he will recount the stories. For now, Oloru tells you this: Of all the stars, the flowers, the songs of earth, or beneath or above the earth, you are the brightest, loveliest, best. What is there to fear? There is all time to meet again."

And then he walked away from her, under the black, light-touched waves of the wood. Out of which there soon came the braying cry of an ass, and then a strange wavering shriek and the splintering of branches. And birds that had slept there burst upward to be gone in haste.

Presently Azhrarn, who had stood looking off into the dark, said, "I am satisfied. For the moment." And he glanced at the girl and said to her, "There is the road he took, if you mean to go after."

Then she did begin to go that way. And as she went by Azhrarn, Sovaz spoke to him, one word of Underearth which the crude filthy-minded dwarfish Drin, lowest caste of demonkind, sometimes wrote up on the walls of each other's habitations.

"That I call you," said Sovaz, "and that you are."

"For your mother's sake," he said, "I will restrain my hand. But there will come some midnight when you will make amends for it."

"When the seas are fires and the winds seas and the

earth glass, and the gods come down on ladders to lick the feet of men. *Then* I will. Perhaps.''

Azhrarn said no more. Nor she. She had said surely enough.

And turning from him, she fled away through the trees after Chuz, like a frightened child.

PART THREE

Fair Is Not Fair

1

MADNESS there had always been, in one form or another, on the earth. When first it came, it was nameless, as were all things. But soon men coined a name for it, since there must be names for every mote and seed. And after the name came the name's Being, which was called Prince Chuz, and became Prince Chuz, and *was*.

One of his own subjects now, Chuz. All Azhrarn had said he would be. No longer fine. No longer, at his own choice, half shining bright, half eerie sinister shadow— like the lunatic moon. Now a lumbering fear-shape at which to slam and bolt the doors, to say, *What beast passes?* But the beasts themselves flee from it, the forests sink silent. It flounders through mire and swamp, through the high palisades of thorns. The ducks rise from the reeds, exclaiming. In a dead tree it halts to rest, if rest it must. In a village street it appears, and the men fling stones at it, even take their bows and hunting spears and let fly with those. Till, quilled like the porcupine, it absconds, squealing, hurt, but hit in no vital spot—for its time to end is far off. Did Azhrarn not promise?

Madness has gone mad. Truly mad, and utterly. And Chuz's princely kingdom of the mad—they know it. It drives them to worse excesses, to more comatose declines.

They pine, they take up knives, and fall down in fits to prophesy the world's ending, or that some colossal lumbering elemental, slick with blood and mud, prickled by arrows, is sweeping through men's lives like a wind from chaos.

But only the mad understand this. And who heeds them? If the times are out of joint, were they not always so? When was the world ever perfect? Speak of golden ages, ages of Innocence and Dream. Those are tales for children. Thus runs the philosophy of the Flat Earth, bearing some resemblance to that of the round one.

But where humanity had hidden and muttered *What beast passes?* now it openly stared and said, ''What maiden is this?''

Sovaz went by without a look.

The earth—what was the earth to her? A birthright so long denied, a treasure house, an alien desert—

Some saw her as a maiden, a white dress, bare feet, no ornament but her eyes, and her long hair for a mantle. Some saw her in male attire, striding fierce as a panther. Some did not see her, sensed her, a fragrance, the mark of one narrow foot in the dust. . . .

There was an anecdote. A young lord, finding just such an exquisite footprint, fell in love even with that, dreaming up an exquisite foot to fit it, so a limb, so a whole body, face, and personality. And then, sleepless and wildened, he sent his soldiers over every inch of that kingdom, to bring him all the women, young or old, virgin, nubile, prepubescent. The married, the celibate, the hag—all were brought, many weeping and protesting, their husbands, lovers, religious orders, and relatives in uproar, and hurrying after. When the procession came to the lord's house, he had them taken, the women, to the forest path where he had spied the print of the foot of Sovaz. ''It is sorcery,'' he said. ''She has disguised herself to tease me, for that is ever a woman's way, to flirt and run off and say No, since a man's part is to demand and pursue and tell her Yes. Even the elderly women, one may be *this* one, hidden by her powers. But I will find her out. Even if she seems a child of twelve.''

So then the women, angry or afraid, or hopeful and willing, were made to set each their left foot in the footprint. None matched, and the lord grew pale, and paler and more pale. Then at last a girl came, among the very last. She put her foot into the footprint, and see! It was a perfect fit.

The lord leapt up and upon the track. The maiden was of a seasonable age, late spring. And she was, as he had known she would be, very beautiful. He took her by the hand. "So, you can elude me no longer." "No, my lord," said the maiden, and lowered her eyes. She was a poor man's daughter and had spent her days so far in herding sheep. She agreed demurely and apologetically with the land's lord that she had set him this test, to be sure of him, and that certainly her ragged appearance was all part of a mischievous plan. "But believe me," she added, "it was not my aim to vex you. My kindred and I have for long years been under the sorcerous curse of an enemy. My father was once a king." "I will not treat him as less," said the land's lord. (So we behold here not only the foot of Sovaz, but the hand of Fate.) And he wedded the maiden and raised her father and brothers also up to the rank of lords, where, let it be said, they all lived righteously.

Meanwhile Sovaz followed the mad, mindless animal that had been her own lord and lover, sometimes losing the trail.

Her purpose set but also grew dull. He had abandoned her, like others. It was a perverted adventure for him, to be tortured in this way. He had preferred Azhrarn's justice to her love.

But it seemed there was nothing else left to her, but to follow. Her powers were vast—she knew them without much trial of them. It might be she could negate Azhrarn's malice. Or would Chuz, reveling in punishment, deny the healing spell?

There was, it is true, a tradition for such a wandering search. The legends had several examples—for instance, how Shezael the Half-Souled had gone to search for the insane hero Drezaem, in whose body dwelled the other half of her spirit. How Simmu, when a girl, had followed her lover Zhirek—before he became a mage, when he was only a priest, exiled and tormented, and mad with anguish. After various trials and tribulations, Shezael and Drezaem had been united. Simmu and Zhirek also, for a little while, till Fate, and the demons, parted them. Though long after, they met again. Simmu (who could be man or woman, now a man) had stolen a draft of Immortality, and so incommoded Uhlume, Lord Death. Thereafter, Simmu came to rule in a demon-built city of immortals at the earth's easternmost corner. Here, Zhirek came back to him, but no longer as a lover or a friend. And Simmu's city, Simmurad, of rosy stone and jade and silver, Simmurad lay under the sea, now.

Very likely, these memories attended on Sovaz in her long walk.

While following the crazy mindless thing, she came into the murkier regions of the earth, prone to unreasonable happenings.

The romantic sheltering forests lay far behind. There were hills, and mountains, where only the passing cumulus gave shade. She could outface the sun, the Demon's daughter, and sometimes, at sunbirth or sundeath, she could fall in love with the solar disk. Yet there were days the sun beat upon Sovaz, and then she suffered in hidden, deep-rooted ways. And she came to travel much by night, through the tall lands, under the moon for a white sun, and all the tears of it, the stars, her motionless continual companions. Nor did she journey always on foot along the ground. She dared all her abilities, and sometimes she walked in the very air, laving her feet in its coolness. Or sometimes she rode on sorcerous carpets, or called black birds from their rocky sentry posts to carry her. And once, discovering a stone lion carved from the hill, the marker of some forgotten tomb, Sovaz made the beast rise up, and she rode on its back three nights and the days between, before she returned it to the dead.

It was a deserted district. None saw.

Only madness had gone before. She noted the evidence of that progress. There was little to be seen, much to be felt. Then she had walked up into the highest terraces of the high mountains, and emerging onto a deep balcony of granite as the dawn began, she found the land fell away before her, the jagged walls of the mountains leveling to a blanched barren plain. This spread to the horizon.

As she stood in the mountain balcony, some people, clad like destitutes, appeared along the neighboring ledges, out of caves and holes there.

"Maiden," they called to her, one after the other. There was something annoying to their voices. And then, an elderly man stepped forward. On the breast of his wretched robe he wore a pectoral of gold, and a circlet of gold around his head held his dusty hair from his colorless face. He pointed a thin finger at her, on which a heavy ring took fire.

"Maiden," said he, "travel no further. Do not seek the plain. It is a wicked zone, and accursed. Beyond, by the river—which is now a canal of foulness—lies a city which is a city no more, but a sewer. Turn back. Or, if you are weary, rest a space with us."

"You are too kind," said Sovaz. "But maybe you are also untruthful, the city beauteous and wholesome—which, being the outcasts of it, plainly, you revile to strangers."

The spokesman sighed and frowned.

"Truly, we are outcasts. Hesitate among us, and I will tell you the cause."

"Again, you are too kind. I am uninterested in your city, or your tales of it."

And saying this, Sovaz went on along the shelves of the mountain, not attempting to go down to the plain, but only seeking still for him she sought.

Behind her, the refugees from the city muttered and lamented.

The risen sun kissed Sovaz viciously. She was weary and sick at heart.

Close to noon, she entered a cave for relief and rest.

It seemed to her Chuz had spent an hour or so in the cave. It was filled by an unseen noiseless scentless awfulness, and in the softer rock ragged nails had gouged a pattern. A little water ran down there, and Sovaz drank from it, as a human drinks who is thirsty. For some needs are not needful, yet they are.

Later, she slept. And she dreamed, but in the general way of the Vazdru, abstract fabulous dreams, though, waking up as the sun began to go down, she dreamed for one half second as a woman might have done, and she saw Oloru-who-was-Chuz, handsome, strong, and cunning, and her beloved. But then he was gone. *Forever I may go after and never catch up to him. Is that Azhrarn's punishment of me, also, for my birth that now he regrets?*

There framed in the cave mouth the sun burned out on the plain. And there were, too, several other smaller suns which did not set: torches. The destitutes who had stayed her earlier had come and found her here, and sat in the cave's entrance. The man with the insignia of gold was seated across from her, glaring. Sovaz noticed they had bound her while she slept with thick cords. There was some raw but effective magic on the cords, for she had not been aware of the binding, and she knew at once it would take some powers of hers to break the knots. She did not immediately perform the feat.

"And now," said the man, "you will listen, insolent girl."

"Then," said Sovaz, "I will listen. Take care not to be tedious with this story you insist I must hear."

But the man only went on with his glaring.

"Out there," he said, "miles off, where the sun perishes, lies the river, and by the river the city which is called Shudm, though that was not always its name. Tiered and darkly gilded is Shudm, and six masters rule it, and three mistresses. But it is my class which was wont to make the governors there. Now, like a vulture, I sit up in the caves and watch the city in my mind's distance, and warn from it those travelers I may. But all I inform of the history of new-named Shudm—which means the Portioned One."

Sovaz yawned behind her white hand, and with a slight gesture broke one of the binding cords in two. If the man saw was not certain. It was black now, but for the torchfire, and he leaned nearer. "What do you seek in Shudm?"

Sovaz said: "You try my patience. Go on with your story or have done."

But she thought, *My goal is lost to me. I may as well be here as anywhere. My summer of love is ended. Winter arrives.*

But the man said, all-importantly, "We call the tale *Liliu*, or *Apples of Fire*."

After which he told it her, in much detail, so her own life seemed to withdraw into the shadows.

2   *The Story of Liliu*

THERE HAD lived then, in the tiered city by the river, in the days before it was known as Shudm, a rich merchant-lord. He had one son, his heir, by name Jadrid. For this son the merchant would, as they said, have plucked apples of fire—he loved him so much and could refuse him so little.

In due course, a marriage was to be arranged. But none of the prospective damsels satisfied the ideals of this young man, though he was shown several portraits, and was even, in some cases, permitted to gaze through curtains and hedges upon the hopeful candidates. The merchant was at his wits' end, for riches and power must pass on.

One day, near sunfall, a man came to the gate. Despite his lack of attendants, the stranger was finely dressed and bore himself like someone of consequence. He was accordingly admitted. On entering the presence of father and son, who had happened to be playing chess together, the visitor spoke in this way: "Sirs, I hear that this house requires a bride for its heir, but that to be fit for him she must be both highly accomplished and of surpassing beauty. Know then, that I serve a mighty master, and that his daughter is of just such a sort. He whose mouthpiece I am has therefore sent me to tell you that should the lordly heir venture this very night to follow me, he shall secretly be

shown the girl, and may make judgment whether I have
offered truth or lie."

Father and son were each taken aback.

"Who is he then, this mighty one you serve?" demanded the merchant.

"That I may not, at this juncture, tell you. You will
readily understand, in the unlikely event of your son's
refusing her, my master does not want his daughter or his
house dishonored, and there is slight chance of this in
anonymity."

The merchant did not seem inclined to smile on these
words. But already the young man felt a curious excitement and desire to try the adventure—and turned to murmur to his father. Apples of fire—

Perhaps half an hour later, as the fire-apple of the sun
itself lay red and low on the river, Jadrid was walking
along behind the stranger-servant. Who had advised him
thus: "Keep always some seven paces at my back. Utter
no word to me, nor to any other, neither let any distract
you from our course."

Indeed, they were not two streets' distance from the
merchant's doors when some friends of the young man's
were seen approaching with garlands and torches, en route
to an entertainment. Noting Jadrid, they called to him to
join them. But he, faithful to his quest, shook his head
gravely and moved on without stopping.

A while after, as he and his guide were turning into the
narrower byways near the dock, a beggar woman lying in
an arcade cried out softly to Jadrid for alms. It was in his
mind to give her some coins, but in the dark red dimming
of the light, he thought he saw the servant make a sharp
gesture of remonstrance. So Jadrid ignored the beggar, and
left her maligning him.

The next minute, a group of priests from one of the
temples appeared on the narrow way, ringing bells and
chanting. As they drew close, Jadrid stepped aside perforce to let them by, but one of the priests turned to clasp
his arm, saying urgently: "The body is only dust; why
then do you seek to joy the body? It is the ever-living soul
which should be your care—" And a ready theosophical
retort sprang to the lips of Jadrid, and he crushed it down

and dumbly, if politely, disengaged himself, before hurrying on in the wake of the mysterious servant.

Shortly after this, the sun sank altogether.

Jadrid found that he had by now followed his guide into the oldest quarter of the city. Soon they came on a deserted boulevard between high walls, above which rose the tops of many great mansions, but all unlit. The night was everywhere, and dark, but strung with stars, which made their white music of silence. Not a sound was to be heard from the city's heart; only sometimes there would be a rustling in the trees which overhung the walls. Jadrid, who had persuaded his father, now began to suspect villainy, and put his hand to the long dagger at his belt. But the servant had paused beside a small door, and unlocking it, intimated that the young man should pass through alone.

With some caution, Jadrid did go to the door, and peered inside. What lay beyond the wall was only a garden, rather overgrown, but with a variety of sweet-smelling blossoming trees. Even as he hesitated, a light bloomed out in the midst of them, and there came the lilt of a long-necked harp, most skillfully played.

"Why do you wait?" whispered the servant to Jadrid. "Each evening my master's daughter plays in the arbor. Go only as far as those three peach trees, and you can view as much."

Just then, there came winging through the air the notes of a female voice, exquisitely singing. And as if enchanted, Jadrid stole forward to the peach trees and looked between them.

There in a little pavilion burned three round lamps that flashed with jewels. But under the lamps there burned the brightest light and jewel of all.

It seemed to Jadrid he had never seen such fair beauty in any mortal thing, and probably he had not. Trellised with golden ornaments, her hair was the same dark red color the dying sun had been, and it splashed in a cascade across her shoulders, and shone all gold too where the lamps burnished it. Her skin, ringed with gold, was paler than the finest white paper. As she played her song to the stars, the gems on her slender fingers dazzled Jadrid. But her eyes, which did not see him, smote him almost blind.

For some while she sang, and surely never did a maiden sing so perfectly. Jadrid stood rooted to the spot. At length the girl set the harp aside, rose on tiptoe to blow out the lamps, and almost slew the watcher with her grace. Then she stole away toward the house, and vanished in darkness.

Slowly, Jadrid turned from the peach trees and went to find the servant, who was waiting for him at the door, arms folded.

"I—" said Jadrid.

"Say nothing now," said the servant mildly. "There on the road waits a chariot, whose driver has been instructed on the quickest route whereby to attain your house."

Jadrid looked and saw that a chariot had indeed arrived by the mansion's wall, with three proud horses in the shafts, and a driver who huddled to his business more like a monkey than a man.

"We shall hear from you, it may chance," said the servant.

"At first light," said Jadrid.

"Such haste is not needful. We are fond of the night, here. Send at tomorrow's dusk, if you wish." Then the servant himself went into the garden and closed the door.

Jadrid, all bemused, walked to the chariot, entered it, and sat down. The journey went by in a dreaming whirl, so that the bridegroom—who now wished to be nothing more vehemently—scarcely noted any of it, its unusual speed, the wild agility of the leaping horses, their thinness, the odd monkeylike slave who managed them.

Returned to his father's house, and going straight to that father's chamber, Jadrid made his confession.

"I will wed this one, or none."

The merchant was troubled, but—apples of fire.

Now the whole affair was rather bizarre, but not unseemly, and in the end even the merchant had put off his doubts as satisfied. It transpired that the strange servant's august master was a very learned but a very old man, for years in wretched health and now near death. He, having vast wealth and one charming daughter, wished to dispose both wisely and well before his departure. He had therefore made inquiries, and it seemed to him that a particular merchant-lord, the father of Jadrid, would be a suitable father-in-law, the merchant's house an excellent and worthy one, and the merchant's son, Jadrid, a noble husband. All this the girl's father communicated to the merchant by means of elegant letters, accompanied always by gifts of surpassing magnificence. That the elderly invalid did not himself appear was due, as he said, to his illness having made him feeble and reclusive. His child, nevertheless, he was eager to bestow on Jadrid, and upon Jadrid's avowal she had been enlightened, and declared herself, dutiful daughter that she was, willing to abide by her father's choice.

Her name was Liliu. Besides her loveliness, she had been gently and ably reared, could read and write in many languages, was a musician of no slight art—yet also was she childlike and innocent. And because of this, on a single point the father begged indulgence. It would seem that, virtuous and loving as she was, the girl had spent most of her time with her ailing parent. And his illness had made him unable to bear any but the rays of the moon or the subfusc of candles; sunlight worsened his condition. So her new protectors must, if they would, be lenient at first with Liliu's aversion to the sun—for, living by night with her father, and taking against the sun for his sake, she might wish to eschew the hours of day for a time, rising at sunfall as had become her habit, sleeping through the morning and the afternoon.

This seemed most understandable. Besides, the idea of wakeful nights did not displease the young man. He, too, had something of the sort in mind.

So letters and presents were exchanged, priests were consulted, the proper sacrifices made to the gods (who, as ever, ignored them), necessaries laid in, furnishings made ready. And at last the night arrived when, lit by torches, Jadrid went to claim his bride—for convenience' sake, since the old father was at death's door, from the pavilion in the garden.

There she sat, veiled and demure, among flowers and perfumes, her dowry (which was truly wondrous) piled around her. The sick parent, as was expected, was nowhere to be seen. Oddly, neither did she have any attendants. It was assumed they modestly stood back in the surrounding trees, consigning her to the bridegroom's care.

Jadrid had no worries on this score.

They were accordingly married, Liliu and Jadrid. Seldom was a bride more fair, more circumspect, or more winsome. Seldom a bridegroom so envied.

Aloft in the bedroom, having disrobed his wife, Jadrid learned that her perfections were as all-encompassing as he had been feverishly dreaming they were. And though she was a virgin, and rendered him the proofs, yet she seemed, perhaps from her erudition, to have gained many wisdoms which—with proper timidity at first, but seeing that her actions were not amiss, with ever greater assurance—she practiced on him, so that his pleasure was doubled and trebled, and actually went beyond all such meager mathematical limits. So much so indeed, that late revelers, who happened to eavesdrop under his windows, were highly gratified. It was in fact at the crest of one such delicious excursion that Jadrid, flinging out an arm unwarily, overturned a ewer that stood by the bed. The ewer, in breaking, cut him.

"Oh, my dearest lord!" exclaimed Liliu, as he sank back spent, to discover that his wrist bled.

"It is nothing at all," said Jadrid.

But Liliu, not unfittingly for a young wife, was most concerned.

"No, no. Who can tell what infection there may be on the edges of the broken thing." (*Yes,* thought Jadrid, full of tenderest sympathy, *she has been too long with a sick man.*) "Now, if you will permit me, here is the surest remedy, which will cleanse your veins of all poisonous stuff." And saying this, she put her mouth to the wound. Jadrid was amazed, and touched at her solicitude. That venoms could be removed in such a way, he knew. But how well she must love him so to tend him! When eventually she was positive all harm had been sucked forth—it took a little while, she was very conscientious—Liliu smiled, and set her lips to other work. Soon, she mounted him lightly, and with an abandoned dancing beautiful to behold and of a divine anguish to experience, began to draw him toward the seventh gateway of the night. *Ah—what a wife*

I have been blessed with! thought Jadrid. Anon, his loud groans brought a new toast from the revelers below, and shook several fruits from the damson tree that grew against the wall.

When he woke at sunrise, Jadrid saw his wife had already vacated their bed, and sought the daytime seclusion which he had, kind husband as he meant to be, prepared for her. He himself slept well past noon.

The first weeks of the marriage, then, went by in harmony. The only discord sounded in the area of the young wife's preference for night over day, from which she, so meek in all else, would not budge. *That is the great love she bore her father,* thought Jadrid. So, he restrained his discontent. (Ah, yes. Apples of fire.)

But in this way, Jadrid, having business affairs he must attend to in the daytime, saw rather less of his wife than was customary, for he could not keep awake all the night through, as it seemed she did.

There was one other slight peculiarity. At the nuptial feast, Liliu had eaten nothing, and drunk nothing save a sip or two of water. This had been taken for timorousness, or sorrow at leaving her father. Yet, even now, Liliu would eat nothing in her husband's sight. She assured him, living as she had so long with an ailing man who could partake only of gruel, she had got in the way herself of eating one frugal meal a day, and that alone. Jadrid remained amenable to this custom, though it subtly discontented him.

After a month had gone by, Jadrid became irritable over little things. One morning he had woken a space before sunrise, wishing very much to embrace Liliu. But though the sun was not yet over the horizon, his wife had already left his bed. Accordingly Jadrid broke his fast alone and in an ill humor, and it happened that one of the servants spilled a dash of salt, and Jadrid cursed her, because it was unlucky. Suddenly the woman burst into a flood of tears. "Oh, my lord," she wept, "unlucky you may well say. Only let me go on my knees and tell you the thing I have kept hidden these past three days, and which has filled me with such distress, I have been nearly out of my mind at it."

Jadrid, astonished, forgot his bad mood.

"Speak at once," he said. "Do not fear my wrath. I have none, unless you continue to keep silent."

Then the woman told Jadrid this, as follows.

Owing to her tasks in the house, she was frequently obliged to get up before cockcrow, and one early morning, when it wanted some half hour of dawn, she was filling a water jar at the courtyard well when she heard a stealthy noise, nearby and, as it seemed, underground. Something made the woman cautious, indeed, rather afraid. So she left her jar and took shelter behind a bush against the privy wall. After a moment, her heart almost started out of her breast. For what should happen but one of the big old paving stones in the yard began to lift by its roots, and presently it stood on its side, and up out of the place undernearth came gliding a dreadful apparition, in the predawn dusk all glaring dark and white. No sooner was it clear of the hole than it set back the paving stone as if the huge thing weighed like a feather. Then it turned and looked carefully about it. (Never had the woman been so glad to bloom unseen.) For sure, the arrival was a ghastly sight, a female being in a white shift, but all dabbled and filthy with dirt and—could it be with blood? Going to the well, it let down the bucket, and when the bucket came up again, the creature washed itself. And then for the first time the woman saw that what had come up in blood and filth from under the earth was none other than her young master's young wife, Liliu.

"Where she had been I do not know, nor do I wish to know. But surely something had delayed her—she was all anxiety lest any come out and catch her at her washing. Then, when she was clean, and had wrung out her long hair, she went into the house and away to her own chamber that she cleaves to by day. And now," said the woman sullenly, folding her hands, "I suppose I shall be slain for witnessing the misdeeds of my betters."

"Not slain for that, but whipped for lying," said Jadrid in a rage—he was frightened, too.

"Well, I have proof of what I say," announced the woman.

"Show it."

So she did. Leading Jadrid to the courtyard, the servant woman requested him to kneel down by one of the paving slabs. At a glance he could see it had been disturbed, but anything might account for that. Not, however, for the strand of hair, poppy-red, which was caught under it.

"She went out again last night and returned again an hour before sunrise. I heard her and looked from a hole in the privy door. She was not canny enough this time. As she set back the slab her hair was caught, but she cut it through with her own sharp teeth, and then ran in haste, not bothering to take the evidence from the stone—for who would glimpse it if they did not come looking for it, as I did. Now you, strong lord, try to lift that stone, and see whether any of us are playing tricks on you."

Jadrid then did try to lift the stone, but even working till the sweat poured, and with his dagger as a lever, he could not shift the piece of paving more than half an inch. Certainly not sufficiently to come at the strand of hair still trapped beneath, clearly on an occasion when the slab had risen freely. . . .

Eventually he rose, and said to the woman, "You will stay quiet. Tell no one, not even my father. You have watched and seen her come in. Now I will watch and see where it is she *goes*."

If truth were told, Jadrid had a notion already, nor did he much relish it. It happened that the cellars beneath the merchant's house abutted underground on some ancient catacombs, supposedly haunted, into which, by his own boy's means, Jadrid had penetrated once or twice years before. These forays had revealed nothing very terrible, aside from rats and mummy-dust. In their turn, however, the tunnels led out of the city to an antique burial ground, no longer much used save by the very poor, and itself of ill repute.

Unbeknownst to any, then, Jadrid spent that day enlarging, with iron bar and mallet, the exit point in the cellar which had accommodated him as a boy. By the afternoon, he had got through into the foul warren beyond, where it was always night, and choking on the dust, he lifted high his lamp. He soon found, as he had unwillingly imagined he would, a weird tearing in the tangled webs of powder, and a mark on the stone roof high overhead—here was the place which corresponded to the loose paving in the courtyard. Going up and down awhile with his light, Jadrid next beheld on the tunnel floor and on some of the shelves that went toward the ceiling, the muddled imprint of many footfalls—or of one person's journey many times repeated. Small feet they were, with ringed toes, but they had been dipped in something to leave such a mark. And what they had been dipped in had been very red—

Oh, horrible. And more than horrible, most strange. Never having suspected her, having been so long her dupe, Jadrid now felt everything coming clear. As if, in some way he had concealed from himself, he had known *always*—

"Forgive me, sweet wife. I cannot enjoy you tonight. I am weary."

So saying, Jadrid lay down and feigned the most abject slumber. Yet she was prudent. She did not steal away till moonrise.

When he was sure she had gone, Jadrid leapt up, flung on his clothes, and belted on his sword. He ran noiselessly through the house and into the cellar, and so came out into the pitchy vault of the catacombs beyond.

He had prepared for himself a dull lamp, by which he could just find his way. For the rest, he knew the passages from before. He went forward with enormous stealth nevertheless, shielding the vague light also with his cloak. And as well. At a turning among the cubbies of disintegrate bones, he caught a flicker of brightness—it was the hem of her shift, the shimmer of her white instep and a white ankle with a chain of gold upon it. So certain she was that none had tracked her here, and so eager for her destination, she went easily, never looking back. And he, taking pains where she did not, pressed after.

Suddenly the tunnels ended and came up through a quantity of caves into the open air. Here the bats took exception to Jadrid's light (*she* had needed none), and he put it out. Still without a glance over her shoulder, the pale flicker of Liliu sped on before him, and through the ruined wall of the old burial ground.

The moon stood high and made a silver twilight. On all sides, among the funeral trees and weeds, the tall tombs rose up, the houses of the dead—and it reminded Jadrid in an awful way of the boulevard of mansions where he had first followed to find his love.

Presently, they drew near a very large tomb, in parts crumbled and fallen down, but elsewhere pillared, and sculpted in historic ways—it had been the resting place of a mighty prince. Out of cracks and holes, and between the carvings of this, there streamed a greenish glow, and as Liliu approached, abruptly the door grated wide. Up the steps she ran, merry as a maiden running to greet her husband, and in. And the door howled shut again.

Jadrid stood awhile. His blood was ice, and many another man would probably have hurried away. But anger, and love-gone-rotten, can work wonders. In less time than it would have taken him to offer a prayer for salvation to one of the deaf gods of the Upperearth, Jadrid had climbed a tree which overlooked the prince's bonehouse, and so got on its roof. Here he quickly discovered an aperture to look through, and availed himself.

What a scene was that, down below, and which he saw in such detail. A great stone catafalque, from which the skeleton had long since been rolled, and great stone chests much despoiled—only those of a superhuman strength could have opened them to rifle them—yet still with skeins of pearls, rubies, diamonds dripping down, and marvelous instruments (such as a long-necked harp) leaned by, and books of erudition centuries old, all green like the putrescent phosphorus which made the light, yet supposedly readable, and held in covers of pure gold. On high, threescore filigree jewelry lamps, with the nasty substance burning away in them. In the midst of it all some nine persons who passed around between them nine golden, gem-encrusted goblets, each containing a different colored wine. And as they did so, like guests before a feast, they laughed and joked with each other, kissed and intimately fondled each other. They might, for a fact, have been a family, and in a manner of speaking, they were, doubtless. Each was of exceptional good looks, slender, pale, and with that red-black poppy hair Jadrid knew so well and had admired so much. And each was clothed, too, as if newly escaped from some bedchamber. And the ninth of them, of course, was Liliu, his wife.

"Then let us drink," said one of them, a man who could have been brother or cousin of Jadrid's wife, yet who held her to him in a way Jadrid himself would have been shamed to do in company. "Let us drink to our immemorial lineage, our destiny, and our success, and to our genius when compared to the clay-brains of ephemeral mankind. For it transpires we have each succeeded. Who are lords then, but ever we?"

And they did indeed some extra drinking, and toasted each other again and again, in the green and yellow and scarlet and white and even the black wines. And tickled and caressed and lipped each other as never before, making all the while obscene and uncharitable comments on the sexual ableness of humanity they had, apparently, every one of them recently had to endure.

And then another door opened to the rear of the tomb and their servants came out, some rather like monkeys, some like men, and one of the latter was the very servant who had conducted Jadrid to Liliu's garden. He it was bowed low, and proclaimed that the feast had been brought.

The nine diners were very much delighted, and more so when this feast was laid before them on the catafalque. They fell to with appreciating cries and smacking of lips. But Jadrid, who also saw on what they banqueted, had fallen prone among the ornaments of the roof in a deathly swoon.

When he came to himself again, the sky was gray, the dew was down, and the great tomb in darkness. Trembling, Jadrid gave some prayers of thanks to the gods (who were not at all responsible) that the ghoulish feasters had not discovered him.

Now, Jadrid saw it all. Demonstrably their race was old, of "lineage" and "destiny" as the male ghoul had remarked. It would seem that for some reason they sought to live among men, and so tricks had been played—not only Liliu's upon himself. In her case there was no elderly father, no house—the mansion deserted, the chariot some dead king's, the horses—phantoms? Only the dowry, the plunder of a hundred graves, was real. Probably it was a variation of this theme they had played elsewhere. Nine in number, they had now, it would seem, snared nine families by their deceptions. From eight other beds, some of hapless wives, some of trusting husbands, these fiends stole out on certain nights to meet together and rejoice. Small wonder Liliu did not care to eat with her lord. Small wonder she abhorred the wholesome sun.

Jadrid's course was sure. He would go home and wait for darkness. When she came to him with her wiles, he would kill her.

As he strode from the cemetery, tears and rage on his face, the sky was lightening but the sun not up. Dwellers in hovels under the city wall, seeing him emerge in this way from the haunted burial ground, fled indoors screaming to each other he was the very devil they had feared all these years, who caroused in the tombs all night and ate their deceased relatives. Which irony was lost on Jadrid.

It happened that Jadrid's father had been away a day or so on business. And that night, which was the night of his return, Jadrid gave orders that there was to be a dinner of especial magnificence.

Accordingly, about sunset, all came to the table, the merchant, and also the guests and relations, every one of whom had been at Jadrid's wedding. Presently Jadrid entered with his wife. "I have entreated her to dine with us, for once."

Everything was laughter and smiles.

Jadrid sat beside his wife. He begged her to take some wine.

"Pray excuse me," said she.

"No. Tonight you must drink with us."

"But you know, my lord, that I never drink wine."

"A wonderful wife," exclaimed one of the guests. "So abstemious."

"Then at least," said Jadrid persuasively, "you must taste a little of this meat—"

"Pray excuse me."

"This fruit—"

"Pray excuse me."

"A pastry then. A spoonful of honey—"

"Excuse me, dear lord," said Liliu. "I have already eaten. Alone, as is my custom."

"How frugal," said another guest. And another: "How charmingly bashful."

"Yes," said Jadrid, smiling upon his wife, "it is true she eats elsewhere, and not with me. But tell us, gentle Liliu, what *is* it that you eat? The servants say they bear you dishes of food, but mostly these dishes go back untouched. Another has declared that he suspects you of throwing what food is gone to stray dogs under the house wall."

The guests laughed. Liliu lowered her eyes.

"A sip of wine now, to bring some color to your pale cheecks," said Jadrid, with vast concern. "A morsel of bread, to please me."

"Excuse me, I pray you," said Liliu. "I am not hungry."

"This," said Jadrid, "is probably a fact. For last night, I think, you ate very well."

Something in his voice then caused a silence in the chamber. Even the flames straightened in the lamps as if anxiously to listen. But Liliu did not raise her eyes.

"What can you mean, Jadrid?" the merchant asked his son. "You say she does not eat with you, and then you say she has, to your knowledge, eaten well. The poor maiden will be distraught. You must not tease her so."

"No?" said Jadrid. "An end to the teasing then." And now his face and voice were very terrible. "Last night, having had a warning, I followed my wife, who often, it seems, leaves my bed in the depths of the dark. I followed her by way of the tunnels under our house, out to the burial ground beyond the city wall. And there in a tomb she met with acquaintances of hers, her kindred, and together they mocked the silliness of mankind, as they tore off the breasts of a dead women and devoured them. And there they drank to the inferiority of men, as they guzzled the blood and bile of corpses."

Horror struck the company. Not one moved, till Liliu jumped up, and rushing to the merchant, she threw herself at his feet. "Save me, my father," she cried, "for your son has gone mad."

"Mad, yes, very nearly," said Jadrid, whose face was now if anything paler than hers. "If you, my own kin and friends, doubt me, I ask you to call in the servants. Among them you will find one at least who has seen this thing I took for wife coming up at morning through the courtyard stones, to wash off the foulness of her feeding at our well."

Then Liliu jumped to her feet again. She turned and gazed at them all, and her beauty was gone, her face ugly and ravenous. Not one who looked on her at that moment but did not know Jadrid had been honest.

"Oh, you, so cunning and so clever the world reels at you, oh dear husband, what will you do?"

"Why, only this," said Jadrid. And going straight up to her, he plunged his dagger into her heart.

She shrieked once, and then she fell to the ground, while the candles sank low in the lamps, as if afraid to see.

3   *The Tale Continues*

EVERYONE in the house was sworn to secrecy concerning the events of that awful night. The oath was a terrific one. It was given out that Jadrid's young spouse had died tragically and suddenly at table, by choking on a bone. (There was a gruesome humor to this of which Jadrid himself may well have been aware.) Of the other houses in the city which might have fallen prey to the company of ghouls, no heed was taken. They must look out for themselves.

Liliu was buried next day with much pomp and lament.

Jadrid was said to be overwhelmed by grief. He had commissioned for his beloved a special monument, and this was why she was first to be laid in a burial chamber unconnected to the family mausoleum, and on ground beyond the family plot.

Out of respect for the family's sorrow, the whole street where stood the merchant's house was closed for three days and three nights.

During this period, too, the house itself stayed shut up and its inmates indoors. It may be true that Jadrid grieved, but his misery was of a feverish, furious sort. In dreams the alarmed father heard his son cry out that he wished he might slay the foul witch a second time. Such is love.

On the third night, some hours before dawn as the moon was sinking, Jadrid roused out of a leaden sleep.

Waking, he knew himself still unconscious. For a nightmare crouched at the bed's foot. It had the shape of Liliu, her perfume even, her long hair of blackest red which poured across his feet, and it leaned to the vein in his ankle and sucked the blood from it.

Jadrid struggled, and would have shouted for help, but he was weak with horror. And even as he tried to free himself of the vile dream, the vile dream itself raised her head and smiled at him, while his blood ran from her teeth. "Be still, dearest lord," said Liliu. And she set her hand on his chest and pushed him back. She had the strength of a giantess; he could not resist. "Why so surprised?" said Liliu. "Is it not right a wife should be by her husband in his bed? Ah, you did not think you killed me? Such flesh as I am, nothing can kill it for long, not iron, nor steel, nor stone nor bone nor water, nor fire. Did we not boast our greatness in the tomb?"

And then she stood up, and laughing at him, became a column of spinning smoke, and this vanished into the air.

"Then, thank the gods, it was a dream—"

But lighting the candles, Jadrid saw, and felt, the bite in his ankle, and how it bled.

Three mages were called to the merchant's house. The first came with much show, and a retinue of servants. His own chair was set for him in the merchant's hall. His page lay down under his feet to be his footstool. The robes of the first mage were sewn with orichalc, and he held a wand of gold with which he casually toyed, though lightnings seeped from its end.

"The young man," said the first mage, "is beset by a vampire. She is thirsty not only for blood but for revenge. She will destroy him if she can."

"So much we are aware of," said the merchant.

"I am glad to find you educated," said the mage. He snapped his fingers. A green toad bounced into his lap and poured for him a sherbet from a flask of emerald. "The chamber where the young man sleeps," said the first mage, "must have branches of the wild thorn tree piled at door and windows. He must be anointed with blessed oil from a temple given over to the worship of some god who is reckoned to have arisen, at least on one occasion, from the dead. (There are several of these.) If the vampire is still able to manifest, he must recite a mantra, which I will teach him."

Things were performed as the first mage directed. Wild thorn brought from the country and laid at the thresholds, sacred oil smeared on Jadrid's body. He lay awake through the first and second hours of darkness, but in the third hour slumbered exhaustedly. He woke to find the devil-woman seated at his bed foot, biting at his ankle. Then Jadrid exclaimed at her the mantra the first mage had instructed him in.

Liliu raised her head.

"Not iron nor steel, stone nor bone, water nor fire. Not scratchy thorns not sticky oil. Not *words*," said Liliu. And before he could stop her, she raked him across the breast with her long and pointed nails, and thrusting him down began to lap his lifeblood like a famished rat.

At this Jadrid let out a cry so loud the house seemed shaken, and the merchant's armed guards, waiting in the passage, rushed into the room. But Liliu sneered at their swords and spears. She began to spin, she became smoke, then air. She was gone.

The second mage came in black and was cowled in black. He wore a mask of thin wood that revealed only his eyes, and these not well. He groveled to his gods constantly, to show them he remembered them. He groveled also to the merchant.

"If you will allow this wretched person to advise you, exalted sir, the efficacy of which advice is only valuable in that it was obtained by study of holy lore, then you will do this . . ." And his treatment was as follows. The young man must fast that day, and bathe seven times in the coldest water. An hour before sunfall he must have arrived at the segregated unresting-place of his late wife, with what helpers he had selected, who must also have fasted and bathed seven times in cold water. Going into the tomb, they should wait by the bier until the sun was almost down, then snatch off the grave coverings. Ignoring the dead woman's appearance of healthy life, her opening eyes, or any pleading she might make, her husband must then lop off her head, cut out her heart and set fire to it, and to the rest of the cadaver, separately.

"But she has told me," said Jadrid, "iron, steel, fire—such things cannot harm her."

"Where is your faith?" said the mage. "My gods know all."

Jadrid was not convinced, but he was desperate, and so obeyed in everything, even to the seven baths.

Just before sunset, disguised as priests, he and his band of retainers entered the small dilapidated tomb where Liliu had been laid.

As the sun began to sink, they approached the bier and snatched off the coverings from the body—finding only what they had expected, that she was firm and fresh, with every appearance of voluptuous life.

If Jadrid was disposed to hesitate was not recorded. Undoubtedly Liliu opened her eyes and glowered at him. In that instant, he smote off her head, and next went on with the rest of the procedure. When a torch was set to the remains, it seemed a jeering female laugh rang around the tomb.

As they paced back to the merchant's house, it occurred to each of the men, and to Jadrid, that something walked behind. They entered the house and barred its doors. Jadrid and his father then kept vigil, with all the guards and the male servants standing by with drawn sword or heavy stave. The black-robed priest knelt in a corner, praying and scourging himself.

Presently there was a dreadful crash—it was the outer door being flung wide. After this the door of the chamber flew open and in came a smother of swirling ashes which spun and roiled and *laughed*. And became Liliu. She was entirely whole, not bearing any mark to show where she had been so frequently and mortally smitten.

"Not iron or steel, stone or bone, thorn or oil or words, not the sword, not the torch, not aesthetics, rituals, traditions, faith, *prayer* can rid you of me, dear husband," said Liliu. "I love you so well I will drain you dry. Not tonight, for you are not private enough, but tomorrow I will come to you. No man set to guard you shall I spare. One scratch of my nails shall be fatal to them. Defend yourself as you will, you cannot deny me. I will have your blood, I will have the marrow of your bones. Look forward to our meeting, sweet lord. For now, a token—only this—" And suddenly she flew at Jadrid and bit from his hand the first finger, and vanished with it into nothingness.

"The gods help me, I am damned!" cried Jadrid. And taking his own sword would have slain himself at once, had his father and the servants not prevented it by force.

Soon afterward, the second mage was thrown from the house, and, at dawn, the third mage invited in.

This third mage was plainly dressed, neither flamboyant nor obscure in his bearing. He looked at Jadrid and said to him, "Do not yet despair." Then he sat down with father and son and discussed matters as though debating on the price of grain. Finally the mage spoke to them, in this way.

"I regret yours is not the only house in the city to be plagued by this confederacy of devilkind. Nevertheless, in this fashion, something has been learned of them. It is true they are an old and, in their own lights, estimable race. They despise man, but must now and then have recourse to him. In the beginning, they believe, their race and man's were one, and man still carries certain of their tastes which he has suppressed from an egomaniacal squeamishness, and refuses to eat, in certain parts, even the flesh of pigs, since it is said to resemble that of men. And so he has lost, they say, his strength, but remains fatally attracted to their kind, which, when necessary, they exploit. He has, too, abilities which they, for all their superior talents, have not. She who named herself to you *Liliu* is, like all her clan, impervious to violence. Her body being always partially etheric, it can never properly be dissipated by any physical means. To strike her with blade, even to burn her—these strategies only strengthen her, for it is *practice* in reintegration which makes such a creature perfect in the art of rebirth."

"Then I am lost," said Jadrid.

"Not so," said the mage. "If you will be resolute but one further time, you may gain such power over her she will cease to annoy you."

"By what means?" cried Jadrid with understandable urgency.

"Listen well to me," said the third mage. "There is on the earth no mortal thing that does not have a shadow. The making of such a shadow is only this, that a solid object impedes the path of light. Now, there are some beings, too, which may pass as mortal, until it is seen that, as they are discorporate, light shines quite through them and they have no shadow at all."

"Liliu?"

"Not Liliu, for would you not have been wary from the first if she had had no shadow? Shadows Liliu's kind do have, but they are not of the nature of the human shadow. The human body is flesh, but the body of one of Liliu's kind is partly nonfleshly. Just so the shadow, which in the human is no more than darkened air, in the vampire is partly corporate. Where light strikes them, it does somewhat pass through, and so forces various particles also through into the substance of the shadow. Why else, do you imagine, does this race so fear the blast of the sun, who is the king of all lights?"

"Then?" asked Jadrid.

"Tonight, do not go to your bed. Stand ready in the chamber. Let her appear, as she will, but be sure there is a bright lamp burning and a knife hidden to hand. Cajole her, then, and promise her rewards, and beg her on your knees—for her people love flattery and terror in equal measure. But all this while, manage it that the light shines upon her and so her shadow is cast out. Then suddenly run to the shadow and slash through it till as much as may be is separated from her. For from her it can be ripped, and it will bleed and she will scream and set on you—but you must resist and tear the shadow free. Now, when you burned her, it was into the shadow that all her atoms fled, but since her flesh is whole, you will have divided, at the first stroke, those atoms. And from that first stroke she will grow weaker, and at the last will fall to entreating you as you had entreated her, promising you all manner of riches and miracles. You will naturally pay no heed. But take the shadow, which you will find limp, skinny, and slimy to the touch, and thrust it in some bag or jar, which you must then tightly seal. Neither air nor light must get in. Keep it so only a few moments, away from her proximity, and the shadow will wither to a harmless husk. And as for she herself, as you will learn, she will have lost all her power.''

''And may I kill her then?'' asked Jadrid, with blazing eyes.

''Her kind do not die easily,'' said the third mage, ''but you will find her docile and much altered, unable to perform against you anything. Imprison her or drive her out, as you will.''

The day blossomed, faded, fell. The night returned, and Jadrid stood ready in his chamber, all alone, one bright lamp burning, and a knife hidden in the cushions of the bed.

He paced up and down, up and down, from the last red drop of sunset, until the windows were black as if the whole city lay inside a tomb. Then there came a fluttering in the midst of the floor, like feathers, then a spiraling like a pillar of dust. And then there stood Liliu.

''Beloved,'' said Jadrid instantly, ''I know you are here to kill me. Have you not vowed it?''

''Just so,'' said Liliu, and raised her claws.

''Give me then,'' said Jadrid, ''a few moments' grace to make to you some act of contrition.''

''Your blood and split bones will satisfy me,'' said Liliu, but she had paused.

"Let me speak; I will be brief," said Jadrid. "Let me tell you, beloved, that my fear has gone from me. I am in a sort of ecstasy that makes me glad to die at your hands. I have loved you with such passion, I would not desire to die in any other way. That I tried to betray you first, and then to destroy you—these were foolish childish deeds, to which others bent me. I had a secret faith besides that you, being of a kingly race, could not succumb. Yet forgive such transgressions. If my agony will please you, take it. Your beauty is beyond all beauty in the world. To have drunk such wine, from such a cup, I have been fortunate as it is given to few men to be. Better to have been your lover a month and perish, than to lie whole centuries with mortal women who are dross."

Now this had its effect. The devil-folk of the ghouls had a further weakness—it thought itself unsurpassable, and so was swiftly able to credit others might think so too.

"For these words," said Liliu, "I will cause your pain to be a little less."

"No," said Jadrid. "My pain is my last gift of love to you. Take as much of it as you wish, and spare me nothing. For to serve you, my goddess, is my only longing."

And then he beckoned her toward the bed, and Liliu came to him, and as she did so the lamp shone on her and her shadow was flung across the covers, clear and blue.

Out then he swept the hidden knife, and with it he slashed at the shadow—and it frayed and tore like ruptured silk, and glittering transparent ichor fountained up. And the devil-woman screamed. She shrieked and threw herself upon Jadrid, and scratched and bit at him, but her strength was not as it had been—

And then all the clinging threads of the shadow were cut away, and Jadrid seized it and rolled up the slimy thing, which was no thicker than a roll of seaweed, and sprang with it from the bed, leaving Liliu sprawled there. And when she lifted herself, only a few vague wisps of shadow lingered, reflected on the wall.

"Oh my husband, pity me. Pity me," said Liliu, "and I will bring you great treasure—"

"Yes, you are not so cunning with your enticements as I, it would seem," said Jadrid bitterly.

"I will make you a king," wailed Liliu. "I will love you always."

"You are stupid now as well as filthy," said Jadrid, and he plunged the crumpled rag of severed shadow into a leather sack, and tied the sack's neck. And when Liliu came creeping toward him, he kicked her away.

Shortly the slight weight in the sack was slighter.

And Liliu lay at his feet, under her black-red hair, shuddering with feeble hate and weakness.

"Well, it seems I may not kill you," said Jadrid then, "but your life will doubtless be more irksome to you than the quick kindness of a sword. You shall be driven out into the mountains, or the swamps beyond the river's delta. There live or die as you choose."

"Oh, Jadrid," said Liliu, lying under her hair, "you have made nothing of me, and I am powerless, but there is one further thing you must know."

"Of you? I would rather hear the nightbird rattle, or the wind through a grating."

"Remember," said Liliu, "how we boasted, my brothers and sisters and I, in the tomb?"

"That I shall never forget. May you and your kind be forever accursed. As you are."

"Remember how we toasted, in the liquors of men, our success?"

"Foul bitch, you sicken me. Can I cut out your tongue, now? And shall I? I have heard enough."

"Not quite enough. Did you never wonder to which success we alluded?"

"Your ability to deceive mankind."

"Not merely. For all its wisdom, my race, so close-bred as it is, cannot bear children of its own loins, unless the seed of our men be sprinkled in a human woman's womb, or the wombs of our women quickened by the seed of human men."

Jadrid stood then like the stone. In his hands, her severed shadow shrank lighter and lighter. Liliu lay before him, seeming shrunken and fragile, too, her hair and skin very dull, her long talons all broken. But her voice remained to devil him. Her voice said:

"Oh Jadrid, you may work against me as you will, but your son is in my body. How shall you deal with *him*?"

The third mage had gone away. The household of the merchant-lord deliberated, and perhaps not sensibly.

It is hard for a man to outlaw his firstborn.

They locked her in an apartment of the lower building. Loyal servants of the merchant and his son, these tended her. It was quite safe for them to do so. For sure, the vampire-ghoul-devil Liliu was wasted now, and burning down like a flame which had no oil to nurture it. Like a blood-red flower without sap, she paled and failed. Her wits seemed addled, she was an idiot. The merchant's son never visited her. But every day the women must make a report to him on how the child fared within her—for each day, as she flickered and sank, her womb grew larger. Strangely, the sunlight seemed no longer to trouble her. She had lost the precious part of herself; there was nothing else to scorch away.

At length, the labor began, there in the locked room. A while before daybreak, she brought forth.

They came to tell Jadrid. The devil-creature was dead, all flaccid, like an empty garment. Its hair had turned colorless and its teeth fallen out, and when they moved it the bones clinked together under the loose skin, like coins in a pot.

But the child—oh the child.

Jadrid said to his father, "I will go now and look at the child and make my decision. It has in its veins, after all, the blood of the living dead. How else could its atoms have unnaturally survived, with the mother's death, dismemberment, burning? If it is like her, then it is hers, and must be destroyed."

And the merchant, gazing at his son's cold graven face, did not argue.

So Jadrid went down through the house and came into the room where now the sun flamed golden. And there the child lay in a patch of sunlight. It was a beautiful boy. Flawlessly formed, already with a look of intelligence and perception in the tiny face, the great eyes. Its skin was transparent pale as the sheerest paper; its hair, for already there was hair upon its scalp, was darkest red.

Jadrid bent over the child, frowning and cruel, and stretched out his hand from which the forefinger had been bitten. But three sound fingers remained, and the boy lifted his small arms and, laughing, grasped the middle one of these in both fists. "Oh my son," said Jadrid. "You are also mine."

And as he took up the baby in his arms, the sun ripened in the window like an apple of fire.

4

"NOW," BEGAN the storyteller, "when some years had gone by—"

"Enough," said Sovaz. "Your story is predictable, and the remainder I discern. Darkness has grown pale, listening to you."

It was a fact. Another morning was near.

The man, though, looked angrily at Sovaz, who had by now broken all her bonds, and sat before him in that rock hole like night's bright symbol.

"If you can fathom the rest, then say the rest," he muttered.

"Very well. Though some of the fraternity of nine perished, some did not, while all the babies were sentimentally spared. These then grew up" —she spoke of this strangely, cruelly; she had had no childhood herself— "and less and less were the foolish parents able to refuse them. At last these ghoul children came to adult estate, and each exercised all the habits of the ghoul parent, and next drove the human parents out, or suborned them, took charge of the city, and warped or won it to their own graveyard ways. And they have by now no doubt spawned other ghoul infants by consent, seduction, and rape. And meanwhile they renamed the place for their manner of portioning the dead they devour, and other spoil they take. And you, old man, are Jadrid, once the wife-seeker.''

''Woman,'' he said, ''do you jeer at me? You have snapped the cords we bound you with, but we have greater magics. Mighty is Shudm, City of the Portioners. It draws hosts and companies to itself, to be its fodder. They come they know not why. Fat merchants and brawny robbers, the entourage of lady and sage. Shudm sucks them in across the plain. Shudm is always hungry and always fed. But even the lone traveler is welcome. And I will be rewarded for you. Look. Where is the omission from my finger? I have none. As a gift, my son gave to me the digit of an emperor, and this finger has been mine some years, though this priceless ring, another of his gifts, hides the adhesion.''

''Since you are yet your son's friend,'' said Sovaz, ''why warn me from the way?''

''That is my humanity,'' said old Jadrid. ''Such mobs arrive, we can afford now and then to be merciful. But the stubborn ones and the jeering ones we take to them, even into the ghoul city of Shudm, for their pleasure.''

And then the rags fell from him and from his accomplices. They were clad in some magnificence, of a tawdry sort, but many of them were revealed as crouching monkey things, not men at all. Then Jadrid spoke to the ropes that had bound Sovaz, and they coiled about her and held her fast again, and at another word of his they became steel.

''You are a witch,'' said Jadrid with venom, ''but your small sorcery cannot match the sorcery of *their* kind. As I have discovered. Come now. We are going to the city.''

At that the monkey creatures snatched Sovaz and bore her away, by leaping bounds, down the sheer mountain ledges toward the the plain. A human girl might well have died of fear. But Sovaz kept her own counsel, made no resistance, and uttered no word.

*   *   *

All day tirelessly they traveled over that blanched bare plain, until, near sunset, they reached a great cemetery. Every tomb of it was despoiled and the earth upturned everywhere, and bones hanging in the trees. Beyond this horrid area stood up the city walls, with the river beyond, but the river was thick and dull, though the red dying of the sun smeared on it. High in the fading sky carrion birds wheeled around, and in the dead trees where the bones hung, and on the wrecked tombs, such birds had chosen their perches, and stood watching with baleful eyes, and one or two of them held perhaps in its beak a human hand, or a hank of human hair.

And the closer you came to the city, the better you heard the sounds of it, the wild strains of pipes and cymbals, or laughter, or loud cries. And its smell filled the atmosphere, of burning resins and sticky oils, and smoke, and under and over all, the tincture of death.

The gates of the city were shut, but it seemed Jadrid had been spied approaching, and in a few moments, the portal was drawn wide. They went through, the old man and his company of men and unmen, with Sovaz hurried along in their midst.

Whatever it once had been, it was a dark city now, Shudm. The streets were black, narrow, straight, and of many corner turnings, and on each side blind black stone platforms went up, and the black tiers of the buildings, out of which dark windows stared. Here and there dark columns arose, carved and gilded, and bearing the writing of several tongues—which Sovaz might read, but which told only the lineage and legends of the ghouls, whom they had conquered and how mighty they were—in terms that seemed always lying. And sometimes, set in the walls were grinning or silently howling masks made of black bronze, with the greenish corpse phosphorus inside them. From the doors and porticos of palaces and temples, or the buildings which had been such in the days when men ruled the city, issued terrible groans and screamings and the notes of blades, whips, mallets, and other instruments of torture and butchery.

Few persons traversed the streets. Those that passed were muffled and veiled, but as Jadrid's gang went by,

there would come a glint of eyes or pallid greedy snouts
turning to look after. Now and then a livid hand would
pluck at Jadrid's sleeve, and the nails of the hand would be
long and pointed. But Jadrid never halted, nor his attendants, and the captive was borne on with them. It was a
route they had borne many captives, no doubt. Soon, some
of the veiled and muffled ones stole after them, hissing to
each other softly, pawing the darkness, but respectfully not
slinking very near.

What did she think, Sovaz, having allowed herself to be
brought to this grisly slough?

Make no mistake, her thoughts were not those of a
frightened girl, or even of a sly and arrogant sorceress.
Pressured by the emanations of this hellhole, her brain had
become purely demonic. She was all demon, now. Therefore, not to be read.

At length they came into an open square which descended on one side to the sewerlike river. The space was
dominated by a huge black edifice, lacking windows and
all apertures but an entrance, this being formed as a vast
and mindless face, and in the face a gaping mouth crowded
by fangs of stone. Within was a red light. And up the stair
to it, and through and under the fanged mouth, and into
the redness, they bore Sovaz. And so into a hall more like
a colossal chimney than any other thing, the walls of it
soaring up to a roof lost beyond the hectic flames of the
torches that burned there. But now and again a shadow
crossed the vault above and a shriek came down, or a dry
black feather: The carrion birds of the city flew freely also
here. The lower part of the hall was decorated with every
gaudy and expensive item imaginable that might be obtained from the hoard of a sarcophagus. Among the inlaid
screens and gemmy hangings, on carved couches and embroidered rugs, sat or lay a quantity of men and women,
all alike for their paleness and their dark cinnabar hair.
Their clothing, though costly, was as rabidly unaesthetic as
the rest. Some even affected graveclothes. (It was perhaps
foolish to expect good taste among ghouls.) Their pet
slaves, who walked or crawled about among them, were
naked, that the owners might the better caresss and savor
the flesh, sometimes even gently biting at it. One of the

ghoul princes had stationed himself before a ten-foot pitcher
of glass within which a woman had been drowned in wine.
She floated, in a cloud of hair, and the ghoul prince,
turning a tap in the side of the glass, drew a cup of this
concoction. But having sampled it, he declared the brew
not yet ready to be drunk.

From which it would appear these, who had human
blood mingled with the other, could tolerate wine and such
human refreshments, though their preference was clearly
for traditional delicacies. Likewise, no doubt, the sun did
not harm or inconvenience them very much (in the story,
the baby had been left lying in a patch of sunlight),
though, no doubt again, they avoided the rays on principle
if left to themselves—there was a decided sense of the new
day in the nighttime city, sunset being still dawn to them.
(Part demon, all demon at this moment, *she* could hardly
miss it.)

But now the ghoul who had tasted the wine turned and
gazed fixedly at Jadrid. Jadrid fell down on his face.

"Beloved son," whined Jadrid, "see what dainty I
found for you, in the mountains."

"By my dead mother's shadow," said the ghoul, "you
have earned for yourself a sojourn in the city by this. For
all the thousands I have sampled, here is one in thousands."

And he came to Sovaz at once and looked at her and
stroked her.

Presently the ghoul said, "And are you not afraid? Do
you not understand your destiny, here?"

Sovaz smiled. The ghoul checked. He was unused to
such attitudes. "You may," said Sovaz, "tell me what
you think it to be."

"So lovely," said the ghoul. "I believe I will delay and
keep you one night and day alive. But when another sunset
comes, some means will be devised for your slow death, at
which I, and my brothers and sisters, will preside. Then we
will dine upon you, as is our way. But I shall keep this
hair," said the ghoul fondly, playing with a long coil of it,
"to edge some fine robe I possess. And your beautiful
eyes shall be set in crystal. I shall wear them as rings, and
remember you often, and lovingly. Indeed, I may compose a

song upon your merits and render your name immortal. What is your name?''

All about, the others of the fellowship, who had been looking on jealously, now tittered and whispered. It was not often they asked a dish upon the table how it was named. An honor for that dish. But the honored one seemed not to realize her bliss.

"My name is nothing to you," said Sovaz, "and your song nothing to me. Nor your night and day of delaying, nor your diet. I am only taking my leisure here, considering what I shall do with you."

Then, there was distinguishable another tone, another voice, in hers. You are all my daughter, Azhrarn had said. This moment you might hear how true it was.

Yet the City of Portionings had forgotten Underearth, or thought *itself* to be demonkind (mankind had occasionally confused the two races). The ghoul prince only widened his eyes and chuckled, captivated by insolence.

"Does the first sorcery still apply?" inquired Sovaz, in *that* voice still. "Nothing may injure your tribe—fire, blade, stone, bone?"

"Oh, yes, sweetheart. We are impervious to all such."

"While to the sun you are somewhat inured by reason of your mixed blood."

"We tolerate but do not care for the sun, which is an ugly mistake of the gods."

"And for your shadows?" said Sovaz, and her voice was nearly flirtatious.

"Behold," said the ghoul, and he raised his arm so its black reflection fell across the torches to a painted screen. "They are now as the shadows of men, and have no substance. Go scrape at that one with a knife if you wish, and see."

"How then," said Sovaz, "may I kill you? Where is the vulnerable spot?"

"Ah," said the ghoul, "do not trouble your pretty head with that. Ponder rather how I shall deal with you."

And he took her hand and kissed it and mouthed it, and softly tongued her flesh. Sovaz did nothing to prevent him. So confident, Shudm city, not one of them grasped meekness was never so meek.

"Dear Father," said the ghoul prince, "for this diversion brought me by you, I will feed you myself, from my own board."

Jadrid groveled. Yet the little graveworms and beetles, which still kept house in some of the floor coverings, may have seen his eyes as he writhed there, upsetting their domestic arrangements. And the eyes of Jadrid had a peculiar expression.

Sovaz said to the ghoul, "So you instruct humanity that it too eats human flesh, here?"

"We are never stingy. We feed our flocks and herds as well as we feed ourselves. And they get a taste for it. The old fellow there, he will be dreaming of what I shall give him of yours. But I shall keep you all for myself, and for a certain sister I am affectionate with."

Then he led her away through the chimneylike hall, while his kin made signs of humor and envy. They passed then through a door into an underground tunnel—the city had always been riddled with them, and by means of them, even in the days of human rule, the ghouls had come and gone about their business quite discreetly.

It was a black journey they now undertook, but the ghoul prince saw well in the dark, and, as he could have noted, so did his victim. Behind them stole only one of the monkey beasts, to guard the prisoner, or to denote the rank of the prince by its presence. Presently a stair, or a series of humped shelves, went up. Kicking aside ancient bones, the prince ascended, and Sovaz followed before the creature at her back should urge her to it. They came out into the basement of a palace by the river.

It was like no palace mentioned in the father's tale. Little had been; the city was much altered. A riot, or some other mayhem, seemed to have passed through the building. It was gloomy and unclean, littered with breakages and also with those tasteless tomb goods the ghoul race loved. Shards of red glass clung in the windows. Phosphorus sputtered in the lamps. No sooner had they, by dint of climbing decaying staircases, reached the upper rooms, than by the shine of such illuminations Sovaz might see bony, hungry faces pressed at the openwork windows, and hear the scrabbling of long-clawed hands and feet venturing up the walls.

"Fear nothing from them," said the ghoul prince. "They are part children of ours by humans, weaklings, having only a fraction of the true blood between them. They grow to our desires and appetites, but not to our strengths and beauties. We permit them to watch us, sometimes. It amuses us."

But he conveyed Sovaz into a windowless cubby, the door of which he closed—the monkeylike attendant left outside—and so to a couch of rotting finery, overhung with curtains of golden stuff.

"Disrobe for me," he said. "Let me see all the feast I shall have."

Then Sovaz smiled once more, and something in that smile caused the prince to hesitate, though beyond the door, they at the sharded windows scrabbled and snuffled eagerly.

"As my lord desires," said Sovaz.

And she untied her sash and unfastened her bodice, and as she did so, the whole garment fell away, and there emerged out of it something that was no longer so entrancing to this prince.

"Delusions," said he haughtily, though he stepped back a pace. "You cannot dissuade me with that."

It was a kind of creature, not wholly identifiable, shapeless and sinuate, most like a serpent, but standing upright, and with glowing eyes. And the serpent said to the prince of the ghouls: "Pardon me, beloved. How have I offended you? Come, embrace me. We shall have much love, and then I shall die for you and you shall consume my succulent, tender flesh."

"Your trick disgusts me," said the ghoul, yet haughty, and yet standing back a pace for every pace the monstrous serpent flowed toward him. "Put on your rightful shape."

"So I have," said the monster, "to enhance your delight."

Then the ghoul prince drew a curved blade from its sheath at his thigh. It was not the weapon he had intended to loose on her, though they lived as neighbors.

"It seems I must slay you at once."

"Do so," the monster answered. "If you can."

At this, the ghoul swung his blade upward and down upon the apparition. And the blade, taken long since from the burial mound of an ancient ruler, split in three pieces.

"Delusions," repeated the monster softly, and it began to wind itself lovingly about the ghoul prince, even as he struggled out a thin dagger and stabbed at its eyes, but the dagger melted and ran on the floor all molten. "I have known one who is the master of such, and he taught me many lessons. Delusion and delirium—O Prince-Portioner, which portion shall be yours?"

And by now the monster, whatever it might be—illusion, delusion, figment of delirium—had completely entwined the prince of the ghouls, so he could not move hand or foot, nor any limb. And it squeezed and strangled him so he had not even the breath to cry aloud for aid. He could only glare into its unnatural eyes and gasp, "Discommode me as you will, you may not kill me."

"How you wound me," said the hallucination (and now it had, most ironically, a voice like the voice of a handsome youth named Oloru). "You smash my heart in fragments, to speak in this way of my amorous clasp."

And with that it wrung the last whisper of air from the ghoul and let him fall senseless—not dead, as a mortal man must have died in that grip, only, as he had mentioned, "discommoded." Though rather more than somewhat.

Sovaz stood over him. If she had changed her shape, or merely caused him to see and experience such a shape in lieu of her own, certainly it was a strong sorcery, and the first of its sort she had practiced on or through her own flesh. Now she flinched at an awareness of victory, how it must be, and how it would alter her, too, more surely than the form of the reptile.

To the ghoul prince she said, and though senseless, he heard her, "Alas for you and yours that I was brought here. I will cast down your city and all your people, and with them those you have corrupted to your ways. No vulnerable spot? One. The very thing you vaunt, there is your undoing. That which you are shall destroy you."

Demon pride, to the pride of the boastful ghouls a

mountain to a pebble. Capture, rape, slay, devour her? She, the child of utter bright and utter dark? And she had other griefs and rages. This, the last drop of water which overspills the cistern.

She walked from the antique rotting cubby of lust, and meeting the monkey thing that had been standing guard there, she raised one finger and it was crushed into a pile of cinders. As she crossed the floors beyond, the scrabbling dribbling watchers at the windows gaped and squeaked. Being stupid witless beings, some tried even to come down and get in her way. Then Sovaz clapped her hands. Lightning bolts sprang from her palms and whipped these lesser ghouls away and left them in black heaps. The last of the monkey slaves she met leaped in terror for roof tops and sewers to escape her.

Leaving the palace, she continued to walk aboveground. She was a strange sight in Shudm, not fitting. Again and again her way was barred, she was menaced, so as she walked, the route became littered with dead scorched things.

She retraced her steps through the black streets, under the platforms and the pillars of lies. Overhead, the sky of night was dull, save now and then catching some red sheen. The noises of the city were as before, though louder, for the revelry was reaching its height. The various sights she saw, high in windows, deep in doorways, under arches, behind grills—these sights shall not be written down.

But as she drew near the gates by which old Jadrid had brought her in, there came the rattle and roar of wheels behind her.

Sovaz went on, she came to the place before the gates, and into the tall gateway itself, and there she waited.

Soon some chariots dashed in view. Horses pulled them, the phantoms it was said the ghouls could make by flinging horseskin over bones and animating the assemblage. In the chariots were whirlings of sparks, which quickly resolved to the figures of the ghoul princes and princesses. Drawing rein, they stood and leered at Sovaz and pointed with their taloned fingers. While at their backs the multitude of their half- and quarter-breeds came snuffling. The ghoul princes cried from their chariots: "We thank you for the novelty of this chase. But now we shall take and rend you."

Sovaz said, "Approach then, take and rend."

At which the ghouls became mirthful and said, "We only savor the moment. Good wine should not be gulped."

But Sovaz said, "I am glad you are here to bid me farewell."

And she turned and struck the gate one blow with her slim fist—but at the blow a flame bloomed upward and the gate crumpled like a paper.

As this happened, some of the ghouls flung spears at Sovaz, but the spears spun in midflight, and plunged back toward the chariots. The phantom horses reared. One prince fell with his own spearhead between his ribs. As he did so he screamed "Tomorrow I will live again—then let her beware of me!"

"Oh, tomorrow," said Sovaz.

But the gate now entirely disintegrated, and she went out of it.

The ghouls chased her a considerable length over the barren plain by night. But though she walked on her naked feet and they rode like the whirlwind in their chariots, they could not make up the gap, and besides, flames and thorns and storms of stones burst up in their path, and they swerved madly and in all directions, or else were overthrown.

So she left them, and so she might have left them. But so she did not leave them.

Sovaz stood on the plain beyond Shudm, as the sun rose.

She raised her white arms, as if she persuaded the sun upward from its sleep in chaos deep below the flat hollow earth.

All the hours of morning she communed with the sun, or seemed to. Her mother had held this gleam in her very veins; her father had once outstared it, as it blasted him to ash. There was such ambivalence in the relation of Sovaz to the sun, but still, she communed with it, or seemed to, until midday. It may have been a part of the magic she made, or only a chastisement of herself, a purgation before the spell was fashioned.

Though it lay miles off, no doubt by one such as Sovaz a glimpse of the city might be obtained. Or else she only visualized the city.

Over the day-smitten towers and walls of Shudm (uglier by day, all its black filth and spiritual garbage too openly displayed), the air began to sing and to ripple, and then grow oppressively silent and motionless. And then the air hardened, like cooling lava. And like lava, the air darkened, until it let in the fierce glare of the sun, but nothing else. Nothing—no lesser light, no noise, no breath of wind or vapor, neither dust nor rain—no wisp of anything. Even the vagrant corpse-eater birds could no longer get in, or out. Shudm had been sealed. Like a tomb. Above, and also beneath. Even the labyrinth of catacombs and tunnels was later found to be blocked up, by those inhabitants who shortly attempted them.

Inside—not simply a dome but an egg of leaden crystal, there was Shudm now, and the afternoon went by, and sunset, which was true dawn to the ghouls, and night, and midnight. And in the first overcast minutes of the new morning, there was not one sensible thing in the city that did not know it had been trapped.

The atmosphere, thick with smokes and aroms, turned swiftly stale and choking; long before sunrise they panted, and the more humanly feeble of their number sank down.

Then they tried obvious and inventive ways, by ordinary or magical means, of escape. And failed. And called out to whatever gods they owned. (It is maintained that some of them worshiped Naras, Queen Death, down in the Inner-earth.) But whoever it was they called to did not answer. Then they raged and lamented, and the roar and moan of this was heard in distant places, not least maybe on the plain beyond, where Sovaz waited, now seated on a smooth high rock.

It is said Sovaz kept vigil there for many months, for a year, watching over the fate of Shudm of the ghouls. That sometimes she journeyed nearer and looked through the tall poreless sides of the egg, and witnessed herself what went on. Or else, climbing to a higher rock, she called the hawks of passage and asked them, "What are they doing now, in Shudm?" And the hawks told her what they did.

But otherwise, word has it that Sovaz left the vicinity, resuming it would seem her search for Chuz, who was Oloru and mad. She did not therefore watch their plight but only sometimes imagined it, or summoned up a view of it. How, locked in with only each other, and that eternal hunger of theirs which was their boast (and vulnerability), the ghoul race soon came to butchering and partaking of the only available meat. Firstly their mortal pets, who were slaves and destined for it anyway, and next their mortal pets—their parents, who were not. Their partly mortal children they preyed on after that. But at last none were left to them save their own kind. So they fell to upon their brothers and sisters, and in the end they came to hacking at their own bodies. Nor did any resurrect, or if they did, it came again to the same pass, till they were wise, and stayed dead. And finally the black birds picked at the bones of what was left, which was not much.

So she paid them out strictly for thinking her only a girl, whether she watched or not, Sovaz-Azhriaz, Azhrarn's daughter.

And one night, perhaps seven months after the day of the sealing of Shudm, Sovaz met another woman on a descending mountain road. The river which had gone by the city still moved below, down in a chasm, but here it was pure, and the mountains were bone-picked clean, in the starlight. The woman had, however, hair of poppy-red, and she crouched on a stone, casting no shadow. She might have been a ghost, or not. She held up her hand, on which gold rings shone (and there was gold on her feet and her neck, and in her tangled hair, but her clothes were rags that barely covered her).

"My son," said this woman. (Liliu?) "You killed him."

"How do you know?" inquired Sovaz. "Did Jadrid scream some prophecy of it to you, when your son's knife was in his vitals? And was Jadrid then sad or merry?"

"In my heart I saw my son's death, and the name of the murderess is carried by the night wind."

"What is that son to you?" said Sovaz. "You died at his birth."

"My child," said the woman. And she clasped her

hands, and her claws clicked together. "I gave my life that
he might have life."

"So, even your people love their children. Apples of
fire. O dearest Father, how is it you can deny me anything?"

And at the acid music of this cry, even the ghoul ghost
faded and shrank into the stone and was gone. And conceivably in any case, Sovaz too was subject to delusions,
and the ghost only one such.

Sovaz walked on along the track. That night she came
upon him that had been her lover—Oloru, Chuz, Madness—
in a cave of the mountains.

5

WHY HAD SHE sought him still? She had known
how it must be. It is not always possible to behave intelligently, or even to avoid the pain an unintelligent act will
bring. The child sees the fire bright on the hearth and feels
the heat of it, but must touch the flame and burn herself
before she is certain.

In this way Sovaz came to the cave mouth and passed
into the fire.

At first, there was only a lump of darkness in the dark,
which moved.

Sovaz stood motionless, but she made light blossom.

The lump of darkness huddled down out of the light,
and it mumbled a noise, but in no language.

"Speak to me," said she. "I command it."

And then the dark lump lumbered upright and came out
at her, and stopped a pace away and capered, tearing at
itself with nails the ghouls would not have disdained.

There was nothing anymore of Oloru, nothing but the

bloodshot eyes and filthy hair held a memory and made it obscene. Of Chuz, there *was* some evidence. Every line of face and body—of the very spine and muscles—seemed to have altered. The back hunched, the arms dangled or lunged, the legs buckled, the feet splayed. The mouth formed itself into a rictus, squawked, relaxed, formed another rictus and another subhuman cry. It drooled and foamed and bit at its own gray warty skin. It did not like itself. Or anything. This then, her lover and protector.

Sovaz showed no hint of an emotion. She was like staring ice.

She said, contemptuously, "Greetings, Master of Delusions, Lord of Darkness, Prince Chuz. You are all of your own left side now, it seems, the side you kept from me, a male hag gone crazy. Come, where are the finger-snakes and the thumb-fly that cracks its feelers? Where is the brass rattle that sounded through Bhelsheved when my mother died, or the jawbones of an ass which declaim?"

At this, Madness the madman brayed. The cave recoiled, and the night. Sovaz only remarked, "A fine love gift for my father. Unbrothers, each closer than ever either was to me. Fool. Do your penance then. I will no more bother you."

And having said this, attempting no argument or counterspell, she went out of the cave.

But behind her the thing was scampering, not to follow her but to go higher up the walls of the mountains. As it fled it shrieked and gibbered, and laughed—at her?

"Oh," whispered Sovaz, "oh, Chuz, be hated of me."

They say the smoke of burning rose from her footsteps awhile, as she walked on over the descending road.

In the morning she came down at last to the delta of the river. The teeth of the mountains sank in this ground, and where the rocks gave way to swamp, reeds grew tall as the tallest men, and the most slender of them were as thick around as a man's strong wrist. As the winds blew, the reeds wailed, or clashed angrily like swords.

All day Sovaz wended across this land, and all night, when a faint flushed moon glowed through the vapors and behind the reeds. And, though she had left him so instantly and with such words, the image of Oloru stayed at her side. She ached with her pain, yet nothing in the swamp dared to trouble her, not the great-winged insects nor the long-headed hunting dogs; the wildfowl feeding out on the waters rose like flung shawls at her coming, and hastened away.

At dawn, when the dull russet moon went out and a dim russet sun stole up from the earth, Sovaz stood looking at her reflection in a pool, one straight beautiful reed among the rest that were crooked and stark.

"Be vile," Sovaz admonished the terrain of the delta. "Beauty is no use."

Just then a second (damson-colored) sun began to rise— out of the pool. It was a lotus, and as it came up shimmering, it opened wide as an offering hand. And on the palm of the lotus lay one single unlikely object: a die of amethyst.

Twice it had been tendered previously. Out of the heart-lake of Bhelsheved, for the unborn child, when Chuz volunteered to be her uncle. And later, in the heart-temple of Bhelsheved, to the born child. The first time Azhrarn refused the gift on her behalf. The second, she had left it lying. But now she was a woman, and alone, and she reached into the lotus's heart and took the amethyst die. At which the lotus itself flickered and was no more.

Sovaz looked closely at the die, turning it in her fingers. It was unmarked, as they often were, the dice Chuz bore about with him, yellow, purple, black. And yet, there was a kind of shadow-marking on the sides. It had fallen, this gem, into the possession of those who later fought over it and tried to fight with Chuz over it—and in the flurry, the death of Dunizel had been prefigured and inaugurated.

They had stoned her, that religious crowd at Bhelsheved. The stones had done no harm. Then some hand chanced upon another thing—a tiny bit of darkest adamant. It was a drop of Vazdru blood, the blood of Azhrarn himself, lost some while since in the desert, found there by Chuz, kept by Chuz, and now seemingly loosed by him. The drop of blood, the only element which could make nothing of the safeguards Azhrarn had set on Dunizel, pierced through all psychic shields, and killed her.

But perhaps this purple gem was another of the dice of

Prince Chuz, nothing to do with that particular event. Dice were ever about him. Had he not been himself a topaz die, for the sake of Sovaz?

Whatever the facts, a strange token of love. For love token it was.

When the dusk came down again, Sovaz still walked among the reeds and swamp. The die was hidden in her clothes, her thoughts concealed behind her eyes. Yet it was an amethystine dusk, the waters and the sky, and the vague moon, all tinged mauvely with that undemonstrated matter.

Near midnight, the girl paused and slept a space. In her sleep, she must have remembered a dream her mother once shared with her in the womb—for being not created in the usual way, the spiritual essence had come early to the flesh, and lived in the mother's body longer than in the general manner, and so learned things of the mother as it waited. Waking, Sovaz called a beast to her, out of some other realm, or out of some forgotten land of the earth, or simply from refashioned atoms of the air. It flew high over the moon's face, then swept down, frightening the waterfowl and setting the wild dogs to howling. When it settled on the ground it was a winged lion of abnormal size, pale as curds, with a bluish mane and eyes of gold, and having a silent thinking face, as wise as a human philosopher's; wiser. This Dunizel had dreamed. Now Dunizel's daughter conjured it.

Sovaz mounted the lion's back, and sat down crosslegged between the wide wings.

Where would she go? Her brain murmured to the lion's mind. And its owl-eagle wings, white-tipped, powerful as winds, bore them up into the sky, and left the delta and all that country far below and miles behind.

Dreams. Where would she go but to Bhelsheved?

6

A FEW YEARS had passed, not many, since that night they said pieces of the moon crashed on the earth: the night Dunizel died, and Azhrarn declared his war on Chuz, and confiscated the blue-eyed child. Yet in this brief time, the white flower had withered in the desert.

Holy Bhelsheved, the gods' jar, had had a darkening future from that instant Azhrarn first took against the place. The city was uninhabited when one came on it now, in the twilight dawn, as the last stars put out their tapers, and only the queen-star blazed on in the east. Bhelsheved's flower-towers were empty hives. Sand piled in gusts along the marble streets, and no sorcerous mechanism anymore brushed it away. It was the same with the singing roads which had led there over the dunes (they sang no more), and in the groves outside the trees had died or been chopped down, and the statues were rubble, or filched. The very gates had been broken and stolen from for their richness, and the sky-colored windows of the fanes broken or taken, too. No treasure was left. Nothing had stayed sacrosanct. The heart-temple was despoiled with the rest, even the golden altar furniture had been carted off. Various persons had muttered that such a robbery would invite a divine curse, but they were already under it: the curse being of Azhrarn's making. Its ruin was not epic, only utter. A cracked jar now, useless.

Yet, in the pale gateway, King Kheshmet sat in a vivid robe, playing on a pipe.

Something crossed between the morning star and the earth. It was the winged lion speeding over. It alighted a short stretch from the gateway, and Sovaz glided from its back. King Kheshmet, however, did not raise his eyes. The shrill of the pipe went on. And Sovaz, standing near enough her shadow touched his robe's orange edge, recited:

> *"Here the sun shuns,*
> *Unsheathes the wind her claws.*
> *Yet in the gate is one:*
> *Fate remains alone.*
> *Fate with fire-eyes broods at the double doors,*
> *Playing a pipe of bone,*
> *Fate with brown hands unwraps each day,*
> *And casts the husk away.*
> *When each waste night is gone."*

At which Kheshmet, Lord Fate, left off playing and observed, "The doors, double or otherwise, are absent. Nor is the pipe of bone."

"Fourth Lord of Darkness," said Sovaz, "why are you here?"

"The exalted shall be flung down and the lowly raised on high. That is fate's law. Behold Bhelsheved, flung down. I am obliged to call from time to time, for form's sake."

"Why at this hour?"

"You," said Kheshmet placidly, "have come here to seek your own fate. And here you will find it. Or partly do so."

"What is my fate?"

"Do not challenge me, Sovaz-Azhriaz, Azhrarn's daughter. I do not know your fate, I merely represent it."

And getting up, putting away the pipe (which was of pastel jade), he offered his arm courteously to guide her into the city.

"Permit me," said Kheshmet, "to show you your mother's tomb."

"No," said Sovaz, and drew back, while the lion snarled and padded closer.

"Follow them," said Kheshmet. "Or not." And he turned mildly in at the gateway, and onto one of the four roads of the city. "I have a mind to go there myself. She too, Doonis-Ezael, Moon's Soul, was a pupil of mine. Indeed, she had an allegiance to three of us: to madness—it ran in the family; her own mother was an idiot until the comet cured her—to destiny, and to death. Only wickedness had nothing to do with Dunizel. So, of course, she became the mistress of Wickedness.''

Presently, Sovaz entered the gateway after Kheshmet, and did follow him along the road between the temples and shrines. The lion trotted at her heels, pausing occasionally to preen its wings.

Here Sovaz had been born. Here she had been carried about and shown to the people, who believed her, then, to be a god's progeny, and her mother the Chosen of that god. The faintest of remembrances lingered, or returned. Her time in the Underearth, and the throes of sudden physical growth, had wiped away the pictures and deeds of her beginnings, till only emotion, bitter, bemused, hurtful, was left.

The sun rose, and blue lights shot from the smashed windows that nearly matched the eyes of Sovaz.

Kheshmet walked before, and now and then he took up again and played a trill on the jade pipe. When this happened, the ghosts or memories of Bhelsheved's white pigeons transparently poured down from the tower tops to circle his hands and shaven head. (The lion stared and licked its jaws.)

They reached the gardens of blossom trees beside the heart-lake of the city. The gardens were a wilderness; only groves of stumps stood there now, as outside. The water of the lake was unblue, unbright. Probably no fish remained in it.

"Here is the grave," said Fate, pointing to the turf beside the lake.

There was no sign, nothing to show that the ground contained anything, but Sovaz knew Fate did not lie. Dunizel's body had found an unmarked bed; Azhrarn had disdained to cover the beautiful flesh which had betrayed him for death, or else he could not bring himself to throw over it the black soil. Some cautious scholar or some simpleton who had pity, or only a sense of tidiness, saw to it.

Sovaz regarded the turf, then she turned from it, and then turned back. She sat down by the spot, and laid her hand on the bare earth a moment. Today she was dressed, or seemed to be, as a young woman, but for traveling, and she had a knife in her belt, which next she took out. With the knife Sovaz cut some of her long hair, the way hair was sometimes shorn in mourning in those lands, and others. Sovaz sprinkled these black curling tresses over the markerless grave. Soon, black hyacinths began to rise where the hair had fallen, but Sovaz did not stay to see. She had got up again, and walked away around the lake.

"Here she came to him, living," Sovaz murmured aloud as she walked, "and here she came to him, dead. Here they spoke and here they loved and here he swore to destroy the country and here she dissuaded him." Then Sovaz stood still and looked down deep into the lake. The four bridges reflected in it, and the temple at their meeting—everything wrecked and robbed though it was. Then the lion reflected in it, having flown up in the air after the ghost birds. And then Fate, who had come to stand beside her. At this, Sovaz saw her own reflection, and that of Kheshmet in his vivid garment. Yet the images trembled and changed. They seemed to be not those of a girl and a man, or one who took on a man's form—but first a white column and a column of yellow-red, thereafter a white flame and a copper flame—but then two young men shone upward from the water. They were not distinct, but the hair of one was the color of apricots, and of the other, black.

By whatever means, Sovaz knew them from their stories—Simmu, who stole immortality from the gods, and Zhirek the Magician, one of the greatest of his kind, for he had learned the magic of the sea peoples, a thing not often achieved.

"Do you see as I see?" inquired Sovaz.

"Perhaps not," said Fate. "Yet if something unusual has appeared, it will be to do with me. I am its harbinger."

When he spoke, the image of Simmu faded, and only the reflection of Kheshmet rippled in the water. But that of Zhirek continued before Sovaz.

"The fate of Zhirek the Magician," she said then. "What was it?"

"He had been blessed or cursed with invulnerability, but immortality he spurned. He would have taken service with your father, but Azhrarn refused him, for reasons only speculated upon. Eventually Zhirek, who could not die as he then much wished to do, took contrary service instead with Uhlume, Lord Death."

"The tale is an ancient one. Surely, though invulnerable and long-lived, Zhirek will by now be ended?"

"It seems to me," said Fate, musingly, "that though Zhirek is dead in all ways, of intellect, heart, and mind, his invulnerable health and vitality have not yet surrendered him. Somewhere, he does live, or rather, does exist. And he is mad, naturally. The awful punishment of Simmu, whom Zhirek always loved and distrusted and so hated, made sure of it. It is the insanity of Zhirek, maybe, which attracts the idea of him to you. Some nuance of your lover's?"

Sovaz picked up a pebble immediately and threw it in the lake, and the indistinct image of Zhirek vanished.

"But you speak to me of my own fate, Kheshmet. Where is it?"

At that, the image of Kheshmet in the lake also vanished, and Kheshmet with it.

Sovaz smiled in anger. They were all tricksters and wraiths and gaudy showmen, these male part unrelatives of hers.

Up in the sky, the winged lion wheeled fantastically, catching bird ghosts in its mouth—which tasted of sugary smoke, but always somehow evaded swallowing.

Sovaz wandered about the desert city. But she was careful to avoid those sites which it seemed to her she had visited with her mother, nor did she go back to Dunizel's grave.

In the heat of the day, Sovaz lay down in a temple court, under a porch, and slept. She dreamed Zhirek stood before her in a priest's robe, with a collar of jewels. The stories made much of his eyes, which had been the color of blue water in a green shade, or green water under a sky of dusk. But his eyes were darker now, all shadow. He said to her coldly, "It was in my nature to do good, but I gained an evil reputation, and justly. I did much wickedness. Forget the voice of your mother, who told you Azhrarn was the darling of the world, who formed the first cats for a jest, and invented love. Go and do wickedness as I did. No one can escape destiny. It runs behind and before. It is in the breath and the blood."

"And where now," Sovaz asked of him in the dream (a human enough dream, no Vazdru abstraction), "where now do you dwell, diligently performing wickedness to please your conception of destiny?"

"I do nothing now, I am nothing now. Neither wicked nor virtuous. And I have no look of who I was, no powers, and no name."

"How is it that you know of me."

"I do not. It is you who know of me."

When Sovaz woke, the sun was setting. She called the winged lion, and they sped up into the sunset, which turned their paleness blood-red, and made the hair of Sovaz a storm cloud. And they flew over the desert and over all those lands, toward a far-off shore where two seas ran together and were one.

She had announced to him she would never seek him, never obey or pay homage, until seas were fires, winds seas, the earth glass, "and the gods come down on ladders to lick the feet of men." And Azhrarn had said no more.

Now Sovaz stood on the seas' shore and she summoned illusion to her, and illusion hurried to attend.

Inside an hour, a terrible sight was to be seen in that area. The two seas which joined had become an ocean of raging arson over which lightnings flashed and crackled. While from the east and north had flown two winds, and they were salt waters, and waves curled through them, and they swept against the land in breakers, roaring, with thin green fish whirled in their midst. And the land itself chipped and splintered, for it was glass, and under the surface you might see through the mineral trenches to laval pits and the bones of beasts and men some centuries old, all caught as if in crystal resin. Last of all, in the center of the frantic scene, a glowing ladder seemed to uncoil between the lightning and the tempest, and drop down until it touched the glass of the earth. Here stood some ragged dirty savage men with their mouths open in astonishment, and out of the heavens came flitting beings neither male nor female, shining facsimiles of the gods. And the pretend-gods, reaching the make-believe men, bowed low and busily lapped their filthy toes.

Near moonrise, though the moon was not to be seen in the confusion, a dark smolder might be espied rushing upward through the crystal ground. Sovaz kneeled, crossed her hands on her breast, and bowed her head, in the attitude of an extreme docility.

Suddenly some of the glass shattered, and a pillar of black fire burst out. For a moment it towered there against the flames and torrent of sky and sea, and then it died down and a man had filled its place, folded in a black cloak. He glanced about him some minutes.

"I acknowledge your joke," he said. "You are truly Vazdru. You will go to any length, however sumptuous or cataclysmic, in order solely to avoid the words: *It appears I am at fault.*"

Sovaz, kneeling, hands crossed, head bowed, said clearly, "It appears I am at fault."

Azhrarn snapped his fingers, and the winds let go their water on the ocean, which was quenched to sea again. Freed, the winds sped away to the north and east corners of the world. The earth grew solid and dense. It put on sands and grasses and rock. The figures of gods and humans disappeared, and the heavenly ladder became a silver necklace wound in the veil of the rising moon.

Sovaz still kneeled, her head still bowed.

"You were clever enough to engage my attention," said Azhrarn "What do you want?"

"I will do your bidding," velvetly said Sovaz. "I will atone for my insults. I will revere and adore you. I am your slave."

"Changed heart," velvetly said Azhrarn, "tell me why."

At that Sovaz looked up and gazed at him, but not into his face, with unvelvet pride and unfriendliness. "There is no escape," she said. "You made me for your purpose. I will fulfill your purpose."

"You have grown to hate mankind."

"Those I would love or hate are beyond my love or hate. I hate none, and I love none. But I am respectful. I am a dutiful daughter. I cut my hair and left flowers on my mother's grave. And I kneel to you."

"Get up," said Azhrarn.

And he turned from her and beckoned to the air, and out of it came the winged lion. It had taken refuge from the maelstrom of illusions so high up in the ether, its ruff and tail and wings were trickled by tinkling essences of the stars. Or else sky elementals had thrown these collected essences over it, like a bucket of slops, in order to chase the big cat out of their yards. It made landfall beside Sovaz, and regarded her with its grave wise eyes.

Then a chariot came, up from the earth. The edge of the sea seemed to catch alight again at its coming. Of bronze the chariot was, but inlaid all over with silver, with pearls set in and stones of clearest blue, thickest black. Three horses drew it, and they were jet-black with a blue streaming frost on them of manes and tails, and the bits, and the reins and shafts, and the chariot-pole, all ran with silver things and things of diamond, with moonstones and colorless beryls like ice. A Vazdru held the skittish team, making them prance, and then making them grow still as stone. He did this with panache, flaunting his skill. And when once the horses were stones, he looked long at Sovaz, marveling and startled, charmed and irritated. Then, having rendered Azhrarn extreme obeisance, he tendered the woman an exquisite bow. She had seen not much of this upper caste of the demons, her own kin. But the Vazdru, all of them, loved beauty, and were envious of anything favored by their lord.

Azhrarn entered and stood in his chariot; it could be no one else's.

He said to Sovaz, "Though you have no power over the sea, you have pressed an illusion on it which might convince the credulous that you had. The sea-folk may be incensed at this. Also that you seemed to fill the air with their waves and fishes. It is prudent to go far off."

"Does my lordly father, then, fear the sea people?"

"Salt water," he said, "has done me a service now and then."

And far out on the moon-spun ocean it seemed for an instant phantoms rode, a youth on a midnight horse, and these ghosts pursued in turn another opalescent ghost like a ship—but the images dissolved.

"I have heard that story in the taverns of men," said Sovaz. "Sivesh, and the fading of his dream. A lover you tired of and destroyed. It would appear that those who win your love are greatly unfortunate."

"Do not let it trouble you," said Azhrarn. "The misfortune is not yours."

There came the flicker of a diamond whip. The chariot sprang away and aloft—tower-high from the earth, horses and wheels, the Vazdru prince and his Prince—and was lost in the night.

But Sovaz sprang upon her lion. *"Follow."*

They ran then, one behind the other, some hours. A wild sight for those who saw, a racing chariot above the trees and a winged lion going after.

The moon, which had been rising, completed her climb and turned her pale smoky mask toward the world's western limit. What did the moon spy there, over the brink? Chaos claimed her with every descent, yet chaos did not harm the moon, or the sun, only enriched them so they came up from its arms like brides.

Certain aspirations of the winds, too, bounded after the lion and Sovaz between its wings, like puppies eager to resume the earlier play with water and fish. But eventually these zephyrs tired and fell back. Then a nightingale sang below in the gray-purple shadow of a lilac tree, and another from an ilex all black jade. Many nightingales were passed by beneath, singing, or silent in perplexity, and many geographies were crossed over, both magnificent and pestiferous, many, many miles.

And sometimes (it is said) he called to her and bade her be dutiful as she had vowed, and there was a village or a town, or some temple, or camp of malcontents, and she should work some wonder on it to amuse him, submissive daughter that she claimed to be.

And so that night (they said) was riddled with roofs

turned to porridge and cheeses to topaz, with owls which cried in human speech, and men who made noises like owls, or donkeys. With, too, a dread voice that whispered in sleepers' ears: "Beware, for I know your terrible secret, and it shall be told to all." And at the phrases of this soft, awful voice, a thousand hearts missing a beat, and thousand men and women scrambling up in horror. And everywhere lamps lit, and shouts raised, and screams and blasphemies, and servants running and horses fetched, and some at prayer and some at a gallop with torches to fly the spot, and some taking up the means of suicide, and some sneaking out to kill their neighbors. While, in a very small number of dwellings, a very few turned over and slept again, muttering in surprise to themselves or others, "But what terrible secret is this? I have none."

All the night, therefore, was a riot (if what they said was so). Many many miles, and after those, many many miles after, till Azhrarn, letting the chariot of bronze and silver idle at last, remarked to the girl on the lion, "Yes, that is fair. You have a cunning mind, though you are yet a child, a demon's mind. A dutiful and obedient daughter for sure." And his smile froze to hail the fringed icy beryls and pearls along the reins, and the very dew that was beginning to form upon the leaves below, that froze too.

Soon after this a city swelled before them. There had been several such, but this one was mighty, and lay along a river, among fields of flowers. Animals of stone guarded the quays and the city's two gates, and even here and there stood up on a roof. They were white as salt. The river itself was white, kissed by the sinking moon, and on all the spires of the city, the moon had set, in parting, silver rings.

"And here," said Sovaz, "what must I do here?"

"I have heard how you deal with a city by a river. Shudm of the ghouls may speak for you in that. Let this place be. Or shall I give it you to be a goddess in?"

"Am I to want such a gift?"

"Oh, dutiful daughter," said Azhrarn. "You are to be a goddess somewhere, for I would teach this world the nature of gods."

"And what is their nature?" she said.

"Indifferent and cruel. And loving not mankind."

"In Bhelsheved," said Sovaz, "I have seen a notion written on a rock: that the kind gods saved the people there from a monster they call in that land *Azhrarn*. Nor did the gods save them only once, but twice over."

"It is by such notions they have earned the lesson I will teach," said Azhrarn. Then: "I have not rebuked you for your discourtesy," said Azhrarn. The dew which had frozen turned to steel and dropped down the trees to concuss little slugs. "Do not forget that I do not forget I have not."

"I am rebuked," said Sovaz, "by the very life you gave me. And since it is an immortal, never-ending life, I shall be rebuked by it forever."

Then Azhrarn reached out to her and put his hand upon her head, very gently, and he said to her, "The Vazdru do not weep."

"Who weeps? Not I."

"Each word spoken was a tear."

But, though he gazed at her intently, when she turned her eyes to him, Azhrarn looked away from her, out over the night. Whatever he might say, she could not help but recall for him Dunizel. The first sight he had had of her, this child of his, an adult woman, had gone through him like a sword, and there can be no doubt of it. And he could not help but dislike her, too, perhaps; since he had created her to do his work upon the earth, she was his own wickedness, externalized and incarnate. And had Dunizel, maybe, caused him to *question* his wickedness, his character, as it seemed she had meant him to?

The chariot, and the lion, hovered in the air, and the city moon-gleamed below. Azhrarn removed his hand from the girl's hair, revoked his caress (the lion shuddered), but said to her, "What now, then, is your name?"

And she replied, "Azhriaz."

The meaning of which is merely this: the Sorceress, Azhrarn's Daughter.

THERE WAS a king who ruled the city and lands of the white stone cats, the name of which was Nennafir. *His* name was Qurob. The very day that he was born, a witch-woman came to his mother, even as she lay swooning with fatigue on her bed, amid the fans of her handmaidens. "Your son," said the witch-woman, "shall be king of Nennafir, in health and bounty, and no man will raise a weapon against him, and no ill happening come near to him, and his name will be well remembered. Unless . . ." And here the witch hesitated meaningfully, and the handmaids held their breath, and their fans were still, and only the mother of Qurob sighed. "Unless," continued the witch, "when once he is a king, he should ever chance to ride upon a stallion's back. For if he does that, he shall lose his kingdom, and he shall die."

At these tidings the mother of Qurob rested upon her pillows, and she said no word at all for some while, though she might be seen to be thinking. Finally she did speak. She said: "Well, this is wonderful fortune, for I am not even the present lord's wife, but only his concubine. It is a small matter, surely, that my son keep from riding on a stallion's back—he will have geldings and mares in plenty for his use, if he is to be king. Come now," she said to an attendant, "pour wine, and you shall all drink with me to this good luck, and the seeress with us—and in every cup I will let drop one of these pearls from my necklet, but for the wisewoman I will let drop three pearls."

There was much approval at this decision. The wine was poured in the cups and each passed to the mother of

Qurob, who, as she had promised, let fall in each a costly pearl, but into the cup of the witch she let fall three. Then everyone drank, save only the mother herself—she was too weak to taste wine as yet. And in a moment or so, everyone but her tumbled over with a groan and died. For in every cup, along with a pearl, the mother of Qurob had let fall a drop of deadly poison from a ring she wore, but in the witch's cup she had let fall three drops. And this was because she had thought to herself: *Only I must know this thing, I and my son. If any other knows, he may seek to trick him into just such a ride.* In that she may have been sensible. She was altogether a clever woman. No sooner were the witch and all the attendants stretched lifeless than Qurob's mother began to scream. When help arrived, she told how a vile sorceress had entered and offered to make the new mother, a mere concubine, into Nennafir's queen, if only she would work evil against her lord. This she sternly refused to do, at which the sorceress cast a spell upon the wine, so it slew everyone who had drunk it—save only Qurob's mother, who had been too weak as yet to drink. And then Qurob's mother had herself recited a charm against witches, taught her long ago by a priest—at which the loathsome sorceress herself expired.

All marveled at this news, as well they might. And presently the tale was recounted to the king.

"Here is one who is steadfast," said the king. And in a while he went to visit Qurob's mother, and was much taken with her beauty, as he had been that prior night he got her with child and gave her pearls.

Affairs then went as they might be expected to go.

The king raised Qurob's mother; he made her one of his lesser queens, awarded her lands and jewels. Then Qurob's mother became a compassionate and admiring friend to each of the three other lesser queens and to each she said, "Why, my son is nothing to yours." Or, if no son yet appeared, "Why, my son *will* be nothing to yours." And she said "I am a nonentity, but it is my joy to be near you. Always I have noted your loveliness and virtue, and indeed I will confide in you, I believe it is you yourself the king loves best—truly, even better than the high queen of Nennafir, for of course that marriage was arranged when he was but a boy. I suppose that he would cast her down and put you in her place, if he were able.'' And that said, next she diligently advised each lady against the other two, and told how she had heard it rumored that they might wish to poison the favored one, or the favored one's child, or the favored one's child-to-be. And shortly, Qurob's mother did the service, and poisoned the two lesser queens who were least susceptible. But the night before she did it, she sought audience with the high queen herself, and Qurob's mother fell on her face, and then being permitted to kneel, warned the high queen how the lesser queens plotted against her, and of one in particular (the most susceptible), who would probably murder her rivals. So when the two bodies were come on next morning, everyone knew who was to blame, and the lesser queen, the susceptible one, was taken and flogged and hanged, and her corpse left on the gibbet where the three white cats of stone lay by the river.

And after that the high queen raised Qurob's mother and had her as her confidante and spy. This went on for thirteen years, during which the boy Qurob grew, and was taught by his mother to be canny, and to flatter and dissemble, and to be cruel, too, for she assured him, ''There is a secret you must tell no one. You are king here.'' And Qurob smiled, and said, ''Am I, Mother? I shall be glad of that.'' But to each of the sons of the high queen he said, ''I am nothing beside you, but let me be your slave, for I have always admired you beyond duty, more as I would worship a god.'' And then he kindly advised them each against the others and told them plots he had heard of, and gave them access to evidence which he simulated and paid others to simulate. And during his thirteenth year, the high queen died of a wasting disease induced by Qurob's mother's having introduced into her food tiny toxic granules. And then the king's sons fell out and quarreled, and some killed each other. And one night Qurob, a strong handsome lad of gracious bearing, knelt humbly to the king and informed him a plot had been laid against the king's life, and though it broke his, Qurob's, heart to speak, all must be revealed. And next morning the two eldest of the king's sons were torn apart by horses, and their remains left in the square where the white cats of stone overlooked the river. And Qurob became the king's heir.

Now three further years passed, and the king, who had grown old and sick, looked lovingly upon his adoring heir, and that year Qurob was sixteen, he murmured to the king, "Magnificent Father, let me speak to you in your chamber." The king willingly complied. When they were closeted together, Qurob said, "Father, have I served you well?" The sick old king nodded, and with tears embraced him. "Of all my sons," said the king, "you alone were faithful." "Then know," said Qurob, "I alone, of all your sons, was false." And then Qurob explained everything he had done, and reminded the king of what had been done through his lies. And the king started up in anguish, and his heart burst and he died.

When the diadem of the city had been set on the brow of Qurob, his mother came to him privately, in a shadow robe of mourning tear-sprinkled with priceless gems.

"Now attend to me, my son," said she. And she apprised him of the prophetic witch who had come to her the very day of Qurob's advent in the world, and said he should be a king. But when he was king, he must not ride upon a stallion's back, for if he did the kingdom would be lost to him and he would die. "I have told no other living soul," said Qurob's mother, "and all who knew, I have made certain they are eternally silent. For if any are aware but us two, they may turn the chance against you and trick you into just such a ride."

"Oh my mother," said Qurob, "I am blessed in you. Oh most sagacious of women, and best. I will heed your caution. None shall know save you and me."

Now it may be thought strange that Qurob should distrust his mother, who had all this while kept the dangerous secret flawlessly. But most men measure most matters by themselves. The woman had weaned her son to trustlessness, and the trustless seldom trust another. Supposing he had one day been at odds with her over something, or even that, growing older and infirm, she muttered the story of the stallion's back in a fever or in sleep?

So Qurob kissed his mother and gave her presents, and when she was in her own apartments, he sent one after her to drown her in her bath, so it should seem to be an accident. For had she not taught him for sixteen years to be prudent?

The length of his lifetime and half again, then, Qurob ruled in Nennafir, till he was forty years. He ruled in prosperity and health, no man stood against him, and, though he was harsh and tyrannical, none spoke ill of him but called him the Beloved King.

And be sure, for all the fine horses he selected, as if carelessly, to ride upon, in all these years he never once took a stallion.

One day, Qurob went hunting. Beyond the flower fields that garlanded the city there was a green plain with waters and spreading trees, and here lived raisin-blue boars and shining white gazelles prized for their skins. Nevertheless, on this day, the party started nothing, and the king became sullen, in which humor he was feared. At last the sun was westering, and there in the tall grass by a pool, Qurob beheld a gazelle drinking, white as the word, and with a black star between her brows.

The hunt at once gave chase, and the animal leapt away fleet as a spear. This was thought excellent sport, and every man shouted for gratification—and relief, seeing the king would now be in a gentler mood. And on and on the gazelle sprang, passing like a wind over grass and stone, leading them toward the eastern sky, with the low sun at their backs.

But ride as they might, and cast spears, and shoot with the bow as they might, they could not get near to her or wound her and bring her down. And they left the hours behind them under their horses' hoofs. The sun went on to the western gate and knocked to be let forth.

The horses flagged. One by one the horsemen drew rein. Only the king surged on. His courtiers dared not suggest to him any other course, but each man but him, to save his mount, now dropped back to follow at a walk. The gazelle they left to the king, and she and he were soon gone from sight into the clear dark dusk.

Qurob did not like anything to elude him. His gelding labored, but he thrashed it and spurred it to greater efforts.

He looked to see the white gazelle tire, but she did not. So he called to her coaxingly over the echoing darkening plain: "Sweetheart, I admire you and wish only to be near you. Let me come close. Let me protect you from others who mean you harm."

After a time, it seemed to Qurob he heard the gazelle cry back to him: "Do not try those lies on me, Qurob. It was I taught you them, and I remember how you repaid me!"

At that the hair bristled on Qurob's neck. He went first chill then hot then clammy cold, for it seemed he knew the voice of the gazelle; it was like his mother's.

Just then the gazelle reached a stand of trees and darted in among them with a white flash. But she did not come out of the trees on the far side. Going in after her, Qurob did not find her.

"Sorcery," said Qurob in some annoyance. "Or that bitch's ghost. I will take offerings to my mother's tomb tomorrow."

He had scarcely spoken when the gelding shuddered and fell dead under him.

Qurob rose bruised, and kicked the gelding's carcass one final kick. Then he shouted for his men, knowing they dared do nothing but follow him. But they were too far off, as yet, to hear, and Qurob did not wish, suddenly, to be solitary in that spot, the Beloved King of Nennafir.

Accordingly he left the cover of the trees, and stepping out, what should he next see down the slope, but a cot with a lighted doorway, and the evening cook-smoke going up. And nearby was a pasture in which a horse was feeding. Going closer, Qurob saw this horse was a splendid mare.

Noting it, Qurob, generally so lucky, strode to the open door of the dwelling. He said to the man he found within, "Down on your knees, oaf. For I am the king of Nennafir." At which the peasant sensibly obliged, leaving his meal to burn on the fire.

"What is your will, mighty lord?" timidly inquired the peasant.

"Give me your horse. That is my will."

"Alas," said the peasant, uneasily, "if you mean the

mare in the pasture, I should not recommend it. She has had such dealings recently she is fractious, and will not like to bear you.''

''What do I care for the whims of the brute?'' exclaimed the king.

''I have, though,'' said the man placatingly, ''a noble stallion who is currently content and docile—''

King Qurob swore a dreadful oath. He had detected sounds without of spurs and hoofs, and understood his courtiers were now approaching. And he was thinking this: *If I decline the stallion, this dolt will question in his mind my insistent preference, and so will they that arrive now, my court. Besides, there are stallions ridden with the geldings for the hunt, and I may be offered one of those and must refuse. And they may wonder at, and may recall I have never sat upon a stallion, and so divine I have some secret reason, and guess it means no good to me, and trick me one day, just as my mother told me.*

So Qurob drew his sword and lopped off the peasant's head, and going out he went after the mare and got hold of her, and when his court came up the king said, ''Go fetch my saddle and the rest of the gear off the dead horse in the trees. I have taken a fancy to this plump mare and will ride her home to the city.''

And that he did, though the stallions of the party were troublesome at her presence, and she herself unwilling, as the peasant had declared, and Qurob beat her.

For all that, she was a lush animal, and Qurob inclined to keep her for his stable. Having forgotten her in other business, it was a while later that, recollecting, a morning came when he called his chief groom and asked for the mare.

''Alas, mighty lord, she died. She was in foal, which foal she dropped before her time, and it came out of her feet-first, having stood all its season in her belly. And, had the foal lived, it would have been the jewel of your yards, for already it was in every particular the most choice of stallions. And it is a great shame that only once you rode on his back, and that unknowing, when you rode over the womb of his mother.''

Hearing these words, Beloved King Qurob went gray as

ash. He lifted his hands and took off the royal diadem, and from his fingers he pulled the rings. ''My sins have hunted me down,'' said he. ''My mother's curse, for certainly she cursed me, has found me out.'' And he called his trembling attendants and had them strip him of all his ornaments, and his raiment, and even his shoes he put off from his feet. And he took with him only one sharp dagger, and walked from his palace naked and alone, astounding the city, and down to the brown river, where the white stone cats of Nennafir gazed away from him with loveless eyes.

Qurob had no mind to wait for death, for he had often sent death to others, or given them death; Qurob grasped death might be unlikable. So he cut his own throat and his corpse fell in the river.

And those many hundred who had come to see and who watched, not comprehending any of it, were filled by terror and amazement, though not, let it be said, by grief.

8

POSSIBLY the tale of the stallion was untrue, or exaggerated. Generally only the warrior in battle chose to ride an ungelded horse, and then not always, for they were untractable beasts. Perhaps there was some other cause for King Qurob's guilty fear and self-immolation.

Whatever it was, there he lay still, on his face, drifting downstream and turning the brown water red.

Several thousands of people watched his corpse on its way, lining the banks to do so, or staring out from high roofs and balconies. And where the harbor was, the birdlike ships were lying with their wings noon-folded and dipped, but men climbed up to the mastheads or hung over the sides, looking out for the throat-cut king of the city. Word had gone fast through Nennafir. "And is it the *lord*?" they cried. "What reason has *he* to kill himself, the ingrate, when I, with so many good reasons, estimably cling to life?"

But if Qurob heard he gave no answer, as he went drifting by on his face.

And some said, "He was a bad master. But who is next may be worse."

Qurob had left many sons, and daughters, lust being his pastime. Some of these were children, but others older. And there were some of twenty-five years and more, that he had sired when he was the heir. These might be expected to squabble and the kingdom not to be the better for it.

Then, far down the river, various sightseers thought they caught another sight, that of a man in an orange robe, walking over the water where there was no bridge. Still others spied him on the quays. He was a beggar, a rich lord. He played a pipe of jade, or merely stood musing, gazing downstream. . . . Fate had come to Nennafir.

A few miles to the west, the river loosed itself into the sea. In that direction the tiered merchant vessels of the city were rowed, and from that direction they returned, some heavy-laden, some light and with the promise of gold. Now, seaward, westward, there seemed to be a sort of fierce flash, either on the water, or just above it in the sky. There came a great radiance suddenly, a second sunrise, and from the wrong place, which brought the people of Nennafir in hordes to their windows and into the streets—or else sent them burrowing to hide in fear. And silence fell, expectant and terrible. Those who had come to watch the floating of their corpse king were due for superior wonders.

The light in the sky turns soft and flowerlike. A day-moon, not a sun. Only look, it is nothing horrible or fearsome, no sea monster out of the depths raging inland, no animate lightning. It is something lovely and fair, something that makes a beautiful music, and the glow on it is rainbows, and the glimmer of colors on the wings of birds and the backs of big fish leaping.

"A ship!" exclaimed a thousand voices.

It *was* a ship. But oh, such a ship it was.

It came upriver, between the banks of the city, gliding. And as it came, Qurob's cadaver slipped down under the water and was gone, from sight and from mind.

Tall, the ship, seven tiers of it, so it should not be able to stay upright or to move, and many, after, declared that indeed it did not rest utterly on the water, but a little over it, on a cloud of bright air. Yet seven oar banks turned, and the tips of their long spoons stirred the river.

It was the shape of a colossal lily, the ship, with a myriad down-folding petals, but the prow was the head of a slender dragon which came out from the flower with looking eyes and parted jaws. What woods had gone into the making of the ship it was not easy to tell, for every inch was plated by poured silver and hammered gold, so it blazed on and dazzled everything that gazed at it. Transparent bubbles like ghost-suns hung over the ship, and rays rang from the golden oars. Multihued, the birds came and went through the sheen of it, and the fish sported in its wake. It had no sail, and no one on its decks, and no cry from within of any directing the oars. Only music played, with no source. It soaked into brain and limb. The listeners felt a delirium fasten on them, they longed to spring about and dance, and quantities did so, clapping their hands and shouting joyfully, although there was no reason for joy, more for suspicion and alarm.

"Only see," said children in the crowds of Nennafir, "there is a lady on the ship."

It was a fact; the only living thing to be seen was up in the prow. A crown of gold spiked from the dragon's head, and there in its circlet stood a beautiful woman, also clad in gold, small as a doll, her long black hair about her.

"That is a mighty sorceress," said the crowds, to their children.

But others kneeled. "A supernatural thing," they said.

Up in the fence of gold, the golden woman did not move, yet her eyes seemed to touch every face and mind.

Then she lifted up her left hand—only that, a gesture remote, out on the river, high in the air.

And the ship stilled, the oars lay like teeth in a burning comb. The birds settled, the fishes sank, and the music died.

But the architecture of the city shifted, groaned, and cracked. Tiles scattered from the walls. Nennafir trembled, with fright or pleasure. And from their places there rose up the white stone cats of Nennafir, yawning and snarling in their carven throats.

Jumping from their high roofs and slinking off their plinths, they loped through the panic-stricken streets. At the river's edge, where the people shrank from them, they gathered with creamy fire in their stone eyes, bowing to the ship.

Then the light of the ship went out. Where it had been began a huge wave, brown for the river, with crystal veins and swirlings of gold and silver, and it swept over with the dragon's head still staring in it, and the golden crown and the supernatural sorceress, and curled down on the land. The multitude fled screaming before it, thinking to be drowned or broken.

Thus, on the emptied river quay, Azhriaz stepped out of the burning wave, and stood in a circle of bowing stone cats.

The poets and scholars would say this, that there she waited, her eyes blue as the sky, her hair the night, dressed in the sun, her skin the moon. And the city fell on its face to worship her, knowing at once that a being of Upperearth had descended.

She was plainly a daughter of heaven, of the etheric regions.

Her name, when they learned it, carried a strange echo, but they would not decipher it. And the ways of gods were beyond the questioning of men.

As she walked up through the streets of Nennafir toward the palace (where already certain of the heirs of Qurob had set to, to stab, strangle, and poison each other), her footsteps indented the paving, which thereafter shone. For decades these footsteps were one of the marvels of the city, and worked miracles. They faded in the end. She had no attendant on her walk but the white stone cats, thirteen of them, which hedged her round jealously. And the awe-smitten people deliriously followed, some yet singing and clapping their hands, some pale and in a trance, some flushed with anxiety.

The soldiers at the palace gate were moved to throw down their spears and kneel. They understood no man opposes the will of heaven.

The doors of the palace opened of themselves.

The gleaming footprints of Azhriaz passed over the court and up the stair and into the halls within.

So fair she was, the poets wrote, who could look at her and not know her for a goddess?

Azhrarn had said: "I will give them a god to adore. Let them discover what it is to be ruled by such."

BOOK TWO

Azhriaz: The Goddess

Matters of Stone

1

IN A BONEYARD of a desert, men were laboring to uproot the slim tall stones the winds of time had sculpted there.

The desert was all of stone, pale and faceless. Its dusts had turned to dust and to a dust of that dust, until they vanished altogether. Now there was a light white powder from the chiseling, and as each of the pillars fell, though the pulleys steadied it, tiny shards flew off into the air.

A road ran over the desert yard to a city which, being a vassal, was about to make its septennial tribute. Precious metal and jewels, herds of beasts and slaves, these were the offerings of this city. But it was requested to send also materials of building, so a forest of trees had been cut down, and here the forest of stone was tumbling likewise.

"Behold this pillar now," said the overseer to his newest gang. "One of the oldest in this haunted nasty place. The wind has howled by it a thousand years, I should not be surprised. And now it must fall to please the Witch-Goddess. Well, they do a lot of building there, I gather. Strike away."

"What is that mark there, high up, like a huge black eye?" asked one of the gang, a comely youth desirous the overseer should notice as much.

The overseer did so. "Well, my boy," said he, "there are holes in some of these stones, and sometimes something fills up the hole. And then time passes and the filling marries with the stone, and turns to a stone itself. Some animal," said the overseer, taking the youth aside, "crawled in there, centuries ago, and died, and became one with the stone. I never knew a hole," said the overseer, inviting the youth into his tent, "that did not, usually, eventually get filled up with something."

The rest of the new gang toiled on in the heat of the day. Their mallets and axes bit into the stone, and their saws ate away at it. In the midst of the afternoon, the stone swayed. The ropes tautened as the pillar teetered in their grip; it swung sideways and plummeted, and the ropes pulled it up before it could beat on the ground and shatter. When the stone was loaded on the cart, two or three men climbed in to look at the black opacity that curved out from it. They rapped on the darkness, to see if it would yield some interesting thing, but it did not oblige them. Their utensils made no impression.

To the city then, this stone, with the others. And then into the caravan of tribute, and away eastward, a journey a year and a half in length, to the wide lands of the Witch-Goddess. Of whom the city heard much, though she had never been seen there.

She had risen in the east like a second sun. Three decades this city had known of her. She was eternally young, the Witch-Goddess, always lovely. Cruel and piti-less she was too, and warlike, and a magician. She de-scended from heaven, and the seas and rivers divided themselves before her. She landed at a place called Nennafir, the Flower of the River Bank, and made it hers in three hours. And then, in three months, she turned the armies of flowering Nennafir outward to conquer the world, in three thirds—and in three years it seemed she had made a good beginning. From coast to coast, isle to isle, the mountains, the valleys, the towns, the cities—one full third, perhaps somewhat more. Only the wastes, or remoter lands, had she, so far, ignored. Where her legions did not go with their brazen tramp and bloody steel, where her magic did not fly like a honey-throated, jet-black bird—kissing blade, kill-ing song—the word of her went, the *gossip*, and that was enough. There had been others like her, it was true. There had been a witch-queen once who subdued many of the lands of the earth and seduced many others, Zorayas, who was now a legend. But Zorayas, for all her might, glory, villainy, beauty, was mortal. This one was a god. To defy her was not merely death, but blasphemy.

A hundred stories were told of her, or seven hundred, or seven thousand. Some were lies, or other tattle (of such as Zorayas and her kind), which were caught up like flotsam in a tide. Some of the stories were real enough. But the deeds of conquest and omnipotence have a sameness, as does the exposition of most evil.

The caravan of tribute ran on, through its initial months of traveling, eastward, and soon the tales lay so thick about it the wheels of the carts and wagons could hardly move for them, and the carriage animals stumbled and perished—stuck and stifled in the swamp of a living myth.

In the third month of the journey, the way became physically congested, by other caravans from other places, all foaming into one enormous channel, as if the dams of countless waters had given way.

All roads now led to Az-Nennafir.

Mere city it was no more, but a metropolis covering so vast an area, thirteen gigantic kingdoms might be sunk in it. A city large as a country, and thereafter a country sprawled through one third of the discovered earth: Empire.

Men sickened, too, coming even to the periphery of that spot. The emanations of its sorcery, though long months and endless miles away, filled mortals with wild emotions. Some men fell subject to fits and to fevers—they danced in their sleep, slept as they walked. The hale declined and the sick grew well. There was a vapor of madness everywhere. And the land changed.

First came a passage through mighty mountains, and the mountains were bald and shone in the distance like pale silver. Nothing grew on them, no tree, no blade of vegetation. Those that passed up and over them saw they were of a grayish granite that in some parts had turned to a kind of mirror. The sun pierced through them, or the moon by night. Beyond the mountains, rolling plains of savage grass, the stems of which were thick and green. The grass was sweet, and brewed in a vat made a green wine which, drunk too often, turned men's wits, or blinded them. Birds drifted over the grasslands on enormous wings, flying parasols of darkness. Sometimes they stooped and took some animal from its cover, or a child—for herders lived on the plains, in huts of grass, clothed in grass, playing on pipes made from the grass stems, and strange in the head from breathing always the grass scent.

Other lands followed, steep and steepled, low as trenches, desolate, populous. There was a sea over which a bridge had been built, and supported partly, it must be, by sorcery. Its legs were sunk down deep into the bedrock under the water. Many days on the bridge the caravans must go, seeing only ocean on either side of the high parapets, or the spurling sea-sky overhead. And seafowl rose before the caravans in a white wind. Or sometimes huge creatures were sighted in the water, swimming by.

In the sixth month of the land voyage east, the towns and cities lay on the ground as thick as locusts, each with only a short stretch of free land between, and over this land the cities fought for possession, but the caravans passed, inviolable, since they carried tribute to the Witch-Goddess. There was not a city now, a town, a village, that did not have a temple dedicated to her, and her looming statues arose on the highways. They were all unalike, yet all similar, white as snow or ice, the hair of black—ebony, agate—the eyes of blue—great sapphires, or blue emeralds— and the offerings made before the statues lay there and decayed; even the birds of the air would not steal from her, or the coneys or the foxes. Heaps of fruits, and vials of perfume and amphorae of liquor, and on the white stone altars the bones stuck up like drawn swords through the rotting carcasses of sacrifice. The dizzying stench of all this filled the atmosphere everywhere around. Sometimes priests were at the altars. Flames burned and smoke lifted, through the loud hymns of praise. It had a blue robe, her order, blue for the eyes of the Goddess, a blue like no other blue on the earth. By night in those lands, you saw the fires of offering burning on every side, dotting the darkness, which otherwise glowed faintly with the lamps of the crowded cities, or glared where one of them was on fire.

In the ninth month of its traveling, the caravan which carried the desert stones—along with those other caravans which had traveled a smaller while, or a greater, but a trek of nine more months still before them all—came to the edge of the country known now as Az-Nennafir, the heartland of the Empire of the Goddess.

No man had ever gone on this expedition more than once in his life. Once was enough. And in most families, the onus of the adventure was passed from father to son, a destiny that could not be avoided.

The outskirts of the heartland of the Goddess, locked in sorcery, were mostly empty. Here were deserts, of a sort. After the teem of the cities, it seemed all life had hidden itself. There were many differing accounts of these regions, and probably they did differ vastly, from one sector to another, for of the large numbers of men who approached, each saw only that landscape he traveled through, and, undoubtedly, so much was sufficient for him.

The stone-bearing caravan, with its companions, then, came in over a rocky precipitous height, and down into a hollow smooth as burnished copper in the dawn. Long pans of metallic ground lay before them, some with pools of metallic water in them, where none would drink, not even the thirsty animals. Days they moved on the face of this geography, under a sweeping sky. When the nights came, there were curious shapes in the heavens—not to be confused with clouds; vague misty forms that went to and fro, ghost-giants, or phantom gods. Stars shot from their moorings—if they were stars. Some crashed on the land, rushing over the encampments of the travelers, lighting the sky with dreadful colors bright as noon, making a sound of screaming, or tearing cloth. Where they fell, over the dim metallic hills, there would come thunder and a blast of fire, and out from that place would roar a sudden brief gale, hot as a furnace, blowing the tents from their pegs and men off their feet, and smelling of essences that had no name.

A month or two then, in this odd environment, unsafe with falling stars. And then the desert of metal gave onto a desert of blue sand under a drenched blue sky. Fountains sprang here from boulders of violet quartz. The water and the blueness refreshed and did no harm—or seemed to do none; who could be sure? (No man, they said, goes that road and returns as sane as he went. They were resigned to it, mostly, having no choice.)

Another month or two in the blue deserts, track of time already being somewhat approximate. And then a white desert, where streams of milk ran from boulders of alabaster. And next, black pastures running black beer—or ink; best be careful when drinking. And then pure water, a land of it, a lake going from the foot's edge to the horizon, with here and there tangle-haired water-forests or primeval trees in which fish nested, flopping from out the lake to tend round eggs like opals, sitting upon them and panting gently, with solemn wintry eyes. A causeway led over the lake. It stopped at a wall.

The wall had become visible some miles off, and even those who had heard of it had stared. It was a wall of tiles, enameled with winged beasts or tailed beasts—it went up and up, and up and up. It seemed to hold off the sky.

The caravans crowded the causeway, piled against the wall. The day had melted into the lake, and the fish dived from their nests and played, gleaming, in the water. The moon had come up, unseen beyond the wall, in the east. She lifted higher and higher until she could crest the wall. When this happened, the tiles whitened, and a door appeared, unlocked by moonlight seemingly, gradually gaping wide. The caravans went through, to the last wheel and pack animal, and the last man. After which, the wall closed itself.

It was pitch dark inside the wall, for the moon had now got over the top of it and lay outside to please the fish in the lake.

But a glowing road lay on the inner side, a road like golden fire. They saw it coil and wind away before them. Wearied out, yet obediently they took this road, and were laved in its flaming aura, which seemed to give no light above or to either side, but which nourished them furiously. The exhausted animals pranced and trotted and galloped. The tired men laughed and cried them on.

So they raced toward the city thirteen kingdoms vast, and entered it.

*   *   *

There was an opinion it was not, after all, sorcery, that made Az-Nennafir the way it was, but rather the fantasies of mankind concerning the place.

Those that returned (not all did so) murmured of size and hue, and the manner in which things were contrary, and, too, of a beauty which had upset them, driven them forever insane in little ways. Or huge ways. Dull men sometimes became poets, or hanged themselves, after Az-Nennafir, but that was the least of it.

The sun there is blue, they said. It is like shimmering dusk at midday. This is due, they said, to a canopy of sapphire which overpanes all the kingdom—the Goddess-dom. Or it is a gargantuan lens set in the sky. Or plain magic. Here and there a hole has been manufactured in the canopy, lens or magic, and under this the sun is to be found in an oasis of fiery brightness.

By night, there are seven moons, of various largeness and shade, and varieties of stars—they are clockwork, or sorcery, or both, and they may be seen to move, slowly, in wonderful formations, occasionally passing each other, when—if they touch—they make a melodious chiming.

All growing things excel there. They attain uncanny burgeonings, and tower in the air. There are rose trees whose roses are so great a girl may recline in them. The petals are waxy, but they exude a perfume sufficient to render one unconscious. Cedars there are which reach the height of a hill, or small mountain, and the lower moons, passing through them at night, scatter their boughs to the earth, frosted with peculiar incandescence. The buildings, meanwhile, are as tall, or taller. There are stairways which it requires a whole morning to ascend. There are spires which vanish from sight into the blue sunshine—they have stained-glass windows in them which stretch down to the ground, as broad as three gateways, but above growing narrow as a beaded thread.

And while the returned travelers speak or write or screech or babble of this, someone or other, not properly fearful, may ask: "But did you look upon the Goddess? Did you gaze at Azhriaz, the Daughter of Upperearth?

And one who had returned might answer in this way:

"After we had journeyed some months through the built

country of the City of Az-Nennafir, we came to the bank of a little brown sinuous river. Oh, it was a good quarter mile across, the river, yet all the things about had dwarfed it utterly. Nevertheless, on the farther bank, there went up an edifice which was a temple-palace of the Goddess. The priests came, and we laid down our tribute. It was weighed and counted, but I hardly heeded what went on. I stared only at that edifice, which might contain her, she that holds us in thrall. Now, she is cruel and pitiless and indifferent (which we have learned, through her teaching, the gods are to mankind—and indeed, have not the lessons of our lives ceaselessly informed us this was so?). We know she may strike us dead with a look, or send any one of us to a hideous torture, which has happened in the past, yes, to those who fear and reverence her. While to ask her for anything is without point; she will not grant the boon. And as for pleasing her by prayer or by oblation, the gods take no note, nor any pleasure in such, though omission they may punish. Yet, she is supernal and she is among us, and none, I think, stands at the entry to one of her palaces and does not dream he may catch a glimpse of her.

"Well then. Certain of the towers of the palace soared so high they dimmed from my view. On others, the blue sunlight trickled like rain. Three of the white stone cats of the city, big as elephants, prowled on the farther bank, before a flight of steps more than three hundred in number, and every tread laid with a mineful of sapphires. And above the sapphire stair was a golden terrace, and above that were two golden doors—each itself the height of a king's house, cellar to roof, out here in the ordinary world. And on the doors was written her name in symbols so beautiful one could not bear to look at them.

"By now the crowds on the bank, where the tribute was being weighed and counted, had swelled to a million persons or more. Suddenly a trumpet sounded, out of the very ether. Such a silence fell that a man might think himself deafened, save he hears the tumult of his own heart.

"There came a perfume, then, that all the swooning roses of that miracle of cities could not rival, and the waters of the river turned to gold and silver, and fishes of

jade sprang up in it, and azure lilies bloomed. The great
doors of gold with the name AZHRIAZ upon them opened
softly as two butterfly wings. And there was a blue fire
burning between them. And out of the fire, she came.

"Perhaps I may find words for all things in the City, but
for her I can find very few. There is needed a new
language to describe her. She is very beautiful, as the
statues show her, dark and pale, with eyes of the sky. But
she is the Goddess, and so human words can never be
enough. She wore a silver garment, but it was also gold.
Such jewels lay on her breast and arms and in her ears,
upon her feet and fingers, at her waist and in her long hair,
that seeing them, jewels ceased to mean anything at all.
She wore a high diadem of gold, set with diamonds, and
from it floated a veil colored like a blush, sprinkled too
with diamonds as if with water drops. Her arms she held
outward from her body; the nails of her hands were long,
and white as snow. On the palms of her hands were gold
and silver patterns, or they may have been infant stars. Her
feet did not rest on the ground, not even on those sapphire
steps. She stood in air, and a soft gleaming cloud curled
under her soles. Her hair spread out like rays of a black
sun. She was a vast distance from us, yet by her power she
was close enough one saw her blink, and when she did so,
there was a flash of fire, as if her lids struck sparks out of
her eyes.

"Then, she spoke. Her voice was low, and sweet as
music. I heard it in my skull, but not in my ears. She said:
'*Do you know me?*' And falling on our knees and our
faces, we cried out that we did, and we worshiped her.
Some thrust knives into their flesh, others slew themselves, or cast themselves down into the river, where the
fish ate them, and we saw it and applauded. I myself
slashed off my left hand—see the stump. That was my first
offering. I felt no pain, only ecstasy. But it was not
enough to give her. I was about to plunge the dagger in my
breast when again she spoke. She said: 'Remember, to the
gods you are nothing. To Azhriaz, the Goddess, you are
only grains of dust or sand. You do well, however, to sculpt
our images from stone, for stone we are, we, the gods—stone
that cannot be broken, stone-hard-handed, stony of eye and

mind, having stones for hearts. Yes, the gods are stones, and you are sand. So it is and always shall be. What then is your answer to heaven?' And we loved her and groveled down, and swallowed the delicious mud of the river bank. That was our answer. And once more I raised the dagger to give her my life, but I felt her whisper in my soul: *Not that*. And she told me what it was she desired, without desire, of me. And so, I have returned and done her bidding. That which I am satisfied she carelessly required and has forgotten. Go to my house; you will discover there my wife and children, murdered for a sacrifice.

"Blessed be heaven, and the Goddess-on-Earth."

2

THERE WAS a boy who had traveled with the caravans west to east, and had charge over the pale stone pillars from the boneyard desert. He came on the journey because his father, who should have had the mission, died of the fear of it a month before. The boy was not in happy mood, and worn down himself with fright. It was not surprising he should often have bad dreams throughout the journey. However, it seemed to him the dreams were worse when he lay near one particular stone, and that when he slumbered distantly from it, the dreams were flimsy, or did not come at all. There was nothing remarkable about the stone, except it had a black blemish at one end. What then did the boy dream, lying near the stone pillar with the black blemish? He dreamed someone flung him into a fire, or else he dreamed that it was he who did the flinging of another, and the victim was one he loved, though he never saw who it might be, nor, waking, had he ever loved any with such intensity. Then again, there was one dream where the pillar stood upright and became a slender dark-faced man, in a robe of white, who touched the boy, and the boy mourned, for he wished to die and he could not. And there was also a dream when he beheld a city tinted like swans and blood, and the sea covered it and turned it to coral.

He was an ill-educated boy; he knew next to nothing of the legends. The living legend of the Goddess-on-Earth had, let it be said, somewhat overset the balance in these matters. But if he had known more of the old tales, he might well have said to himself, "Why do I dream the dreams of Zhirek the Magician, he that killed Simmu, or meant to do so, and gave Simmu's city of Simmurad to the seas of the earth's eastern corner?" But, unknowing, the boy only said to himself, "Alas, this journey!" And moved farther away from the pillars of stone.

So the caravans came in, like wrecked shipping, on the shores of the marvel of Az-Nennafir.

And at last on the bank of the brown river then, with the gigantic spectacle of the temple-palace over the water, under the spectral shadows of seven moons, expecting to be maimed or die in the morning, and all around the tribute of a hundred lands, and their people—every one of them with much the same thought as he—the boy climbed up on the supine stack of columns, and slept that night lying over the very damned stone, from sheer defiance. For what could a dream do to him worse than Azhriaz the Goddess?

But a dream came which was not like any of the others.

It seemed to the boy he woke, and he lay all alone on the river bank, under a gentle sky with a single crescent moon and some mild singing stars. And nearby, through the blue water flowers, a woman walked. She was veiled, yet she seemed to have a radiance on her. He thought: *It is she*. But in that moment the woman came up to him, and he looked into the deep clearness of her eyes, and understood no goddess—for the gods were unloving—would look so kindly on a human thing.

"Lady," he said, "what is it you want of me?"

"I will tell you a riddle," she replied. "You must try to guess its meaning."

Then the boy forgot it all, his father's death, the journey, the place, and the delirious horror to come. He smiled and sat waiting attentively.

"There is," said the woman, and her voice was beautiful to hear, "a casket set with fabulous gems, glittering and hard. And within this casket is a casket of gold, and within that casket a casket of silver. Open these three in turn, and you will find a casket of crystal, and inside the casket of crystal one of pearl, and within the pearl a box of velvet. And within the velvet an exquisite jewel. But within the jewel, what?"

The boy thought. He said, "Inside so many rich wrappings, only something more rich can lie."

"Ah, you must read with your heart and not your wit," said the woman, so tenderly tears started to his eyes. "How rich is the body of any mortal creature, yet under its fine covers, there is only bone, and only bone remains when all the jewels of the flesh are gone. Bone, and one other item, better than the rest, but unseen. Now, open the six rich caskets, gaze into the jewel. There you will find a child, weeping."

The boy sighed, comprehending nothing, save that this did not need comprehension.

"Get up now," said the woman quietly, "and cut the rope which binds the stone you lie over. At dawn, when the priests come to examine the tribute, this one pillar will roll away and fall into the river. Do not let it distress you. You shall go home safely."

The boy turned eagerly, and with his knife he cut the rope which secured the baleful stone to its fellows. When he looked again for the woman, she was walking away along the bank through the flowers. Though it was a dream, a night breeze had began to blow, and a wing of her hair was tossed shining from under her veil. And this hair, though young as she herself, was whiter than the moon. But the boy was unversed in the stories. Her white hair told him nothing.

Dawn came, green and turquoise, lifting its blue cornflower of a sun.

The river bank roused, the boy with the rest, recollecting nothing of what he had dreamed.

The priests of the Goddess came over the river to shore on a raft of gold, and the oars rowed by themselves. The priests, in the robes of that blue like which there was no other, chanted in a shrill groan, and bells rang, and incense smoke, blue on blue on blue, unwove into the sapphire-lidded sky.

The tribute of the many lands was laid out like a market, oddly quiet, and the blue priests passed silently amid the tribute, weighing, counting. Among them were both old and young, and there were female orders, priestesses of Az-Nennafir, but in truth they each wore the same face, ageless and lacking a gender. They had given their spirits to Azhriaz, or to the ethos they recognized by her name. They had relinquished all identity, and gained in lieu of it no other thing. Pithless gourds. They worshiped, knowingly, the indifferent hatred of heaven.

But all this while, the vaster part of the multitude gazed only across the river. They wondered if *she* would appear to them. She did not always do so. For all the swarms of people who came to her City, only a fraction witnessed her. The majority were bitter all their lives, cheated by being spared.

Six white stone cats, big as elephants, patrolled the farther bank. The jewelry of the stair glittered like a glacier. The high doors of gold did not quiver.

The boy who had had the dream was also gazing, his heart in his mouth. He was aware a priest came by him, eyeing the scores of white natural columns, bundled there like huge posts. As the thin hand of the priest reached out to one of these bundles, its topmost column, resting some thirty feet in the air, suddenly leapt free. It flew outward like a live thing, and then came hurtling down. The priest, making no move to avoid it, raised his arms and shouted aloud: "*Azhriaz!*" And the column struck him in the chest; as he fell it ground over him and on, toward the river.

Other men scrambled to safety; only the flowers were in the column's path, and did not stop it. That stone from the desert one and a half years away dropped into the Goddess's river, and the water gushed upward and poured down again, but the stone, having gone under, reemerged, and lay afloat on the surface like a long white bone with one black knot in it. The boy, still remembering no iota of his dream, had flung himself flat to wait for death, but the priests took no notice of him. One cried in a great voice: "An omen! The gift itself rushes to meet the Goddess."

But they did not attempt to fish out the pillar, bizarrely floating there and, borne now despite its weight—which did not seem inclined to sink it—to drift with the current downstream.

And that was all. Presently the boy, shaking with trepidation, got up. The portion of tribute he had been in charge of was declared in order. The golden doors of the temple-palace did not open, and the Goddess did not appear. No attempt was made to salvage the dead priest who had allowed the pillar to crush him. It was thought offensive to treat the sick or to display pomp in funerals, since punishment through illness and death was the casual will of Upperearth. Corpses were dragged by the heels and hair to pits, and burned there. And in a while, some did this office for the priest. Others came to deal with the treasures of tribute, and soon the bank was empty, but for all the people and their much-lightened beasts and wagons, and their hearts—emptied also.

The boy stood and sobbed with raging disappointment, one of countless others. He wished to swim the river and immolate himself on the sapphire steps. He shivered with resentful ire that he had not been asked to murder or to die for her. Nor was he alone in this seizure.

And it was months after, on the tedious journey homeward, that his hysterical craving gave way to a sulky gladness. And it seemed to him then that he *had* seen her, all alone by night, but that was in a dream.

3

SOME QUANTITY of air there must have been, trapped in the sealed cavity of the pillar stone, to keep it afloat. Unsinking, it wended through the blue day on the river. The flowers of the bank brushed it and sought to detain it, but it slipped easily from each embrace, though showered by petal-tears. Spangled flies pursued the stone, wanting to alight, but found the texture not to their liking, buzzily discussed it to its detriment, and flew away. And as the day declined, and dusk began to purple the river, the pillar came between great gardens on the shore, and here armored crocodiles of prodigious size slunk from the reeds, and approached it. "What manner of beast is this?" they sinisterly mumbled. "It moves as we do, graceful and leaden, but where are the jaws of it? It has only one dull eye." And they snarled their teeth of white and yellow, and closed up their lazy-lidded hellish gaze, and rowed away on strong spiky legs.

But the blossoming rushes of the gardens, whose dusk-colored lily heads stood up from the water, had made a net beneath the surface. Here they caught enormous jewels that were sometimes thrown in the river, unwary fish of startling girth, and the corpses of men who had sacrificed themselves to the Goddess through drowning. Now, the net caught the pillar of stone, gently, and held it fast as chains.

When the first moon of Az-Nennafir's night flew upward from the east, and the first dance of the first stars began across the sky, the stone lay still, white and grave, among the crowns of the purple rush iris.

And the water sipped and lipped the pillar. The water said: Taste, drink of me, hard desert thing. Be wet as never before. The river can dissolve, in time, almost anything. I will lick you away, and you will become water, too. Taste and drink, as you are tasted and drunk. Soak up the river's wine as it melts you. I am full of death and life. I carry the magic of this metropolis like an artery. I know black caverns where neither the sun nor the moon ever shine, but they are light as day to those that dwell there. And I know lairs of weed where little creatures swim about that are like tiny lions and horses and cattle, but with fishtails, and where there are tall shells that scuttle on fringed spider legs. And I know where the crocodiles go to die, and their bones have made a temple of calcium, but their eyes only crystallize and become lamps of pale green topaz. And I flow in and out of everything that pauses or that passes here, through its very body, and so learn all its secrets. Flowers grow far down that no man has ever looked on, not even Azhriaz the Goddess has looked at them. They have no color, here, but if they were brought up into the light, they would be found to have a color never seen before on the earth. And there is a place where there exists an invisible race of insects, who build complex cities of their own in the slime. And there is a forest of dead women's hair, where ferns grow that sing in female voices. Ah, then, said the river to the pillar of stone, when you become one with me, we will travel together and all these things you will see and know. But it may take a short while, a few hundred years. Be patient. Taste and drink. Soak up the river's wine. . . .

High as sky, the temple-palace on the river bank in Az-Nennafir of the Goddess. Few have entered it, and of those that have, fewer come away, to tell. Yet the moonlight of seven moons falls now in through the painted and stained windows. What does the moonlight say?

The outer precinct is a hall of jewels. Every gemstone of the earth is represented in it. There are columns built of butter-yellow beryls and beryls yellow as a cat's eyes, or greenish as the eyes of crocodiles. And there are columns of crimson faceted corundum and polished corundum of dragon-red. There are blue columns also, of transparent aquamarine, that seem to hang suspended, and jade and emerald columns that seem to grow like trees or spouting waves frozen in viridescent ice. The walls have scenes depicted on them, made all of these jewels, and others, and the floors are a jeweled mosaic. The ceiling has seven carbuncles in it larger than cartwheels, of bloodiest green and most astringent violet. . . . The moonlight spins and grows giddy and hastens through a half-open door into an inner precinct, which is of gold.

There is a carpet in this room, on a floor of gold so malleable it is runneled and pitted like mud. The carpet is made of the wool of golden sheep, so it is said. Golden swords, each the stature of three brawny men upon each other's shoulders, uphold a canopy of golden disks. Gold, *gold*—the eyes are numbed and see all things golden. Even the candles are gold in golden sconces, and burn with a sheer gold flame. The moonlight flees through a lattice of gold lace, into a room of silver.

Aloft, a silver web. Beneath, the floor is a pool—of fluid silver, boiling and bubbling. Silver bridges cross the silver pool, but the moonlight falls in love with the silver room and falls fainting with desire into the molten liquid.

Imagination, or hearsay, must go on alone.

Up a stair of silver flanked by silver gryphons, to a silver door with a silver keyhole, and through that into a room which is crystal. Part milky the walls, and part lucid. You may look up into the sky—so close, for all the while, the enormous rooms have subtly ascended. Stars dance on the roof of this one, twirling their skirts of tinsel. In crystal columns, which are slim as a girl's arm, crystal water seems to play, and sometimes fish—that have no visible bodies, only crystalline spines and little crystalline skulls and bright, bright eyes—flit about there.

Beyond and above the crystal room lies a room hollowed from a single pearl. Heaven alone knows (if it bothers) what monstrous oyster could have been afflicted by what horrific boulder of grit to produce a result so large. Smooth, the pearl room, and slightly flushed, but with no furnishings, save another long stair—each step of which is, too, a single pearl, but, of course, infinitely smaller. The stair ends at a pearl-crusted door; these pearls are only the size of hand mirrors. The door is firmly shut, and will not yield to pressure, to a demanding cry or to a courteous knock.

So far, there have been glimpsed no attendants. Sometimes priests may be found on the outer stair of this sacred house, but they do not enter even the room of jewels, though they have spied it. In the temple-palace, hordes of human slaves of all the peoples of the conquered world-third may be supposed to come and go. Yet, in this succession of chambers at least, they have left no evidence.

Nevertheless, by the door of pearl, something waits. It is not to be looked on, has no form, makes no sound, gives off no odor. But it is there. A guardian. And by night, surely other things come to pass within the door of pearl?

They say she has supernatural handmaidens and pages more beautiful than any mortal. Gorgeous, as she is, and with black hair, though they do not have her eyes. They tend her only after sunfall, being children of the night.

But by day or by night, oh what splendors must manifest inside that inaccessible room—

The room within the jewels, the gold, the silver, the crystal, the pearl—was bare. It was built of nothing important, it would seem to be constructed of wattle, and the floor was wood. Fat candles burned prosaically on iron spikes. There was a window half a mile up from the ground, that saw only sky, but the wooden shutters were fastened by iron bolts, and the sky, also, was shut out.

A girl of seventeen years sat on the floor, drawing on the wood, with a wand of ocher, strange symbols. She wore a gown of vermilion velvet, as if she were cold in the hot night. Her black hair made her veil and diadem both. Her eyes were sapphires; she had no other jewel that was to be seen: Her beauty was enough.

Three and thirty years—at the very least—she has ruled a third of the earth. And she is seventeen still, the immortal Goddess Azhriaz.

Azhriaz finished her work with the wand of ocher, and taking up instead a wand of brass, she struck the near edge of the drawn symbols three times.

Smolder burst there.

In the smolder stood a man of brass, with brazen hair and batlike wings. His feet were the claws of an eagle and he had one eye only, set at the center of his forehead.

"I am here," said he.

"Speak," said she.

"There is nothing new," said the brass man. "I have searched about and looked diligently and long. Cities burn and men die, as ever. And, as ever, they call out your name and worship you."

"Go," said Azhriaz.

And the smolder perished and the brass man with it, draining down into the floor.

Then Azhriaz took a wand of leprous turquoise and struck the symbols three times with that.

And a second smolder shot out, but more like water than smoke.

There was a bluish man-being, with two alligator tails for legs, and he was horned like the young moon.

"I am here," he said.

"Speak," she said.

"There is nothing new," said the bluish man. "I have searched about and listened and pried. Harvests are reaped, of corn and flesh. And men sing always hymns to the Goddess."

"Go," said the Goddess.

And he went.

Then she took a wand of ivory and smote with that.

Steam blustered.

A white horse with the head of a woman cavorted in the drawing.

"Here I am," said she.

"Speak," said Azhriaz.

"There is nothing new," said the woman-headed horse.

"Go," said Azhriaz—

—And the apparition went.

Then Azhriaz the Goddess took a rosebud, a bud of Az-Nennafir, large as a caldron, and threw it among the symbols. There came at once the slow explosion of a rose, the bud unfolding, the flower like a flaming torch, blooming, full-blown, stretched on its veins like a sunshade—till the layers of it shattered.

And from the heart of the rose there stole a coil of rose-red incense.

From behind the incense appeared a beautiful maiden child, clad only in saffron hair, but her eyes were the heads of two snakes.

"Am I here?" asked the child with her rosy mouth.

"You are," said Azhriaz. "Now tell me of my love."

"Oh," said the child, "your love. I have seen him fleeing over hills when none ran after. I have seen him screaming at the heat of the moon and lying parched under the sun to be cool. I have seen him pluck thorns and dress and garland himself in them till his blood made streams on the ground. I have seen him eat poison and vomit it forth. I have seen him squealing and hopping through the years, and men curse him and shun him and fling stones and blades. And after the sun goes down, sometimes some come to him like slender dark shadows, and tease and torture him, setting the night flowers to sting him and the forest hares to bite him. And later these shadow ones spit in his face, and their spit is like a holy blue flame."

"I would spit upon him, too," said Azhriaz, but she held her side as if a knife cut into her. "And does he remember ever that he is a prince?"

"Yes. Then he is worse. Then he makes himself crowns of rusty nails."

"And does he ever remember the lovers Oloru and Sovaz?"

"No. Once he passed two lovers in a field, a man and a girl, he fair, and she raven-headed. But they started up in fear of him. Then he only climbed a tree and tore the leaves with his teeth, laughing. He does not remember Oloru. He forgets Sovaz."

"Go," said the Witch-Goddess.

But the child lingered.

"Give me a night of time to wander the world," said the child with snakes for eyes.

"I will give you nothing. Go, or I will blast you, and with those powers you know I have."

"Yes, you are very powerful, exalted mistress. But give me only then one half of the night to wander, for I am weary of that region wherefrom you summon me. I watch mad Prince Madness at your bidding, and I glimpse the world and I long to enter the world with all my essence, not merely with that little wraith of me that is your servant.''

"I am pitiless,'' said Azhriaz. "Have you not heard of it? I am pitiless even to the pitiless. You shall have no night and no half night in the world.''

"Give me then but one hour, Mistress of Madness and Delirium, and I will lead you to a spot downriver where lies a white stone from a desert that the rushes have captured fast. And the stone shall charm you, for it holds the dream of one who once spoke aloud a curse against the Prince of Demons.''

Azhriaz lifted her head. Her face was a dagger. She said, carefully, "Azhrarn, Lord Wickedness, is my peerless father, and I his obedient heir.''

The child shrank at the voice of Azhriaz and at her look, but still the child said, "I heard the river singing. The river sang as it caressed the stone. I only tell the truth.''

Azhriaz rose. She stood and gazed upon the child, who said plaintively, "Give me an hour in the world, and I will guide you.''

"I need no guide,'' said Azhriaz, and she clapped her hands.

At once the ocher markings on the floor blew in the air and the child with snakes for eyes was caught up by them and dashed away, back into the psychic junkyard from which she had been sprung.

Azhriaz stood alone in the bare room high in the sky. In her look were thirty-three years at least of arrogant dominion, of the sea-waves of war and encompassing unkindness, and of an unremitting chastity. Demon women had no wombs. The womb of Azhriaz, also a mortal woman's daughter, was now a closed dumb winter fruit of ice. She had taken to herself mage-craft, battles, an empire, but no lover, since Chuz.

Yet she was seventeen years still, as on the eve of their parting. And still she was a weeping child, within the sparkling jewel of sorcerous might.

She glanced at the shutters and they clashed wide. Azhriaz took on the form of a somber moth—she was long since accustomed to such changes.

Between the mountainous peaks of the City she beat her way, past the stupendous colored windows with bold lights behind, and the darkened panes that reflected back the moons. To such calumnies as were practiced all about, she paid no heed, as she paid no heed to the suicides and butcheries perpetrated in her name, and seemingly at her instruction.

Her parchment wings were strong, but presently she settled on the water of the river, a black swan with one hyacinthine ring of plumage at her throat.

In this guise, she caught the strand of the river's song which pertained to the pillar of stone.

She followed then that strand, and came to the net of the rush iris.

One by one, the moons were going down in the west, and they lit bright pathways on the river. In the shadows the iris crowns showed black as the swan herself, but the stone was pallid.

Azhriaz moved up along the length of it, until she reached the curving blackened blemish. Here she felt the pulse of something pounding slowly and insistently on and on.

It is a heart, the heart of Azhriaz informed her.

The sorcerously embued water, washing the pillarbone, stony dry so long, had already worked magic on it. There had come about a loosening, the rock letting go what lay in it—or what lay there letting go the stone of its hiding place.

Like an insect prisoned in white amber, the being in the stone. Yet alive, in certain ways, since unable so far to be dead.

And there was the scent of a madness grown luminous and calm through its brush with eternity.

The swan came close and touched the eye of the stone with her nacre beak.

There was neither crack nor crumbling. There was a sigh. In the water a further darkness flowed like blood. A cavity showed in the white, and the stone, losing balance, turned over.

It lay face down among the irises, and then, its buoyancy and its soul quite gone from it, mourned by a storm of bubbles, the pillar dropped down and down to the river's floor.

And the last of the sinking moons was able to describe, adrift in the rushes' net and three handspans underwater, the naked body of a man, white as the stone, but for the black hair flowering at his loins and pillowing his head and shoulders.

His eyes were shut. The lids of them said, *Do not waken me*, clear as if it had been printed there. The lips were firm; the nostrils waxed and waned, breathing the water with no trouble.

He had known the depths of water before, and perhaps recalled it. But he did not stir.

And the last moon fell, and when it had fallen, Azhriaz took her own form, and stood in the dark on the river.

There was a desert place, where even the powders and the dusts had ground away to nothing. This was the site he had chosen for his exile.

He had climbed one of its pillars of stone, and entered a fracture there. He sat down on the bone floor and he bowed his head, and so he stayed for many years.

By day the sun beat in at him, by night the blue winds. He ate only what came to him, which was the air; he drank the dew, the infrequent rain. He lived because deprivation could not kill him, any more than a spear or a sea or a flame. But he became a blackened wire and his beauty left him.

Men visited him, and birds of prey. Both stubbed their intentions on the walls of his invulnerability and despair. Death came to him only in sleep, those fearsome sleeps the Lord Uhlume had granted him in return for erstwhile service— slumber like a tomb. And this way of sleeping wiped his brain clean of everything at last. Even guilt and anguish and agony of mind were gradually spent, and almost forgotten.

Then one night demons came to taunt and seduce the hermit in the fractured stone. And in their vicious play, perhaps only by accident, he discovered a curious redemption from blame. The splinter of steel he had driven in through his invulnerable heart was, he discovered, only a nightmare. Where he had spread venom, gardens flourished. His curse became a blessing.

Then he wept. He wept away the final vestige of himself. And when that ended, he curled himself within the stone. The blackness of the deeds he had done sealed him round, but it was charred and vitrified, with all the energy gone out of it, though it lay heavy on him as most rubble does.

Invulnerable, stone-dead, he lived, lived on, while the hurricanes of centuries blew by.

Till they hacked down the pillar and brought it to Az-Nennafir, and a boy dreamed Dunizel came and told him to cut that one stone free, and the stone rolled into the river and among the rushes. And so lay there until Azhriaz came upon it.

The boy who dreamed had not known the legends. But Dunizel, the priestess of Bhelsheved, had known esoteric lore, and most myths, both veritable and false, and she had related stories to her child in the womb. Azhriaz was schooled.

Azhriaz stood on the river now, like a tall lily. She wore after all one jewel—a square of amethyst inside a little silver cage, fastened on a hair-fine silver chain. It reposed and warmed between her breasts, but now she had plucked it out, and held the jewel to her lips, as if she kissed or requested council. Then she let go the jewel again and the velvet covered it.

"You may sleep no longer," she said to the pale, dark man under the surface of the river. "That is over."

The closed lids of the eyes said to her: What is over? I may sleep for ever. I am unknown.

"You breathe the water," she said. "Any peasant who ever heard the tale, would know you. You are the one made a pact with the people of the sea, and broke the pact, but not before you had learned their magic."

Then his eyelids raised themselves.

They had been once but were no more the sky-reflecting color of the oasis, those eyes. Now, they were black.

He had shriveled and shrunk and become a rock. Rebirthed, he had again the youthful physical being of a man, but though this was a handsome man enough, still the beauty of his first life was gone, with the green-blue of the eyes.

"*I* did none of those things you speak of," said the man, perhaps truthfully, sitting up in the net of rushes, cleaving water to breathe air. His thick wet hair streaked him now like ink, and water drops flickered on his lashes. But his eyes were hard stones, well tutored how to be. He was, ironically, of the racial coloring of the demons he had once attempted to serve. But as unlike demonkind, even in his handsomeness, as dead coal is unlike the lit volcano.

"Then, if you are not who I say, say who you are," mockingly prompted Azhriaz.

At that he smiled, though he did not look at her.

"I am the one who is stone-born," he said. "And unwillingly."

"So be it," she said. "Then who am I?"

"Some woman," said he, "from that king's house I see upstream.

"You have been a long while out of the world in your pillar," said Azhriaz. "Tomorrow you shall meet with the king of this city. Do not seek to evade the honor."

"Everything is nothing to me," he said. And now his open eyes also appeared closed. "I shall not evade, I shall not seek."

Then Azhriaz burned brighter than a moon—and was gone into thin air.

But he, who had named himself, in one of the seventy tongues of men, *Dathanja*, waded up from the river to the bank, where the flowers overtopped him and the trees flared thousands of feet toward stars that danced in patterns. And paying no heed to any of it, he sat down there and bowed his head, as if meaning to stay so for many years. But that was not to be.

4

AT DAWN, a detachment of the soldiery of the Goddess came to the flower gardens by the river. They were
clad in the blackest mail, every scale of it limned by
white-gold. In the helm of every man was set a precious
stone, and great plumes poured upward as if from the
war-smoke of their brains. Their eyes glittered also from
that fire, furiously empty. Like the black horses, the manes
and tails of which were dyed to red, puce, white, and
bronze, they had been bred for combat and for little else.
They waited, in their lofty barracks, day and night, for the
summons to go out and take another third of the world.
They told each other how it would be, who should be
killed, what cities would fall. Now they rode down on the
naked man in the garden, and grinned at him and gathered
him up among the plumes, caparisons, weapons.

They carried Dathanja along the banks where pilgrims
and tribute-bringers—such tribute came endlessly—stared
in awe, or failed to notice. Some were imbibing the water
of the river, thinking it a cure-all, which sometimes it was,
or it gave strange abilities, or hallucinations, or sent men
witless. Or it did nothing to them, and then they sulked.

At the sapphire stair by the temple-palace there were
priests, who progressed with the soldiers up onto the golden
terrace, and around it, and so to a ramp of pocked and
pitted marble which slid up into the sky along with the
palace roofs.

At the foot of this ramp, the priests stopped still and
chanted. (The naked man seemed to frown contemptuously
a moment, before both the frown and the contempt faded.)

Then the soldiery made a dead set at the ramp and cantered up it, the brass-shod hoofs of their horses screeching and striking fire. In the midst of the charge one of these men was unsaddled. He whirled to his death on the golden pavement far below without a sound, his arms opened wide as if to embrace fate. The pitting of the marble ramp had been occasioned by countless rushes of this kind, and many warriors died, both ascending and going down. This was one of their means of sacrifice to Azhriaz, when battle was unavailable.

At the top of the ramp, high above the City, there was a platform laid with alternating blocks of ebony, malachite, and orange jasper. And about this checkerboard there waited human and bestial examples of the countries of the conquered. The men and women were of surpassing beauty, fair, or copper color, or black, and arrayed like princes. And there were leashed animals of unusual sort, camels white as milk and having three humps, two-headed lizards, winged serpents, turtles carapaced with shields fit for giants, and older than the oldest hills. Braziers burned with scented fire—to which the winged serpents were sometimes taken to drink. Damsels plucked music from instruments like sickle moons.

Walking their war-steeds through this living forest, the soldiers who bore the naked man came at long last—for it took most of an hour to cross the platform—to a pavilion made of polished bones. Within it was a chair of cut glass, smooth as water, and guarded by two adamant wolves, having each three golden living darting eyes.

In the glass chair sat Azhriaz the Goddess.

Her robe was scarlet, and spinels burned in her hair. Gold was strewn on her like fallen blossom, and she was gloved in gold. It had been noticed long since, curious phenomenon, that the gold worn by the Goddess, however, would insidiously alter over a period of time, becoming harder, cooler, more like silver.

The soldiers gazed long at her, then staggered away, drunk on the sight. Some ran across the platform and flung themselves down, falling between the sky-scraping towers with cries of satisfaction. They had left Dathanja at her feet.

"Look up, Dathanja, O Unwilling Birth of the Stone,"
said Azhriaz. "Look up, and see the woman from the
king's palace."

Dathanja looked up.

"Guess now," said Azhriaz, "who is king here."

And she raised her hand in its golden glove—already
silvered as if with the faintest frost—and all the slaves,
human or creature, fell prone to reverence her. And to the
sudden stillness of that high place came drifting the praise
song of all the thousands of priests of all the countless
temples of that metropolis, even from a hundred miles off.

Dathanja looked at her for a great while. There was a
quality to his look that demonstrated a firm concentration
of the mind. The glamour of what he gazed on did not
distract him. And seated before her now on the rugs of the
pavilion, naked as he had come from the pillar, he neither
vaunted nor sought to conceal his body. He wore it as a
garment.

Eventually, he said: "They call you a goddess. But you
are not of the generation of Upperearth, I think. You have
about you the quality of another race whose land lies in the
opposite direction. Yet they shun daylight, and here you
sit, blue-eyed under the sun."

"How wise you are, Dathanja," said Azhriaz. "Do you
hear the name my priests are crying?"

"Yes," said Dathanja. "By your name then, I know
you are his child."

"How wise, how wise," said Azhriaz.

"He got you on a mortal, or you could not endure the
day."

"Oh, a blue-eyed mortal, with day in her very flesh and
soul. But now," said Azhriaz, "enough of she that I am.
Tell me of him you are."

"I have told you. I am a newborn infant. I am an
unmarked stone sloughed by stone."

"Zhirek," said Azhriaz. "The Dark Magician. Invulnerable, terrible. Simmu's lover and Simmu's murderer.
Zhirek who learned the magic of the sea-folk. Zhirek who
offered my father his service. But my father said to him, 'I
need no service of yours.' "

"That was a former life," said Dathanja in a low and almost silent voice.

"Let us see."

And removing the silvered golden glove from her left hand, she showed him a dagger, which next she threw into his heart. But the dagger fell broken on the rugs. He was unharmed. Then she took a cup standing by her and gave it him. "Drink this poison." He took the cup, and drank, and set the cup aside. Azhriaz kicked the goblet, and where the wine in it ran out, a fearsome scorch seared along the ground. But the man was not affected. And then Azhriaz took the glove from her right hand and touched the head of the three-eyed wolf at her right knee. It came alive, every inch of it, and padded to the man and gaped its jaws for his throat. But something pushed the wolf aside, and it rolled away and went back to the chair and grew instantly rigid again, all but its three eyes.

"Behold now," said Azhriaz. "This way Zhirek was, for his mother had him seethed in a sorcerous well. . . . And this way you are. How is that?"

"Azhriaz," he said, "it is to me a memory—less visible, far less actual, than the glass of your clever chair. For I am done with Zhirek."

"The earth rings yet with tales of his arrogance and wickedness, nevertheless. In remembrance of that, you are well suited to my City and my Empire. And now I am sure of this: Unless you had consented, the soldiers would have had some problem to bring you here. Thus. You were willing."

Then Azhriaz rose and clapped her hands.

The pavilion dazzled into the sky and vanished. The crowds of beasts and humans also disappeared, either spirited elsewhere or canceled, never having existed at all. The checkered platform remained, void, with the smothering gentian sky hung over it, and the City round about too bright to gaze on, and the towers going up as it seemed to very Upperearth, to illustrate how the gods were mocked.

Then two huge creatures came flying, like doves.

"They are my slaves, as all things are in this place," said Azhriaz. "Go with them, if you wish. For if you do not desire it, I will not tussle with you to see if my magic can crush yours—between strong powers such fights are so tiresome," said Azhriaz, "even Lords of Darkness do not engage in them, as I have witnessed."

The dove things alighted, and cooed to Zhirek who was Zhirek no more, gesturing how they would bear him kindly through the air to some wonderful prospect.

"And if I go with them, what?" he said.

"You shall be a prince here. You shall enjoy the luxuries of Az-Nennafir; its learning will be at your disposal, and its dower of curiosities."

"And by night, the living image of Simmu will be sent to me, perhaps?"

"If you desire it."

"I do not. Simmu is no more, and no more anything to me. But it would be a demon's trick."

"I am no demon," she said, "but a Goddess-on-Earth."

Dathanja, who had been Zhirek, regarded her. He said, "Yes, you are a goddess. So strung with riches and enchantments you might as well be destitute. And so beautiful you might as well be faceless."

"You are wise, as I said," replied Azhriaz. "Do not be too wise."

And she was gone, but for a second, a slender dragon filled the whole sky, and the City whispered in its stones.

Dathanja lived then some months of his new life at Az-Nennafir of the Goddess. He had been once before in a tall, tall city, the prize of a woman, but that was in the former life, and besides, beneath an ocean. It may have seemed to Dathanja that Azhriaz put no watch on him, that he might proceed where and how he wished. But he must know also that since every person and being of the City, its every brick and tile, even the waters and dusts of it, were hers, she might at any time have news of him, if she was inclined. But it was a place of wonders, and some of these he inspected. He walked the thoroughfares like other men, and for weeks wandered far afield on its hills of marble and through its obelisk woods. He spoke to travelers who came there, and no one stayed him. He watched unhindered, and uninvited, the orgies and revels, the sorceries and dramas and festivals that were its daily and nightly fare. The extravagant sacrifices he saw, and how easily death claimed them. He came to be known by sight, himself, for some mark of hers had been left on him, to protect him from annoyance, or only in the way a favorite dog is given a collar. For himself, he remained grave as the stone, and though the lensed sun tanned his skin, no other hue of him was altered. Black of hair and blacker of eye, and in plain clothing of black, this way he went. Yet he walked barefoot as Zhirek had always done.

None, asking or learning his current name, addressed him by the old one, and perhaps they did not know it. Neither did the determinedly lascivious women and men of Az-Nennafir approach him, nor any tricksters, nor any sage or scholar or poet. And this was not solely the mark of their Goddess on him, but some branding of his own. Dathanja did not entice lust or hate or love, as Zhirek did. No one begged compassion of him, or sought to adore him, or cast him down. And when, rarely and in seeming error, some might speak to him, his calm stony eyes drove them off, as once his invulnerable fearful flesh had driven off the spears and lions.

There was an avenue of statues, each representing the Witch-Goddess, and to one side of it, high up, was a grove of olive trees, higher themselves than a house of ten or twelve stories, and with leaves like tarnished water. Dark ferns flourished below, whose heads would brush the ears of elephants. Golden fruits scattered the ground that had fallen from no tree, and which, after a space, hatched out butterflies.

At the center of the grove had been built a shrine to the Goddess, where every dawn young women and young men would come to pour, from vials, the blood or tears of those they had injured during the night. The butterflies fed on these substances, and immediately turned black, and flew awhile, then drifted down and died. But from the little corpses would presently spread a golden stain that, as the day wore on, hardened and rounded, until by night it had become once more a fruit of gold.

To this grove Dathanja found his way, and here he came to sit, day after day, and sometimes to sleep on the grass under the ferns. He watched the eternal circle, how the

fruit hatched, how the butterflies flew about, how the
blood and tears were splashed on the shrine of Azhriaz and
the butterflies fed and blackened and fell down. How there
came to be again golden fruit, and again the fruit hatched
butterflies. On and on, the cycle toiled, around and around,
and never ended.

One twilight just before the dawn, Dathanja took up a
golden fruit from the earth, and, at the warmth of his
hand, a butterfly straightaway hatched itself. It flew up to
sit upon his shoulder.

Soon the sky bloomed and there came the notes of a
reed, and singing. Into the grove, preceded by a piper,
strolled three youths of great attraction, who nodded to
Dathanja and passed by him to the altar. "Here, heavenly
Goddess," said one, "is the blood of a man who died in a
tiger's jaws because I asked it of him." "And here," said
the second, "the blood of a girl who paid me to kill her
since I cared for her no more." "And here," said the
third, "the tears of a fool who weeps on my feet as I
caress my new friend." Then they linked arms, and struck
the piper to make him resume the song. And so they lilted,
singing, away.

Then at once came three young women in garlands of
poppies and orchids, and they poured out the contents of a
single phial between them, gaudily large as a bucket.
"Behold, O Goddess of goddesses," said one, "here are
the mingled tears and gore of those who have worshiped at
our shrine through the dark, and whom we scored with our
nails and our knives." Then they kissed the altar and each
other, and two coupled like lionesses under Dathanja's
very eyes, while the third watched him, but her face was
shut like a fan. And then the three of them went away.

The butterflies which had hatched in the grove lifted in a
spangled spray and settled on the shrine.

All but the butterfly which had hatched in Dathanja's
palm, and this crept into his hair and hid itself.

When the others had done feeding, they blackened as
usual, and flew up to hang like thunder under the trees.
Then the one butterfly which had not fed left its shelter
and fluttered out among them. The black butterflies, seeing

its difference, turned on it and tore it in pieces, for they had claws in their mouths.

The fragments of the butterfly lay in a bright heap beneath the fern, but when the black butterflies flopped down, the fragments, also, began to issue gold, and by nightfall, a fruit lay where the one bright butterfly had lain, as with all the rest.

Dawn returned; the golden fruit opened and the butterflies flew and played about the grove. Then there arrived young men and maidens, who made joyous and foul confession at the altar, and the stone was given its libation. But when the butterflies settled there to feed, three flew another way, to the spot where the man sat watching them, and they gathered instead on his robe, and he sheltered them. So bright they burned, like little papers written by the sun. But later, when the other butterflies rose from their feast, black as if burnt, the bright butterflies flew among them and were ripped to bits. When these bits were on the ground, they issued gold, and turned to golden fruits.

And this happened day after day, for seven days, or nine, or more. But each day more butterflies abstained from the nectar of tears and blood, although they were then slaughtered by those which had not.

One morning, a handful of minutes before the dawn, as Dathanja sat in the grove of olives, and the butterflies were just beginning to break free of the fruit, a girl stole into the grove alone, and stood at the man's left shoulder.

She was a poor girl, dressed in rags, and with neither a precious stone nor a garland on her hair, but only a mean cloth to hide it and muffle her face. Dathanja had seen many destitutes in the City. Generally they stretched dead in gutters, having brought themselves to ruin with excess in pleasure, sadism, or ill-conceived magic. None would help them; it was not religious. Nor did they entreat. This girl might be one such, on her descent to the crematory pits. But still she murmured to Dathanja in a low dulcet voice, "Why do you stay here, lord, to watch butterflies, when there are so many marvels in the City?" Since he did not answer, she continued, "Today there is a celebration. Mages will fly with wings and women will dance themselves to death. Eastward, a new palace has been erected. The casements are of colored rain, but it has, too, its own tame sun, that lives in a cupola of cedarwood—which every day will be incinerated by the heat, and so will have to be replaced every day. Westward there is a bull of electrum that has trapped a moon between its horns; it speaks awesome prophecies. And south there is a garden grown from one seed. It is only seven yards in length or breadth, but whosoever enters is lost among its walks and arbors for days on end. And north there is to be a marriage between a virgin and a statue of chalcedony. And there are other matters. Why sit here and stare at butterflies?''

But at that instant the sky lightened and there was a noise of bells and tabors. The butterflies rippled on the ferns. Youths and maidens ran between the olives and poured their libations at the altar, relating what they had done, then laughingly went away.

Presently every butterfly in the grove fluttered upward, and came to rest about Dathanja, and some to sit upon his shoulders and his hands. Every butterfly—but one. And this one butterfly rushed to the altar and fed on the blood and tears, and turned black, and then it soared about the grove and alighted on the bough of a tree. Here it folded its wings, and trembled, for it seemed to see at last it was alone.

For a while, this stasis. Then the one black butterfly shot into the air, and thrust itself upward through the leaves, and battered itself and mangled itself, and floated down dead to the earth. And where it fell, gold spilled and hardened and rounded and became a fruit, all in a few moments. And then the fruit burst wide and from it came the butterfly like a paper the sun had written. And when this had happened, the butterflies flew in ones or twos, or scores, upward into the trees, and left the grove behind. They vanished into the sky like a trail of sparks. But the last butterfly came to Dathanja and looked into his eyes with its own that were like jeweled pins, before it sped away.

"I see it is a parable," said the poor girl to Dathanja. "But I cannot read it."

"Azhriaz," said Dathanja, "put off your silly disguise."

And sure enough the delusion dropped from her like a veil. There she stood, Night's Daughter, and she said, "But still I cannot read the parable."

"I am not priest or teacher or magician any longer."

"All three you are," she said, "and will ever be."

He sighed. He said, "Each finds his own symbols, and can therefore read them. But to another they are the language of a foreign country. So with this grove."

"I have said to you," said Azhriaz, " 'Be a prince in my kingdom,' and you have spurned the rôle. What next, Dathanja?"

"I shall leave your City," he said.

"Will you? Do I premit it?"

"Yes," he said.

Azhriaz said, "I have not told you so. But if I did, where would you go?"

"Where I am able."

"To wander, like all madmen."

Azhriaz went to the altar of her shrine. She looked at the liquors there. She spoke a word, and the shrine split. Out of it sprang a bush, which lashed and spat, for every twig of it was a serpent. "Let them offer here now," she said.

Dathanja laughed. It had a bitter sound, before the laugh and the bitterness both faded. He got to his feet and he walked from the grove. Azhriaz stood in his path, before him, though she had been at his back.

"*Him* you would have served," she said. "Serve me. Azhrarn's murky ichor is mingled in my blood. There is not a man or woman in these lands," she said, "who would not give their lives for three hours' such service as I propose to you."

But he looked at her at last with his blackened eyes.

"No," he said.

"I can bewitch you," she said. "Your magic you have renounced, and in any case, I doubt it would match my own."

"You can," he said, "bewitch the world. Where then is the victory in bewitching me?"

"It is true," she said. "Go, wherever you will."

5

IF IT WAS the room of wattle, how it had changed. Perhaps the luxury was illusion, or illusion had been the poverty before. There were fountains there that were cascades, of scent not water. There were rugs that were lawns of flowers, draperies that were midnight sky. . . . In the midst a dragon lay asleep. It was a couch, and on the cushions of it, Azhriaz lay in turn, awake, while her maidens combed through her long, long hair with combs of silver. Entirely lovely, these maidens. They were Eshva. And Eshva played music on the moonlit hills of this room, such music, like starshine rippling over glass. Nightbirds came to the opened casements of the valley which was a chamber, insomniac owls, dumbfounded nightingales. The moons of the City passed and repassed the windows like pale lost ships.

Occasionally now Azhriaz allowed the Eshva to soothe her, like a drug. But the Eshva males who came to her now and then, and whose touches were—to mortals—a life's desire, these she turned uncivilly away. Some of the Vazdru princes had also come to her, every one most profoundly handsome, but she had laughed at them coldly. She was prejudiced, she said, against her own race. And coldly smiling in return, they left her, the rings glaring on their fingers and the daggers in their belts. A number made mischief, but it was nothing against her powers. Their malices withered at her doors like dying bouquets. They dared not do much—she was Azhrarn's daughter, and fulfilled his wish in the world. There was a sentence spoken in some crystalline darkness below: Surely she couples with our kind. It is with her lordly father she lies down. This unnovelty reached the hearing of Azhrarn.

He left his palace and went slowly through his city underground. He said nothing to any of those extraordinary subjects of his, as they bowed before him, but a shadow fell, and in the faces of some he looked, and their Vazdru hearts turned to water. Finally, one of the magnificent princes of the Vazdru came out and met Azhrarn's chariot in a thoroughfare of black ruby.

"Lord of lords," said the prince. "I am told you take exception to a jest of ours. But you are Wickedness. Why does wickedness perturb you?"

Azhrarn said, "Do you question me?"

The prince said, "By philosophical mortals, who are ants, incest is not counted a sin, Lord of lords, when willingly performed and inducing no mishap. Is it that you are ashamed, O Terrible One, to have caused so little terror lately? Is it the slightness of the sin which angers you?"

Azhrarn leaned from his chariot and set one hand on this prince's shoulder. The whole street turned chill as if snow had fallen. "Let mortals," said Azhrarn, "err or philosophize as they wish. She that was born of me is not my lover. I am not the clay of humankind, and their muck does not stick to me."

Then the prince said softly, though he shook, "Do not be angry with one who loves you."

"Love?" said Azhrarn. "There is no such commodity. There is carnality, our plaything. There is worship, and there is obsession. Death you may see walking the world, and Fate, and Delusion, too, in a form I have kindly lent him. But no man sees love, and no demon sees it." The prince who had accosted Azhrarn closed his eyes. Azhrarn took his hand from the prince's shoulder, but the prince remained as if turned to ice, there in the ruby street.

Later Azhrarn came to the shore of an ironine lake where the Drin forges dully thudded and infrequently chimed. Activity was sluggish. The Drin, recently disliking the sorrowful climate of Underearth, spent much time abroad on the earth above, in the employ of the foremost sorcerers, whom they tricked and wheedled and ultimately wrecked wherever possible. But some Drin came now and rubbed against the chariot wheels of Azhrarn.

"There is a rumor," said Azhrarn. "Who began it?"

The Drin squeaked and squabbled. Several made up fantastic lies to gain his notice only for a perilous moment. But one crept near and touched the black-and-silver sole of Azhrarn's boot. "An insect flits about the gardens of your city, and sometimes it makes a small sound. I can never understand the voice, but some do, and from this source all kinds of rumors start. The insect is green in color, and on its wings is the symbol which, in the Vazdru High Tongue, is the letter V."

Then Azhrarn went up to his palace again and into a tower like a silver needle. Standing in the eye of it, he summoned her, and she came. Vasht, who had been herself his lover once, Vasht blasted to the shape of a tiny green-winged leaf, at the transmitted memory of that other love of his—by the one who now said: No man sees love, no demon sees it.

"I discover," said Azhrarn, Night's Master, one of the Lords of Darkness, "that Vasht is green-winged not only through her pain, but also with jealousy and ignorance."

The butterfly shimmered in the air.

"Do you still imagine that we may be reconciled in love, Vasht?" said Azhrarn. It was a fact, his voice had no love in it.

The butterfly started toward him. It paused.

"You love me," said Azhrarn. "How much?"

The green butterfly came to him; it brushed by his hair that shone like midnight waves, it lit upon his hand, strong and pale as a carven stone. Then it lowered itself until it reached the paving by his foot. There it folded its wings, and waited.

"Truly, Vasht," said Azhrarn, and his voice was softer than the nap of velvet and it lanced to the bone, "you have learned love's lesson well. For if any do see her walk the world, love is a hag, worse than plague or famine, or even Death with his ghostly show. Love in her robe of rags with her heart torn out and sewn on her breast, love with her eyes wept out and only the blind sockets staring. Love is a bitch, but she suffers, and so she knows best how to make all things suffer that she kisses with her sickness. Vasht, I thank you for this love of yours I do not want, and I give you love's reward.'' And he put his bootheel down on the butterfly and crushed it.

Now nothing could die in the Underearth, it was said. And demons were numbered among the immortals. Yet only this remained of Vasht, after Azhrarn had left that place: an impression, as if of the thinnest jade, seared into the paving—of a butterfly's two wings, like the two pieces of a broken heart.

But in Druhim Vanashta they said, "As he did with her, so he does with his kingdom." And some of the Vazdru, a great many of them, put on yellow clothing—which color to them was the shade of mourning, being like sunlight—and they stood beneath his walls, and lamented in the seventh tongue of the demons, out of which their chants and melodies of sorcery were made.

But Azhrarn paid no apparent heed. And they did not then dare approach him nearer, remembering the reward of Vasht.

They spoke together. They mockingly said, "Where is Azhrarn? Who has seen him?" And some of them took the shape of black lions, but with yellow eyes, which eye color, again, was a sign of unease or sorrow or extreme outrage among their caste. They prowled the black lawns of Azhrarn's palace, going in over the walls, and snapped the bronze fish out of the trees, maiming them, so they flopped horribly in the grass until the fantastic air and emanations of that area healed them.

At the center of Azhrarn's garden a fountain played; it was composed not of water but of fire, scarlet fire that gave neither light nor heat. But the lion-Vazdru dug deep in the strata of the lawn, and they cast the turf and soils in upon the fountain, tirelessly, for more than a mortal month. Until at last the flame was choked and lay under a black compost, which yet smoldered still in parts like a cold red coal.

But even to this, Azhrarn seemed to pay no heed.

The lion-Vazdru leapt back across the walls and resumed their male and female forms. Then they rent their yellow clothes and cried in anarchic voices, "Azhrarn,

where is Azhrarn, the Beautiful, the Bringer of Anguish,
Night's Master?'' And they answered themselves stonily
thereafter: "*Azhrarn is dead.*''

But Azhriaz lay on the dragon's back, and the Eshva
combed her hair and sang in wordless voices. And she
heeded them nearly as little as Azhrarn heeded the Vazdru,
miles under her feet.

Years ago, in the first decade of her reign over men,
Prince Wickedness had sometimes paid a visit to his
daughter.

In those nights, she had lived in the marble apartments
of the former palace of Nennafir, merely with Qurob's
luxuriousness. Two of Qurob's sons had, in that time,
attempted to make war on her, but she had destroyed their
armies as a hurricane breaks a branch. And one of Qurob's
female progeny, who had laid a plot to murder the new
Goddess, Azhriaz had fastened to a wheel of silver that
was sorcerously flung about the sky over the city all day,
and hung above the tallest palace tower after sunset. The
screams of this wretched woman became familiar to the
ears as the cries of particular indigenous birds, for, by
magic, she was not permitted death. Eventually the victim
went mad. Then Azhriaz had her taken down and sent
away into some handy wilderness, with the reported words:
"Go seek your prince." Various had been the cruelties of
the Goddess in the early years of her reign. At Azhrarn's
instruction she performed many deeds in order to educate
the earth in the viciousness of the gods, and, more important, their indifference to all human suffering.

Mostly, the visits of the lordly father to the dutiful child
comprised such instructions. Azhriaz had placed for him a
silver chair intricately molded, with a canopy of silk, and
with inlaid steps leading up to it. She kneeled before him,
arms crossed on her breast and head bowed. It was a
parody, and soon bored them. Now she was polite and
now he had got his way, they had nothing at all to say to
each other. And to be sure, they were like many a mortal
father and daughter in that.

Probably, at the beginning, he tested her, to see if she
was faithful to his edict. Once the tests were accom-

plished, he let her alone. Next, some of the Vazdru were
sent to her and taught her demonic magic—or they refined
her skills and lessoned her in the proper rituals and occult
language that should ornament such art. (As callers, the
Vazdru were proud. And she, the hostess, prouder.) But
the mellifluous Eshva came at her whim, to please her.
And the Drin came, to fawn and bring gifts, or to fashion,
out of the tributes of the Empire she had begun to estab-
lish, diadems and collars, clockworks, mechanisms. They
built that pillared room of gems (of course), and the gold
room, and those of silver and pearl. And the Drindra she
fetched up, too, the dregs of the Drin, and spoke to them
in their gabble, and found access through them to the
bizarre supernatural tips where such weeds and flowerlets
burgeoned as the four things she summoned to tell her of
her worth in the world—the man of brass and the man of
alligator legs, the woman-headed horse, the snake-eyed
child. Meanwhile, her human legions milled more and
more lands for her bread.

So in the end she dwelled alone, surrounded by everything a third of the world could bring her, and played at
appalling sorceries, while, in her sprawling Goddessdom,
men did incredible mindless evils, each in her name.

For herself, she had done directly very little evil. And
what she had done, mostly, at Azhrarn's incentive, was
her duty. For the rest, accepting her as a goddess of
wickedness and carelessness, men let loose all the rubbish
in themselves for her sake. They supposed she came to
them in dreams and visions and requested of them slaughter, rapine, and sacrifice of animal and man, suicide, and
other items less succulent still. But this she did not do;
they managed it all themselves most adequately. And the
delirium which fell on them like a ravening panther at the
invocation of her being—that was their creature, too.

But Azhrarn, who had made her to chastise the earth, he
might have been said to be satisfied. Yet it appeared he
was not so very much concerned, having set the toy in
motion. Once before he had inadvertently unleashed havoc,
and gone elsewhere, to some other interest, and not seen
the mess till almost the last hour of mankind. Now there
was no other interest, but regardless, the mighty endeavor

palled. He, who had invented this play, in which millions were overwhelmed, continents tottered, men perished as autumn leaves in a forest—he had turned his head away.

And for Azhriaz, the fount of the pandemonium, she lingered on her couch-dragon, and let her City go about its riots under the high windows. And lingering in the flesh on the couch, otherwise she passed through a mirror she had been staring into, and stood before Dathanja on a hill at her kingdom's edge.

Brown and barren the hill, even the sky was brown, and a tannic rain fell, with sometimes a brown frog or two in it.

But Azhriaz came clad in lights, with stars in her hair.

Dathanja, who sat on the hill in the rain, glanced up at her.

"Is your journey charming?" she asked him.

"Perhaps," he said.

"And do you think of me?" she said.

"It now and then chances that I think of you, for you manifest now and then, do you not, to remind me?"

"What have you seen since last you looked on me?"

He said, "Misery and want, and fear, and death. I saw a beggar begging help from a muddy stream. He told me it was as much use to do that as to beg help of heaven. And I met a girl who lay down and said that I should rape or murder her at once, as I wished, for she could expect nothing else of me. And I met a priest who danced in delirium for the Goddess under an altar piled with the dead pilgrims he had given her. But he found he could not seize me, since I am yet invulnerable, so he ran away in a poor temper."

"By day," said Azhriaz, "you set your face to the sunrise. You travel always eastward. Now what lies in the east, O Zhirek?"

"I am not Zhirek," said Dathanja, and his black eyes burned cold, before the fire and the coldness faded.

"Simmurad lies east," said Azhriaz, "under the ocean."

But the rain and the frogs smote down, and Dathanja bowed his dark head, rather in the way she had bowed her darker head before her lordly father. So she returned to herself through the mirror.

From the room of landscape and scent, once wood and wattle, the Eshva women had all gone, leaving behind a glorious wafting inexplicableness. Someone tootled on a pipe, out in the air below the window, where the moons were sinking.

"Kingly Kheshmet," said Azhriaz, "it is a long while since I saw you. Why are you here?"

"To offer a warning," said Kheshmet, integrating in the midst of the room, and putting away the pastel pipe. He was arrayed solely as a king, and blared so bright that the room filmed over and reverted to wood and wattle.

"You have warned me previously. Is it sensible Fate can give warnings?"

"You see he does so," said Fate. "Besides, you are sorceress enough to divine your likely destiny, without any clue from me. My apparition is superfluous here, though here, as everywhere, I pay my respects from time to time. Therefore I appear to you as a king and present the warning modestly, as a keepsake."

"Warn me, then," said Azhriaz.

"In one direction, the sea," said Kheshmet. "In another, the sky. Though you may conquer all the world, the seas have their own masters, who may be your equals. And the ether is the floor of others who, stepping there, begin to notice you."

Azhriaz looked at Fate with some attention.

"I beheld the building of Baybhelu Tower," said Kheshmet. "Few saw me, so circumspectly did I comport myself, and such florid cousins there were about besides, Lords of Darkness thick on the ground as beetles when a stone has been disturbed. Nevertheless, the Tower rose, to breach heaven, and heaven bethought itself, and stirred, only as a feather stirs on a pigeon's back when it sleeps. But because of that feather, Baybhelu fell down with a crash that rocked the world."

"I," said Azhriaz, "do not build so high. I excavate rottenness, digging downward." Her face expressed disgust as she said this.

Kheshmet said, "You are a goddess, and adored as

such, and you have the powers of what you claim to be.
What will the gods think of that?"

But, musingly, she said, "In the east, Simmurad . . ."

Kheshmet came close. "Not east, but in your eyes, I
was wont to see Chuz like an amber figurine. Now I see
Zhirek who is Dathanja, like a figurine of black basalt.
When will the blue come clear again in your blue eyes,
Goddess-on-Earth, Soveh-Sovaz?"

But Azhriaz reached out, and with a laugh she plucked
the tiny chameleon from Kheshmet's sceptered staff. It
came to her a furiously growling orange, then lay upon her
palm white as a dove, making a purring noise.

Kheshmet smiled; he allowed her to fondle the lizard.
He was an uncle of sorts to her, after all, and the rest of
the family did not seem to have been too familial with her.

In a while they went up, King Fate, Night's Daughter,
and the chameleon, to observe sunrise at Az-Nennafir.

The sun rose like a bud unfurling.

Fate snapped his fingers, and against its disk, the glory
of the great nightmare of a City crumbled, and only its
skeleton remained, the heights smashed, like Baybhelu,
the tall temples and mansions roofless, and gaunt dragons
moved over the desolation, and carrion birds with dusty
eyes blew out of a desert that had been parks and palaces.

"Where the gods shall walk," said Kheshmet, "perhaps
metaphorically. But at each footfall, another tower falls."

Then he moved his hand across the scene, and the City
returned, quite whole.

"It seemed to me once," said Azhriaz, "that I might
one day die."

"Ah, Soveh-Sovaz," said Kheshmet, taking the lizard
up onto his staff in the moment before he vanished, "for
more centuries than you could ever dream of, so, it has
seemed to me, shall I."

PART TWO
The War with Sea and Sky

1

AS USUAL, it was a clear winter morning in Upper-earth.

Nothing ever changed there, or very little. The ground of heaven was sky, and the sky of heaven was sky, and time, like the sky, hung everywhere and did not move and did not stay still. Tomorrow might be yesterday, and next year three mortal centuries ago. But to the gods this gave no cause for concern—and men never came there, or would never come there, perhaps. . . . Thin blue morning, lit crisp-to-brittle by an unseen sun which neither rose nor set, never shifted, yet shone from all sides. Not cold, nor hot, that endless day. It described the Well of glass, containing the fluid of Immortality, which Simmu once had contrived to borrow from, and in which, once, Azhrarn had spat—making the leaden liquid sparkling and beautiful for a second or so. Against the Well, the two fearsome one-eyed Guardians slept, in their gray cloaks. The story went there had been long before, or would be long in the future, *three* Guardians. The third had been, would be, lost, in some curious maneuver, defending the Well (unnecessary), or falling in the Well (unlikely), or falling through the floor of heaven (less likely), or by incurring the displeasure of the gods: unthinkable.

For the gods were far off—both in their unphysical physicality and in their supernal spirit-minds.

To that limited number of beings, of whom Azhrarn was one, who had walked the Upperearth, it was a formless and mostly markerless country. It had its Well, and here and there some evidence of possession might be descried by those with exceptional vision—the harpstring dwellings of the gods, for example, eons abandoned, the various esoteric intellectual exercises, such as checkered squares of unknown colors, pavilions of indescribable structure, a flight of steps, waterfall or archway that neither word nor pen would or can award any idea of. Distantly on the horizon were mountains, or the frozen souls of mountains, the shade of the sky, outlined by delicate snows of impervious adamant. Even should you walk toward these mountains for seven years, you would not reach them. They remained always that exact distance on the horizon as before. To the gods, however, these inaccessible crags were easily to be gained.

Awhile then, in this region, some of the gods had been congregated. Since the location was otherwise never entered, it can only be conjectured upon. But there they were, the lords of Upperearth, who had all genders and none, transparently robed, translucent of flesh and aflow with the palest violet ichors. In high excitement, glassy flutterings would sometimes erupt from their garments, hair, or brains—and now continuously did so. For the gods, this was a most savage clamor. But their polished eyes gave away nothing. And they were voiceless as Eshva, more so. Yet it has to be supposed, as on other occasions it has had to be, that the gods did communicate with each other, and that a dialogue was in progress. Which, to render it in sentences and phrases, went somewhat like this.

"Ages past," a portion of the gods stated, "we were volatile. We dressed ourselves in heavy skins, and descended to the earth, and there indulged in uncouth adventures, and left behind a selection of legends, and even, in some instances, progeny. Which last were counted as heroes or monsters by mankind. And indeed, it was in those foolish eras of our extremist youth we first made man, to amuse us, and for a little space he did. But later we grew out of him, and out of ourselves, and, purged of all such nonsense, we retreated to our upperworld to spend the rest of time, as time is now reckoned, in contemplations, and other astral athletics. Let us, therefore, only continue as we are, ceaselessly purifying our purity. And let the world also go on until it destroys itself by its gross randomness. The earth is no longer any concern of ours. And as for man, he is a mistake we made. And if we notice him, he will naturally offend us, as one's mistakes always do.''

"But," intoned another portion of the gods, "though for the most part the doings of man have no bearing upon us, yet sometimes his willful innovations strike a discordant echo even here. And this is one such, their new religion. A human thing, even one of their sorcerers, investing himself with godhead is only ridiculous. But this woman, being ab-human, has vast powers, and may, through their stupidity—in which state all men perpetually are—be taken undeniably for a god. It is true, when we roved upon the earth in our adolescence, we behaved quite often in such ways, and the legends we left support the woman's claim. And this resonance of our past, and this affront to our present (though neither past nor present any longer trouble us), is a hindrance to our inward seeking. Therefore we may not ignore the discord. It must be silenced.''

Then a solitary god speechlessly spoke, and said this:

"One ascended to our country and walked here. He was no mortal, for such cannot ascend or enter. He was of an immortal race men call *demons*, and these we did not make, and therefore they may not be bound by us. And this demon, who was their prince, is a magician beyond all imagining. And when he had talked insolently to us, he kissed me, and I remember still the kiss.'' And the god lowered his head (or her head, or its head), and flying crystals sped from every fold and pore and hair. "It is a fact,'' continued the god presently, "that this woman mankind call a goddess is none other than the offspring of that demon prince. Such an adversary may be said to be worthy of our attention, and deserving of a supreme conflict, and we, inescapably, must offer war to such.''

Then the gods stared, or did what amounted to that action, but there is no source which reveals what that might be. This one god had now (unvocally) uttered the very concepts of their youth. So there came a pause, which undoubtedly lasted many mortal years. After which the gods affirmed that this one of their fraternity should take on for them the onus of retribution. He should do all—and it did seem that he was now masculine, though how it seemed so is not told, nor was it probably by any straightforward means. And in this way, too, the rest of the gods punished him, for the vestiges on him of outgrown things, not to mention for having been kissed by a demon.

Thus, the god—who carried within himself all the gods, though a rogue member; they were at heart intrinsically a single entity—thus, *he* set forth. And crossing Upperearth he arrived at a place like every other, but here he grasped the invisible substance of the air and wrenched it free and molded it, invisibly, between his hands—then cast it from him, where it broke invisibly into three shards.

These the god breathed upon, one after the other, and next gathered them up again, though still they were not to be seen.

He *spoke* then, or he made some positive, audible sound. It was a phonetic the like of which no sorcerer of the world had ever compassed, nor, let it be admitted, any demon magician-prince under the ground.

And the blue of Upperearth split, a small vent, and through it, miles away and a little below, was a raging thing, like many million furnaces melded into one, from which rays and streamers and breakers of flame reeled and exploded. Then the god, who had breathed his divine breath into the three invisible shards of the fabric of heaven, flung them down yet again, one upon the other, into the core of the sun.

The first shard struck the sun. The second shard struck it. And the third. At each impact there came a surge of light and heat more dreadful than those which the sun already shot and flailed about itself. But when the third fire spasm guttered and died, there was only the flaming mass of the sun disk, terrible enough, but not more terrible than it had ever been.

And then. With a violence that caused the upper airs to judder in a skyquake, the sun *disgorged*. Once, twice, thrice, a torrent of scalding matter reared upward and soared over heaven in a roaring arc, led by a dot of brilliance unbearable to look on, if any had looked, a shooting star of cosmic arson—which, ending its flight suddenly in mid-ether, stopped still and hung there, slowly cooling moment by moment to a stab of diamond. Until:

They stood high up, between earth and heaven, like three stooping hawks, their feet upon the winds and their wide wings spread. They were the Malukhim, the Sun-Created. They were made to be the scourge of men, the warrior-priests of the gods, their messengers and envoys, the shining sheathless blade of that which had outgrown battle.

The first who sprang from the solar fire was Ebriel. He stood on the right hand, and he had been calcined to yellow-gold. His skin was the metal of a king's goblet, and his eyes like topaz, and his hair was a lion's mane of the hue of the tasseled wheat in the field. His garments were of that pale creaminess of the asphodel, and the sheen of his flesh shone through with a golden radiation. His breastplate was hammered gold gazing with blond citrines. His wings were whitely gold as those of a young eagle. He was like the spring sun at noon.

The second who sprang from the fire was Yabael, and he stood on the left hand, and he had been seethed for a greater while, and his was a gold dark as darkest bronze. So the metal of his skin, but his eyes were like tawny amethysts, and his hair a stallion's mane the hue of the scorched rufous leaves of autumn oaks. His garments were fulvous, like honey in beer, and the burnish of his flesh burned through with a somber radiation. His breastplate was of hammered brazen gold wounded with copper zircons. His wings were shadowed gilt as those of a vulture. He was like the late-summer sun in thunder.

But foremost, and nearest to the world, with the solar disk behind his head, there stood Melqar, who had stayed within the fire until it seared him white. His skin was the fairest gold, the metal of a sacred chalice, and his eyes were kindled lamps, and his hair a sunburst. His garments dazzled white as all white things, the newborn snows, the bones within a child, and the sunshine of his bright golden flesh soaked through with the radiation of a torch. His breastplate of hammered white gold was sunned with golden beryls. His wings were white as a swan's, yet golden white, a swan that flew always at the day's rise. And Melqar was like the sun of midsummer dawning.

But the sky itself turned black. Dismayed by the ethereal disturbance, storms formed in every quarter. Shocks tolled, and the clouds ran in like tidal waves upon a beach. The whole roof of heaven was blotted out; only the sun spiked through like the tip of a white-hot spear. Night closed on the day. And in every land of the world, down in the flat earth's dish, they saw it. Men trembled, and sages and mages forecast dooms. Priests offered to the gods, guessing, almost accurately, that they were angry. But in the third of the earth where the Goddess was worshiped, they would do nothing, for they knew the gods to be indifferent, or hating. "They will smite us anyway," men said there. And so slew themselves for fear of worse, or ran to hide in cellars, or else performed the most hideous villainies of their lives, frenziedly and rapidly, in order to get everything done before annihilation swept them up.

But in a far country, where the grim teaching of the Goddess had not yet gone, there was a scholar who watched the stars through a mighty lens large as a palace dome, mounted upon four sculpted tortoises of brass. And this man, though his vertebrae rattled with terror, stayed to see. Many hours later, the sky began after all to clear. It was midnight, and a moon rose in the east, a slender bow, yet fever-flushed. Then the scholar-astrologer was summoned to the house of his king, who asked questions.

"My lord, I can only say this. That I saw three arrows of light fired out of the sun, and from these lights came three winged men, one gold, one brazen gold, one white as gold that is molten. They stood in heaven, and the darkness followed, but yet *they* blazed bright, and rode upon the clouds like great and awful birds. And then it appeared that he who stood to the right of the sky drew a sword with a blade which sizzled like yellow lightning, and he in the left of the sky drew a sword which dripped red, like blood. But he that stood foremost with the sun behind his head, he drew a sword like white flame, and he raised it high, yet with its edge down-pointing to the earth.

"And I would venture to suggest," added the scholar-astrologer, "that this bodes no good for us."

2

THEY HAD neither mind nor soul, the Malukhim. They had no heart. They had spiritual will and purpose, but these came from the gods' own. Though they were beautiful, so are fires and leopards.

Some nine days they were, falling to earth, so leisurely and so fraught with meaning their descent.

The passage may have been heeded, but, closing with the vapors of the world, they had shuttered their brightness. Those golden feet, naked as swords, touched initially the bare shoulder of a mountaintop. An emblem, the choice of landing. The most high to the highmost. And three days they paused upon the mountain and from miles off might be glimpsed there, glinting like jeweler's work. But none saw it save some animals thereabouts, or envious ravens.

Below the mountain lay purple deserts with rocks of quartz and gullies veined by costly minerals, and here and there a long-armed tree that turned to flint.

The warrior-messengers came down from the mountain. It was emblematic also that they should walk a short way, that they should inhale the air and tread the back of the world. For they scarcely needed to.

At sunset, they paused again on a high place, and looked down, and Az-Nennafir lay before them, the City wide as an ocean, twinkling with the first buds of its lights.

Gods do not soil themselves with deeds. That requires angels.

Yabael took up a pebble, and hurled it toward the City.

213

It flew so fast for so far, it caught alight, and a sparkling tail went after it. Over the City, over the river of the City, it raced, and crashed through a tall window of glass that had still the blush of dying sun upon it. Below, among pillars of incense, a multitude started and shouted. But the pebble flashed into the midst of them and tore downward through the body of a man, from cranium to instep, and buried itself in the floor beneath. The slain man burst in flames, and fell across the altar. He was a priest of Azhriaz. He had been offering the thirteenth human victim of the evening, it having been thought proper to give thanks, since the lifting of the storm. Now the worshipers wailed in their temple, blessing Azhriez for her disdain. They believed, of course, the thunderbolt was her doing.

> *"Oh kind is she in her unkindliness,*
> *And lovely in her evil.*
> *Let us be worthy of your hatred,*
> *Azhriaz! Azhriaz!"*

Yet, whole kingdoms! lengths of streets and concourses away, three strangers now stood at one of the large gates of the City.

It gaped always open, night and day, the gate. The leaves of it, in any event, were made of glass.

When the three strangers passed beneath, galvanics scored the atmosphere. But only a sick man lying in the gateway noticed this.

They were cowled and cloaked, the strangers, one in singed cloth that took shadow, and one in blond cloth that took light, and the third in blanched cloth that sang on the eye.

Fools, thought the failing one under the gate. (He had been a magus once, exalted and proud, and stayed arrogant though he perished of hunger and disease.) "Oh, wise masters," he cried aloud, "give alms to a wretched destitute." He did this to see if they were idiotic—and irreligious— enough to do it. And at his words, to his surprise, contempt, and hope, the traveler in the blond cloak turned and cast down to him something that gleamed. The sick magus scrabbled for it eagerly, then cursed, for it was only another pebble, and besides, it had burned his palm. Then, from the burn, there flowed through him a frightening sensation—it was health and vigor leaping back on him like two rabid tigers. Soon he got up and ran away in horror, leaving the pebble to blacken in the gate.

All night long the three strangers went through Az-Nennafir, and some beheld them, and some attempted to detain them. But a great heat played about them, and those who caught the sleeves of their garments felt a touch like a desert wind, and those who plucked their flesh seemed to have dipped their fingers in scalding sand. And though they were seen in several parts of that gigantic metropolis, both on its mountainous heights and in the chasmic lanes between, they did what no mortal could do, traversing the whole City in that single night.

Near dawn, they came to an inn on the river bank. It rose story upon story, like a coiled dragon, with windows of primrose green. And in the court, which was strewn with the petals of bruised white myrtles of unusual size, there posed a statue of chalcedony, a man in form, that held clasped close a beautiful dead girl whose hair streamed to the ground. Her body did not mortify; she too was altering to a chalcedon. At their feet was a message written in silver, which read: *Such is love*.

The three strangers approached the inn door, which, like the gates, gaped wide. The hall within was loud and busy with carouse, despite the weary hour. Caged fires enlightened riches and riot, in the middle of which a chained beast crouched, that had the face of a wolf, the hind legs of an enormous hare, the figure of a serpent, the breasts and tresses of a woman.

The white-cloaked stranger tossed down a last pebble, among the couches. The pebble chinked and grated, bounced against a winepot, and spun to stillness. There was no other sound anymore in that room. Every man and every woman stood or leaned or sat or lay in the attitude adopted at the instant of the pebble's flight. Some had their arms raised aloft in dramatic gesturings, others humped in crazy positions, suspended in the fiercest performances of lust. But the fires in the cages were also motionless, every flame glistening like a dagger. And a number of cups had been spilled, and hung in air, with the wine half splashed from them like beads of tinted glass.

The composite beast alone was not affected. Nevertheless, it deemed it prudent to cower down and howl, and when the three travelers moved by it, it crawled away until its chain groaned and creaked and suddenly snapped. And then it crawled on into the dark beyond the door.

Upward through the motionless inn the travelers took their way. Over every formerly vociferous floor they wended, and were gone. In the top tier, at the very peak of the new silence, they sat down, and under their cloaks stirred an uncanny restlessness, as great wings were folded.

It happened that a magnet began to exert its influence in the City of the Witch-Goddess.

They were drawn, the citizens, they could not help it. Sometimes there was a dream they could not remember, or explain. Or it was only a mute desire. Sometimes they did not even wish to go—*there*. But there they went. They left their comforts, mageries, and their studied wrongdoings. Worship and sacrifice they left also. They abandoned the luxury trades of Az-Nennafir that had made them wealthy, and its debaucheries that slowly killed them. They left off even ritual murder and suicide. They trooped along the wide roads, steered along the river, under the blued sky. They came to a building, once an inn. But the inn had become peculiar, putting out oddly graceful protuberances, galleries, spires . . . growing like a heavenly vegetable. Within this inn's radius, which seemed to increase with every hour, the winds came by and did not move the grasses of the lawn or the leaves of the myrtle shrubs. Flowers lay on the ground and did not fade.

In the courtyard, a chalcedony statue had toppled over and broken into chunks, none of which had been pilfered. A clean female skeleton was mingled with these.

Mostly, the bemused arrivals sat down about the inn and wondered and murmured. As days and nights wore, some would fall silent, and presently get up again and hurry away. These might subsequently be seen dashing through the City toward one of the several gates—a journey of weeks, or months. But others lay down and slept, and did not waken, though the whole area sighed with their concerted regular breathing.

A few ascended through the inn. From the top tier of it, which now resembled a gorgeous diadem of filigreed lettuce, a quantity of these, in a short while, threw themselves off. Others came down by the stairs, and yet others did not come down.

"What is *there*?"

"I . . . cannot say."

"Or will not? Is it some fresh magic of the Astonishing One, Azhriaz? She has been unseen by us a long while."

"No. *No*."

One man stood in the courtyard and said, "The sun waits three times over in the upper room. Six-winged is the sun, with golden feet and hair of fire. Evacuate this kingdom, or die here."

"A punishment of the gods? Then we are honored by their attention."

"*We* are nothing to the gods, as we are told. It is for the Goddess they cast their shining net."

Then the aesthetics marveled. Did the gods seek to upbraid one of their own?

Still, some went home and got their goods together in a rush, and soon were to be seen, like the others who had done so, dashing for the exit points of Az-Nennafir. But the majority stayed where they were, and the streets around the erstwhile inn, and the river bank and the river, were thick with them, while far and near whole sectors of the city were deserted. Yet, so populous was that huge place, it teemed on around each vacuum. And there were plenty of persons so stupid, or so erudite, they never felt the magnetic force laid upon them.

3

AZHRIAZ the Goddess was walking westward, by the river. It was traditional, when she roamed abroad about her own business, for the vicinity to be emptied by her soldiers, a duty they cherished. The living and the corpses then removed, no human thing was there to annoy her. Only peacocks spread their fans along the avenues and uttered their soulless scream, and the ibis and the crane lowered their long necks to drink from garden pools. While two cats of white stone turned their heads with an unnerving rasp to watch their mistress going by.

The Goddess-on-Earth went down in the sunset to the harbor basin, where once, more than three decades ago, the merchant ships had ordinarily come and gone. Now only one vessel lay there. The bark of Azhriaz.

It was not that half-delusory ship in which she had first plied upriver from the west. This was a seagoing galley, resting on mighty chains at the center of the river. A man-made ship, or mostly, with enamels blazoned upon her, and bannered with furled sail. She had three terraces of decks, and when once her ports should open to let out the oars, they would quill her like a porcupine.

Solid, the ship, if nameless. And not quite natural. Those that had seen her assured you she could vanish—like her lady—at a word. Only those who had toiled to make her truly knew of her—shipwrights, joiners—who had been struck dumb for the duration. And, too, certain unnormal bipeds summoned generally by night. Although the demons had not been called on, not even those genius metalsmiths the Drin. Azhriaz had not, it seemed, wished to inform the Underearth of this venture, despite the fact that she would know nothing could be kept from Azhrarn her father should he look about for it. Maybe she had become assured of his uninterest.

Now Azhriaz, having observed her fine galley, stepped on the water. She walked over the river, past the sun as it sank, and lifted in the air to attain the highest deck, under the great rolled clouds of sail.

What was the ship for? Why, the sea. And *why* the sea, then? Standing on the deck, Azhriaz traced, for momentary amusement, a name on the air in watery letters. *Simmurad.*

But immediately, the letters died. Now she poised like an orphaned child, this fabulous woman-girl, dwarfed by the stature of a mere ship, her long-lashed eyes downcast.

Was there not a futility in everything? Why then attempt anything?

But she must rein back these thoughts. There was all time, and she damned with it. Best not to dwell on the centuries, or the minutes.

Just then it seemed to her she heard a strange music, or some other stranger sound, reverberating from the depths of her City. Had she perhaps heard it before? Attuned to the auras, notes, nuances of the thousand spells that went on here, she had paid this oddity slight heed. Yet, it did not harmonize, it was discordant.

The sun had set behind the sapphire lens; the afterglow lay along the mirror of the river. Azhriaz raised her eyes, and saw three golden stars fly up the sky.

No sooner did she see them than extraordinary feelings welled in her. She was not accustomed to excitement, for her powers had, inevitably, deadened her emotional senses. So, for a moment, joy clawed at her heart. Yellow gold and russet gold and gold that was white, the three stars sliced through the firmament. Could she not, putting on such wings, too, soar upward and meet with them in confrontation?

Yet all about a weird moaning began from every side, the lapping of the river—a moan, the rushes moaning at the water's edge. The very chains that held the ship groaned as they rubbed against each other, and the boards of the young vessel groaned as if they ached. No fish surfaced from the water. The glowing flies that came to the luminous night flowers of the garden and made love to them in error—thinking the flowers to be flies—put out their lights. An assembly of cranes took the air and flew low along the river and away, *away*. What perfume was this? A soft attar of fear.

Then Azhriaz was angry. Not in the manner of men, or women either, in the Vazdru way, flawless clutterless rage, with a razor's edge. Her lips parted to speak words like drops of bane. But a hand, light as a pane of the darkness, was set upon her head.

"No," said the voice, black catspaw silk, out of the night where nothing had been.

"You have made me a goddess," she said, as silken. "Is there then something a goddess dare not do?"

"It may be so," said Azhrarn. "Wait, and be still."

And so they waited, shut in under the umbra of the sails, while the flaming stars quartered the sky on their wings, then drew away together inland, over the river.

"There is after all a novelty in my City," said Azhriaz at length.

"Do not be charmed by it, little girl. I did not make you to be spoiled in fire."

Azhriaz turned, and so beheld her father, the Prince of Demons, and even she for a moment took breath at his magnificence. He had come there as prince and lord indeed, clothed in the armorings of midnight, a mail glassblack as dragon plates, girt with battle ornaments of bone and jewel and staring silver. Even a sword at his side cased in black and itself all blackness, with a blue tongue running on it. About each arm there twined serpents with bodies black-armored as his own, eyes like curses, teeth for swords. Behind him and the halo of his clarified light were seven of the Vazdru, dressed after his fashion, their faces masks, their hands wicked on the gracious hilts of blades. But his face was like the sword stroke, so beautiful it was, so steeled, so sovereign.

"Which fire is that?" said Azhriaz. She spoke haughtily, and upon her the raiment of a queen began to bloom. She did not like to be humble in such company.

Azhrarn told her which fire; of the angels with their flaming swords hanging high up like three thoughts of golden death burst from the brains of the gods.

They say he knew by having watched in one of the magical looking glasses of the Underearth. But they said, also, that perhaps a ghost passed over some lawn before his palace, and glimpsing it, he went to find such a glass.

Azhriaz may now have said to him, "I am nothing to you. Why come to me with this? I have had a warning. My darling un-uncle, King Fate, brought it some months ago." Azhrarn would then have answered, "I am not here to warn you. I will do more than that. I have told you endlessly, as I told another, you are mine, and what is mine will be chastised only by me."

"So you have come here armed to fight?" she said.

Neither he nor those who followed him replied.

In a second, Azhriaz was clad not only as an empress-queen, but like a prince.

"I will fight too," she said. "It is my Empire, my godhood at stake. Those gifts you gave me that I hold so dear."

Azhrarn ignored her irony. He said, "They are sun-birthed. Their strengths flourish best by day, and the stamina of my kind by night. The sun is down. You, meanwhile, go to the river shore and wait."

"No, I will fight."

"Did I say it was a matter for war? Do as I bid you."

"Oh inimitable Father, and lordly Lord of lords, what name shall I get in the works of men if I hide myself?"

The face of Azhrarn had not changed. It was the countenance he had put on, with the battlegarb, to come here, and he would not alter it.

"Azhriaz," he said, "not only shall you hide, you shall fly the City. You flatter me by your estimation of my power. But the gods are the gods." And saying that, he turned his head and spat in the river, and the water spangled as if fireworks raced from end to end, then went black. "Chuz would not duel with me," said Azhrarn. "Have you forgotten so soon? And heaven is not to be fought with. It is a gesture, on all sides. But by these gestures, mountains are tumbled and landmasses sunk in the sea.''

Azhriaz turned from him.

"You are too young and have not learned to be afraid," he said.

Startled then, she looked at him once more. "And do you fear?"

But he awarded her only a terrible smile. The night opened, and the Vazdru were gone, Azhrarn before them.

Azhriaz frowned, but her heart, which had the tissue of mortals also in it, quickly beat. She flickered out in one place and reevolved amid the rushes of the bank.

And does he fear? Why then take the risk, why begin it? In order to sample the fear in its due season?

The atmosphere was electric. Not an awareness in Az-Nennafir that did not feel it, even to the beetles under the stones, even to the *stones*.

And suddenly there came a wild blunder of wings, and a torrential scurrying—the birds, the lizards, the rats, coming forth into the night, running away through it. And the sleek pet beasts, those leashed and caged, these might be heard tricking and wheedling their ways to freedom, and next running too. Pads and talons on the streets, the walls, tails and wings, feather and fur and leather and scale. And in the river the fish winging west toward the sea, as the birds did through the sky between the mindless dancing of the sorcerous stars and moons—

Then the dark was slashed open again, and out of it poured an army of undersized and hideous monstrosities, on whose swart unlovely limbs incredible adornments coiled. The Drin, who—passing by—licked the ground about Azhriaz, then fell upon her ship, the sea galley. And it seemed they tore it assunder.

"Now," she said, and tapped her foot.

One of the Drin approached her, crawling. "Mistress of Fevers and Fantasies, Lady of Constellations, Moon Queen—"

"I am *his* daughter," she said. "One compliment at a time will do. But speak of the ship."

"It is to be made worthy of you, Black Dream of the Night."

"So it was, worthy."

"To be made safe. And wondrous. Mistress of Delusions."

"How?"

"Let me go, and you shall see, Ebony Honey from the Silvermost Wasp of the Gardens of Druhim Vanashta."

Azhriaz kicked him lightly away. And the Drin bounded and squeaked as if he had been fondled. Then hurtled down toward the disintegrating ship.

I have no power. Helpless as a falling star am I, thought Azhriaz as she stood on the river bank. *When has it been otherwise?* And she too spat in the river, and spangled lilies rose which the Drin hastily plucked, biting and punching each other for possession, as they ripped apart the galley of the Goddess-on-Earth.

Night ranged black above a filigreed comber, the metamorphosed inn. It was like a jade mountain where it reflected in the river. No fish rose there, and in the reeds no frogs crackled, the crickets did not harp.

Black night on the roof, then, piercing its openwork fans. And night black in the room beneath, Night, armored, mailed, jeweled—the Vazdru. And there, before them, merely three cloaked figures, three pilgrims from some other land.

Nothing said. Time stopped.

Then, to the challenge of darkness, three cloaks unfolded, curved upward, and were wings, and a fount of light flooded the chamber. Some of the Vazdru turned their heads a little aside at it. Not Azhrarn. He stared straight upon this nocturnal sunrise, at Ebriel the eagle, and Yabael the vulture, but hardest he stared at swan-winged Melqar that the sun had seared white, and behind whose sunburst hair the solar disk seemed yet to stand.

"The gods," said Azhrarn, "are the gods. I say nothing of them. They are not here. But the rabble of the lower skies, it seems, has some quarrel with me." Long, long since, Azhrarn outstared the sun. It had duly blasted him. Now the twin suns of the eyes of the angel bored into the black and oceanic eyes of the Demon. One could not dry up the other, nor the other quench that one. "Who am I?"

said Azhrarn. "Can it be my modest name is known to you?"

The Malukhim did not speak. But the eyes spoke in their own way. And the golden hand, the sword of bleached flame. And in the hand of Azhrarn, black-gloved, the sword of indigo.

"But you," said Azhrarn. "The sun has sweated off three drops. And there you are. The foul orb of day was ever my enemy."

At which the points of the swords touched each other, nearly delicate, as if they kissed.

But brilliance shattered through the room and into the sky, and broke the clockwork stars so they rained on Az-Nennafir below.

When the first concussion divided the sky, the Drin gibbered, but did not cease their labors. They went at them more swiftly. It had been a while since they had had much heart to make anything. The magnitude of this assignment frightened them, filling them with creative delight and doubt.

They had one night to do it. The task should be impossible. Yet demon-time was on their side. They could not shift the framework of darkness, nor keep the sun down in chaos for a second more than it was habitually kept. Yet, within the bounds of the night, the scope of time—or its scope for them—might be a little rearranged. So, they accomplished complex feats.

The galley, only slightly supernatural, had boiled and bubbled, and sorcery gushed in. By the hour the heavens began to ignite and roar, and splintered stardust showered; a curious *thing* lay in the harbor, with the Drin swarming over it.

They must have plumbed the shelves of the seas, to get the model right. Or they had gone out by moonlight and attracted the blue-skinned dolphins and the umber whales. Or maybe some had plummeted amid the reefs, popping out to scare polyps and to become amorous with reserved females of many legs, and wish to court them in their shells, and not have the space, and so come back above the sea bulging with information and unsatisfied longings. . .

Some great fish had been the inspiration of design. Quite properly, for where such fishes swam, there this ship would go swimming, presently.

It was said to be glamorous, and more so than the original galley which had vanished somehow into it. For the revolting Drin could make nothing that was not wonderful.

But there was scarcely a means of regarding the new ship at this juncture, what with the river now in spate, and with the sky every now and then exploding. It must suffice to say that there it was.

Azhriaz, standing upon the bank, was no longer clad as empress or warrior-prince, but plainly, in black. And but for her beauty she seemed slight and small, unfit for a world of such drama.

Finally one of the Drin came to her, and lying on his face, put the tip of a finger to her ankle.

The girl looked down.

"Supreme Mistress, we have done all he told us to do. The sorceries are gelled, without and within. The rivets closed. All secure. Come now, board the vessel. I entreat you. There is only half a glassful of the lovesome darkness left."

"But," she said, and glanced about her, "who is to be with me?"

"None is needed."

"The City—" said Azhriaz.

"Let go the City. He will hang cities on your white brow like pearls."

"A vast quantity of lives," said Azhriaz. Her face was white indeed.

The Drin, puzzled, gobbled politely at the bank. What should she care for human lives, the Demon's daughter? Though, even *he*, once—

"Beloved of Glooms and Shades," said the Drin at last, "we seek only to serve you and so *him*. Come aboard."

Then, Azhriaz glanced at the sky, where the lightnings came and went and all the clockworks had perished.

"What causes that?"

"The Great Quarrel, Mistress of Delirium."

"Whose?" she said, childlike.

"Oh come aboard," pleaded the Drin. "Have pity on us."

"*You?* Have pity on you, but on no mortal? And he is embattled with sun-creatures? Not for my sake," said Azhriaz, beginning to drift toward the metal fish in the river. "It is his game, of course, and he does not like to lose."

There was, in the fish-vessel's side, a round high door. Azhriaz the Goddess went up to the door through the scalded air, and the Drin chittered. But at the doorway she said, "And where is Chuz?" Not loudly enough that they, who were deaf in any case from all the millennia of hammerings, could hear. "And my mother? Where is she? And cold Dathanja, that priest from a womb-temple of rock—where? I am alone."

Then she went inside the mysterious ship. The mysterious door shut tight.

It is not to be thought they contended as men who are skilled with swords. They fought in the way of what they were, dark and light, earth and ether, though something too in the way of dragons, and something in the way of a tempest turned upon itself.

The first blows, even if they slew stars, were foreplay. They danced, as lovers do, along the edge of death, Azhrarn the Demon, Melqar the angel. And the strokes of the black sword were lilting, nearly tender, and the Sun-Created—who had no soul, no purpose but the will of the gods—seemed induced by the presence of this adversary to copy and to match him. So the Malukhim also played, and the sword of golden whiteness teased, tempted, and the last agonized stella objects shivered to bits nearby.

And somewhere in this terrifying prologue, the inn roof fell away or was destroyed, and then they moved in the sky an instant, and then they passed into some place within the night, or beside it, a second dimension as close to the world as the skin to the skull. And close enough certainly that the incendiaries of conflict tore through and cracked the moons, now, like plates.

There is this to be borne in mind. Azhrarn had announced: *I say nothing of the gods. They are not here.*

And in this way, by this pious formality, he made pretense he did not know it was against the gods he fought. Such then the gods, as he had said, that even Azhrarn was politic. But yet again the Malukhim, though not in precise terms his equals, yet they were sufficiently puissant. And they were sun-beings, while the substance of demon stuff could not endure the sun—

The first and second angels, Ebriel, Yabael, had risen and gone up the sky, sentinel now on two precipices of masonry, one westward and one to the east. They waited there, and did nothing. Only they gazed inward behind their eyes, after the dueling of their fellow. For the Vazdru, they also stood high up, their mailed feet on black air. They kept between the two angels and the fabric of the other dimension, guarding the gate in absolute if inexplicable ways. They were pale as dead men, the Vazdru. They had not been among those in the underlands who put on yellow discontent. When Azhrarn called them, they galloped after him on their steeds of night, without one word.

The sky rang and coruscated.

Flung upward on the forming cumulus, great shadows, one coldest black, one boiling white.

The two swords met now not to kiss or woo. They scraped, rammed, impacted, mauled each other, clashed free, spraying fire. The clouds and vapors of that inner alter-place were tattered by the onslaught. The two antagonists bore no mark of having been touched, either by the other. Yet the swords themselves would seem to be living things, containing and sustained by the force of what wielded them. Each metal length sang and throbbed as if with hidden blood. Phalluses of spiritual death, then, organs of ungeneration.

Suddenly (miles away, next door through the thin skin separating the dimensions of night and fight) came the shining whistle of a silver Vazdru pipe. No less than a signal: The reerected ship was whole, and had been boarded: moved. Time was vanquished—yet time conquered. For the pipe said also that dawn, invisible, perceived in other fashion, dawn walked up the stairway to the earth.

It would appear the Malukhim, too, read the message. On the towers they opened wide their wings and turned their heads, Ebriel, Yabael, eastward. And Melqar opened also his wings, and like a spear of smoking snow, he whirled upon Azhrarn. The two swords embraced for the last, and split each other lengthways. The dying weapons, fixed together by the blow, smashed downward, gouging a channel through the churning dark.

Then Melqar had grasped Azhrarn by the shoulder and about the waist. Azhrarn in his turn caught the Malukhim by his wrist and by the rim of one foamy sinuous wing.

They were exact in stature, tall and slender, yet with a strength no mortal could attain, be he a giant of his tribe. Their features were alike, perhaps, in transcendence. In no other way.

There was no struggle, not a movement now. The muscular tonicity of each denied any further act to his opponent. They were locked, breast to breast and eye to eye, in stasis, but the foliage of their hair, the very garments that were on their bodies, streamed back as if from the thrust of a hurricane.

Again—far off, within the hollow of the ear—the Vazdru pipe shrieked its urgent summons.

Azhrarn spoke quietly to the angel.

"I have gained what I wished. It is my notion now to depart. Am I to take you with me?"

And then the angel also spoke. He had no voice, and so he thieved the voice of Azhrarn, though the darkness of its notes was altered, pitched from that golden throat.

"Descend with me," said the angel Melqar, "and all your kingdom will be blighted."

"You are too boastful," said Azhrarn. "Only a little ground will char."

"You cannot take me there," the angel said. "I will detain you until sunrise."

"You cannot detain me," said Azhrarn. "Take you there I shall."

And then, where they had grappled, was a black whirlwind with a white, a fiery avalanche with an avalanche of ink. These forces plunged and enwrapped, mingled, burst into a column that spun, that writhed and ribboned and was many-headed as a bush of cobras. Then, the tumult ended. And there they were once more, the angel and the demon, locked together, eye flaming upon eye, unchanged.

"Then," said Azhrarn, "I cannot."

He smiled. Gently, he let go the wing of the angel, and next the wrist. He stood in the angel's arms.

Azhrarn said, "One bright flower has unfolded in the east."

The angel said nothing now.

Azhrarn spoke once more, but to the Vazdru. He said: "*Go.*"

Not for anything would they leave him. They prevaricated there, the other side of the dimensional partition, until the eastern edge of the sky began to grin. And then, cursing themselves, fled. They could not bear the fireball of the sun.

But he, he had outstared the sun. He had been incinerated into ashes. And from the ashes, risen again.

"Here is your mother," he said finally to the angel, but in a tone all music. "That which formed you, warm and dear to you. For me, she has only hate. You will see."

The angel did not loosen his hold. He clenched Azhrarn to him, and the swan wings beat slowly, and the eyes burned on and on, the gold upon the black.

Then the curtain of that second dimension melted, and only the air over the city was about them, pierced below by its towers and terraces. The lens or the sorcery that had tinted the sky, this had been smashed. The atmosphere swirled with motes, with clouds and steams and enchanted clockwork debris, but through it all, and through the piercing towers, inexorable, came day.

The horizon overbrimmed, and out of the light stabbed suddenly the sun.

Azhrarn and the angel hung in the midst of the morning and flamed together—and in that instant, Melqar, he the gods made, loosed his hold.

There was a flash, a spasm of blackness. Azhrarn was gone. Swan-hawk Melqar wheeled across the dawn. Expressionless, he alighted on another high place, the winged warrior of heaven. His eyes were so golden now, they seemed sightless, opaque as blackest onyx.

*   *   *

In those ultimate phases of strife, the angel had become a mimic, in the manner of most newborn things. He mimicked the flirting swordplay of Azhrarn, next its violence. When he must speak at last, he mimicked the vocal range of Azhrarn, and facing him, was like a mirror image, a shadow's gleaming shadow. So, as Azhrarn loosed his hold on Melqar, Melqar, become so imitative, had slowly been impelled also to loose hold. Azhrarn's strategy.

But. The sun had come up. It stared upon them—upon *both*. In that gale of light, Azhrarn had blazed—but was not extinguished. This was impossible. It mocked the laws and the lore of demonkind and of mankind alike. It must therefore be discounted and reported differently. Thus: Azhrarn had tricked the angel. He fled as the Vazdru had fled a moment before the sun's disk came visible. Truth must be silent with her cry: Not so, not so, the sun discovered him. And he—he flamed for a split second as golden-white as Melqar—and at this phenomenon, deceived or amazed, or purely upon some instinct still ripe in his beautiful and soulless shell, Melqar released the enemy. Since the enemy, shade and shadow and night and black wickedness—*was also the sun*.

Truth is at the door, howling and stamping her foot. Truth is not always decorous.

Then best botch up an explanation. Say this: Azhrarn had met with the sun before, and the first meeting, which killed him outright, and from which, being immortal, he resurrected, toughened his supernatural fibers. A second meeting, since it was so brief, he could by a feather's breadth endure.

Besides, go down now after him, into his kingdom of eternal night that-is-not-night-at-all. Behold. Is Azhrarn kindred of the day?

They were able, the Vazdru, to enter their underworld at any point of the earth above. Yet, wherever on earth they were, their arrival was always at the same spot, directly outside the three gates of Azhrarn's territory. It was a matter of discretion. One may assume Azhrarn himself was not confined by the rule—however, on this occasion, the rule had had its effect.

He is on the borders of his own lands, at the base of the

first outer gate, that of agate. He lies like some wonderful discarded toy, one arm upflung over his head. The plates of mail are cloven from his body. There is no wound, not even a scratch or trace of blood upon the peerless flesh. Yet, through the pale clear sheath of it, you see the glimmer of jewelry knives, the bones of Azhrarn, Prince of Demons.

Three of the Vazdru kneel beside him—the others have been lost, sun-struck ash, or else have run farther to conceal their shame at leaving him. These three remain, snarling, like great cat that smell burning, and are afraid.

4

AND IN THE world the sun, coming to Az-Nennafir, brought darkness.

To the east and to the west and at the center of the sky, now, the angels took their posts. The day itself was so strange and horrible that even thick-witted man had ascertained it boded ill. Over the huge cloud-pointing City, thirteen kingdoms' width and length of it and more, the dawn had turned to blood and the sun to tarnish.

The groaning and the screaming, the prayers—useless and known to be useless—the exhortations, scrabbling attempts at exodus, the burrowings that would yield no safety, the ecstasies of madness and immolation—each and all occurred: the correct paraphernalia of catastrophe. But, seen from the heavens, what was it but a fomentation in a hill of termites? That which is so small cannot be important.

From the fair sword of Ebriel there beamed a line of sunflower light, and from the rust-tinctured sword of Yabael a spurting stem like gore. The sword of Melqar not being about him, he spread his left hand, and from the very palm of it a white ray pillared forth, and met the others, and there was a sound, not loud, yet audible perhaps to the earth's four corners. A sound like no other, and after this sound, a soundlessness, on earth and in heaven.

There came down first a rain of dirt and large stones, and hail which flamed. Seen from the sky, the destruction was solely a pretty pattern.

After the rain of boulders, filth and fire, a fog more dense than night; that too went down upon the lands of the City. And it swallowed them. They were gone.

Then the three Malukhim lifted their heads, feeling for the purchase in their unminds of the wishes of the gods, or for that premier wish. For by now who was to say that the gods had not already forgotten what they wanted, the angels they made, the Goddess they had disapproved of, everything—and, soon to be disturbed, by a vague bang far below, would wax displeased a minute at the interruption.

But the Malukhim, primed automata, did not lose track of their mission.

There came a detonation. There came a brightness. They were one. They cut out a piece of the substance of everything, and were finished.

When the finish passed, there was no aftershock, no afterglow. Nothing. And beneath the heavens, nothing also. A dull cavity, going from one horizon's edge to another, with a faint movement of dust about it, hard and featureless, blank, and void. Not a fleck of interest in it. Not a speck of life. *Az-Nennafir*.

Then, in the uncolored sky, the blaze of the angels winked out. They had dealings elsewhere.

Only smitten sky then, and the dead pit in the world's side.

They remarked this of Az-Nennafir:

They said, We are rotten and will revel in rottenness. *And rottenness was theirs*.

Then they said, See how vile we are and how well we deserve punishment. *And punishment heard them talking*.

And they said, We are helpless before destiny, let us have no hope for ourselves. Let us be sophisticated and say to Death: See, we are doomed, let doom claim us. We are waiting. *And Death listened.*

Invoke and be answered.

And the worst of their sins was the sin of *default*.

There was then no more ghastly place than that crater, after the dust had settled.

What of the fish-ship and the Goddess-girl? Her city of wickedness had been, in traditional mode, razed by the outraged gods, and in a cataclysm vital enough to dig a hole through the surface of the world. Could even an immortal thing survive intact this escapade?

Because she had already had built the great galley of decks and oars, and her magic was woven through it, a kind of spirit or astral element had come to be in it, which the Drin were then able to employ, and which therefore eased their labor.

The Drin were moreover artificers of genius, the magics powerful, while the ship had besides a kind of double life upon and about it.

As the Vazdru pipe gave its warning, the ship already fled. It had two means of motivation, and of these it used the second, to which the Drin, before they vanished, ordered it. This means was solely sorcerous. The ship ran fast as lightning, which was all the speed of which it was capable. It broke through the river at this rate, and had reached the egress to the sea, even as Azhrarn stood eye to eye with Melqar. And when the sun came and the duel so oddly ended, the ship forged eastward through the western sea, and as it went, it dived. It hid itself under the waves, but even there, it *ran*.

The boulders and hail fell, but behind it. And the black fog fell. And last, the light. Where by now the ship had taken itself, that final thud was not heard. There was only a quiver that hollowed all the water out, so the most abysmal oceanic caverns twanged at it, and the spiny corals cracked, and little sea animals, only catching a whiff of the indecipherable noise immediately died and left the husks of their small bodies fluttering in the currents, like the leaves on winter streams.

For the fish-ship, it too rocked, its great speed slowed, it slewed, it bucked and rolled and went hugely toppling downward through those deaf deeps of the waters.

5

HAVING walked many months and miles, Dathanja, black of hair and eye, and clothed in black, and barefoot, reached a land of woods and waterfalls and valleys. He had, as he went by, seen the periphery landscapes of the Goddessdom. Various highly tinted deserts equipped with smashing meteors, a selection of seas with bridges over them, plains of intoxicant grass—such as these had met his gaze. The altars too he looked at, and the delirious worshipers. He heard the ceaselessly repeated philosophy of the uncaring gods, just as in the City. He did not deny it. Memory, fragmentary and transparent as a painting on broken glass, informed Dathanja of old rites and prayers—which had brought only disillusion and grief. It was another life. He did not dwell upon it, though inevitably it tutored and guided him.

In due course he moved beyond the boundaries of that domain. Then there began to be, at long last, only the usual anomalies of human thought and religion. And thereafter, more primitive ground, lonely of mankind.

Eastward. The dawns out-combed their yellow hair. The sunsets hurried. The earth had a youth about it. It cleansed Dathanja's soul, or so it seemed to him. He had not often tasted calm—a serenity that was not embittered loss of feeling, numbness passing for peace. What secret lay behind this cool and quiet state? So, he reached the land of watered, wooded valleys.

Between one valley and the next, on the hillside, at the mouth of a waterfall, there stood an ancient shrine. It was not devoted to any particular god, nor, perhaps, to the gods at all. None tended it. Trees and shrubs rooted in its court. Birds housed and discoursed in the roof. The hurrying sunset had commenced and slid down the waterfall in its haste to be away.

Dathanja entered the court, and seated himself on the ground to eat a feast of gathered roots and fruit. He had been a wanderer in the former life. He had had no need to prepare himself for this journey. To some, the habit of itinerance is ordinary.

The dusk came, the night came after. Stars unfastened windows in the sky and began their watch of the earth.

On a paving stone, Dathanja built and kindled a fire. He, who had been a mighty magician once, and would bring the elements at a snap of his ringed fingers. He who might have produced a palace from the hill.

As the flames played together, Dathanja beheld a woman standing the other side of the light. He took her, firstly, for Azhriaz, who had met him at irregular intervals on his trek, a thing so astonishingly fair he did not find her beautiful. (She was a demon, too, and of all the races he distrusted their kind the most.)

However, this was not Azhriaz, either in disguised person or projected form. This was a human girl, humanly fair, so he recognized as much.

"Do you see me, Dathanja?" she superfluously asked him.

"I see you," he said.

She had the later summer's hue; roses, malt. Behind her was another, taller, and a man, who said, "And do you see *me*, Dathanja?"

"I do," he said.

The man came from the shadow. He had the hue of kingship; metals and dyes. Behind him—

"And that one also," Dathanja said. "I see him."

But the third was wrapped in the dark, and he had no hue and did not speak.

"Which of us is to begin?" inquired the summery girl of the kingly man.

"I," he said. And she stepped away. "It is not," she muttered in her hair, "always so."

But the tall man moved to the fire and beckoned Dathanja. "You must come with me," he said. And Dathanja must.

They were high up then, above the shrine, and the fire looked tiny as a sequin.

"Ah, Dathanja," said the kingly one, mockingly affectionate. "You have disappointed me." And he seemed many men at once. He was sometimes like a priest in costly yellow robes, and sometimes like an azure-bearded king. Or sometimes he was demoniac, and took on a Vazdru air. Or else he resembled Dathanja himself, save his features were rather altered and his eyes were blue, or green. But whatever or whoever he might be, he came to rest on a ridge and Dathanja with him. "Such power was yours, beloved," said the kingly one, coaxingly. "Do you not recall? Emperors went in fear of you. The very oceans did your bidding. *Do this!* you told them: It was done. And your sorcery is still spoken of. Your unspeakable cruelties, your mighty deeds. Ah, do you not even recall a mite of it?" "Yes," said Dathanja, in a low, clear voice. "I do recall." "Acquiesce," said the man. "I will give all back to you. You shall be again Zhirek the Dark Magician, and rule men, and make a new legend."

And at this, the kingly changeable one unrolled the night like parchment, and there lay—illusion or truth—the kingdoms of the world, its seas. And men kneeled to Zhirek, or to Dathanja. And sorcery came like a perfumed wind, and cloaked him round. He might do anything. His brain took flight with the sciences he had once kept like his dogs.

"Acquiesce," the kingly one repeated. And he was now most like Zhirek. He was Zhirek, and he cajoled Zhirek. "Take your glory back again. Be again a mage and a lord, so that every footstep of yours is written of."

Dathanja looked at the illusions or realities of his earlier life, and of his proposed future, and a terrrible pang, like pain or pleasure, cut through his heart. Before it faded.

"No," said Dathanja.   "Ah, beloved," said the tempter. "Do you reject this summit because it is a sin?"

"Is it a sin?" said Dathanja. "I only know that this I have done. It is past."

"And you will walk powerless in the world, the butt of every accident, at the mercy of men? *You?*"

"I am at no man's mercy save my own," Dathanja said. "My apologies I offer you, for you do not tempt me with this."

The man shrugged and he laughed, and he was gone. Dathanja sat before the fire in the courtyard.

"Which of us, now?" inquired the girl, of that figure still wrapped in obscurity. *He* did not reply. "Then it is to be me," she said.

She moved to Dathanja's fire, and when she was near, the glow of it was netted in her hair, wetted her bangles, and soaked her thin garment so all the shape of her was to be seen, and she was well made.

"Ah, beloved," said she. And he was in the fire with her.

Like a drum the night pounded, red and bright, black and red. Sometimes her hair was of a watery sheen, sometimes an apricot shade, she was a sea-princess, she was a girl who danced with unicorns. And sometimes she was a youth, her breasts flattened to hard pectorals under his hands, her loins upflowering where a full-fleshed anemone had closed him round. They writhed upon the bed of fire, and her hair streamed out along the earth. Her limbs clasped him, fierce as a lioness, yet her fingers came and went as soft and slight as grass. Her waist made motions like a snake, her mare's pelvis galloped. They plunged together through the fire into another fire beneath. The stars were whirling through his brain, and at her core a silver star tipped now the spear he rode upon. And into him in turn the silver sped, and quickened in a shivering wire, along the thrusting of the lance, through the taut shield of the belly and the striving groin, to the sacrum, where the atom of eternity lay buried in the spine. And he held her fast, though now she sobbed aloud and struggled and was transformed—to beast, to sprite, to conflagration and to waterfall. He held her by her snake's waist, by her thrashing limbs, drowned in her mouth and carried upward on the curved wave of her abdomen and her breasts flowered upon their flowers—riding the winged horse of lust, blinded, slain, born, disemboweled by ecstasies, until the silver probe pierced the atom of eternity itself, and the water of life was flung forth.

The winged spasm fell through the dark and shook Dathanja from its back. He lay beside the fire.

"You have betrayed yourself. You have shown weakness and need. Your soul lay naked as you suffered the fit of pleasure. You have sinned." This is what the girl said, out of the dark.

But it was Dathanja who laughed now. "*That*," he said, "is not a sin." And turning his shoulder to the fire, and the still-waiting, still-unseen, third figure (for the tall man and the summer girl were gone), smiling, Dathanja slept.

Yet, in the hour before the dawn, Dathanja roused, and sitting up, beheld the third figure seated across from him, by the ashes of the fire, against the starless sky.

Robed and hooded in white, handsome black-skinned Death, the Lord Uhlume, regarding the mortal man with immortal opal eyes.

"You must forgive me," said Dathanja after a while, "if I say that all this I believe to be a delusion. Fantasies sent to aggravate or dissect me, by another, or conceivably by my own self. And this being so, you also, lord king, are a figment of my mind. It seems to me Uhlume, who was kind to me in his own way once, and once my master, would not put himself to the bother of this visit."

The vision of Death—Dathanja was correct—responded.

"It may be you are wise. Nevertheless, I am your third and last tempter, and as such, I have validity and you must listen." (And Dathanja must.) "You have lived out your years of invulnerability, that blessing-curse awarded you by witchcraft long ago. Like everything of the earth, sorcery decays, or it is altered. Centuries have passed, and you have slumbered, and you have woken, and you are not as you were. It is the residue of your own lost magery that keeps you currently from harm. While you consign yourself to safety, safe you will be. But the armoring enchantment was sloughed within the pillar of stone. Should you desire otherwise, Dathanja, than for comfort, now you may be harried and hurt. Now, if you choose, you may die."

Then Dathanja sat in silence, looking into the face of Death, or of Death's image. At length Dathanja said, "Can it be so?"

"A dozen means of proof lie all about," said 'Death.'

Dathanja considered. Zhirek, a world of time before, had searched a valley for slicing stones, had drunk from the morbific water of it, had sought to hang himself on its tree and to throw himself down from its overleaning height. To no avail. Now, Dathanja reached out one hand, and taking up a raw flint from the courtyard, he stuck it in his arm. And the flint wounded him. His blood flowed crimson. "I am glad of it," he said. And he closed his eyes, and the calm within him seemed to flow outward with the blood, to surround him, and to comfort him, as the barrier of invulnerability had not. "Then," said Dathanja, "the last temptation is certainly to die. And it is a cunning one. But, Death, I have learned. Men, too, are as immortal as the gods, and as invulnerable as Zhirek, who was dipped in the well of flame. And therefore it does not distress me to remain alive a little longer. For he that I was fled wickedness and did good only out of fear, and then fear overwhelmed him and he did only wickedness. My debts are many, but wickedness has no more sway over me. I have used it up. I am not, therefore, afraid to live." And opening his eyes, Dathanja saw that Death too—or death—had left him, and the long and passionate dawn began.

Going out of the shrine, Dathanja went to the waterfall, and cupping his hands, he caught the water and drank. Presently a deer approached with her faun, and he offered them the water, and they too drank from his hands. The faun allowed him to smooth its dappled head. Untroubled, the mother ate the moss that grew on the rock. And Dathanja remembered Simmu, youth and maiden, calling the deer and the hares to race with him, communing with birds and serpents.

But Simmu was no more, and Zhirek, the invulnerable sorcerer, was no more. It was Dathanja who soon strode away into the morning.

6

DARKNESS had its abode in the depths of the sea. Nor did it dwell alone there. These uterine cellars teemed with life, yet it was a life that existed lightlessly for the most part, and when light came upon it, the stranger was unwelcome.

Light rays entered the upper floors of the great trench in a gentle blush. There came a swirling and lashing, as of a legion of whips, and larger entities, like huge black ghosts, blundered softly away. But the light sharpened. It would not be held back, or avoided. It pushed through the water and the dark, and suddenly the sea deeps burst to visibility. A forest lay along the top tiers of the trench. It was composed of a million tendrils, oil-black. And in the forest perched fish nests of flaxen floss, and their makers—finnily sprinting to conceal themselves—were each like a rainbow prism. The huge things which had already careered into flight, they were enormous slothful sacks of billowing skin, and where the light sluiced over their bodies, they glimmered acid-blue and bronze. Farther down the steps of the trench the illumination, striking like a bell, showed beds of oceanic flowers, hot coral and rose, chill melon-pale or sour melanic green, all slamming their portals in dismay, and here or there on them a slim startled creature like a gold-leaf worm, bolting a last morsel of grazing before it dashed from view.

Behind the light and the upheaval, a monster swam.

It seemed most like a whale, of giant proportions. Smooth as a silken egg, and, seen by its own corona, of a sea-washed silver. The mouth of the whale gaped slowly as it

swallowed the water. Everything was sucked in, helplessly—
fish, fish nests, loosened tendrils, grazing worms, and
straying flowers. Yet, from the stern of the giant, a crystalline defecation almost spontaneously shot them all forth
again in a tremendous gush. What tales these animalcules
might hasten home to tell. How they had been eaten by a
whale, flailed through its guts, and emerged unscathed
once more into the mothering ocean. The whale, meanwhile, never ceased to ingest the sea, and to expel the sea
in drafts of purest flatulence.

Above the maw of it, two eyes beamed wide, both
round and bright, but one only with a black vertical pupil
in it.

So the unconscionable thing went on, staring and causing affright and picaresque heroics along the trench.

Now and then its one vertical pupil moved, and even
crossed from one eye into the other. Azhriaz (the pupil)
looked out upon the water world which the lamps of her
ship revealed to her.

When the blast of annihilation rocked the ship and
plunged it downward into these deeps, she was stunned,
her brain, like the ship, whirling. Then she had called on
Chuz inadvertently, and even once almost cried out a word
which had no meaning for her (which word was "Father"). Soon enough the deep-sea ark steadied. Then the
Goddess arose from the bottom of it and shook off her
feebleness.

She would not consider her City, wiped like dirt from
the earth by an angel rag. She would not consider how she
rode under the waves. She stood before the casement eye
of the fish-whale-ship and frowned upon submarine marvels. Nor would she consider these. She was alone. She
was a Goddess. This was the sea. Well, well.

The craft progressed, when not by means of preset
mantras, through an engine in its entrails, Drin-built, which
gasped in fluid and expelled it, so making for a tireless
forward propulsion. Within the hub was a palatial suite, to
which the Drin had pretentiously added examples of their
finest or most obtuse smithery. This included, ringed about
the main chamber, a series of grotesque silver heads. Like
the whale, these *breathed*. And by breathing, gulped away

the stale air, puffed out, suitably scented, the reviving gases of the dry land.

Whatever the submarine sailor wished, she had only to demand it. A quantity of genies seemed to have been hammered in with the rivets. Should she need a sumptuous repast, music, one more satin pillow for her couch, these attendants supplied the item. They additionally guided the vessel and maintained it. Azhriaz was asked to do nothing, either with her magic or her wits. Sometimes, her new servants might be glimpsed: tinted wisps, bodiless spirals of smoke, protruding delicate hands, or half-seen childish faces. Whatever were they? Efflorescences of Vazdru science, or the uncouth Drindra in the process of refinement—it was not to be guessed.

The sea had its own masters. . . . Fate had warned her, if she had even needed such a hint. Though she had cast illusion on it once, now she was the ocean's uninvited guest.

"Why," said Azhriaz imperiously, to her part-seen servitors, "do these depths have color? They are always in the dark."

A genie flittered forth.

"O Mistress," said it, "the sea-folk are magicians. They came beneath millennia since and learned to prosper here, after a spat with the gods. It was they, then, who made the vegetation colorful."

"Again, why?"

"Because the sea peoples value lights. They go about with them, and then they can admire the colors, which they enticed for this purpose."

When she slept, after her questionings, banquets, on silk and satin, she dreamed of cities flattened and the death of men. Not Vazdru dreams, not artistic. She woke screaming. She called the genies and had music, or stood in the eyes of her ship, regarding the water, and put sleep from her like a faithless friend.

They say she traveled in the sea for a month or a year.

The oceanic trench continued for a time. It was a sort of valley of the region, and mountains soared above and beyond it, cliffs of aqueous purple granites, out of whose steep caves weird fish-mammals peered, and mooed at the ship, unheard. The crests of these stupendous mountains, thousands of feet overhead, might break the sea as little islands.

The ship had turned already eastward, as much as the valley permitted. Azhriaz had not given any direction, but the earlier ship of oars and sail had been bound on an easterly voyage; its spirit, held in this one, bore the impress still, and the genie crew humored the motive. Eventually the floor of the valley-trench sloped upward. The ship accordingly ascended.

Between the shadowy heights appeared, then, a cup of glowing water, into which the ship propelled itself. Azhriaz, in the whale's sinister eye, presently saw she had come upon a city of the sea peoples.

There were many of these, and most of them different. This one lay in a honeycomb of grape-green sunlight, that seemed to spill straight down through the thick tons of ocean aloft. It was a black and iridescent city, very tall, with enormous arches and apertures set stories up. Black shapes that might be sharks hovered in its "skies," and here and there some chariot or other conveyance sparkled as it soared across the aqueducts.

Beneath the ship, pastures of white anemones stretched down toward the suburbs. On the pastures herds of elephantine lobsters were browsing. Mermen shepherds glanced up and made averting gestures at the metal whale. From the beginning, the sea kings had bred such slaves. They wore garlands of salty barnacles on their weed-wild hair, and carried knives of coral and electrum, but they were timid and ingenuous.

Azhriaz did not stay her vessel. It swam on, until it hung in the funnel of green sun close to the city of the sea lords. The black-crow sharks had dispersed, the chariots withdrawn. Nothing stirred.

Azhriaz interrogated the genies, and learned from them that the light came down via a system of lenses arranged higher up to catch and focus the sun. But as they spoke, another genie trickled out like paint in milk.

"O Mistress," this genie exclaimed, and pointed with its long-fingered hands.

Far across the city an apparatus had elevated on one of the arches. Now it lurched and the water tore. Burning darkness with a train of bubbling white came rushing upon the ship. A catapult had been fired.

"Do not exert yourself," chorused all the genies to Azhriaz. "It is not required."

At this moment a pore of the ship sorcerously opened and a levinbolt sped forth. It intercepted the missile from the catapult some distance off, and hurled it away so that, erupting and ablaze, the ball crashed back on the black city. Fire and smolder poured into the water at that point like blood.

Another ball had, however, already been launched at them.

"We fight no more," said Azhriaz. "We will run away." The genies chirruped.

"It is unnecessary, Mistress. All that they send we can destroy, and level their proudest towers maybe."

"Just so," said Azhriaz. "And angels do that. We will not fight but fly."

The genies obeyed her. They seemed neither sorrowful nor glad, not even surprised at her curious whim.

The mantras were activated and the metal whale dived from the sea-skies of that city like lightning. The second missile flung itself harmlessly by below, and was lost in wet green space.

She had come among the cities of Tirzom of the eastern oceans. She did not know it, but would learn. Black and beauteous were these cities, and between them lay the fertile plains and marine woods of the shallower shelves. All which territory the Tirzomites claimed.

Jungles of kelp and branching coral afforded cover for the ship as Azhriaz stole upon the hem of each metropolis. She saw the black cupolas and pinnacles of olivine, as the shy fish saw them.

My father is not here to guide me, said Azhriaz to herself. *I need do nothing. I need not make war.* And her dreams of battered Nennafir— which had become mixed with others of the ghoul city Shudm—were eased.

Yet, though she hid modestly, many in those sea cities

of magicians knew that something passed. And some crept upon it, more crafty in their forests than Azhriaz. By their own abnormal means, the sister capitals of that country sent news and warning of the thing which trespassed there.

All this time, the ship ascended as the ocean floor itself went up. And soon it was possible to tell in those waters the traffic of night with day above, as the aquascape faded or grew bright.

One day the waters were very clear and most crystal green. The subsea ark was nosing among the glades of a great weed wood, when the shining eyes of it, one with a slender pupil, saw away over the plains beyond a tall rock, and on the rock's top a city. It happened that this was Tirzom Jum, Capital of all the capitals in that part of the world.

Even from a distance, one could tell it was a city of especial size and import, while a colossal silvery half-moon rested over the crown of it, the two points going down among the walls.

Azhriaz questioned the genies. The genies, their wells of knowledge seemingly floorless, replied that certain of the sea peoples—though thoroughly acclimated to the ocean—had a nostalgia for the airs of earth. And these they might distill and set to play in various chambers or gardens of their dwellings. It would appear that this city (and despite the floorless wells, the genies did not, it seems, know enough to name it) had given over to earth air whole sections of its upper streets. They were contained, therefore, under a dome of magical glass.

Azhriaz said, "I should like to see it."

The genies told her she did so.

"Closer to hand."

The genies told her the ship would go closer to the city.

"No," said Azhriaz. "I do not mean to make war—this ship is taken as a threat. I will go out alone."

The genies gazed upon her with their vague childlike eyes. Their incorporeal concentration was such that Azhriaz asked of them: "What now?"

"O Mistress, though you are Night's Daughter, and though you are a Goddess-Witch, yet, these are the kingdoms of the ocean."

"Will my mage-craft not avail me here?"

"Perhaps," they said.

"Then, let me see."

A pore of the ship loosed her, like a dark tear. She had made herself a bubble of air, inside which she stood. And when she moved the bubble clung about her and went with her. The air of the bubble stayed fresh, renewing itself constantly, and in its wake drifted other slighter bubbles sloughed from the whole. Delicious with the Vazdru breath of Azhriaz, they danced among the fish and the fish lovingly pursued them.

Azhriaz rejoiced in her sudden freedom. She had not thought to venture out before. But long inactivity—as once before—had worn her down, making her depression weigh the heavier. She played about the passing creatures, and though she could not touch them through the bubble, nor they her, she gazed into their eyes and made circles around them, chased them, allowed them to give chase to her.

The plains below Tirzom Jum were of the sheerest sand, where lay incredible shells. Striped and spotted they were, like ocelots, creamy and resinous as amber, or whorled like the spikes of unicorns, or pure as the thinnest porcelain— and of every color imaginable. Azhriaz paused over these, and contemplated piercing the bubble a moment to take up some of the most beautiful or strange. But the murmuring of the genies clouded her mind. The ship was her protection. She would not risk undoing her magic in the liquid element. Could it be she might not then be able to reinstate the spell? And although it was inconceivable she should drown, the living breathless struggle was a horrible idea. She had never doubted her powers before, never had cause.

Yet she idled on, and soon the rock cliff of the city loomed above her.

It was a fact, the Tirzomites were nostalgic, in a scornful way, for the earth. The sun itself, though removed through layers of water and sky, might incoherently be *seen* here. On the earth it must be high noon, for a faint goldenness burned in the apex of the waters, and under the rock a little frill of shadow lay on the sand.

Azhriaz drifted up the cliff with caution, keeping her

distance from the city. Midway along its slopes, ornate buildings began to appear, black as jet, with lynx-eyed windows. She glimpsed the momentum of vehicles, and sea-blown clouds that were enormous trees. . . . Like a child she stared at this, and kept away, and would not fight.

One third below the cliff's summit, the curious dome began. It too was a bubble, transparent, discernible only by the crescent gleam of filtered sunlight limning its curve. Under the dome, up in the *air* and gilded peridot light, were the massive oval archways of the architecture of Tirzom, and the streets and steps needful where swimming had no place, the stalking towers and emerald minarets.

The Goddess floated, and looked her fill. She felt her sadness and her guilt, her confusion in the face of the wishes of others, of eternity—and one short second. *What is this city to me?* Should she go to her ship and fire lightnings at it? *I slew Shudm.* She had given the ghouls to each other to gnaw. She was the daughter of Wickedness.

A blackness was slowly detaching itself from the rocky masonry of Tirzom Jum. It flowed toward her.

Azhriaz, interrupted in her guilt, becoming aware of it, thought it mundane. It was a beast resembling a black bladder, with optics of blue, like a jest at her own garb and eyes. An octopus with the snakes of its tentacles about it.

"I am not for you," she said to it, though it could not hear and would not heed.

It came on, and Azhriaz spread out her hand. A glare ripped through the water and rapped the octopus smartly, so it was packed off in a succession of somersaults. In its fury it released a wave of ink into the sea.

She had meant to kill it, and had not done as much. It did not think her very dangerous, only irksome, and it came on again through the ink. Then Azhriaz resorted to the magic which would vanish her from that spot and bring her out inside her safe ship. On earth, it had been hardly more momentous, this, than to blink her eyelids.

But she was in the sea.

There was a surge that buffeted and slung her down into the sand. And that was all it did.

Azhriaz kneeled among the shells and felt the sea on her

body, and tasted it in her mouth. Her casting of power had broken wide the bubble.

I am invulnerable. I am Vazdru. The ocean cannot murder me. Yet the salt sea filled her nostrils, her throat, her lungs, and the agony of it was not to be borne. *Then am I less than Zhirek?* she wondered in terror and outrage.

And she cursed her father and her mother, sun and dark, for what of *this*?

Her sight grew blind. The octopus hauled her up into its multitude of arms.

7

THROUGH perforated screens and lucid vanes soaked the amphibian dusk of Tirzom Jum: It was sunset in the world above. Lamps were being lit along the upper levels of the city, a nightly ritual. Fire was a specialty here. Slaves gracefully slunk about the palace halls, dipping their tapers to orbs of vitreous and sconces of verdigris.

Illumined in the sea-dusk lamplight, the court of the king looked on the animal which had been captured.

Like their cities, the Tirzomites were black, and green. Their skins were pantherish. The hair that splendored their heads was the hue of apples, and equally so the not-white whites of their eyes. When they spoke or laughed (as below water it was not comfortable to do, it subsequently becoming a fashion up here), the insides of their mouths and their tongues were darkest green, their teeth like pure green pearls. Other more intimate parts of them would have been seen to be green, had they revealed them. Cut these persons, they would shed blood like drops of tourmaline. They were wise, though, not green that way, the

Tirzomites. Educated, clever, and arrogant—and cruel, as all the peoples of the sea—which was, despite the fashion, no laughing matter.

The king himself sat in his orichalc chair, with his two cats at his feet. They were of a bibred species, cheetahs that had never tried the acres of earth, but rather coursed the floor of the waters. They had the fins of golden carp, and spotted scales for pelts. They had recently hunted sharks; now they glared at the shackled thing on the carpets below their master's feet.

"It is not ill made," commented one of the courtiers. He spoke in the language of Tirzom. "Yet, so beautiless."

"It is truly quite foul," agreed another. "Yet, it has some value as a curiosity."

"It breathes the sea, despite having no gills, and is unharmed."

"It is a female. It may belong to some other kingdom. With whom are we at war that might send spies?"

"With three or four states, as is usual. Though their peoples have just such hideous white skin, they have other proper characteristics of the ocean races. This creature has none, however hard it breathes water. Besides, there is the ship. We do not understand the magical mechanics of it, and though it has been surrounded by our soldiery, it lies still in the woods—we have been unable to gain access, so strong are the sorcerous protections. We have had word from Vesh Tirzom that their catapults did it no damage, but that the ship itself smote back an exploding missile into the city. While from Tirzom Bey came the message of those who perused the ship when it, or its occupant, slept. And the message told of workmanship thereon that the forges of mortals do not produce."

"Enough," interrupted the king sharply, and the mer-cheetahs growled. "We will question the captive thing. It swoons too long. Go, wake it up."

"I have awakened," said a voice from the carpets, and also in the language of Tirzom.

She reclined, Azhriaz, only as if at leisure before them, not deigning to stand, let alone to give obeisance. The king she regarded as if he were some supplicant she had permitted to sit down. The rest she did not bother with.

It was a truth, she was a goddess and had grown used to homage, and not to get it irked her. And she had been besides conscious always of her beauty, if indifferent to it. Here, her white skin was reckoned the depth of ugliness, overriding all other consideration or feature.

"How is it," said the king of Tirzom Jum, "that you, a deficient foreign animal, can speak our tongue?"

"How is it," said Azhriaz, "that you, so erudite and all-wise, do not know?"

For another fact, her Vazdru training of recent years had taught her every tongue of the earth (of which there were seven root languages, and each of those split into ten sublanguages), and the seven undefiled speech modes of Underearth. The teaching of these had been a relatively simple thing, involving touches of nephrite and nacre. . . . Time hanging heavy in her Goddessdom, however, Azhriaz had summoned the Drindra, and now and then the Drindra had even breached the seas for her, and brought her relics, including certain stone tablets or sewn books of the aquatic folk. The magicianry that pulsed in her very blood had not deserted her; such would be absurd. Her powers were only severely mitigated by the environment. They enabled her now, from the linguisttics she had formerly studied, to piece together Tirzom's vernacular. Indeed, though there were a host of languages beneath the waves, yet they too sprang from mother roots, and were not so unfathomable as the sea lords opined.

Something of that, this sea lord now seemed unwillingly to comprehend.

"Then you are," said he, "by the terms of the earth, a great sorceress."

"I am, by the terms of the earth, a peerless goddess."

At this, the court of the king laughed extravagantly.

The king put on a stern face.

"We eschew the gods here, though we respect them. You have neither the manner nor the aspect of a god."

Azhriaz met the king's cat eyes unrelentingly, but she knew, with sulky amusement, that this argument was irrefutable. Here, the Goddess of Nennafir was not much.

"I will," she said, "out of tact at your ignorance,

dispense with my holy titles. I shall only inform you of my royalty. I am Azhriaz, the Prince of Demons' daughter."

The king started. The court whispered. And, for their parts, the mer-cheetahs lowered themselves onto their bellies, as if unsure whether to snarl or purr.

Presently the king of Tirzom Jum said this: "Azhrarn we know of, and between all our kind and his there exists a compact of truce for he is mighty in his way, but we also, as he would himself confirm."

"You," said Azhriaz, "are mere magicians, and were human once. It is the sea itself, this element you have wedded, which so swells your power. Shipwreck you a few years on the land, there would be another song."

At this the courtiers put their hands to their daggers, and many discussed loudly killing this upstart foreign *thing* at once. Or, if it might not be killed, of distressing it in other ways.

Then Azhriaz laughed, not from humor, but because she saw it was idiomatic. "I am invulnerable," she said. "I can breathe the sea, though to me it is anathema. What do you suppose you may do to me?" And she rose to her feet, and clad herself by her magic in the trappings of her earthly godhead. It impressed them, this vulgarity, as she had divined it might. "Consider also," said Azhriaz, "if you attempt to harm me, my father may forgo his truce with you. Have you, such bold warriors as you claim to be, ever fought a war with the Vazdru? Insult me, and the joy shall be yours."

Then a man came to the king and muttered in his ear. This one wore a long robe of black, and on his breast hung a pectoral of green bones.

Azhriaz attended to the mutter. She waited till the man drew back and then she said to the king, "Your scholar tells you, if I am Azhrarn's, I must prove it."

"The request is not unjust."

"My father," said Azhriaz, "has his own affairs to tend to. I may call to him, and he not hear the cry, no, not for some while. Rest assured, nevertheless, that at length he will hear it, and that if you have inconvenienced me, it may not gladden him."

"You have made your threat," said the king, "and your

boast. We are ready to extend all politeness to you, provided you demonstrate yourself worthy. Any cunning witch, who had gained an ability for breathing water, might come here and say what you have said. Should we be gentle with you for Azhrarn's sake, and the parenthood be discovered as a lie—such, too, might offend the Prince of Demons."

"To call to him requires a spell," said Azhriaz.

"I shall set at your disposal my own mage-chamber, and only I and my scholars shall be by."

"Let me do it, then," said Azhriaz. But her heart beat heavily, and cold.

They ascended on foot—it was all the rage to walk, since elsewhere in the sea one did not—between high-pillared roofs of the palace. It was night on earth, and night in the domed city. Stars had also been lit, far up in the dome, by slaves, who must climb bizarre scaffolding each sunset to do it, and often fell to their deaths on the streets below. The king strolled amid burning torches, and now and then paused beside some flowering shrub—for the upper city was mantled with plants, to supplement and enhance the air. "Sample this bloom," he said to Azhriaz, so courteous now it boded ill, for it seemed he thought he could be lavish with such manners; soon there would be no need for them. And Azhriaz said, "Pretty enough, king. But black flowers remind me of pathetic human death."

"Oh, Death," said the king of Tirzom Jum. "We believe he is a relative of ours, sprung from our stock but debased. His green hair and eyes whitened in disgust at his exile to dry land." "I deduce you have never met the Lord Uhlume," said Azhriaz, who had not properly met him either. "For you are only black as the black men of the earth are black." "Theirs is a red-blackness," said the king, contemptuously. "Or a brown blackness, or the purple black of damsons." "And you are only black as jet," said Azhriaz. "But the Lord Uhlume, my un-uncle, is black as *black* is black, and no other."

The mage-chamber of the king lay a long distance up in the dome. It was a sphere of obsidian stuff, windowless, and held by three towers in claws of brackish brass.

The king, and seven of his chosen scholars, entered, with Azhriaz, and the door was shut on them.

No sooner had this happened than soft light filled the sphere.

"All is at your disposal," said the king. "Commence."

"Stand back some way," said she. "Such things may occur as will dazzle or scorch you."

"Pray do not be afraid for *us*."

Yet, back they stood, and made eight figures against the curving wall. Azhriaz went to the wide room's center, and was alone.

Mortals called to Azhrarn by means of demon pipes, either given, filched, or come across. Then he did not commonly answer. Only myth said that he did. With those he loved, such artifacts were rarely necessary. With Dunizel, in the final months of their liaison, a thought would have brought him to her side. And it must be he had longed for this thought, but she, for the sake of his child (for in her own way, she was adamant against his proposed employment of it), had resisted. And now she was dead, and Azhriaz had been put to use exactly as he vowed—

What did Azhriaz need then, his unloved child, to call her father?

Nothing.

Yet she stood in the sea king's mage-chamber, and made a vast show. To attract Azhrarn's attention, to flatter him, maybe. Or only to delay the inevitable.

She knew her phantasms could not reach her here. So she invented phantasms, which flooded the area, moping and meowing, and some, in psychic fright at being created in such a spot, psychically made psychic water on the floor. Thereafter, many magic fireworks were let off. And in the wake of the colorful confusion, Azhriaz summoned the Drindra, that she knew must come, for several of them she had chained to her as her slaves, a deed the Vazdru could accomplish.

The Drindra came. What a sight *they* were.*

---

*While the name *Drin* may be roughly translated as meaning "they that have no women"—the Drin kind being only of the male sex—the subname *Drindra* would seem to mean "they that have no women—and no wits." This statement, while not strictly veritable, yet provides some notion of Drindra looks and personality.

Foremost stood a great clod-hopping thing with a lion's body, horse's feet, the head of an owl, and the tail of a pony—which tail was plaited with ribbons. It made noises harmonious with its appearance, but additionally vocalized the gabble-slang of the fellowship. There were also others, in the forms of bears crossed with bats or dragons, oxen with dogs, toads with goats and gazelles, and parrots having long hairy hind legs.

Azhriaz, seeing the sea king shrink in (laughing) loathing, addressed the Drindra twice over, once in their gabble, and once in the tongue of Tirzom.

"Valiant servants, you have braved the seas for me. Say who I am."

The ridiculous owl-lion spoke for the rest, who augmented its oratory by emphatic grunts, burps, and squawks.

"You are she that is *his* child."

Azhriaz glanced at the king, but the king, spurningly shrinking and holding his nose, evidenced either no understanding of the slang, or no belief in its import.

Azhriaz said to the Drindra: "Know me then. Now, take me hence."

At this, though she spoke only in the gabble, guessing a trick the king grew alert and his scholars with him, and they too began to weave glimmering sorceries in the air.

But the Drindra boiled and burbled. The lion-owl said in a hiss, "O Mistress, O Lovely One, it may not be. These are the oceans, and have other laws. For all your power, and ours, you or we can do nothing here that goes against *their* plans."

"Fools," said Azhriaz, with a lashing glance, so the Drindra rolled in a debauch of agony across the psychic urinations on the ground. "Go away then, and tell my father what you have told me. And say to Azhrarn the Beautiful, his daughter is here in threatened peril, and she requests he will come to save her from it."

At these words the Drindra entered paroxysm. They writhed and screamed and raved and hooted and brayed, until the mage-sphere quaked.

"Alas, alas," said the owl-lion, blushing with anxiety.

"*Alas?* Go do my bidding," said Azhriaz.

"No, it cannot be done," said the Drindra. "Alas, alas."

And so saying, in a storm of fur and feathers and uproar, they disappeared, and left her there.

Azhriaz waited a while in the silent chamber, and the black-green king of Tirzom Jum gave her space to wait, out of his victory.

No other demon manifested. The Drindra did not return. While their cry of *Alas*, their cry of *No*, these had somehow an all-pervasive meaning to be understood by any.

Eventually: "It seems he does not deign to come to you," said the king. "Or else, as you have said, he is—*busy* at other affairs."

Azhriaz pointed at the floor of the chamber. A brightness wrenched from her hand and struck the paving and cracked it. That she could do. But in another moment, one of the scholar-mages had muttered, and the crack healed, might never have been. This *they* could do.

Azhriaz turned. She went to the king and looked in his face.

"Behold, your captive," said the Goddess Azhriaz.

Some days and nights went by before they decided her fate. At first they kept her at the court, as an interesting freak. They mocked her, but she would not answer or seem to hear. Or sometimes she did answer more cleverly than they cared for. Finding they might tether her with spelled cords, they did it. She broke the cords. They retied them. She broke them. It grew tiresome. She seemed aloof, as if she lived within a pane of steely glass. They did not know if she was afraid, or angry, or in despair. They did not know if she feared them, or admired them properly. It seemed perhaps she did not. Her equivocal vulnerability infuriated them, and her useless powers, and her ugly beauty. She quickly ceased to please. Since such a captive could never be let free, what was to be done with the wretched thing?

The scholar in black and bones muttered again to his king. Azhrarn had not claimed the woman, yet patently she was supernatural. Best be a fraction cautious. Cast her down, yet leave a margin in offense. Do nothing irretrievable.

So, in the end, Azhriaz, the Demon's Daughter, the

Goddess-on-Earth, was thrown out of the palace of Tirzom
Jum, and left on the middle streets of the city, a destitute
foreign beggar.

The middle streets lay between the air of the dome and
the waters of the lower streets. Being neither completely
watery, therefore, nor aristocratically gaseous, they were
reckoned a slum. Here too were to be found the semimagical
tubes by means of which the air from above was cleansed
and revitalized, and the large cubicles via which it was
necessary to journey from the wet habitat to the dry one,
or the reverse. And in the middle streets, about these
valves and pipes and the inadvertent canals they sometimes
formed, the outcasts of the city lived.

Since the sea races were all descended of magicians,
even the lowest of the low among them had some magic
aptitude or skill. (For this very cause, the slaves of the
undersea regime were for the most part sub-breedings
between men and fish, or stolen human stock adapted to
the watery life. For the mage-aristos preferred the service
of beings that could work no spells, and had, preferably,
no true intelligence.)

The rabble of the bottom air levels of Tirzom Jum was
exotic. There were pride-stung illegitimates of the princes,
and revengeful lamenting legitimates flung from high places
for some crime, or by the connivance of enemies. And
there were schizophrenic half-blood Tirzomites, got by
mistakes with other peoples, some even with pale skins,
which made them targets for aversion and abuse.

Azhriaz fitted but too well inside the messy nest, and
made slight stir.

There was a sloping street that lay beneath the steep,
windowless, back black walls of three palaces, whose tops
flowered into apertures, and proper existence, some four
hundred feet or so farther up. High over the street crossed
bridges, where slaves teemed, day and night, on their
onerous duties. Sometimes they also dropped in the street,
when falling from the nightly star-lighting half a mile
overhead. The dwellers in the street found it easy to avoid
being flattened by these downfalls. One heard the screaming from a long way off, and the bothersome sound of a

fleshly object driving through atmosphere. The persons in the street took cover accordingly, though sometimes their possessions were crushed. The passage of a falling slave was never impeded by any of the bridgework: It repelled each flailing body by magic. The princes did not wish even their lower avenues to be spoiled by corpses. Once the body had arrived in the street and was still, there was a universal stealing out to rob the cadaver of any worthwhile thing. And in this way, the street in which the star-lighters fell so regularly was considered something of a prize.

The rabble of Tirzom was aesthetic. A man might barter a dish of food for a dainty carving, then the food-gainer change his mind, and clutch the other to him: "No, no, better hunger of the belly than a starved soul. Retrieve your slops, and return my valuable." Before the robbery of a dead slave, too, the thieves might pause a moment to consider the angle of its limbs, if it had died couthly. The facts were related presently to those who had the job of collecting such corpses and disposing of them. Most were fed to the octopus guards of the city, to help them keep a taste for man-flesh. Presumably those who had expired at a pretty angle fared no better.

Azhriaz built herself a house at the street's nether end. It was not made of debris, shells, or the hides of sharks, as were the other dwellings. It was made of bricks, and swank. What was solid she had formed by marshaling her powers, and then dressed it by the same powers to look every way grander than it was. The house had a white skin, and casements of painted glass in blue and deep red—the height of unacceptable unfashion in the green-black city.

"Who is that haughty subwoman?"

"She is a hostage-spy from some inferior nation. She came here in a ship of metal which is kept in durance, at the whim of our wonderful damnable lords, accursed be they, and blessed above all others."

"I have heard it said they could not best her."

"Nor could she them. Here she is. She cannot escape. She is trapped here forever."

"She has no gills and would drown in water."

"No. There is a tank in her house, large as a room and

full of sea, and she swims there submerged, or dances, and fish accept tidbits from her fingers. This has been seen through her windows.''

"She has said she is Vazdru. I think she lies, for I am not convinced there are such things as demons.''

"And I said a spell as I emptied my bladder against her house wall. The bricks are in reality black.''

"Also, however, urine turns to lilies where it touches them.''

The rabble began to visit Azhriaz in her queenly house.

So she entertained demoted sages and sacked lords— who wore tatters and behaved rudely out of gall. And thieves she received, who preyed on the higher city or the lower wet city, and who garbed themselves like princes and had such sumptuous social graces it was impossible to converse with them. And there came also exiles to the white-skinned house (which had every day more fair white lilies blooming on it, for insolence provokes insolence, and a great quantity of liquid was drunk thereabouts). All the exiles were pale, some green of hair, some blue, and some had fishy eyes, or were scaled, and one even had a fishtail under her long robe, though she pretended she was only lame and her litter-bearers had no tongues.

Azhriaz entertained each and every one with insulting illusory magnificence, like idiot children. Delicacies of the dry earth were served by unseen attendants. Musics played and the air dripped with fragrances of land, sandalwood, balsam, and nard.

One golden-green midday, a lord's mistake, aristocratically black, but dun of hair, came to Azhriaz and talked with her.

"I might increase your station," said Azhriaz at the fifth bowl of illusory but intoxicant wine. "Placed as I am, I cannot do it. But, when I am gone from here . . . Do you know of any way I might take a brief holiday out of Tirzom Jum?''

"You say,'' said the mistake, "you are a demon's daughter. Trapped here hopelessly, as you also are, do you long for the vile Underearth?''

"I do not," said Azhriaz, canceling the wine. "The viler customs here intrigue me more."

Later, when the greener afternoon began, a pale-skinned pale-eyed thief stepped in. His face was painted black, and his gills gilded.

"I have thought over your earlier question to me, regarding a holiday. That is superfluous, for I have decided to take you under my protection, when your every day will be a holiday of joy. You shall be my mistress. Since we are both blasted with pallor, you do not offend me so very much."

"How generous you are," said Azhriaz. "Pray go and be generous some otherwhere."

But in the green dusk of Tirzom, a young black man, with green dusk too for hair, approached the gate.

Up aloft the stars were being lit, and soon there came the shriek and rush of a slave falling to his death.

The princely visitor looked about. Several of the denizens of the street were hastening to move their valuables out of harm's way.

Louder and louder the impending rush of the fall, and thinner and thinner the cries of the victim, almost senseless with horror.

The black lord moved away from the gate of Azhriaz and out into the street's center. The rabble, who already stared at him for his hateful prefection, nudged each other. "*It is Tavir,*" they said.

The shadow of the falling one filled the street.

The lord raised his arms, spoke a word of power, and caught the slave in his grasp. To any but a magician it was a feat impossible. But to a magician, nothing so very much. He did not even stagger, nor shift from one silk-clad foot to another. He put the slave down upon the way, uninjured and gazing at him. The rabble were moved to unapproving impressed applause. The lord took no note of this, and little of the slave, beyond a nod. The fine green head was turned again to the gate of Azhriaz, and in another minute he had returned to it and entered the courtyard of the house. Azhriaz had come out on a balcony and looked down on him.

He bowed gracefully as a thief.

"Madam," said he, "may I come in?"

Azhriaz said nothing, but the door opened and stood wide.

8

*The Story
of Tavir's Dream*

"I AM TAVIR, a prince of Tirzom Jum. Because our high caste is so uniform in coloring and so symmetrical of physiognomy, to an alien we are often indistinguishable from each other. You will not remember me."

"Indeed that is true, that I do not remember you. But the lapse is due solely in my uninterest in the ways of your kind. You are, however, doubtless an intimate of your king. We shall not discuss my notion to holiday outside his domain."

Prince Tavir smiled. In his green locks were woven the blackest agates; on his black fingers and in the lobes of his well-shaped black ears burned the greenest agates. His shirt was vermilion, which was not the vogue at all.

"I had heard," he said, "the entertainment in this house was lavish."

Azhriaz clapped her hands. Stringed instruments rilled, incenses uncoiled from sudden lamps, pitchers of wine came sailing through the air.

Azhriaz clapped her hands again. All vanished.

"You will be entertained better," said Azhriaz, "by your king. Why are you here?"

"If you will indulge me, I will speak first of a dream I have had continually since childhood."

"Speak on," said Azhriaz, "my indulgence being immaterial."

But Tavir gazed at her and spoke seriously, as to a respected equal. And Azhriaz sparred with him no further.

Thus, he told her of his dream, which was this:

That he, a creature able to breathe both water and air, had drowned. There he stood, his lungs bulging with saline liquid and drawing neither in or out, and his skull seeming flooded too, yet not his brain. His mind worked on in a dreamy way. And it came to him he was a statue, fossilized to limestone, which had endured there in the depths for centuries, and was, moreover, one of a company. Like a crowd of petrified ghosts they were, feet planted in an old mosaic, and dimly, on the shores of sight (for the eyes of these statues did not move), were vistas of a wrecked palace. The ocean bustled in and around, and went off again, and with it fish, and long cold sea serpents. Sometimes some wandering aquamite would pause among the statues, and make its home in a convenient crevice—the dip between a woman's breasts, a fold of rocky robe or hair, or the cupped palm of a hand forever open. But even these slithery nomads did not remain. Altogether, the statue-Tavir concluded, this was no life for an adventurous spirit.

At last, the sense that he should leave his jail became so insistent that he made as if to run away. And in that instant he did run, and found himself at large and at liberty. At first this surprised him. Then he came to see that it was some mental or astral part which had slipped the leash. The stony body stayed behind, blank-faced, and would not look at him. He was glad to be rid of it. It was so good to move about after the endless years, and he darted through the sea, losing all awareness of place or time, or even of self, flighty as a fish.

How long this spree lasted he could not be sure. But after a while, he began to take note of things and to reason again, and he grew once more dissatisfied, and yearned for the expression, and the limits, of a fleshly container.

How to get one? He might invade the physique of some other, but who could guess what battle would ensue? To find some corpse and occupy that was not to be relished. Another means occurred to him.

He came on a city soon, and that city was Tirzom Jum

upon its cliff, beneath its dome—though at the hour he did not know its name, nor care.

Invisible and weightless, he skimmed about the place, and when he wished to, seeped in through the dome itself, and blew around the upper streets.

Now it seemed to Tavir, who in the dream was not Tavir, that he had been formerly a prince, handsome, and schooled in sorcery. Therefore he concluded he must be again a prince, handsome and a sorcerer, for old habits die hard. And to excuse this sameness he remarked to himself that he could be all that again and do differently with it—as before, let it be whispered low, had he not rather wasted his gifts?

Presently Tavir-not-yet-Tavir beheld a gorgeous girl carried in a litter. Black as night she looked to him, with reseda hair. Such a mold could only make handsome sons—

He followed the girl. He dared even, intellectual air current that he was, to sit in her lap and murmur *Oh, dear Mother!* to her from time to time. Then, however, the litter came to a mansion, and the girl was borne in. Who should greet her in an inner chamber but a stooped fellow, princely black and green as she, but missing most of his teeth and those remaining as black as his hide, while his hair was streaked by white. Worse, he looked on the girl and said: "Good day, Wife. I have been reading in my library— which is, as you know, my only pleasure—and the sage says this: 'How privileged the bride that her husband has not deflowered.' Are you not then gratified that I have laid not one finger on you, and that you will stay a virgin all your years?"

"Whatever you will," said the girl, listlessly.

But Tavir—and so he shall henceforth be called, for so he had now determined to be—Tavir flew up in the air like a wax bung out of a shaken bottle, and hitting the chamber roof, exclaimed: "Never, on my life!"

The aged pedant sucked his un-nice teeth and squinted at the ceiling. He was a sorcerer, naturally, and had detected something amiss.

"Can some air-inhaling fish have got in?" inquired he.

"Old fool!" raved Tavir from above. "I will show you

what a fish it is!'' And flapping down he gave the old man a sound blow. And though not corporeal, his shot had the strength of passion behind it, so the pedant leapt and clutched his nose. Waving a stick of carved black vitreous from some submarine lava flow as cooled now as his own, he cried: ''A haunt! Some fiend let loose by others' careless conjuration. Have I not warned you before, Wife, that you must curb your witcheries. *I* am the husband and *I* will work the magic. Go to your apartments in disgrace, and peruse there the improving books I have sent you!'' At which the lovely girl shrank and trembled and crept from the room. Tavir pursued her, pausing only to inflict upon the old pedant another savage blow. Leaving him howling, Tavir rose with the princess up through the house into some demure little chambers of great richness.

''Hush, Sweetheart-Mother,'' he consoled the virgin-wife, flitting affectionately about her. ''There are other men in this city.''

He remained concerned at her dejection until, having locked her doors by both key and charm, the black princess proceeded to arrange a spell upon the floor. And when the genie of it appeared, she stamped her foot and railed at it with some spirit. ''Did you not promise me a handsome husband and a handsome son?'' screamed she. ''Where are they, pray, and how much longer must I endure this *wait*?'' The genie looked abashed, but Tavir, ever resourceful, dashed into its open mouth, and by cleverly manipulating the big tongue against the palate and fangs, in proper rhythm with its attempt to speak otherwise, caused it to announce: ''It shall be done. By tomorrow's sunset, Fate shall rap the door.''

Then, leaving both genie and princess dumb with amazement, Tavir dived out again and so through a succession of closed windows, and through the city to find himself a suitable sire.

This deed was not so very taxing for Tavir. He merely selected from among the highest of the high princes of Tirzom Jum the wealthiest, best-looking, and most accomplished specimen, luckily wifeless. This prince was disposed to walk in his gardens, and Tavir accompanied him.

"You suppose," said Tavir, unseen, unheard, invidi- ous, "that you are happy. But you are not. Here you are, and no one by. Can it be your scholars and your friends now bore you? That your concubines no longer wake your pulses? But you are wise. This is safer. Go out into the city, you would find your heart's desire."

Now, though he was a mage, Tavir's father (and there is no use denying that is what he would become) was young, and did not always measure every act or idea. And so, sensing the import of Tavir's wheedling, the prince came to believe these fancies sprang from a sort of sorcerous intuition. And thus this educated and astute young man let himself be led like a bull by the nose.

Out into the city he therefore went, and so came, in a sea-green sunset, under the window of Tavir's mother (and no use denying that, either).

"Do not look up at that casement," exclaimed Tavir to his princely father. The prince naturally at once looked up at it. "Beware," insisted Tavir. "Your heart's desire lies in prison within. See her, and you are lost. Best leave the spot instantly." Tavir's father accordingly lingered in the street, beset by strange emotions.

Tavir then flew up the wall and into the room of the princess. He found her in the process of tearing to bits and burning the improving literature given by her spouse. Hast- ily blowing a white smut or two from her face, Tavir propelled the lady to the window: "Do not dare look out into the street. Your fate is below—"

So she reached the window and looked down with a wildly beating heart, and there she saw the prince looking up in much the same condition.

Soon she puts her hand to her brow. The prince starts forward. "Madam, are you unwell?"

"Quite well," she answers. It is a lie. The sword has gone in her heart. As for him, never was fish more hooked.

Just then a series of appalling crashes, thuds, and yowls shock through the house. Tavir is about other business, chasing the aged pedant around his library and hurling books and scrolls at his venerable head, now and then getting in a hearty bite with incorporeally impassioned teeth.

"Save me!" cries the pedant.

"Madam," says the prince in the street to the princess in the window, "you are the moon clad in black pearl, your casement is the east and you rising in it to give me light. I would say more about this, but I think your household to be in some trouble—" And so saying, he goes to the house door and thunders on it.

"Oh, fate," faintly says the princess.

The pedant's alarmed servants have already drawn the bolts and let in the prince, who rushes upstairs to the old fellow's assistance. Flinging wide the barriers of the library, the prince strides in.

"It is a conjuration—a fiend—" shrieks the pedant, perched on a bookshelf and batting volumes with his stick.

The prince utters an admonishing incantation. Tavir, who is not of course at all affected by it, with a parting kick, desists.

"My rescuer," says the old man.

"Her father?" asks the young one.

"Whose father?"

Prudently the prince falls silent.

At this moment the princess comes hurrying into the room, having combed her glorious hair and donned an attar of sea blossoms, to sink in a helpless swoon in the arms of the young prince.

"She is my wife," the pedant introduces her.

Much too late.

Mischief-maker Tavir, soul on the loose looking for harbor. Less to do now the wheel is rolling of its own volition.

But it is a fact, whenever the prince is from the house, the pedant is set on. No sooner does the young lord go from the porch than some servant of the old lord's must run to call him back. Or a messenger be sent across the city. At any hour of the day or night, the mad elemental is ready, to break and burn (even instructional books given one's wife), to rip and ruin, to trip and tweak and bonk and bang, and punch and thump and slap. And there are times when the only escape is for the old man to go out. Yes, out of his own house, for the persecution ends always at the door, just as so often it begins there. In the streets and parks, in the mansions of others, there is safety. When he returns home it is uneasily, and with mixed feelings does he find his rescuer so frequently already before him.

"I have lain in wait whole hours behind the fifth column in the annex where it sprang on you with the hot water," says the prince. "I have gone into each room, intoned the incantation, and burned rare incenses." Doubtless this is why he is so out of breath, and the virgin-wife out of breath for a similar reason, having dutifully followed him.

But it seems the young couple have a furtive glance. Why has the elemental never struck at *them*?

Well, Tavir has done a thing or two in that quarter. He has said to *him*, "Do not touch her. One touch leads to another." He has said to *her*, "One touch of his hand and you are will-less. Run away." And the young prince has touched her and the princess has not run away. And after much persuasion, denial, acquiescence, doubt—on both sides—and not even a prayer to aid them, since their kind does not reverence the gods, Tavir has had the smug joy of seeing them embraced upon a couch of spilled potions and unsaid exorcising spells.

And after this, all air and aspiration, Tavir keeps watch. While, all ire and perspiration, the old pedant does likewise.

And one night the princess is agitated, and Tavir peers in at her womb, as the pedant peers in at a window. Tavir's gaze passes easily through black pearl flesh and heart-of-apple bones, and sees in the sweet and secret inner room, a bud no larger than an eyelash's tip. The view of the pedant is impeded by a lattice.

(*Mine,* quoth Tavir, staking claim to what he has seen, unimpeded by anything, so all the wandering entities, wisps, and psychic wiggles in the cosmic crowd scene should be aware who owned the vacant lot.)

But the princess is revealing her delicate condition to the prince, who clasps his inamorata, and swears to protect her. "By a spell of my mother's," adds the prince, "I might rid you of this burden."

Rid? Burden? crows Tavir inaudibly, hitting against the ceiling once again.

Unwitting ally, the pedant chooses this moment to fall through the lattice.

"Villain!" says he to the prince, who is helping him up. "Did I not all this while suspect it was you yourself set that fiendly thing on me, to gain entry to both my house and my wife?"

And stick awave, he is howling now for his retainers, and so forces the lovers to flee into the night of sea-murmurous Tirzom Jum. From one rich house to another, richer, they go. And at the threshold of the second, the princess says to the prince, "Long since a genie divined for me that I should bear a son. It is fate."

Which leaves the way free for love and birth, and the bruised, battered, bitten old husband to instigate legal proceedings. And this, after some to-do, he does.

Worse than all other hurts, that one.

Spitting and choking with rage, the toothless pedant, before nine judges: "I divorce her, the ingrate. I divorce her, the slut. I divorce her, and the craven thief is welcome to the baggage." After which he went home to his mansion.

Tavir, who was by now nearing the end of his dream and vaguely guessed as much, had intended to hasten straight back to his mother—having decorously overseen the divorce. She was at this time big with the fine garment destined to be his. At any minute, it seemed to the anxious expectant child, the interior call might reach him. Then he must rush in and rouse the fetus from its soullessness, blend with it, and pass out with it to seek the light of life. Yet, something made Tavir stay awhile with the pedant, to see what he would do, and he had done indeed, only as imagined.

There he sat in his library, huffing and muttering, referring to this sage and that one on the inconstancy of women, their worthlessness and wickedness. Until, all at once he laid the books aside and tears rolled from his eyes, so the watching soul was astonished at it.

"Alas," said the old husband. "Now I am alone. Was it not enough that I must suffer the shame of impotence, which even my magic could not cure, then that I must meet her and love her in old age when I repelled her? Yes, bad enough, this. And the harsh means and words I used to conceal my shame and the lies I told her and the scrolls I misquoted, bad, too. But now she is gone, and I am a laughingstock, and will die loveless. I deserve no better, and no better did I get.''

Than Tavir, having had all his own way, was also ashamed. He approached the pedant quietly, and even so, from intuitive memory, the old fellow braced himself for some pinch or nip. But Tavir said at his ear, "Hush. Do not grieve. There is no death. In fifty years you will be younger than you are today, and there will be many loves to comfort you. Let her go; she deserves a life. Read your books and revel in your learning. Who knows but next time you may be the handsomest of all men—or," and here Tavir slyly smiled, "the prettiest of all women."

The pedant staunchly sighed, wiped his eyes, and selected a book of lore.

Then the calling sounded for Tavir, and leaping up he darted away—but even as he did so, he *woke*.

9

AFTER SHE had listened to all this, seated with her chin upon her hand, Azhriaz awarded Tavir a rare courtesy. She drew from a table a jar of sea-colored wine and poured it into two glass goblets. The wine was, or seemed, quite real. Maybe one of the rabble, who admired her as a quaint animal, had brought her the gift.

"A truth for a truth?" inquired Tavir. "You seem to say that you believe my dream is a reality."

"Perhaps."

"Because of this dream," he said, "I learned the unfairness of treating with others as if they are only shadows."

"And so pity cuckolded spouses, and catch down-plummeting slaves in the street."

"And reckon none should be held in our city against her will."

"I might leave at once," said Azhriaz carelessly. "Save, like you, I begin to dislike the shedding of mortal tears and blood. I will not make war on Tirzom."

"Nor will your demon servants, who are no altruists at all. Did they not tell you? You are a prisoner here."

"Unproven," said Azhriaz. But she poured the wine from her goblet on the floor, untasted, while in the goblet of Tavir the cool liquid began to bubble and smoke.

Tavir put the wine aside. "One other thing," he said.

"I thought," said she, "you would be all night coming to it."

"Upon your ship, which the lords here have taken from you, there is a sorcerous impression. Of a journey eastward. Of a human city smothered in sea."

"Simmurad. Where the immortals who defied Lord Death were turned to coral, even as they lived, and left to brood forever on the fact."

"And in my dream," began the Prince Tavir.

"You were at first confined alive inside a limestone case, in a sea-surged palace."

"Can it be," said Tavir, "my soul, refusing to be held within the stagnant immortal body, escaped it, and came here for rebirth?"

"What are souls? I have no soul," said Azhriaz. "I am Vazdru, an immortal myself. Nor did the immortals of Simmurad, either, have a soul left between them. Immortality devours the spirit, fusing it with the flesh."

"Is such a doctrine false?"

Azhriaz said, "Rather say to me what you mean to say."

Tavir glanced at the bubbling wine in momentary irritation, and spoke a word to it, at which glass and contents shattered into thin air.

"I am curious to look on Simmurad," he said. "But though my parents are entombed and I have no kindred to whom I must defer, the conventions of Tirzom and the edict of the king would not favor me in such travel. I should be prevented, and perhaps taken for an enemy of the state. Yet, now there is your sorcerous ship, capable of such speeds our own magicians are surprised. Once aboard, who could catch up with me?''

"My ship will not obey you."

"So I guessed. Nor are you able to approach it."

"I might," said she, "take on some illusion and go there at once, unseen by the guards of your king."

"There are other guards about the ship than fleshly ones. They would detect you. You know it, and have not gone there. Only a prince of the city, such as myself, could subdue the magics of Tirzom."

"I do not know," said Azhriaz, "that I am inclined to leave this charming domicile. I am quite comfortable. No. Let your princely brothers keep my ship they cannot use. I will stay here and live quietly."

"What is that sound?" asked Tavir, turning toward the outer door.

"Another hapless slave falling to the street? Go out and catch him."

But this was not the fall of a slave. Some other thing bore down on them, with a taut, rumbling drone. Presently the upper levels of Tirzom Jum quivered underfoot and all about. The foundations of the black palaces were vibrating above, and the street of the white-skinned house trembled as if in fear.

Then came a frightful booming impact. The walls of Azhriaz's building, of which she had just spoken so much praise, collapsed—as did those of a thousand other dwellings. The atmosphere itself had addled. Draperies and cups, things literal and phantom, burst through the air.

The outer wall having ceased to be, Azhriaz might look forth, and directly into the street, where a scene of mingled terror and astound went on, all under a peculiar light. Upward from the thoroughfare the palace-sides ascended their four hundred feet; beyond the dearly lit stars within the dome, and after these, and that, the sea, in which soft night had lain but lay no more.

There instead, plastered and flickering like a muddy fire all about the dome, was a type of burning meteor dashed from heaven. So huge it was, so ravenously ablaze, for some while you did not tell it had the body of a man—a giant man, all burned himself to bloodiest bronze, with darkly blazoned wings that beat, like ten hundred vultures, with hair like the many-rayed comet, his mindlessly beautiful and savage face pressed so nearly upon the encapsulated city, just as a pitiless child presses and stares upon a jar of ants. Oh what a face it was, alight itself with the great eyes of a storm. But worse than all, upraised through the sea, a red flame, blistering and sizzling, reflecting bloodstained glare upon the street and all the streets of Tirzom Jum: the swollen sword of the giant-grown Yabael, second of the Malukhim, a sword of blood and smoke coming down like screaming thunder on the city.

10

FIRE IN the air, fire in the sea. The earth cratered by it. The gods were angry. Or had been. Or had felt that they ought to be. A sword in the world's heart—

Deeper than the earth, however, deeper than the sea, and a little deeper yet, down into the shady demon country—what swords are glittering there?

See, like a sword, a male body in the black velvet sheath of a hill.

The eyes of Azhrarn were open, like two pools that had no floor. They mirrored, but did nothing else. The lids, the lashes, they never stirred. He breathed, so slowly, depthlessly, it was not evident. The pulses of demons, detectable by their own kind, were not detected by those three that guarded him still.

Once or twice, in what would have been the space of a day, an evening day of Underearth, one of these three would go out of the deep cave, from its recess of velure moss, through the curtains of creeper. Descending through the trees that clad the hill, the Vazdru warrior came to a stream where opals blushed and sang and sprang in the current like fish. Taking some of this water in a silver cup, the demon would return again up the hill, into the cave, and rest the cup against the mouth of Azhrarn. Perhaps, though liquid was not essential to demon life, the waters of Underearth were, to its inhabitants, restorative. Or possibly the act of moistening the lips, or of accepting the drink—had he done so—was a necessary symbol. But Azhrarn did not seem to drink, as he did not seem to breathe or to live.

They had brought him here, those three princes who stayed loyal to him in the face almost of the sun itself. At the gates of this land, summoning the black-blue horses, they had lifted him and carried him—and the skin of Azhrarn burned them. He had touched the sun-thing, the Malukhim. He had touched sunlight in a morning sky and fallen from heaven like a severed star—

As they neared Druhim Vanashta, its slender spires on the horizon, a presence blew upward in their path.

The horses shied. The Vazdru clenched their brows in maddened anger, for they had cause enough already to be desperate. The apparition was pallid, with eyes like cornflowers through a mist, and its golden hair hung down its back. If it was masculine, or a female, is unresolved. Some say it was the ghost of Sivesh, or of another youth who had been the beloved of Azhrarn. Or yet that it was a woman, one he had destroyed or ruined, who spoke in vengeful satisfaction. Others named it for Dunizel. Others said it was all of these persons, and more. To the frenzied demon princes, doubtless it took a form, perhaps out of history or the future. Or it may have been only a safeguard of Azhrarn's magic, autonomously alerted, in a shape of energy—shapeless.

It said: "Do not go on to Druhim Vanashta. Azhrarn's city is his city no more. They have said of him: *He is dead*. And now they say, *Let him be dead*. Others of the Vazdru have usurped him. Go elsewhere, wherever you will, but do not go on to Druhim Vanashta. His moon has set.''

At this message, the three princes of the Vazdru looked at Azhrarn, where he lay, to see him wake at once in coldest ferocity. But he did not wake. So they rode away from Druhim Vanashta, and into the dark countryside. They passed by the River of Sleep, where the leaden flax grew. Through meadows they went where crystal flowers brushed the stirrups, and over water where horses' hoofs struck like bright bells.

After much traveling, they selected a place which seemed to them suitable.

They laid Azhrarn inside the velvet cave, on a slab of rock they found there.

They stood guard thereafter, the three princes, one at the couch of Azhrarn, and one just within the cave mouth, both with drawn sword; while the third worked magic, a ritual which, with mankind, would have amounted only to a prayer. And at certain junctures, he that guarded the couch would take his turn at constructing this magic, or he at the cave's mouth would do it. And once or twice each twilit un-day, one of them would go to the stream where the opals sprang, and come back with water. . . . And so time passed, a great deal of it. Time in the Under-earth, time on the earth above, and nothing altered in or about the hill. Till time herself grew weary of making no impression there, and even she stopped calling on them. Not even the winds of the underworld blew by. And then at last even the three Vazdru ceased to do anything. They let ritual fail. They did not go out to the stream, and the cup was left on the ground by the creeper, and only the dew fell in it with an occasional silver *chink*. One stood at the head of the couch, and one at its foot. One stood just within the mouth of the cave. They leaned upon their swords and bowed their heads. Like icons they became, the Vazdru.

And *nothing* moved then. The blades of the grass, the foliage of the trees, each was static. There came to be a kind of substance which grew together over the cave's entrance, like a membrane.

Only the stream ran on below, with the opals prancing in it.

Once a cup was dipped in me, sang the stream, *a cup which had touched the lips of a young god*. For the stream, being untutored, did not seem to know the difference between the lords of its own country and the lords of heaven, nor between youth and immortality.

Who had *dared* take Azhrarn's princedom from him? Long long ago, when he had become cinders, they left the chair vacant, and lamented him the earth over. But he had loved them then; his cleaving to mankind was just a fad. Now, lovers unloved, they grew vicious, which condition was an art among the Vazdru.

He was of the princes of Druhim Vanashta, and he had dressed in yellow. And later, with eyes of cold yellow hate, he was a lion and clawed the soil of Azhrarn's garden, and cast in on the fire fountain there the first clod of dirt that smoored it.

This Vazdru lion sat now in his man's form, beautiful as night's morning at the heart of Azhrarn's palace, which was iron without, marble within.

His name was Hazrond. On his hands stared black rubies. No longer did he dress in the color of the abhorred sun, but in the sable beloved of demonkind. Yet the sable was slashed across the breast with one band of yellow silk, heavily fringed and embroidered with yellow jewels and metals (all but loathsome gold), topaz and amber and bleached bronze.

"Play," said Hazrond. And some of the Eshva came into the courts and smote the satin tongues of their seven-stringed harps. The songs were wonderful, and sad, as befitted the aftermath of a lord's demise. The Eshva wept continually and exquisitely. No one stayed them. Many Eshva did not come anymore into the city, but wandered the outer places, lost in somber dreaming, their wild hair harp-strung with silver snakes. They were the servants of the Vazdru, but Hazrond let them be. "They will return in due course," he said. His voice was so musical, the flowers which were dying, or attempting to die, in the gardens, craned their stems toward its notes, and started inadvertently to live again. The Eshva too raised their pale and flowerlike faces from their harps. Even far off, on the hills as they wandered, they caught the distant melody of that voice. In due course, they must, they would return.

The Vazdru were marvelous to look on, nothing in that. But of them all, Hazrond was of the most marvelous. Perfection perfected. They said, and it is not sensible to disbelieve them, that of all his caste, after Azhrarn, Hazrond was the strongest, the most gifted, the most fair. Like Azhrarn, maybe, as Azhrarn had been in the adolescence of eternity.

Thus Hazrond sat in the chair of Azhrarn, and paced about Azhrarn's halls under the caustic windows. He rested his long-lashed eyes, and tapped his long ringed fingers, did Hazrond, upon the books and adornments of the palace. He reviewed the hounds and horses in its yards. He waited high up in the needle's eyes of the towers, and gazed over the city like an eagle.

Now there is this to be mentioned too, of Hazrond, that he stalks out suddenly from among the Vazdru, into the mansion of Azhrarn, and assumes the palace and the city. But until then, nothing is said of Hazrond. Perhaps it was he that Azhrarn spoke to in the ruby street, pausing in the chariot to remark that no man saw love and no demon, either. And perhaps he had been often, this one, with Azhrarn, his charioteer even on the very night the Demon claimed back his daughter from the earth. And it is possible that when the yellow was donned in Druhim Vanashta, Hazrond had sought an audience with Azhrarn and stood before him slightingly. And Azhrarn, preoccupied, had dismissed Hazrond without comment. And there is one tale, told with hindsight, that when Azhrarn called the Vazdru to him, before he fought the angel at Az-Nennafir, Hazrond sent to Azhrarn a finely wrought sword budded with clear jewels, Drin work, and the sword itself had said: "Hazrond dispatches me to you and bids you look upon me as your defender, for he himself is engaged elsewhere." At which Azhrarn had cursed. And the sword had said: "Hazrond bids me say that he learned this tactic from his lord, Prince Azhrarn, who rules Druhim Vanashta in image only, his heart and mind being engaged elsewhere."

Yet one black flame from a black fire, Hazrond appears at once and there he is, upon the tower, his black hair streaming, looking about him like an eagle.

No other of the demons had opposed him. His method was simple. He walked into the palace and sat down there, and—word getting around—when his fellows came he nodded, and smiled upon them, as if never another had owned the house. Until there had been the whisper—*What of Azhrarn?* To that Hazrond had replied: "Of whom do you speak?"

Had they resigned themselves that the angel had vanquished their lord? Unarguably, no search was made for him through the Underearth, or above.

Slow but sure, the sad songs flowed away, and the wandering Eshva on the hills drifted toward the city. While, down by their sluggish lake, the Drin forges began to flare hotter than for a great time, and now and then the noise of squeaks and quarrelings arose there, as they made glorious presents to lay at the new lord's feet, Hazrond's feet, and then stole the items from each other.

And as for the uncouth Drindra, they were in a turmoil, for, enslaved by Azhriaz and summoned to her, they had not dared tell that her father, whose aid she invoked, was fallen farther than she. For Hazrond, doubtless he knew her straitened circumstances in the sea, and that the god-primed Malukhim had tracked her there. Had he wooed her once, and been rejected? Or did he only hate her as Azhrarn's child, a debased demon, partly mortal? (Mortal hatred being the fashion now, below.)

Certainly Hazrond did not trouble himself at the perils of Azhriaz.

"Play," said Hazrond, and the Eshva performed their voiceless songs, like nightingales of snow. And with the black wings of his cloak folded about him, Hazrond looked down from the towers of the palace.

11

THE SWORD of the angel Yabael crashed upon Tirzom Jum.

To those beneath it was apparent as a scarlet blast that smashed equally both ground and air. The buildings of that city tottered and went down. But the dome itself, its glass and sorcery riven, exploding, spewed up the world of atmosphere into the world of sea, amid a million pyrotechnics.

Azhriaz was cast upward too in a plume of black water, green fire, red steam, and debris of all sorts. Her instinct had been immediately to mesh herself within a bubble of breathable air. This she succeeded in doing, and in maintaining, despite the tumult, and presently she located herself inside it still, and Tavir with her, for a gallant impulse had caused him to seize hold of her, the moment the Malukhim struck.

For a minute or more, nothing was to be seen, or at least to be deciphered by either of them, beyond each other's outlines and the margin of the air bubble.

The ocean was in ferment. It rocked and collapsed and upheaved itself exactly as the city had done. Arrow flights of fish tore by, slabs of architecture, but mostly bloodied smokes. While beyond it all, the creature of destruction showed only as a dull red glare, where even the water *burned*.

The concussion had tossed them far away, Azhriaz, Tavir, that was the inadvertent helpfulness of it. And by this fluke of nemesis, many escaped. The angel itself, mindless golem that it was, stood over the blasted mousehole in a long interlude of triumph, and so the mouse it sought, the demon goddess of all mice, rode in the upsurge farther and farther to safety. They had been hunting, it would seem, the Malukhim, at least two of them. Who knows how this one—Yabael the blood-sworded, the vulture, the second scorched—how he learned to pierce the sea for her, but learn he did. And, worse than at Nennafir, unreasoning, he took a cleaver to a mote of light, missed it, and decimated all the other life around.

They swung now in the bubble, high up amid the greenest water, over which one might tell the distant earthly dawn was spreading her mantle. Their arms had stayed about each other, even their hair had coiled and clung, the magician-prince Tavir, the Goddess Azhriaz, for it was a fearsome thing they had experienced.

The bubble bobbed them into the top fringes of a wood of weed, and here, the sea quietening somewhat, they were able to rest. They looked back toward the city and its cliff, but neither was any longer to be found. Instead, the sea was full of unnatural scenes. Half a mile away there sailed by, like a strange ship, the upper tiers and cupola of a tower, seemingly unscathed, and in the cage of its long windows, Tirzomite sorcerers and scholars were soundlessly railing against fate. A mile off, whole stories spun slowly through the water, on the stairways and roofs of which, or what portions of these remained, lords and slaves alike scrambled about in fright. Nearer there passed a succession of islandlike gardens, or the treed walks of the city, coming unraveled, the great roots alone like trees. Among them three or four octopuses were forcing a way, darkening the sea with a panic of ink. And nearer yet came floating a princely bed with painted curtains, and lying on it like a black statue, tethered by her long yellow tresses, a dead beautiful half-breed, who had not possessed either the gills or the spells to survive immersion.

"Oh, alas," said Tavir, staring after her in grief.

"Blame me for it," said Azhriaz, sullen as a child. "I am the reason. The sun-thing lunged at me, and your city was only in the way."

"You are not the reason. The gods, as ever, are to blame.

"*I* am a god."

Tavir shook his green-haired head, and from his lustrous eyes, tears fell. Then Azhriaz wept also. They wept together in their little globe of air, which neither needed, while all around those they despaired for meandered by, some dead, some live and weeping too, for Tirzom Jum, nostalgic for the earth, had never lost the knack of tears. But the sea, itself all tears, the story went, the tears the gods shed eons ago at the evil of mankind, the sea scorned Tirzomite crying and drank their tears and filled their eyes again with its own.

As for Yabael, seen from the cover of the weed, he was just visible, for his giant height and girth seemed to have been lessened—voluntarily, or in the expending of power. There he loomed over a heap of clinker and glass, above a plain of broken spotted shells, and the smokes and sea-borne ruins revolved around him, and his wings rose flightlessly behind his fiery head, his soulless eyes saw nothing.

"Let me be gone," said Azhriaz, "before he wakes out of his dream of death-lust, and his masters tell him the stroke missed."

"Your sea vessel is exactly here," said Tavir. "Fate was on your side, for the disaster threw you down in this wood, close by."

"Yes, Fate is kin to me," said Azhriaz. "One may anticipate an occasional favor. Blessings on you, dear un-uncle," added she, with some venom. And then she whistled, like a silver pipe. And by some means not normal, the genies of her ship heard her.

It had been captive all this time, here in the wood of weed, and had never granted access, or a hint of its secrets, to Tirzom Jum. But flee it could not, nor come to the demoness, until, at the chime of destruction, the guards themselves, and all their magical accessories and provisos with them, fled cityward, or away to more secure climes. Now, released, and ever sensitive to the mistress it served, the ship came quick as a pulse through the weeds.

"I shall accompany you," said Tavir.

"Once the way is open, I believe I cannot prevent you."

So they swam to the porelike door the ship now offered, and in a few moments were inside the belly of it, among the fragrances and breathing carvings.

And while the angel still stood over the city's ruins, the great fish flashed away.

In less than an hour, some countless areas of distance lay between Azhriaz and Tirzom.

Tavir sat on a couch and grieved. Azhriaz would grieve no more. *Men are fools,* she thought, *and their magicians worse, and demons and gods more stupid than the stupid. Had I warred with them from the ship, I might have harmed the city, or their city done some ill to me. But I would soon have gone from it, and so the hunter would not have wrecked it for my sake. The thing that wished me slain slew them and liberated me.*

The genies had appeared in large numbers, as if to greet Azhriaz, or inspect her. She marshaled them to create soft music and to serve wines and dishes for a feast, all to tempt Tavir. But Tavir brushed the genies aside, and turned from the food and drink.

"These are no illusion," said Azhriaz. "Here, all is real. Or so we must suppose it."

"How can I drink, or lie listening to songs, when some thousands of my brothers are dead or dispossessed?"

"Go back to them, then," said Azhriaz. "I will let you."

"Permit me to stay," said Tavir, gazing at her. "I am an outcast now. Permit me to stay, for your loveliness is some solace to me. But permit me also to grieve."

"To you I am ugly," said Azhriaz. "As you are, in my eyes."

"This I do not credit," said Tavir. "For all the while I told you of my dream, you looked at me with excessive attention. And for yourself, any man not sightless would acclaim you."

"But you are grieving," said Azhriaz. And seating herself beside him she found an interest in an earring of his, which was green agate. So interested in it indeed did she become, she took the earring into her mouth, and so, too, the smooth dark lobe of his ear, and with her teeth she measured all the balance of it, how the earring was made, and next how the ear was made, and how they fit one into the other, and with her tongue she described for herself the ear, so finely channeled like some black shell, even with a pure black sea cave in it—and against her eyes lay his sea-green hair so she might think she lay upon a bank of fresh green grass, spiced with the spring of earth. And as she did these things, her hands found out his throat, which was like a column of black marble, but with a heart-sound drumming in it, and wide shoulders and strong arms the same, warm marble, and hands which caught at her hands, and letting them go, encircled her. And the hands of each moved upon the other then, as if they both would form the other out of water, or from clay.

Then they lay down together, firstly he black upon her whiteness and in turn upon the blackness of her hair, but in a while, she lay above him, pearl above jet above jade. Then sometimes he was a black bow upon a white bow reflected beneath him, or she a white moon's crescent over the black crescent of a nighttime world.

Now he had been an immortal, or thought so, and was at least a mage. But she was solar comet and midnight, and a demon, her only lover a Lord of Darkness, and for all her chasteness, she was Vazdru, and the Vazdru had invented love.

In the first phase of his pleasure, it seemed to Tavir that he rode a chariot of flame toward a gate of flame, but passing through the gate, he became fire itself, and yet rode on. And now he was winged, and he flew across the sky. He was the winged sun, and he held the earth in his arms, and that was the second phase of his pleasure, but the earth kissed him with perfumed lips, and drew him down by her silver hands. He plunged, and was a levinbolt, he was a sword that clove a city to its core, and his hair blew backward in the whirlwind's rush and his winged body blew from him—he cried out in an agony of joy and drove to the earth's center, the third gate, to die there—but did not die, nor was the flight ended.

Then, he held her still, by an effort of his brain, and he gasped upon that pinnacle, forgetting everything, even to his name, his nation, his sorcery. "Truly," he said, "you are a goddess," but he spoke only with his mind, for he had no breath for words upon that height. "This chase you lead me is for gods, not men. Let me fall, Azhriaz."

"Not yet," she said, and her eyes were cruel with love, all the earth's skies in them, and her hands moved on him, and at each touch each inch of skin, each bone, became a living separate thing which followed her in frenzy, and he could not remain.

So they traveled, and clung together, and wept, as in the terror of the city's death. And they were in ocean and in air, in the heart of the world, and the womb of fire, and deeper yet they passaged on, and going in at a fourth gate, and a fifth, and through a sixth, it came to Tavir that he was no longer anything, but All, earth, sky, sea, the sun, the moon, the day, the dark, love and death and quietude and war, innocence and erudition, immortal, finite, damned, forgiven, and delivered. And far away he heard his own cries flying under him like wild birds, and far above he felt his shadow smite the golden roof of his brain—but between, his soul flung free.

Thus to the seventh gate they came and through the gate they sped, locked and silent now, and scarcely moving in the body, while all else shimmered and spun, faster and more fast.

Tavir, Tavir no more, felt that his heart had ceased to beat, the clockwork of his flesh had stopped. And even Azhriaz was gone from him, or had become for him not only All and Everything, but Nothing, beautiful and utter.

Then came the eighth gate, and in the gateway he was stayed. Before him and within him boiled the total dissolution of all worlds, all space and time. He would no longer resist, yet he was reined, chained, anchored there. He yearned and strove to burst into a million shards, into stars and suns, into new worlds, a cosmos, the last scream of ecstasy, which none would hear, half formed upon his lips—but yet, but yet, the fetters would not let him go.

Then came a gentle murmur within him, a caress far lighter than a leaf. And he was still once more, ceased to travel, to strive, and only waited. And from infinity, unsought, the ninth gate itself came upon him, rushing through space, like a wave which breaks, and he broke, shattered, and the universe was born of him.

Senseless, wrung and cleansed, he lay in the arms of Azhriaz and did not know he lived, and was only a man and a mage. Nor did he grieve any longer for anything.

But Azhriaz lay quietly, and perhaps she did grieve. For to the demons, who imparted such pleasure, pleasure had not the value of the shock it rendered mortal fiber. It could not stun them, nor surprise. And so it was for them a little less.

So she lay with her lover, thinking well of him. But her tears fell again, with none now to comfort her.

The fish-whale-ship dazzled on, having nowhere else to go but drowned Simmurad, one more city that had been cast down.

Through sea and time the vessel ran, quick as thought, or only quick as a great fish-mammal breathing in and out. And often now its glowing eyes had each a watching pupil, Tavir being one, Azhriaz the other. Or else the pupils were away, practicing the arts of love—not only in the demon climacteric, but in various delightful human forms. (And the first terrible grandeur was never quite repeated; such things seldom are, since after the first all must be compared to that first, and besides, as is sometimes the way of the most accomplished lovers, Azhriaz was thereafter more and more easily bored with ecstasy.) And they discussed and debated, too, and played games of learning. And they squabbled. All of which was of interest to them.

The genies meanwhile flitted about and saw to the luxurious rudiments of living.

And beyond the skin of the ship lay the sea, always.

But the sea they now went through, Azhriaz and Tavir, began to have an emptiness, not merely of fish and aquatic beasts, but of all robust things. Huge forests of weed and coral grew there, it is true, massive flowers bloomed, the currents ran, but each with a kind of deadness. And where they might glimpse a fish, it shone like a tinder, and all the rest seemed flat and cold against the slight ignition.

It had lain in the farthest east, Simmurad, and lay there yet, at the world's dawn corner.

"Will the vengeance of heaven seek me even there?" Azhriaz asked her sleeping lover. "And does Dathanja wander the sunken streets under the water, looking at what Zhirek did for Death?"

"O Mistress, tomorrow, when the sun above rises, we shall come to Simmurad." So the genies announced, in concert, journey's end.

Simmurad, once the red rose, cameoed from crimson rock and white mountainside. Simmurad, an anemone now, bottled in brine.

They came to it in the sea-dawn, sea-dyed morning that had been rose-dyed when the city stood on land. Yet it was most often dawn here, even now, the prolonged sunrise of the easternmost edge.

The demon ship entered the city slowly, barely breathing, eyes wide and both attentively pupiled.

The gates of brass had long ago come down. But in any event, traffic might advance over the walls, as the tide had done. The high towers, and the higher mountains, the ocean covered all their heads. And the vast plazas and the terraced walks, the parks where ever-living deer and leopards had sported, they were no more than bowls of water. Not only everlasting immortality, but mere life had gone from Simmurad. Its proper colors had been washed out, so the glimmer of outer sun, or even the lamps of the ship, did not wake them. And the stone itself, endlessly mouthed by the water, had worn away. Not a monument or a carving was distinguishable. The pristine columns and spires, they were like melted candles.

From a mass of kelp and primeval fern, an unburnished dome or two stubbed forth. By a matted doorway was the stump of an obelisk. Centuries before, there had been letters in this pylon. A message was, after some pains, still to be discovered there. It read:

I AM SIMMURAD.
HEREIN FOREVER, DUST.

"Is it always so," asked Azhriaz, "that men must be ridiculed by their own legends?"

Tavir stared silently.

Azhriaz said, "This wonder is finished, and we shame it to gaze on it. We will depart."

She was angered, and disappointed, in many dissimilar forms. But Tavir said: "Humor me, and the recollection of my dream. Let us at least remain here until one day and night have gone by. To do less is to add another shame to the place. Besides, it was a long journey, and beyond is world's end, at the eastern edge. Only chaos lies over it, where men will not or cannot enter. In the face of such a symbol, it is only correct to linger, before turning back."

"I would not stay another minute," said Azhriaz.

But, to humor him, she did not urge the ship away.

They continued to patrol the avenues all that long, weary morning and dismal afternoon, looking on desolation, and the vanquishment of human ideals. Nothing was to be seen that lived, for even the most embryonic fishes of that deep kept aloof or had been scared from the vicinity by the ship. Only a facsimile of life, their own bold shadow, moved beside them on the rotted walls, or sometimes some splinter of a bloodless jewel might leeringly wink at their lights.

No man strode or swam about the streets. Not even a ghost cared to haunt the ruin. Sigh then, as the songs exclaimed, for the decline of Simmurad.

And Tavir himself, for the princes of Tirzom were accomplished, had summoned for himself a lyre, and sat there melancholically singing in the fish-ship's left eye.

> "*The glory is crumbled in dust,*
>   *the swords of delight sheathed in rust,*
> *And off from the precipice thrust,*
>   *the scapegoats and saviors fall dead.*
> *Behold now the wreck of our lives,*
>   *the honey spilled out from the hives,*
> *The pageant of Hate and his wives,*
>   *in their garments of choler and dread.*
> *Beseech then no gods—they are blind;*
>   *destroy that poor hope of the mind,*

Kneel rather to stones in the wind
      and ask them for music and bread.
We have woven our dreams for a cloak,
      our bright towers we have mortared with smoke.
It is Death, it is Death we invoke,
      and the wolves of his pack we have fed."

At which Azhriaz, turning to speak to him in unfriendliness, started. For where Tavir had sat, all sea shade and dark, was another young lord, pale, gold-haired, in a damson garment, with gloves—

But before even she could catch her breath to curse him, the vision faded. *Unreal,* thought she, less friendly yet. *He roams elsewhere, cackling and cawing. But I take due note. Surely the apparition implies my lovesome lover, touched by the dawn-decline of Simmurad, is making a pet of madness.*

Therefore she did not upbraid Tavir, but she keenly observed him. *Of course, he will in some way betray me, abandon me. When I look for a shield, or a brother, to defend my back, all they that swore to be beside me are gone off on errands.*

"There are knives in your looks," said Tavir. "Knives of fairest sapphire. But still knives."

"If my eyes do not please you," said Azhriaz, putting her hands tenderly about his neck, "close them with your kisses."

This Tavir willingly did.

Their amorous dalliance concluded the day, and seemed to put out the sun. Sunset was so swift in that region, one moment the sea was green, then ashen, then black.

Azhriaz, who had held Tavir as a flower holds its own shadow, now let him go and pretended to sleep. She had sensed, even in the pangs of his rapture, a restless energy that was not wholly appeased.

Presently, as she had supposed he would, Tavir, despite the most adoring of parting embraces, left the couch, and went away through the suite. The sorcery of Azhriaz was always unhampered within her ship: She stole after him smaller and less visible than a mote of that glory-dust he had elegized.

Soon enough, he stood next the ship's skin and craved of it an exit into the sea. And the ship, commanded by Azhriaz to obey him, did so. In a short while more, Tavir was speeding through the blackness of the drowned city, airlessly and effortlessly breathing in the manner of the gilled princes of Tirzom, and accompanied only by a tiny glow of phosphorus, which he had enchanted from the water to light his path.

Azhriaz was filled by anger, and the unhappy satisfaction of being in the right. She took up her own sorcery, with two or three sharp words besides, and clad herself, still little as a mote, in a second mote of air. Then she sprang after Tavir and the receding light.

If Simmurad was sad by day, how much more depressing in its robe of night. It was no place for poets, though songs had been made because of it. True despair is only a blank wall; there must be rage or foolish hope, or at least a shout, to make anything of it. But Simmurad. Oh, Simmurad.

Yet Tavir swam on, and Azhriaz went after. She foresaw his quest. Of course, he went to find the one he had been, or believed he had been, if his dream were a fact.

So, in an hour or less, they came again to that dissolved obelisk, and passed through the tangle of sea wrack (Tavir hacking the way) into the citadel.

There had been a domed vault, a floor of mosaic and silver. Fountains had played, and at great tables, the nightly feast of the immortals. . . . Now the water feasted. All was blurred by water. And a tainted severe light fell, from high up, like a rain through rain, where luminous filaments embroidered the dead choked windows.

Caught by the unmerciful gleam, here they were, the immortal ones of Simmu's city. They had won their slice of eternal life by feats of wizardry, wisdom, or exotic cheek, surgeons and mages, artists and courtesans, the luscious, the cunning, the unhinged. Now, they were white coral. Simply that. For these miniature builders of the seas had been industrious over the centuries. No longer was any shape recognizable, not a feature, nor a gesture. They were limstone blocks. Where now the flaunting dreams? The water washed away, the coral makers built. Soon, even the legend would fade, and those that came here seeking it—they would find melted stones, a few lumps of the coraline detritus of the sea. They would say, Simmurad, that was some lie we were told. There is no Simmurad, was never such a place. Nor Simmu, and no theft from heaven of Immortality for men, no heaven either, no life eternal. Only this and here and now. Only what we see and can put our hands on. Would there not, otherwise, be evidence?

Tavir, having come in, let his torch die. He moved as if he swam in sleep, about the limestone pillars. It seemed he did not especially remember any one of them. Should he seek for one in particular, how would he find it?

There was a means.

Suddenly a voice spoke out loudly, there in the sea—through which, unless sorcerously aided, you could hear nothing at all—sorcerously then.

"Well," it said, "is liberty good? Pray tell me of it. I forget."

Tavir, quite naturally, turned and stared about.

"Here I repose," said the voice. "On your right hand—" And it directed him zealously on how it should be come at. Tavir followed the instructions, and after a minute he hung in the water by a pillar of coral resembling exactly all the rest.

"How is it you can speak?" asked Tavir, himself not with his vocal cords, but through the mechanics of sea magic.

"Speak? Who says I speak?" retorted the voice. "I impart my thoughts by an effort of magicianry, as do you. Do you forget also? I am a mage."

"By my query I meant to inquire," said Tavir, "if I am you and you are me, how is it I am here and you are there, and we have dialogue?"

"Tush," said the coral block testily. "It seems certain that when I waned to youth again, as you, I gained in silliness what I relinquished in years. Pay attention. For this is the mighty theosophic paradox which I, and other genius sages that the monster Zhirek trapped here, long since grasped. All men possess souls which are immortal. But some men prefer longevity or eternality of the body, seeing that with each new life we are forced to undergo once more the idiocy of birth, childhood, and unknowledge, not to mention the discomfort of physical demise. For example I, that am you as you were when me, joined the immortals, partaking of a drop of the divine Elixir. Now, it is thought," prated on the block, "that in a mortal made immortal, the soul infuses the flesh. This may be the case. However, by petrifying the flesh to stone, Zhirek, in his overcleverness, separated the soul in each of us once again from the earthly atoms—for no soul can ever be bound indefinitely, being itself a fabulous thing. Therefore my soul flew out—as, for a truth, did all the souls of all those prisoned in Simmurad. And, getting itself reborn, it became the dweller in the body of one Tavir, prince of Tirzom Jum, and of a scheme of colors, I will say, strikes oddly on my eye."

"But you," said Tavir. "If you are not me, who, upon the bones of our two mothers, are you?"

"Your former body being immortal, it lives still within the coral. It is a wise sage yet, and has, to boot, the full legion of your former memories, which you, in your greenness, have forgotten. It is the body, therefore, which speaks so graciously and intelligently to you, and which calls itself *I*. As I shall continue to do."

"Upon my life—or on one of them," said Tavir. And fell silent.

"Tut, tut," said the immortal body reprovingly, "if only you had your sagacity back, you would not waffle in this way."

"Recount to me then," said Tavir, "your learning. It is mine by right."

"Not so," said the body in the coral. "By your decision to seek rebirth, you have forfeited anything of mine."

"But had I not lived in you, you would have learned nothing!"

"And now you have vacated me, you must learn all again, by dint of labor and groans," replied the body, with the utmost complacence.

Tavir struck his fist in rage upon the block. The motion was slowed by water, yet its intent was bruising, and so bruised. The coral complained.

"I have learned this," said Tavir, "to respect the life of others. I believe you to have been indifferent to all lives but your own."

"You," said the coral in an injured tone, "have merely acquired sickly sentiment, a fault it had previously taken you many years to be rid of."

"You do not know me; do not presume."

"And you do not recollect; presume neither."

"By my spells, I can return within you," said Tavir, "and experience again what I was, and collect up any superfluous knowledge you may, debatably, retain."

At his threat, the body in the coral turned uncommunicative. Tavir, with a grimace, between fascinated interest and deep chagrin, drew aside a way, and began to prepare himself for such sorcery as would be needed.

Azhriaz was not far off, and had listened to all that went on. Now she could have wished to transform herself to her proper feminine shape, but she believed this must entail an airless passage in the sea, its laws being as they were and inimical to her. So she did not venture change, but went to Tavir as she was, a tiny little mote in a teardrop of fragrant atmosphere.

"Tavir," she said, sending her words into his brain, for his ears would be deaf to her, "do not reenter the coral. Only consider how you have dreamed of the imprisonment, and how that dream has lured you to the spot. Now the thing taunts you, and you are driven to become its prisoner again—that which was your prior body has the stronger claim; there you lived the mostest time, and, too, it is immortal and endures, and even speaks of itself as a proud man does—"

But Tavir did not heed, and perhaps he did not hear, for now he made a magic that shone about him much brighter than the luminants in the roof. And even as Azhriaz warned him, there came a swirling, and a flush as if a huge lamp took light. And then it fluttered out, and only the marine half-light lingered.

Azhriaz, who had known and wielded such power on the land that men cowered in terror at the mention of it, now looked down and knew herself powerless. Tavir lay on the smeared mosaics and silver of the floor. The water fingered his hair; his eyes were shut. The soul had gone, back through the coral into the former body, which it knew better, and which had signaled and called and finally pulled it in by a long fine leash.

"I have been then a servant," said Azhriaz. "My purpose was to bring you here, to this, as your charioteer would have brought you, or your riding ass. And for payment I have had three kisses. My thanks, Tavir."

"My name," said the voice from the coral, "is not *Tavir. That* is Tavir, there on the ground. As for kisses, he kissed you well. I have his new memories to add to the old. But that life is only a mirage. It has been joyful enough to be a youth, and spry and agile in the horizontal art, but age and immobility have their compensations. The adventurous existence will inevitably pall, for the man who thinks."

"Traitor," said Azhriaz. "I will not attempt your rescue. Lie on the floor, greenlocks, and rot, and lie and *think* in your coral, and rot also. You are one more fool."

And when she had said this, Azhriaz saw the corals and the water and the whole dim hall begin to flush again with light. A most poignant excitement went through her, for she imagined Tavir was fighting his way back to her, and she eagerly braced herself to help him. But then she saw, with a heart-sinking not only due to sorrow, that this light was not the same as the first. It came thick and fast, as if wine or blood was poured. It had a reddish glare. The moon or the sun, rising under the sea—

She knew what it was. She felt a strange dark fear, and also a wretched wish to yield herself—and with that an urge to do battle. And again the despair of Simmurad, and of all her confused and blazing years, mired her round, and she hesitated, questioned herself, whether she might be lost.

But it was not in her, after all, to do nothing. And so she spun about, and away from the ghostly ghostless citadel, toward the only chance to hand, the demon ship.

Chuz had failed her, and Azhrarn had dismissed her. Of mortals, Dathanja had barely spared her a glance, though her beauty rocked the world, and for Tavir—Tavir was dead.

How loud the deathly avenues were glowing now, as if they burned there in the sea. Azhriaz fled into her vessel, and next the vessel fled. For behind the reddening of the water, on her scent, came again Yabael the Bloody and the Second-Scorched, that hound of the gods, the hunter.

12

BUT IT WAS Ebriel who walked the mountaintops of the eastern corner.

There were higher crags beyond Simmurad; the sea had not covered them. They overlooked the basin of the ocean, and reflected in it, that was all. When the long dawns warmed them, they beamed, but there was something disquieting in them always. Their peaks masked, and maybe led to, the world's very edge. They were a part of the last fence that ringed the earth. Who could tell what it would mean to travel over them and to the end of them—who could risk the venture?

Even the angel restricted his pacing, he kept to the inner places, though World's Brink, and chaos itself, could surely be nothing to him.

The sunset came and went quick as a careless kiss. Night and a few spare stars tricked out the sky.

The Malukhim gleamed on in the dark. He seemed to be looking down into the ocean, as a man looks for the rising of fish.

"You are not waiting there for me," said Dathanja, as he came up the midnight mountain slope, "but it is I who arrive."

The angel turned, and now looked at Dathanja. Even in

blackness, the eyes of Ebriel *shone*, for the light remained within him constantly.

Dathanja came on. He approached the angel, nearer and more near, until he was within three feet of him.

There were many powers left to Dathanja. He used them. He said:

"Ebriel, do you stand in my way? There has been a conflict. Let us not reenact it, inadequately. I am no demon. And you are not the mightiest of the Sun-Created; you are not Melqar, who came from the fire last."

Then Ebriel, with a whisper of his wings, moved aside. It was a gesture of economy and beauty. Dathanja went by him, and reached the crown of the slope, where the mountain opened to loom above the lake of sea.

He was still a mage when he wished it. He cast his mind into the deeps, like a line. His thoughts, nothing else, walked under the ocean, and through that sunken city there. He, too, had learned economy.

There was a lurid radiance down below. He perhaps did notice it, but gave it no attention, though, all the while, it heightened. He had other business.

The awareness of Dathanja came then into a hall, where there were columns of coral (flushed now very red). And there began to be a stirring in the water.

Zhirek, it said, in several voices. *See how the murderer slinks back to gloat on his legendary deed.*

The thoughts, the mind of Dathanja, ignoring that too, went about and scanned every column with care. A multitude of personalities responded, chaffering and beguiling. But they lived in the limestone as snails do in their shells, and were comfortable: They had evolved their own destiny. It was not these upon whom he had worked the vengeance of King Death. And of the eternal souls which he had incarcerated, all were gone. But one.

And this one presently came and tapped him, as it were, on the shoulder, a human mind and thoughts like his own, essence and personality together. "Here I repose," it said, insufferably. And, once the inner eye of Dathanja regarded it, it added, "You are not as you were. I observe your sense of debt. You must set me free then."

"I accept that I must."

"And at once, *if* you please." In some hundreds of years, in one sort or another, this being had stayed used to getting its own way.

Nothing was said, either, of the feelings of Uhlume, Lord Death, in whose name the work had been accomplished. There would seem to be some assumption a few centuries had healed his wounds.

Up on the mountain, Dathanja murmured.

Below, from the russet dimness his awareness glimmered out.

"Wait, you dog!" snapped the personage in the coral. As the trap split, it was disgorged, and flailed with blathering outcry into the ocean. "Oh base jackal! I cannot swim—" But next a recollection, for what had he been, this one, in the interim, but a gilled sea prince of Tirzom. So, out of the depths of Simmurad the final captive floundered, breathing water and not breathing it, drowning and not drowned. Vestiges of immortality still on him, just, yet no longer an immortal, soul cut loose, returned, staying separate: a testy, cunning, age-old refugee. "How red the sea is. Was the sea here always red? Not so. Something is afoot. Some angry reddened rushing thing. What does Tavir make of it?" (Thumping and leafing through that relinquished body's memory, as if through a muddled library. Followed by an outraged shriek and more energetic labors to surface.) "The angel—the brazen destroyer— oh, you dog-jackal of a Zhirek, to desert me here—what release is this you give me—"

Dathanja, calm as the night, the Malukhim, day in night, they beheld something plump up through the skin of the sea, far below. It bobbed and sank, it scudded and blundered and shook its fists. Then, remembering, it howled a phrase of the ancient thaumaturgy that had once earned it a niche in Simmu's city—and was vaulted high into the air on a carpet with chicken wings.

In a trice, sage and carpet pelted down between the sorcerer and the angel, squawking.

The dialogue was lost. For at this instant, the sea began to cook.

Thunder bellowed from the horizon. The air bristled. A sun of darkest fire arose. Like blood boiling through a vein, the apparition of Yabael came tearing through the water, beneath it, invisible, save as a running gash of ravening scarlet with something man-shaped, vulture-shaped, the gouging beak of it. The mountains shook to their roots, and everywhere avalanches teemed down to splash into the seething ocean. Steam gouted, the waves leapt toward the sky in fear. The world seemed on the verge of ending—

Then it had passed. Like a terrible fever, it drove away, under the very land itself, the crags, all that redness, the bloodstained flare and noise and shuddering. The sea dropped back on itself, turning black. The boomings and moanings died. A quiet fell.

Ebriel had folded up his silent whiteness. Dathanja looked away where the thing had gone, toward the farthest east. The rescued sage was dumb.

As for the chicken-winged carpet, in affright it had laid an egg upon the ground, and leaving it motherless, vanished.

The final sea. It ran under the basements of the mountains. It was the only road. She fled by it, the lost Goddess in her demon ship.

And she knew, flying east and ever east, that there was a limit to her flight. If she had not known, the genies had started up to explain. They foamed about her now, those smoky creatures, as if something were burning. They clasped their slender hands, and their childlike faces were full of woe. They had no nervousness for themselves. It was for her they misgave, presumably, because they were her slaves, and that only proper.

"O Mistress. The earth's edge. The sea flows out beyond the mountains to nothingness and otherness, into the limbo that surrounds the world."

"Exactly," said Azhriaz. "And there is nowhere else to go. Since Simmurad, the channel is too narrow—to fly north or south is to crash against the submarine mountains that abound here. To turn back is to meet red death headlong. May we fly up in the air? The spells of this vessel preclude it. Shall I try alone? Oh, how swiftly then would the destroyer catch me, closer to heaven wherefrom it took its life. But this way, eastward, as you say, is the unknown horror, the opposition to all earthly-living things—

therefore also to that which pursues. Even the Malukhim will be discouraged, and draw back.''

But the hunter did not do this. It came on behind like a long roller of blood.

Azhriaz herself withdrew from the eye-windows of her ship. It moved so speedily, like lightning, she could tell very little from the view. She prowled the exquisite belly of the fish-whale. She ordered music, and a feast—the melodies were weird and unharmonious, the food was slops and the wine smoldered. She tried to envisage the boundary of the world. To believe in it. She was not afraid. She was terrified. She had no fear at all. ''Chuz,'' she said, ''I am your subject, too.'' And she threw the melting writhing apples of the feast against the walls where the draperies whined and tore. And she bit her beautiful nails, like a frightened mortal girl.

The ship sped on, through the last channels of earth's eastern ocean, under the mountains. There was no light down there. Even the water was not quite fluid. The ship began to rustle and to creak in all its joints. The magical lamps expired one by one. The music had the sound of distant screaming.

''O Mistress,'' said the genies.

''Be still. If I am to bolt into chaos, then so must that thing which hunts me. Come, sun-hawk!'' called Azhriaz into the flickering far-screaming motion, into the deaf un-sea behind, the sightless question before. ''Follow, enemy. *Follow*, and chaos shall swallow you, too.''

Suddenly the genies disappeared. Not a wisp of them remained. And then a ghastly rattling din resounded through the ship. The ultimate lamps died like flowers which break apart.

Blackness came and sat in the ship and in the eyes of Azhriaz, and blackness smiled and said to her: Now look about you.

But Azhriaz covered her eyes with her hands.

Then every noise stopped. The ship grew soundless. It grew motionless. It hung suspended.

Azhriaz kneeled down. She held her breath.

She could never die. Yet death was so close. No relative

of hers, no handsome uncle who might bargain. True death, the facts of it. And she was alone.

Then there was a bang that seemed to crack the world itself. And the ship soared upward—so fast that everything was left behind, the metal bodywork, the magical rivets, flesh and bones—and faster and faster, until even thought and breathing lay crushed beneath—and she heard, the black-haired girl alone in blackness, miles off and eons under her, her own voice crying out, like the voice of the infant that still she was and yet had never been: "Mother—O my mother help me! Mother! Mother! O my mother!"

But untenable Nothingness or Somethingness had closed upon the ship. Chaos, or whatever chaos was at the hem of the earth. It gripped, and even as it gripped, it recoiled.

Mother help me—

And now the ship plunged downward, as if into a bottomless abyss. Or into one.

This is death. And I cannot die. I shall live death forever—

A hand held the ship. A hand so huge, so vast, the ship lay tiny there as a shell upon a beach. The hand, weighing the ship, its contents. It could not be a hand at all. Nor, in the black, a face, stooping, staring, somehow seen unseen. Two eyes whose centers were the spinning voids that had no name, have none, the depth from which the seeds of matter spring, the toiling of planets unborn, the sleep of worlds that are done. The tinder box of life, the eyes, empty and full and overbrimmed and open wide. And the face in profile now, its brow all time, its features shifting like pale sands along the slope of space. The mouth breathing out pale flame, a word, a wish. And the hand curving back, as the hand of a boy might curve to fling away a little stone—

But as the hand rises, the great sleeve comes with it, a curling wave with the galaxies caught in the folds—

And under the colossal curving and curling, a redness is running, directly there, like a torn seam.

The great sleeve sweeps over to meet the running red of the tearing seam, meets with it, envelops. Fire and unfire curdling and a million stitches coming undone.

There was a moment of pure electrics, coronas, sunbursts, novas. Each one voiceless and without color. There-after there commenced a deep soft thunder. It stretched and mounted and passed through volume, into a sound that was no sound at all.

Soundless then, the eruption. The world arched its back, the sky leaned. For a second all matter heaved toward oblivion, or new life, which was the same. (Even heaven cratered supposedly, and flakes of sky scattered like plaster.) And then the balance swung again. Smoothly, every-thing came to rest, like a gentle wheel which runs down.

Shaken like a bag of salt, earth's substance settled. Like salt, every grain in a fresh place, yet salt still, thinking itself unaltered.

And the huge hand, with nothing in it now, returning into the forms of unform from which it had conceived itself. No eyes to see, no voids of spinning things. Seeping away. Ceaseless. Ceased.

To the ends of the earth, in the remotest places, drowsy, half asleep, the rumor yawned and sleepily said, Some-thing has gone on in the night. But nothing had happened, surely, for the world looked no different. The trees wore their necklaces of fruit, the goats gave up their milk, now and then with a kick to go with it, the young girls combed their hair and put blossoms and beads in it. The wise men, poring over their scrolls and globes of quartz, in tall towers, shook their heads, puzzled, dissatisfied.

If all are changed, who will feel change in the air?

Is mankind safe? Yes.

Is the world whole? Yes.

Is the earth still flat? It is.

PART THREE

Under the Earth

1

HAZROND, Prince of Demons, took on him, for diversion, the shape of a great black eagle. East and west he flew, beating with his vast wings, north and south, to the four edges of the world. He watched the lighted processions of men crawling by below, and crossed, with a cool glance, over the high stone pylons of cities. Once he folded his inky wings on the roof of a temple. "He has not taught you anything, then," said the wings, the feathers, the eyes—everything but the voice of Hazrond. "Even he, Azhrarn the Beautiful, with his educational plan. But mankind cannot learn. Behold, dead lord, they are still worshiping the gods, though they know now the gods care nothing for them."

An hour before the sun should rise, Hazrond returned to the world's center, and thence under the earth. Through a gate of agate he passed, and a gate of steel, and a gate of black fire. He strode into Druhim Vanashta, and taking out a pipe shaped like the thighbone of a cat, he blew on it. At once a demon horse came galloping and Hazrond leaped on its back and rode, faster than any wind of the wide wild world, to his palace. There, lying supplicatingly across a mighty doorsill, Hazrond found a little Drin.

"Mercy, glorious one!" said the Drin.

"What have you done?"

"Nothing, yet, alas. For my mere existence I crave your pardon."

"I do not grant it. Why are you here?"

"It seems to me," warbled the Drin, "I have lain in the earth hereabouts, in the garden, and been a worm. I did worm deeds. I had fifty worm wives, all of whom bore me worm sons, which was of interest to me, since as a demon I am infertile. Then the one who set me there as a worm—to punish me—forgot me. Or only, perhaps, forgot himself. And then there came a curious hesitation in the whole of Being, as if life herself caught her breath—and so I was sprung, and here I am.''

''Your name is Bakvi. You stole a necklace of tears,'' said Hazrond, musingly.

''I do not remember that,'' said Bakvi with caution. ''But I remember my fifty wives and my five thousand sons. This garden is well worm-tilled, lord, on account of my efforts.''

''Who am I?'' said Hazrond.

''A Vazdru, shining brighter and better than any light of the earth.''

''What more?''

Bakvi licked his lips. If Azhrarn had forgotten Azhrarn, and if this one came like a burnished storm through the door of the palace—

''The Prince of Demons,'' submitted Bakvi.

Hazrond smiled, and petted the Drin, who palpitated with ecstasy. But it seemed to Bakvi he did not palpitate quite as much as he would have done if another had petted him—

Presently Hazrond, the Eagle-Winged, the Beautiful (Night's Master?), went on into his somber house.

Bakvi skittered away through the garden. He had got used to the garden, let it be said. Used to tunneling through it, fornicating in it, to all manner of items which, in demon shape, he would never have dared. Meanwhile his forge beside the lake would have been invaded long since by some miscreant. So Bakvi loitered, and now and then, askance, he would lie on the dark grass and woo the lady worms he sensed were gliding there, lovely as water, through the undercountry of the soil.

After a time, Bakvi came down the terraces between the cedars of silver trunks, restraining himself continually from diving for shelter from the winged fish in the boughs— which, as a worm, has been no more than sensible—and reached the garden's center. Here Bakvi paused, perplexed.

There had played on this spot, formerly—and always—a fountain of heatless unilluminating red flame. Now there was a mound of earth, fissured here and there, and the fissures smoldered like rubies.

Bakvi sat on the grass and looked at the mound. When he had been there an hour, a black worm poked its snout out of the ground and Bakvi caught hold of it.

"Pause a moment, my son," said Bakvi.

But the worm wriggled unhappily. "You are not as I recall, Daddy."

"Never mind that. Do you see that heap there?"

"My sight is poor. But I do see it. It glows."

"Go fetch the rest of your brothers."

The worm remonstrated. Bakvi threatened. The worm cringed and went away and returned shortly with ninety-nine other worms. In Bakvi's worm day he had taught his family to respect him.

"Sons," said Bakvi, "you see I am not as I was." The worms said that they did, and asked if they should mourn. "Only get under that mound," said Bakvi, "and bring me up a good huge piece of the red glowing stuff which is in it." The worms were unwilling. "It will not burn you," said Bakvi. "It may do something worse, but that is no longer my affair," he added to himself. "Have I not," he inquired of the garden, " presented you with five thousand gardeners? A hundred of them will not be missed."

The obedient worms now wriggled into the mound and delved about. Shortly, for they had been lessoned to be *most* respectful in Bakvi's worm days, they all came out again, lugging in their midst a large incarnadine clod.

"It seems to us," said the eldest of the worms, "that the fire in the dirt, though heatless and nonilluminative, has properties."

"You shall all be kings," said Bakvi. "Now, follow me."

And so saying Bakvi waddled away toward the region of the lake, where the Drin metalsmiths hammered. As they went the hundred worms, made drunken by contact with the fountain fire, began to sing unseemly songs (taught them by Bakvi in his worm days).

Now Bakvi, if any had asked him, could not have said

precisely why he did as he did. Indeed, as he came to the lake, and along the rocky banks where the forges rang and the fumes puffed, and scores of Drin out-peered and asked where he went and what murky lantern that was, Bakvi invented stories, and lied, and still he did not know exactly what truth he hid.

At length he located a dingy little vacant cave, and here he crawled in and the worms crawled after, chanting and hiccuping, with the ball of light which gave no light. One last nosy Drin cried in after them: "What is that you have?" "Only a dull coal to ignite my brazier," said Bakvi, again. "It is a magic I experiment with, combusting a pat of centipede excreta."

Having got in the cave, Bakvi further instructed his sons, and sent them belchily forth again. In a state of euphoria they coiled in all directions, and entering the workshops of those Drin who slept or were absent, appropriated implements, and took them to their father.

Soon enough, even as waking or home-wended Drin might be heard screaming *"Thief!"* and throttling various neighbors, Bakvi set to, rigging a bench, starting a brazier, calling up old spells, while the worm sons sat admiringly inebriate all about.

From time to time, fellow Drin would plod to the cave entry, insatiably curious.

"Who is there?" "It is Ikki." "Ikki? It seemed to me I knew your voice. Yet Ikki was not the name that tallies with it—" "I am Ikki, and my mistress is a scorpion whose sting discommodes for a mortal year, particularly in the riding position." "Blessings on you, Ikki, and farewell." And later yet, now and then: "Is that you, Ikki?" "It is I." "How is your mistress?" "Stingful." "Good luck attend you, Ikki, and again farewell."

Bakvi toiled. He made, as the Drin were accustomed to make, an artifact, and duly glamoured it. It was a stoppered vase of silver, in the shape of a bird. Next Bakvi took up the clod of earth and fire, and thrust it down into the bird's neck, and so into its body, and then bunged in the head. Then he turned a key of corundum and the bird flew around and around.

"There, it is done," said Bakvi. And so saying, he fell

over an enormous roll of black carpet. This turned out to be the eldest of his worm sons, grown (unnoticed, for the Drin, when intent upon smithing, seldom saw anything else) to prodigious length and girth. As had all the other ninety-nine that had carried the fountain fire.

"Do not be alarmed, little Father," said the eldest worm, a smooth dragon of blazing eyes. "We thank you for keeping your promise, and making us kings. Now we will take you on your journey."

"Wh—wh—what journey?" inquired Bakvi, trying to fit himself into a crevice, unsuccessfully.

"The supernatural dirt has made us uncommonly wise. We know the way. Come, take the bird of silver and get up on my back."

"Um," said Bakvi. "I have a pressing appointment."

But in the end he was loaded by the other worms upon the eldest worm, which sprawled away over the rocks in such speedy liquid humpings, Bakvi shrieked with horror.

"Ah, there goes that Ikki, calling and showing off to us," said the Drin. "What is that monster he rides? And where is that scorpion mistress of his?"

"Behind you!" wailed Bakvi, with parting malice, and the worm rippled him away with it, he knew not where.

But they came to a stream where opals swam and leapt like salmons and above the stream was a black hill.

"Now I know why I was afraid," said Bakvi. But he did not, truly.

The worm put him off with the barest courtesy. The other worms, which had accompanied them, lay on the ground like some giant's silken ropes. But all their eyes gazed upon Bakvi, and all their eyes indicated he must go up the hill, with only the silver bird of fire to aid him.

"Now why," said Bakvi, "did the earth catch her breath? And why could she not have done so without sloughing me? Azhrarn's punishment of me was no trouble. But this I do not like."

There was a path worn up from the stream to a cave mouth in the hill. The path softly shone. Bakvi thumping up it, the shine muddied over.

Bakvi reached the membrane of Time's Absence, and

the scent of it made him sneeze. It was an uncouth and noisy sneeze. The membrane, offended, tore. Bakvi, knock-kneed, tooth-chattering, bird-clutching Bakvi, padded in.

He could see nothing, or very little. A statue, slim and dark, stood nearby, two others farther off, and on a slab of rock, a figure, bright as a fallen moon, blacker than the blood of night, close as a bone, distant as heaven, a stranger, and familiar.

Bakvi fell to his face and gibbered, and the bird fluttered from his grasp and he did not see where it went.

Then a voice spoke to Bakvi. It was gentle, and very terrible. Yet, at the sound of it, the demon ichor in his veins came all alive.

"I gave you only severity. Why do you do this for me?"

Then Bakvi said, "Pile acrimony on me. What does that matter? Love is love."

And Bakvi thought to himself, *I am possessed and speak like a fool*. But he said again: "Love is love. She cannot be seen because she is everything. We fight her. We turn her away. But we can no more do it than throw off our own life. In the end, love alone remains. In the end, love will inherit the world. But that is not yet."

"Not yet, for sure," said the voice, so wondrous, so awful, Bakvi nearly perished, immortal that he was. "Tell me the reward you would have."

Then Bakvi twittered with cravenness.

"Let me be a worm again. Let me be a *big* worm, like my sons. Let me be the king of the worms of the demon country."

And then he jumped up to abscond—and what was he, Bakvi, but a huge nigrescent perfect worm. And going out and down the hill, he crossed the stream like a river and slid upon his willful sons, and dwarfed them.

"Who am I?" said Bakvi, the worm.

"Our respected daddy," said the worms, respectfully.

"Go beneath," said Bakvi, "and tell your mother, and all my wives, to *grow*. And then, to make ready."

Under windows of sultry sapphire, Hazrond paced to and fro. He had been out hunting, had Hazrond, chasing with his horses and hounds the strayed souls of madmen asleep. But there had been something wanting in the sport. They had not screamed enough, maybe, those souls, or they had screamed with laughter in the nightmare's jaws.

The earth had caught her breath, or the nature of life had done so. With his Vazdru awareness, Hazrond knew of it, unknowingly. Knew, also, he had somehow missed it. The moon had stumbled and the stars exclaimed. One instant. Then all was rectified. Why should it concern him? Was he not Prince Wickedness, mankind's tormentor?

Hazrond seated himself, and drank from a cup of glass a wine more transparent.

A lamp lighted itself across the chamber, and with a deep ruby ray. Hazrond looked at the lamp. Though alight, it gave none.

Hazrond pointed at the lamp, which went out. Looking down, he found a serpent at his foot, with ruby eyes. Hazrond kicked it from him—it was already gone.

Then in the middle of the air, a bird of silver circled. Hazrond tossed a dagger at it and all at once its head shot off—it burst into fragments, and only a flame flowered there, flickering and twisting, giving no heat, illuminating nothing.

Hazrond reclined in his chair, and took another sip from his cup. He was different now. Softer, more vivid. "Oh, are you about?" he said. "You have slept late, wherever you have been sleeping. Have you come to offer me your service? A handsome page to bring me sweetmeats, or a minstrel to pipe me tunes? Which is it to be, Azhrarn?"

Then the flame stretched near. Hazrond sat in his chair and finished his wine. Into the empty goblet the flame ran, and filled it. Hazrond threw the cup away with a negligent gesture. The cup whirled; the flame gushed from it, vanished. The cup smashed against a pillar, and the voice of Azhrarn spoke behind Hazrond's left shoulder: "When the night returns to the earth above, I shall return to Druhim Vanashta, my city, which you borrowed without my leave."

"You will be welcome," said Hazrond, "if any remember you."

But the demon city was trembling around him, like a bride in joy and anxiety, and the very hearts of demonkind might be heard, starting like hares—for there was not a brick or a leaf or an intellect that did not in some habitual form answer him. Even Hazrond leaned toward the voice, his eyes half closing, though the rings cut into his hands where he had clenched them.

"I am lord here now," said Hazrond.

"As much as you ever were," said the voice of Azhrarn out of the shadow. "Which was not much."

"We shall see. I await you with pleasure."

"Do so," said Azhrarn. "Your pleasure will be brief enough when once we meet."

The day dropped out of the world. In the country underground, which knew neither day nor dark, night nevertheless was always realized. A great stillness was already there, in the city. Not a note of music, not a mechanical bird, not a voice. Yet in their porticos and on their towers, the Vazdru stood, and nearby the Eshva, as if to wait on them. Even the Drin had sidled in and crouched behind the window panes, the walls of gardens, squinting through eyelets, unable to keep away, full of misgiving. As night lay down upon the earth above, one bell of bronze gave tongue through Druhim Vanashta.

They had betrayed him, nearly every one of his race. Either in jealous rage deliberately, or by acquiescence. Not one had resisted a new order or a usurper's rule. They had said, *He is dead to us.* They had resumed their artistic feasts and gamings, and when Hazrond passed by them, they adored him. Now, while the Eshva shivered and shook with sensuous emotions, and the Drin squintily hid, the Vazdru waited, simply that, immobile as the reeds when no wind blows. The pale faces, white as the flowers of night, those benighted eyes, were profoundly composed. Though the city silently drummed with the uproar of every heart that was in it.

Then the bell rang out one more time—and was riven in bits. Not an ear that did not catch the commotion. The eyes of the demons turned all in one direction.

He reentered his city, Azhrarn, without ceremony or state. He came neither mounted on horseback nor in a chariot; he was on foot. And there was no one with him, courtier or guard. And he was clad in black, only that. And as he moved there, the very air unfurled like a blossoming rose, the very mosaics blushed, the pillars quivered like the strings of harps. He *was* the city, and the city knew itself. And every one of those therein, they knew it also.

But they were dignified, the upper echelons of demonkind. They did not cast themselves down before him, the Vazdru, and though the Eshva hung in a frozen melting faint, neither did they obeise themselves. (And the Drin stayed from sight.)

So he walked, in silence, along the silent avenues, followed only by dark eyes, and came at length to the black palace where, for numberless generations of the earth and timeless moments of the Underearth, he had been a prince and a lord. When he was half a mile away, the doors, of their own volition, opened wide. You might hear the hounds eagerly panting in the courts, but nothing else. When Azhrarn reached the palace and the opened doors, Hazrond was in the doorway.

Now Hazrond was the most handsome of the Vazdru, and the most spectacular. He had put on mail and jewels and very flames indeed. But Azhrarn had returned to Druhim Vanashta clad only in black, and one saw that Hazrond, beside Azhrarn, was as the great sea is, to the endless, depthless, inimitable sky.

"Well, you are here," said Hazrond.

"I am here," said Azhrarn.

"I trust you are well."

"I am sick, and the disease must be torn out. *Hazrond* is the name of it."

"I will come down into the street," said Hazrond. "Do you wish to brawl there with me?"

"Come down," said Azhrarn, "and see."

Hazrond came down, and set his hand on Azhrarn's shoulder.

"They will be envious of us," he murmured, "that we touch one another."

"Oh, Hazrond," said Azhrarn, looking into his eyes, "do you imagine so?" And in that gaze, Hazrond turned pale enough you saw the skull beneath his skin. Then a force came from Azhrarn, sparkling, and flung Hazrond onto the marble flags before the palace.

He danced back again to his feet, this Vazdru prince who had been Prince of the princes, carelessly, as if nothing had hurt him, it was his jest to be flung and to fall. As he rose, he drew his sword of blackest bluest steel, and springing forward, he thrust the blade toward the breast of Azhrarn.

They were immortals. What were swords to them, and strokes that men used to bring death? Emblems, *language*. Oh surely he had known, Hazrond, in the second Azhrarn spoke to him behind his chair, and maybe even in the second he himself usurped that chair, that he was to be the loser?

Azhrarn stretched out his hand, empty of anything, and let the point of the sword impale his wrist. But it did not, for the sword had disintegrated, and was gone.

And then Hazrond became sheer light. It was the essence of him, the pure dynamic that underlay the beautiful male shape in which a Vazdru prince was wont to adorn himself—sulfurously blue, the vitality of Hazrond, like moonlight seen through fever and indigo. And it dashed itself against Azhrarn. It embraced him, bore upon him.

Where Azhrarn had stood a black fire blazed in its turn, and the fire beat and fanned itself, and heightened to a deep cold red. The energy of Azhrarn, the psychic essence of him, scarlet as the fountain of the garden—it overtopped, it wrapped the blue fire of Hazrond. It struggled with it, but then there came another change.

For the red fire scalded colder, hotter, to an incandescence: white. And the white fire in its turn began to throb and to make a color that was like a soundless ringing.

And Druhim Vanashta, watching, would have averted its eyes, would have cried out. For the color of this fire was gold. It was gold as gold is, and golden things, *and it was like the sun*. Yes, even like the sun of the earth, that to demons was the one true death. Like the sun, Azhrarn seared there, his vital energy, and it burned out the essence of Hazrond the way acid would eat a paper. Until only a thin dust sifted and drifted, and was no more. And Hazrond . . . no more was Hazrond.

Not a noise. Not a cry. Not one eye averted.

So they saw him come back, Azhrarn, their prince, a

Lord of Darkness, Night's Master. He was a man clothed in gold and made of gold, his flesh and hair, all gold, and his eyes were golden suns. He stood there upon the streets of Night's own kingdom, and was *day*. Then the golden scream of his glory transposed. It was all blackness, all coolness. Not morning, but evening.

And without a glance, without a phrase, Azhrarn walked into his palace, and the doors shut softly as two sleeping eyelids.

Say now, city and people, who is your prince, and *what* is he?

2

DEMONS did not die. At least, they did not remain dead. (They were like mortals in that.) And the Underearth could countenance no absolute ending. The Lord Uhlume had never entered there. And so, as Azhrarn moved through his dark palace like a darker thought, refinding it, the ashes of Hazrond, borne by a sudden breeze, made their exit from the city and blew away over the landscape of the underworld.

They were not even ashes, these ashes, but a substance thinner than air—blasted so fine as to be invisible. They were, indeed, actually, nothing. And this settled in a hollow place, in the black grass, and as they or it lay there, three Vazdru princes rode by. These laughed together, and spoke proudly and cruelly, as if they had recently woken from refreshing sleep. They were the three who had stayed loyal to Azhrarn, and guarded him in the hill. They made now toward the city, anticipating generous welcome, rightly.

"But this," said one of them, "let us be rid of it. For it is a memory of despair." And he threw away the silver cup which they had dipped in the living stream, and with which they had attempted to moisten the lips of their lord—but which had failed to restore him.

The cup jumped over the grasses and fell into the hollow where, for want of much better words, Hazrond's *ashes* lay.

There was a hint of water still in the bowl of the cup, which spilled. More, the cup came charged with Vazdru sorcery, that prayer within the hill, that will to revivify. Besides, it had touched the mouth of Azhrarn, like a lover.

The clear unlit light of Underearth lapped everything like a balm, and the dust of Hazrond with the rest.

In the world of men above, perhaps a few days came and went. Below, a few beats of bells and hearts. The ashes, sprinkled with dews of water and prayer, wove together like moss, hardened like clay in a potter's oven. To die in Underearth was a very different matter to a death above.

Hazrond, handsome and splendored, though pale now as one dead, and weak now as one newly born, lay on his back with scarcely the strength to take up and kiss the silver cup which had come to rest under his hand. Then, in a while, he sat, and leaning one palm on the ground from strengthlessness, he drew forth the silver pipe like a cat's thighbone, and sounded it. And presently a demon mare came galloping through the grass. But when Hazrond had mounted her, and turned her head toward the city, she too paled. Her blackness turned the color of ashes, and she trod slowly.

Azhrarn was seated in a hall, beneath windows like a lion's blood. He had been reading from books of ivory, but now he rested one hand upon them, and the other on the carved arm of his chair. He listened and heard, beyond the songs and silences of Druhim Vanashta, beyond all the enchanting audibles currently put forth to placate and enamor him, the sorry hoofbeats on the flags, and then the doors opening one by one, and the footsteps, symmetrically stumbling.

Hazrond entered. Azhrarn said nothing; Hazrond came

on. He crossed the whole length of the hall, while the windows laved him in a dead sunset, and reaching the feet of Azhrarn, Hazrond kneeled there. But, with his swimming, burning eyes, he stared into the eyes of Azhrarn.

"Ask me only this," said Hazrond. "Why I took this city from you in your absence."

"Why," said Azhrarn, "should your answer interest me?"

"Because you fought with a sky-being, and some power of the sun is also yours at last, Azhrarn, together with the might which was yours always. And we—we are less than grass, Azhrarn, and you are everything we may not be. Even the greatest of us. You have nothing to fear. Not even from Hazrond who is at your feet."

"Who told you," said Azhrarn, "I feared Hazrond at any time?"

"Oh," said Hazrond, smiling, "will you not fear me a little, when I have done so much for you? For I kept you in their memory, exhorting them, by every word and glance of mine, to forgetfulness of you."

"Stand," said Azhrarn.

"I cannot. Your strength crushes me."

"Lie on your face then," said Azhrarn. "And tell me why you took the city."

"Because I loved you enough to hate you. I loved you enough, when you removed yourself, to fill the gaping void the only way I might—by myself becoming Azhrarn. Or as much of Azhrarn as any could. And there are not many, my prince, who were ever nearer than I. And you do fear me, Lord of lords, because you see in me your own self. You are the black sun, and I am the dark which was before. I am your childhood. And some long night, I have come to believe, I shall be all of you again, and forever, as forever may then be reckoned."

"Riddles," said Azhrarn. But he rested his chin upon his hand and he gazed at Hazrond, and it was evident that, though no other did or might, Azhrarn had understood each sentence; it was no riddle at all to him.

"What now, then?" said Hazrond.

Azhrarn struck him.

It was such a blow that it dashed Hazrond away, and

stunned him. But when he had recovered from it, he was toughened and energized, and rose to his feet. "That is not much for punishment," he said.

"Your punishment I gave you before," said Azhrarn. "That was my forgiveness."

Then Hazrond laughed out loud. Such a laugh it was— musical, and like the cry of some rare animal of great beauty, that softly kills all it sees. Oh, it was the laugh of Azhrarn. Yes, it was his.

"I am done with mankind," said Azhrarn to Hazrond. "There are other games, or I will invent them."

"Let mankind go," said Hazrond. "Let it rot. They learn nothing. They worship the gods still, though the world was scarred by what the gods have done to it. And that woman you gave sway over humanity, they worship her yet as a god, though she is a god no longer, and even her worship they misremember, entreating her for pity, and calling her loving names, praising her kindness and care for them." And Hazrond, standing by Azhrarn, looked to see how these words would be received, this reminiscence of the girl Azhriaz, his child by a human female.

But Azhrarn said only: "She is an immortal and she lives. If I owe her that, let her live then."

"And I?" said Hazrond, leaning close, that his mouth might brush the hair of Azhrarn. "May I live also? Or must I die again? Only tell me. I will do it gladly. I will die for you, I will endure agony for you. I am yourself, that part of you which loves you best. Only notice me. Here I wait at your side."

Azhrarn, putting out his hand, drew Hazrond down, so he lay across the chair, and so that their bodies pressed one against the other.

"Wait no more."

Druhim Vanashta, that moon-star of cities, filled by her enchanted love whispers, her placatory cajolements, Druhim Vanashta felt that lovemaking, and was made love to, all the vast jewel box of her, and every one of the demons— they felt the caresses of that love, the fierceness of it, and the concourses moaned and the towers stretched them- selves in ecstasy—for by that love he returned himself to them. He noticed them. He was theirs, once again, body, soul—which in him were one.

And for Hazrond, the vessel into which this light and darkness entered, this night sea, midnight sky, black wine, red fire, the intimation of sun and of death, the sensations of it passed through him and into the stones of the city, and into the flesh of those that were there, or perhaps even he could not have borne the pleasure of it.

As chaos had touched all things, so this piercing harmonic shot through and through the Underearth. It was an ultimate possession. Druhim Vanashta, borne upward on a wave, poised in the liquid silver of three seconds lasting longer than all time, then released, flowing down, sinking, one ambient sigh.

And when the sigh was sighed out, a green butterfly might be seen, among the cedars of Azhrarn's garden. Vasht, reborn by orgasmic psychic quake out of the paving where Azhrarn's heel had formerly compressed her.

How fresh the wings of the butterfly. Azhrarn had renounced mankind. He was the beloved, as in the past. He was the Prince of Demons, *theirs*. No other's.

There will come an hour, quite soon as soon is thought of there, when Vasht also will be noticed. The green wings, at his glance, will be a robe of silvered green upon the pearl form of a Vazdru princess. His touch, loosing the clasps of the robe, will turn it black as night—

BOOK THREE

ATMEH:
The Search for Life

1

DOWN THE mountain road walked a man clothed in black, and close behind him another man, more advanced in years and more inventive in dress, this being robes of ocher scarfed with rubric, tasseled with purple, bordered and trimmed and dimpled with gold. Gray-headed, this one, under a plumy diadem, lugging a staff, and with, beneath the other arm, a silken bundle, egg-shaped. . . . Perhaps a quarter of a mile behind these two, a third person made his way. He was hooded in a blond mantle, but the noon sun lit ceaselessly upon him, so he seemed to shine, brighter even than the plumed one with all his gold.

"Now say what you will," said the revived sage-mage to Dathanja, who had, for a great while, said entirely nothing. "That night in the first wretched flea-bitten village, I was aroused near daybreak, aware of an enormous occurrence. And resorting to sorcerous exercise, I divined a change had come about. Yet what it was the spell would not divulge. Being practiced, as I am, in all sorts of occult mathematic, I made calculations. Which informed me that chaos itself had been breached, and, in securing itself, had violently brushed the world of organized matter—an impact felt not only in the narrow confine of the event, but throughout, and to all four quarters. Such a marvel must have consequences. And how else should this cataclysm have occurred but through an action of the entity we glimpsed, tearing eastward under the sea? What was its purpose? Is it destroyed? Meanwhile, that other heavenly bore goes on following us, day and night. A whole month it has dogged us. My wizardrous researches—though not

317

you—have told me what the creature is. But it returns no word to my questions or expostulations. It merely, unmannerly brute that it is, *shines* upon me."

Dathanja had paused, as if to listen. The angel, a quarter of a mile away, paused also. The mage-sage shook his magician's staff at the angel, and prepared to harangue one and all.

Having left the ocean brink above drowned Simmurad, they had gone southwestward. Or, Dathanja had done so and the mage, attaching himself, had done so too, while Ebriel, for unrevealed motives, followed. They kept to the crags, though the roseate shadings of the sea-mouthed eastern reaches were soon bled out. More ordinary, these dry uplands, and here and there were isolate human habitations. Dathanja took his way among them quietly, asking nothing but often given, nevertheless, food, or what shelter there might be. They were innocent, these wayside people, seeming young as the land, with large eyes cloudless as the eyes of loved children. They would bring Dathanja water or milk in a stone jar or rough clay dipper, sit to watch him, and sometimes then usher up to him their infants, and Dathanja would put his hands on them a moment, as if to bless. In one place, there was a baby with sore skin. Dathanja took it from its mother, unasked, unasking, undenied. He patted the baby with the fawn dust, all over, and then carried it to the stream and washed off the dust and the sore skin with it, and there the baby lay, gurgling and brand-new, quite cured. The mage took huge exception to this and berated Dathanja—who, since he no longer recognized the name of Zhirek, the sage would call by no name at all. "*You*, look how you debase the brotherhood of magicians. Could you not, you who have sunk Simmurad, have healed the brat by the touch of one finger—by a single utterance? Why this quack's preamble?" Dathanja said, "A parable is sometimes necessary." "Errant rubbish!" warbled the sage-mage. "Why," said Dathanja, "do you put on clothing when the sun is so hot?" Missing the point willfully, the mage-sage lectured Dathanja for five miles—they had by now left that particular village far behind—on the merits of voguish attire, espe-

cially when it was created by illusion, and so toned the
sorcerous muscles.

And with no comment, Ebriel paced slowly after them.

In other villages, and at occasional lonely huts, many
small wonders were performed by Dathanja. He proceeded
with the modicum of show, yet generally by means of a
symbol, as with the baby. A woman who wept because the
well was dry was told to weep into the well—and water
filled it, salt at first, then sweet. A missing copper pot was
located by arranging the other copper implements of the
house by the doorstep, and presently, out of some bram-
bles, along came bowling the pot to join their meeting.
Everything was performed with care and gentleness.
Dathanja made no exhibitions of passionate tenderness, and
none of aversion. If it pleased him to heal the sick, if it
brought him joy to help his fellow men, you could not
have said. He did these things as a man might sweep his
yard, a needful, simple incident, neither onerous nor fabulous, important only in omission. (Everything the angel
watched also, from his distance, stilly.) And the ingenuous
ones of the mountain lands, they received the benison from
Dathanja as it was given, thanking him without the word,
smiling, not shouting.

But the sage-mage shouted. His exclamations rattled
along the goat paths and the roads made only by the
treading of feet. He had established for himself a title,
compound of his former name and that of the sea prince
he had been in Tirzom. Tavrosharak, that was he. And he
toted the heavy egg his chicken-carpet had laid in witless
fright, always grumbling at its weight, but, "One does
not leave such significant deposits lying. No, no, some
priceless gadget will be hatched, no doubt. For this reason,
too, I must keep it against my person every hour, to warm
it." At night, amid the blank bare peaks, Tavrosharak
fashioned a bed with posts and canopy, and slept with the
silk-packed egg held close. And now and then he rolled on
it in sleep and awakened unpeacefully. Sometimes Dathanja
would depart during the night, and the Malukhim, Ebriel,
apparently more intent upon Dathanja than upon the mage-
sage, would also go by like a straight pale flame. Roused
by this, the magician would aggravatedly tramp after, or,

summoning up some conveyance from thin air, whirl upon them out of the skies. For days at a stretch Tavrosharak rode in a chariot pulled by dragons, and bearing down on Ebriel was always dissatisfied that the blond figure would neither get out of his way nor stay in it, being somehow one second before the chariot and then behind it, not a sublime (hidden) feather ruffled.

"What is it that you want?" demanded Tavrosharak, diving upon the angel time and again. "Is it some message from the gods you must deliver? It is too bad," added Tavrosharak, jouncing along in his car beside Dathanja, the dragons hissing and cavorting. "Why will the thing not speak to me?" And, wishing to lecture Dathanja, and finding charioteering incommodious for the purpose, he would slough the chariot. "So much bouncing," he averred, "may curdle this egg."

Thus they progressed. Then came the noon they stepped onto a road which men had made not with their feet, but with their hands. Walking along it, Tavrosharak complained about chaos and Ebriel, and Dathanja paused, and Ebriel paused, as if to listen.

But it was not to listen.

A mountain rose on the near horizon, higher than its brothers. Azure it was, half submerged in the sky, but near the pinnacle there was a glistening disturbance, and now and then a shaft of light streamed from it, and tore across heaven like a wide-shot star.

"As I have said," declared Tavrosharak, but at this instant, the glistening on the mountain caught also his eye.

"I am," said Tavrosharak, "bound to go near, and to investigate. There may be a miracle or a treasure." He gazed at Dathanja. "But you," said Tavrosharak, winningly, "bold sorcerer, fearless—as the earth knows, even of Lord Wickedness and Lord Death. . . . Should it not be you who will climb the mountain first?"

Dathanja spoke to Tavrosharak. "I saw enough of miracles and treasures long past. You are starved of them, perhaps. The mountain does not itself lure me."

"Ah, now, excellent *Dathanja*—" began Tavrosharak.

Just then a stunning light, like a second sunrise, opened at their backs, ascended, fanned over their heads with a hurricane rush of wings. The Malukhim, unmantled, a flying flambeau, sped up the mountain.

"He has followed us because we led him to some spot he wished to come at," said Tavrosharak, after a swift thaumaturgic calculation. "This I perceive clearly now. And therefore, as we have led him here, we also have been led. Something has pulled us hither. Come, dear Zhirek— that is, dauntless Dathanja—you, more than I, the sun- beast has trailed. You more than I, therefore, were drawn here. The miracle is yours to claim. Dare you refuse it? You are a mighty healer, all compassion. Oh best Dathanja, go up the mountain and render aid or counsel. I promise I shall be close. At your shoulder."

Dathanja had not attended to any of this, but to the flight of the Malukhim he had. And now he felt an inexpli- cable hand laid on his heart and mind, which hand, before, had only beckoned. Dathanja had been aware that some- thing drew him. He had not and did not resist. Only the weak need fear and avoid temptation. And possibly to this man, now, there was a serene happiness in each surrender, since no longer thereby could he lose himself.

He murmured, a syllable only. And then he lifted as if he too were winged, and went after the angel, shadow behind flame.

The summit of the mountain was a cone, beaten to translucence by weather and the sheer proximity to heaven. It refracted the afternoon, and abetted, like a mirror, the other conflagration which went on beneath. There was a natural terrace, tined with thin copses of rock. In this unlikely cradle, buzzing and flashing with strange emis- sions, lay a battered shattered thing, part melted silver on a huge crushed cage of bronze and steel, its sides stoved in, its design unrecognizable. Yet all about the area, a mile or more, lay shapes and shards and chips and crystals of freakish formation, and wide spilled stains that tingled with eccentric colors, sheens, and odors. Over all throbbed a kind of effulgent pulse, which every so often erupted. Yet these antics, visible as they had been from thousands of feet below, were nevertheless growing more feeble with every minute.

The Malukhim Ebriel had alighted eastward on one of

the rocky tines, and with folded wings and golden mask of face, looked down on the monstrous wreck. Dathanja, in turn, stood to the west, under the cone, and there surveyed the scene.

Tavrosharak, speeding up the mountain now saddled athwart a quirky dragon, called instructively to them both: "Behold, it is some mighty magic craft which has foundered, maybe fallen from the air. Beware a detonation."

It was, of course, the demon ship of Azhriaz the Goddess, not dropped from air but somehow ejected from ocean, chaos-riddled, wholly defunct.

Tavrosharak, sensitive to his own advice, circled the peak cautiously. Ebriel maintained the vantage of the tine. Dathanja, after an interval, moved forward.

In the shade of the ruined hull, not to be seen at once, if at all, one might (or not) visualize a series of curves and angles, proportions, densities, that could belong to the figure of a man. And having discerned that much, that could belong also to the figures of two others, neither men.

Under the frame, among the scintillant debris, a beggar sat on the ground. He was swagged solely in a ragged orange cloth, and his brown shaven cranium was bowed. Across from him there crouched a snarling lizard, large as a tiger and tinted like one. This mounted guard, it would seem, upon the man, and upon the girl who lay between them, her head resting upon the man's knees, while he smoothed her forehead, and quietly tidied the coiling flood of her night-black hair.

She breathed, the girl; you might see it, if you leaned close. This Dathanja presently did. The beggar did not try to prevent him, nor the lizard. It only glared outward at the angel on the rock, and lashed its tail at Tavrosharak's circling dragon.

But through the lids of her eyes, the blue irises were scarcely burning. Her face was far away as a note of music sounded from the cold shores of the moon.

"Azhriaz," said the beggar. "Soveh, Sovaz." But he got no answer, and seemed to await none. To Dathanja, in the way of a king, the beggar added, "Did she summon you then? Somewhere within herself she has remembered you. Or forgotten. Forgetfulness might summon, too.''

"I see now how beautiful she is," said Dathanja. "Can that be because some of her beauty has left her.''

"Or some of his fear has left the one who sees.''

King Fate, Fortune's Master, raised his vibrant voice and called to the Malukhim: "Ebriel, you white eagle, you also see what you require—that there is no Goddess anymore. Is heaven content?'' On his rock Ebriel shifted one wing, whitely, that was all. "Shall I inform you,'' inquired Kheshmet, "of what became of Yabael your brother, in the sea, when the tidal wave, vomited from chaos, struck him?'' Kheshmet laughed, a slow, red-golden noise. "Destiny overtops even angels. For that one was borne into chaos just as the sun, his mother and father, is borne each evening. And chaos remade Yabael before expelling him, despite the will of the gods upon him. He has since come forth again, into a distant ocean, and there he blazes and runs on in his pursuit, which lacks now only a quarry. He is a fiery streaming orb, chaos and matter, sun and liquid, a long-haired comet of the seas. And he will haunt there awhile, coming and going over the water-skies of the sea peoples. They will tell their times and seasons by him, as men have done by the comets of heaven. That is the fate of Yabael, the sun-vulture, the holy runner.''

Ebriel spread his wings. Yellow his mane, like wheat; asphodel and cream and topaz was he. And that, it would appear, was all he was.

Kheshmet continued to stroke the midnight hair from the girl's brow under his fingers. "Ah, child,'' he said.

"The wicked are eternally children,'' said Dathanja softly. And he stepped back again, as if to go away.

That crucial moment, the invented dragon of the sage-mage launched itself against Fate's pet, the snapping giant chameleon under the wreck. It was with a squall and a vast flapping that the dragon came, Tavrosharak yet affixed to its swooping spine, while the lizard rose with bladed claws to meet them.

Supposing there was no time or breath for a spell: "Help, merciful gods!' yelled Tavrosharak, who kept old-fashioned ideas.

But Kheshmet only said, "Hush," in a voice mild as the rustle of a parchment. And the lizard shrank down and down until it was the size of a nutshell, and the dragon came undone and was no more. With the result that Tavrosharak fell onto the terrace, nor elegantly. And lying bruised before Kheshmet, Tavrosharak bemoaned the injustice of a world where beggars might also be choosers, attain magic knacks, and use them on their betters. Meantime, the egg had slipped from the mage's grasp and its silken wrapper, and spun on the terrace madly. Cracks spread across its surface.

"It is hatching, prematurely. Whatever misshapen mistake will now emerge, it is the fault of this orange one. All my labor gone for nothing," groused Tavrosharak.

Then the egg split. The bits of shell sprayed out fine as seafoam, and from the center a lotus flower, winged by petals, flew in the air. Damson-colored the lotus was, with veins of clearest gold. It fluttered to the girl who lay on the rock, and settling and rising and settling, light as down, it touched her forehead, the lids of her eyes, her lips, her two breasts—and the heart beneath, it must have touched that too, for suddenly she sighed, her fringed lashes stirred on her cheeks, and she whispered to the lotus in a little, little voice, "If I were a child, I would weep."

But the lotus darted up and smacked King Kheshmet smartly on each ear. And as Fate's fingers reached for it, the magenta flower crumbled into a magenta flour, that showered over him and flossed his bright garment. Fate clicked his tongue, and smiled, with half his mouth only.

The girl who had been the Goddess Azhriaz opened wide her eyes.

She looked at Kheshmet's half-smile, and smiled herself, sadly and silently.

"There," he said, "you have woken up."

"So I have," she said. These were the accents of a young woman, of a Vazdru, yet it was the tone of a child, the very one he had compared her to—this was not Azhriaz the Goddess. It was not Sovaz, the sorceress mistress of the Prince of Delusions.

"Soveh," said Kheshmet, using the name of her babyhood. "Little Flame."

"Where is my mother?" said the child-girl-woman, staring at him in abrupt mistrust. A darkness took her face. "Oh, she is dead. Now I remember. I cried out to her, but she could not hear. She is beyond the world. She would have come to me if she could."

She lay under the torn ribcage of the ship, physically flawless. But the wounds of chaos were on her, for all that. She had had, from the first, almost, the body of a girl of seventeen, and she had lived in it for nearly half a century. But nevertheless, she was now what she had always been and never been, a child of seven years.

And this child, brushing aside the forest of her own hair impatiently, said, "Where is my father? I want my father. He will care for me." And then her eyes, the blue of the soul of night behind the seal of day, her eyes—that had looked on torture and murder and death and destruction—her eyes, so lovely, so incongruously pure—they came to Dathanja. And the laughter of a child's sheer gladness dawned on her woman's face. She sat up quickly, and got to her feet, and holding out her hands toward him, she ran forward. Until Dathanja turned to ice, turned to *Zhirek* in front of her. That halted her.

"Why?" she said. "Why?"

"What does she want from me?" Dathanja said.

"You well know," said Fate, taking the lizard into his hand, like a coal to warm him. "It is a humorous error, such as the gosling may make, waking up beside the cat, and thinking the cat its dam or sire."

"Tell her otherwise," said Dathanja, as he stood before that wondering child's frightened gaze. Black-haired Dathanja, black of eye, clad in black, and pale, handsome: ciphers of the demon country.

"*You* must do it," said Kheshmet. "She is a child. She thinks she is your daughter. She thinks you are another."

"I am not Azhrarn," said Dathanja to her, she that had been Azhriaz, who had had her soldiers carry him to her, in a city large as a continent, a pavilion where a third of the earth had seemed to bow down at her name.

And she shook her head, but once more stretched out her hand to him.

"She is a child," said Kheshmet, again. "She does not

take you for him, perhaps. It is not necessarily as simple as that. But for one of the demon race, surely she does take you, or for one like herself, half demon, half human, an immortal. And for the instigator of her life.''

"She has hated him always,'' said Dathanja, "that one who fathered her.''

"Regard her,'' said Kheshmet. "There is the hatred. Look.''

She stood weeping, a weeping child, crying to her father very low, asking what she had done, why did he not love her, why had he shut her from him, abandoned her, alone and lost in the bitter world.

And Dathanja, who had come so far in his journey of Self, was rooted to the spot, a stone again.

Then a wind blew cold across the mountaintop, and from the clouds, a weeping rain came down. In the rain, the figments of men, angels, rocks, allegorical Lords of Darkness, seemed dissolved and swept away. There had been a valley in deep rain, a gray rain of the heart, too. Zhirek recollected, and with it, all those who had wept in their turn through him. And Dathanja went to the small girl who kneeled on the mountain in the weeping rain and wept, and he too kneeled, and taking her into his arms, he comforted her. He knew nothing of her as a woman, but only as a child seven years old, who clung to him, for it had taken her half a century to find him, to be loved, and to love.

And as he comforted this daughter never born to him, he learned, and he comforted himself, held in his own arms with her. The one he had been. The one he was.

2

LIKE A SEED dropped in untended soil, where conceivably nothing would come of it, so the change in the world. Out of sight and out of mind.

Suns rose and set, cities rose and were cast down. The moon sailed the ether and the ships of men the seas. Time stalked over the world, shaking her hair, disturbing everything. Seasons budded, bloomed, withered. The caravans of days tirelessly set out, and the caravans of humankind, the chariots, the wagons, and the walkers. All with their cargoes of merchandise, and lives. And night, the black hyacinth, closed their eyes, or black Uhlume the Beautiful, he closed them.

A palmful of years passed. How many years fit in a palm? In a child's palm—say then, three.

What it is to be a child. The astonishment of it. All things so curious. What is that? What is *that*? Tell me. Teach me. Let me learn.

In the lands they went through, sometimes she was pitied. So gorgeous she stopped the heart, so lovely the birds sang for her, and the clouds uncurtained the skies—and she a fool, retarded to the age of seven years, or maybe nine years. A bright child, it was true. But still a child. They compared her to legendary Shezael, the half-souled, fair, oblique—unfinished. Though in the places where black hair carried a stigma, they looked uneasily upon both of them, the infant-woman, and the adult man, her guardian. Some heard her refer to him as her father, though he looked barely old enough to be such, and besides plainly he was a priest of some wandering order, and should be chaste, or if ever unchaste then at least circumspect. There was too, in the company, a disgruntled magician (an uncle, perhaps?). Few took to him, since he seemed always irascible, and was in the habit of sorcerously venting on bystanders his inner discontents. Luckily the priest, a healer of extraordinary facility, and also himself a sorcerer, would put right what this hasty mage put wrong. Then again, there was another often of the party. Cracked like the girl and the old uncle, it would seem, for he would walk always considerable yards behind, as if he had quarreled with them, and later sit on some boulder, observing what the healer did. And when the healer had completed his task, after him again went this other fellow, who, it must be admitted, was as fair as the girl, though in a different way, all gold for her snow and jet and sapphire. However, several got the impression that he was humpbacked under his mantle. Oh, they were a strange crew, the four of them.

And over and around those countries they took their way, engendering health and entertainment and—best of everything—gossip. Through the kingdoms, and across earthscapes that were in themselves rather novel and unvisited. Or which, possibly, had come to be so from that iota of chaotic change each devotedly forgot.

And eventually, they came into a land where there were slate-skinned elephants upon the roads, and haughty camels with vermilion tassels about their heads. A parched wind blew, for it was the season of crisp bronzy withering, but along the bronze-brown hills white palaces stared on the turquoise sky. The folk of this region had no unease at black hair, for they were themselves a black-haired race, and with a black that was almost blue. The light-skinned among them were the color of ivory, and the dark among them the color of cloves. The land was railed by mountains, and parted by a mighty river, where played hippopotami like air bladders, and lotuses grew.

Now the sorcerer-priest sometimes told stories to the crowds which gathered about him. One day as he did this, the daughter of the prince of that area happened to be going by in her litter. She was dark as sandalwood and haughty as any tasseled camel, though she had a charming human face. Having heard a rumor of these itinerants, led by a healer-teacher, she ordered her bearers to bring her where she could hear the tale.

When the priest concluded, the prince's daughter called to him loudly, "That is all very well, but if you are a sorcerer, you should also perform tricks. Do so."

The priest, turning his black eyes upon hers, replied, "All the earth is a magic thing. Only glance into the tree that shades us. See how the wild figs have ripened there, and how the leaves cover it. And once, this tree was only a seed hidden in the untended soil. Beside such sorcery, madam, any trick of mine would be a frail matter."

Then the prince's daughter, annoyed, stamped her bangled foot hard on the ground. At once the earth unseamed itself and out of it there reared suddenly a most terrifying snake. Red as dying fire it was, with the fangs of a leopard. It towered up over the prince's daughter, even as the crowd jumped aside shrieking, and opened its jaws to bite off her head.

The priest spoke to the snake in a language unknown in that country. But the snake, which understood many tongues, most of them forked as its own, swung itself about and, seeing who addressed it, bowed itself down three times over.

"O Magus," said the snake, "I know you by your elder name. One of my kin you slew, long ago, under the wasteful waters men call Ocean."

"I am contrite for that," said the priest.

"I see that you are," said the giant snake. "But your debt is to your own kind, and you have slain, too, enough of them. May I not decapitate this one uncivil maiden who rudely stamped just now upon the roof of my dwelling?"

"Forbear," said the sorcerer-priest.

"Because you bid it, I must reluctantly obey," said the snake, and frowning between its cat's eyes, it dropped straight down into the ground like a rope, and the earth sewed tight again.

Then the crowd, which had hesitated to run away, once it found the priest to be the situation's commander, vehemently acclaimed him. And the prince's daughter threw herself at his ankles.

"I am dear to my father," said she, "and he will reward you for saving my life."

"I will take no reward," said the priest.

"Winter is coming," said the prince's daughter. "The leaves will blacken and the fruit become husks. Winged dusts will scour the hills and valleys, and frosts will gnaw on them. Rains will fall. Let my father build for you, for he will do so, a palace, and install there a hundred servants to wait on you, and yours," and here she graciously indicated the carping old uncle, who—lost in a tome—had not troubled even to get up, the mantled other up the slope, and the idiot girl.

Then the priest softly laughed. His laughter said, if any had been able to decipher it, Such palaces and such service I have had as might shame emperors, and could have them again. Here, where the wild fig tree grows, I might cause the very wind to build with bricks and raise a mansion to confound all others. But if I do not do it, and yet still refuse you, it is from a stamping pride like your own.

And so he said to the princess, "Not a palace. But some more modest shelter I would accept."

Then he too looked down, and saw the girl who was a child gazing at him intently. When the snake had come from the earth, she had stayed by him, and taken a sharp flint in her grasp, perhaps to defend him. Now she let go the flint, and he took her hand.

Seeing this, the princess asked if the woman was really a simpleton, as the rumor had it.

"Not so. She has become a child. She was an empress once."

"Fate is fate. Nothing is sure," prosaically appended the princess, as she tiptoed over the snake's roof to her litter.

On the banks of the wide river, then, where the shrinking autumn sun cast bars of amber, there came to be a stone house. The brown shore ran into the brown water, and the hippopotami took their mud baths beneath the house wall. Roses grew there, and vines, and now and then a long-legged crane would pass daintily between, or there would fall a furry dew of bees.

Every morning, shortly after sunrise, Dathanja would leave the house and go up the bank to the spot where another of the wild spreading fruit trees gave shade. From this vantage he might see some miles along the river, and over the land on either side, away into the morning haze from which pierced the tiaras of the mountains, sparkling now with snow. A white city or two he might also discern on either hand, and the white town of the princess's father, and his palace of painted windows.

Sometimes a multitude already waited for Dathanja about the tree. He was famed; men would make expeditions to reach him. All day long, through the whey of morning, the cinnamon of afternoon, into the deep-dyed dusk that quickly gave on night, he would heal and he would debate, for some came to him for a decision even in argument, or to have a prophecy explained which had foxed them. And he sent none from him at a loss, or empty. His patience was boundless, and his strength seemed likewise.

Frequently the girl he called Soveh was with him, and in the early day she would lean by his knee. But she disliked the midday sun, and to elude it even climbed the tree and hid in the branches. Persons healed there, and drunk with wonder and relief, might come away also with a memory of a white flower looking down through the dark leaves, upon the triumph of hope.

At other times, she played along the bank, or swam in the river, for she had forgotten how to walk on water, and to swim was all the instinct left her. Under the river, among the stems of the lotuses, she met the hippos, graceful as swans in that element, who did her no harm, and occasionally let her ride—unseen by mortals—on their backs. When darkness came, Soveh would make garlands for herself and for Dathanja, all clung with fireflies, and so light him homeward to the stone house.

In those weeks, the watcher of the blond mantle was seldom come on. "He must keep to the house," the people of the neighborhood said, "Only let him come out again and show us his unusual hair, which is the color of the summer grain." But it began to be said that one of the two sorcerers had summoned to their service a huge golden bird, for such had been seen, flying over the sky at dawn, or threading the swift sunset, and others declared it had made a perch for itself atop a hill across the river.

For the magician uncle, he too kept from sight, though his carping might be heard from the upper room of the house, as he pored there over his weighty collection of magegoria. "Pray do us no harm, Uncle," said the cattle-herders, between amusement and earnest, as they drove their charges by under the window.

While the priest and the child discoursed below, or ate their simple meals, or were silent together, they too could make out—if they so desired—that muttering in the upper room. And it might chance a whirlwind would be dragged in there by a spell, or some other undomestic item, and the stones of the house would rattle, so at length Dathanja must go out and repair them. (The child was not afraid. The upheavals interested her, and in return she sometimes threw garlands, figs, or mangoes in at the upper window.)

But the sage-mage Tavrosharak, reborn out of drowned coral (twice), he paid no heed. He would have nothing to do with humankind anymore. He had taken up residence in the humble house because said house had occurred, but the upper room was filled to crowding with costly furniture—subtracted from palaces by air-borne devils. And amid it all, Tavrosharak lived, hemmed in by valuables, and served each dusk a fabulous repast whipped from under the very lips of kings. And to his unhuman minions neither would Tavrosharak speak, but sent them about by other means. He would give words now to none, save to his own reflection in a silvered glass, and to this he did talk, and conversed long with it. But even with that he sometimes fell out, and then would not speak to it for days.

Along the margin of the shore, the lotuses had turned to twilight mauve and to magenta. Elsewhere they closed their cowls like hermits; shriveled. The sun waned and a bleak wind breathed upon the earth.

Dathanja saw the color of the lotuses below the house, and how they did not die. But Soveh the child, playing among them and swimming between their stems, only took them for another aspect of all life, which was a constant novelty to her. They did not, therefore, cause her hurt or aggravation, as to Sovaz or Azhriaz they would have done, being recollections of Chuz. And she had not questioned herself if, by the lotus that broke from the insane egg, he had found some way, even inadvertently, to bring her consciousness out of the nothing where it had wandered. Or if this act, as with the coloration of the plants in the river, were random, or chosen, of one who once had been her lover.

The winter came, riding his sere chariot. He flung before him the flowers and fruits, the leaves, the birds, the new-mown days.

A dust wind blew. The shutters of the stone house were bolted fast, as were the ornate panes of all the palaces. Like sticks of brittle sugar, the reeds. The hippopotami had made for themselves long caves in the mud, and slept there, or floated in the river, somnolent, with their round eyes fast locked as any shutter or pane. And the winter frogs, and the lizards, and the grasshoppers, crept in by night to the shore of the fire. Sometimes the sick or weary, seeking Dathanja, were also let in to share the lower room. They went away singing, through wind and frost, careless now.

It was the end of the third year.

The child played by the hearth, making paper garlands for all the frogs and lizards there, and their little eyes were like row upon row of bright beads. Dathanja sat and looked at this, and put aside the precious book he had been reading, which the prince's daughter, along with much else, had given him.

"How old are you, Soveh?" he asked the child in the woman's body.

"I am seven or I am nine or I am eleven years of age," said she. "For you told me."

"What have you learned?"

"Only to be alive," she said, and she laughed, and hung a paper garland on the toe of his shoe. (For the princess, seeing him barefoot, had given him shoes, and sometimes Dathanja wore them.)

But the lizard for whom the garland had been intended came and pulled it off and gave it to Soveh again, stretching out its neck for the token.

Across the river, in the west, a star rose, and later it
flew over the roof. But Tavrosharak had squabbled with
his mirror again and it was quiet in the upper room.

It would seem Dathanja, priest, healer, sorcerer that he
was, must know some witchcraft that could have cured
Soveh of all her delusions. Or maybe he had attempted it,
but the effect of chaos proved obdurate. Or, he had not
attempted it.

One by one, the creatures at the hearth allowed her to
adorn them, and reminded her when she omitted to do so.
They knew, it appeared, she was not only a retarded girl.
And the hippopotami, they knew. Why not, when she
breathed water as she rode upon them under it?

And the lotuses had found out or been told, blooming on
through the gales and the nights of ice. And even some of
the servitors that the mage-sage called up, they had guessed,
and glared down through the floorboards at her, while they
were before him.

And the angel also, that knew, keeping its watch upon
them all.

3

ONE DIM veiled morning, Soveh was under the house wall, playing a game of hers with small stones she had collected. It was a complex game, involving rulers and ruled, armies, citadels, and ominiscient strokes of fate—those few who had chanced to ask her to explain her childish hobby had been mostly astonished, and sometimes discomposed.

As she played she sang, in a voice so beautiful the very air seemed hushed to listen. The sun, not long risen, sent its rays through the stripped trees along the shore, and over the river, polishing as it went the islands of four or five floating hippos. Every night the sun descended into and sojourned amid chaos. It touched the child-woman, who had also entered the Un-ness beyond the world, with a musing finger.

Your grandmother, your mother's mother, said the sun, *once wedded my light. It is already in your bones, and your soul knows it, my power and the powers of chaos and nonmatter. There is no need to hide.*

Soveh won a city with a legion of small brown pebbles. *I am not ready to believe you, yet*, said Soveh's averted head.

Just then, Dathanja came out of the house, and Soveh ran up to him. "Here is the king of all the stones," she said, and gave to him a pebble of a strange and natural stripe, opaque black, transparent blue, a beautiful thing she had saved for him. Dathanja took the pebble, and next her beautiful face between his hands, and he kissed her quietly on the forehead. "What have I taught you, Soveh?" he said. "About the seasons," she said, "and dark and day, and why trees grow, and where the sea is. And how to be loved." Dathanja said, "Yes, that is true. You have learned that very well. But do you know then what you have taught me?" The child looked at him, and the woman smiled. Neither knew the other, but both were for a moment before him. Dathanja said, to both of them, "You have taught me how to take. It was the hardest lesson, the longest missed, and I learned it from you in three seconds."

In the house Tavrosharak might be heard saying to the silvered glass: "Do you not agree that it is impossible to live in such squalor, or to bring the intellect to bear upon deeds of occult science, when there is this constant raucous hubbub under the window?"

Then Dathanja laughed, and the child, and they walked together up the bank toward the tree, where today only the slim gilt figure of Ebriel was waiting—who, at their approach, opened his wings and drifted like a daffodil hawk into the sky.

"How golden he is," said Soveh. "Is he our enemy, or a friend?

"I do not know," said Dathanja. "Nor, I think, does he, now."

"There is a white O behind his head. Is it a cloud that is so round and burns so coldly?"

Dathanja paused and looked at the orb of light in the sky, across which the Malukhim had now flown. At last Dathanja said, "That is the moon, which has risen by day, and follows the sun over the sky."

(Now, it is said that such a thing had never happened before, that the moon of the flat earth dawned only after the sun had gone down. Or, if ever it had happened, it had been in the chaotic primitive ages, before reason ordered the world.)

In another moment, however, the white orb disappeared inside a true cloud, and meanwhile some wagons and carts drawn by bullocks began to come along the river shore, filled by those who sought Dathanja, and behind these, riders on blue elephants. The day's work had begun.

But the day was dark, and most silent. So soundless it was that the speech the healer had with his patients, and the debates he had with those who wished to be tutored by him, seemed the only attest to life for miles. And then again, from time to time, clear as a clarion, you could hear Tavrosharak upbraiding a solitary cricket for the din it made in the vine under his window.

"Healer," said one of the debaters seated on the ground before Dathanja, "this is a curious day. How thick the panes of it."

"The atmosphere," said another, "is charged as if with lightning. Some event is due. Should we fear? Should we entreat the gods for clemency?"

"Why should you entreat them?" said Dathanja.

"Because perhaps our sins have made them angry."

"Sin," said Dathanja, "does not anger the gods. It is we who anger ourselves by what we do amiss. When you do wrong, ask forgiveness of yourself, for it is yourself you have harmed far worse than any other man, and that in proportion to your crime."

"Say then," said one of the debaters, "I kill my own brother. Surely that is a worse sin against him than against myself?"

"Not in the least," said Dathanja. "For, though your sin in wrenching from him his selected life is very great, he will have another life. While you have sullied for yourself that life which is your own, as if you had taken up mud and slime and rubbed them into your garments, and you must live on in that muck until conclusion and rebirth. Nor will you be free of the stain even then, till you have toiled and striven to cleanse it."

"Ah, Master," said the man, "by these words we know, as we have been led to believe, that you are without any sin."

"I am the most sinful among you," said Dathanja. "My soul is thick with the filth of foolish terrible evils."

Those who heard this gasped and protested. Finally one who had come riding there in silk and velvet on an elephant said to Dathanja, "How then, priest, do you dare to invoke healing, or to offer solutions to those events which perturb us?"

"He," said Dathanja, "that drinks from the poisoned well and dies there, do they not leave his skull on a post to warn other travelers from the water? Or, if he survives, will he not know, best of all men, which wells to avoid, and better than those who have never tasted the poison, nor swallowed it down?"

"Do you say then that all men *must* first do evil that they may learn how to do good?"

"There is no 'must,' " answered Dathanja. "I say only that, in most cases, this is how it will fall out. And as with individual men and women, so with mankind itself. Until at last the cruel and selfish stages of infancy and adolescence are finished with, and the peoples of the world—which may not then be any world we should recognize, for the date is far off—these peoples shall be, all of them, grown to adult estate, in heart, spirit, and mind. In which time, which shall doubtless be time's end, there will be no villainy done, no ambition vaunted, no struggling one with another. Nor will it grow from innocence or ignorance, that era of compassion and mildness, but from an enduring knowledge gained by example and experience. And then, in that ultimate time, before the last of the suns sets and the last of the stars goes out, and the endless adventure of existence removes itself to some other finer course, then the gentle, the good, and the knowing, they and they alone, those that we shall come to be, shall inherit the earth, before the earth is no more."

A profound quiet now lay upon the slope above the river, under the tree. It had kept its leaves, the wild fig, though they were worn thin.

"Yet," said the rider of the elephant, "you, a sinner, you have said, say all this too, and are weightless as those leaves over our heads. How can you walk upright, how can you speak so blithely, if your deeds are as you say?"

"Once," said Dathanja, "there was a merchant, who owed money to many other merchants in the town. He kept mighty ledgers, and pored over them day and night. So intent was he upon how much he owed, and so carefully did he groan over the accounts, that his trade was ruined. He was near to becoming not only a debtor, but an impoverished debtor. There came one to him then, and said to him, 'Throw away your books, and go out into the town and earn your gold, for you are talented and will soon be rich again.' 'But,' said the merchant, 'how am I to remember to whom I owe these debts, unless I keep note of them?' 'Do only this,' said his adviser, kindly. 'If you see any that lack, or if any apply to you for funds, where you have it, give it them. In that way those in need you will sustain, and those you owe you cannot help but repay.' And so the merchant burned the ledgers and forgot them, but going out he earned much gold, made himself the debtor of everyman, and did great service for all. And lightly did he walk, that man, having so simplified his life.''

''But for sure,'' cried the elephant's velvet rider, ''there are some bad men abroad, and to do good turns to them would be idiocy.''

''Yet,'' said Dathanja, ''if you would punish them, then you must keep note of their names and carry the long list with you, always taking it out and consulting it, wherever you go.''

''But if I do kindnesses to a wicked man, he will make a fool of me. He will grind me like grain between the millstones.''

''Does he,'' said Dathanja, ''make more of a fool of you by supposing you a fool than you make of yourself by wasting your time and effort in the constant striving to return ill for ill? A hungry man who finds a fruit tree may eat some of the fruit. It is perhaps sour, or perhaps deliciously sweet. Either way, the matter is soon discovered and the man may go on with his journey. Conversely, he may halt under the tree for an hour with his stomach crying to him for food, deciding if it is worth biting at the fruit, since it may not be to his liking. Each has his own life, and came to this place to live it. The easier his dealings with other men, the more time is left for his own pursuits. Now suppose,'' said the priest, ''you sat here by the water, where you had come to think or dream, or contemplate the world, or to sleep. And a man came to you and struck you in the face. What then?''

''Why, I would jump up and clap him back, twice as hard as he had struck at *me*.''

''And thereupon he would strike you most hardly yet, and you would strike him more hardly, and so on, until one had maimed or killed the other. And say you are the victor and he lies prone, then you must fly justice or the revenge of his family. Or you must gain a way to recompense them. And all this while you have been fighting, planning, or flying, you have spent your energy that you had meant to use on your own account. Now, when the man struck you, if you had only said to him, 'Strike me again for good measure, I have no quarrel with *you*,' perhaps he would have struck you, or perhaps not, but the affair would have been finished with, and you at liberty to go on as you wished.''

"Master, I see it is a parable, but nevertheless, some men, being allowed to strike another unchecked, will make a habit of striking there. Is that not also an interruption?"

"Life is a series of blows, in any case," said the priest, "birth and death being the greatest of these, but between them, many of lesser sort. And is it possible to return or mend every smack of fate and life? Sit down beneath the storm, for if you shout at it, it will not hear you."

"Now by the gods," said the velvet rider, "tell me how to get wisdom."

"Leave your mansion and your wealth. Wander the world. Accept only what is given, but where you are able, give away again all you have."

The rider's face fell to his silken boots.

"*Must* I do this? Is there no other method?"

"There are many. They will take you longer. It is hard to run when your feet are tied to a palace gate; it is hard to see through windows of emerald and silver. You put difficulties in your path. That is all."

And then the sky turned the color of the worn fig leaves, a smoky shadow-shade, and the men who had sought Dathanja, one and all, exclaimed in fear. Even the bullocks lowed and snorted, and the elephants squealed. After which, the silence came again, three times more leaden than before.

The elephant's rider drew from his belt a pale emerald set in silver, and gazing through it at the sky, he announced: "The face of the sun has turned black, though all about it streams his bright hair."

It was the first eclipse of the flat earth, or the first eclipse of the sun by the moon which had been seen since the ages of chaos. (For chaos had been brushed, and brushed in turn the world, and changed it. Things would never be quite as they had been. Nature took strides, she raced.)

"It is the rage of heaven," quavered certain of the sick who had been healed, and now felt guilty for being comfortable after years of anguish.

"It is this priest's abstruse teaching, which has upset those gods who control the sky's disks. In a moment they may throw stars at him. Let us run away!"

But others plucked at Dathanja's sleeve, where he sat serenely, and child-girl leaned on him without any sign of alarm. Dathanja said, "The moon has come between us and the sun. In a minute or so the moon take her way onward, and this phenomenon will cease."

The child looked into his face with her blue, blue eyes.

"Tell a story to us," said she softly, "why the moon should approach the sun."

Dathanja motioned all the nervous and frightened ones to sit down again. He spoke a phrase that brought a vast calm upon them, there in the darkness with the hair of the sun streaming from a black hole in the sky. Even the beasts lay down, and even the river smoothed itself.

4   *The Story of the Sun and the Moon*

LONG, LONG ago, and longer ago than that . . .
. . . the Sun had a garden in the east. But he had had words with the Moon, and would not let her into the garden. There came a dusk when she could bear her curiosity no more. The Moon summoned one of the wide-winged moths that fly by night. "Go you into the gar-

den," she said, "and see of what sort it is. Return and tell me."

So the night-flying moth flew down the miles of heaven and over the back of the earth, into the east. Presently he came to a high wall, higher than the sky it seemed. Upward again he flew, but the wall appeared to meet and become one with the darkness. Around and around he flew, but the wall was a vast circle, without beginning or end. At last the moth grew weary and fell to the ground under the wall. Here he found a tiny eyelet. Folding close his wings, he crept through this little space, and emerged into the garden.

How beautiful it was. The lawns were many-tiered and with the nap of velvet, and more velvety even than these were the rock shelves and steps over which rivulets trickled. It was the Sun's garden, and so even by night, the rock was warm, and the air of the garden was warm, and scented with a hundred fragrances. The shrubs grew tall as trees. The trees were like mighty spires, and the perfume of their wood and their moisture nearly drowned the moth, so he must rest on an amber stone which glowed. Everywhere about such stones lay scattered, and each glowed. It was the Sun's garden, and all bright and fulvous things were there. The trees were crowded by golden fruit which shone like lamps; fireflies played above the pools, where creatures with orange pelts and fiery eyes stole down to drink. A fish leapt: It was a topaz.

Eventually the night began to fade. The moth remembered who had sent him on her errand. He returned to the wall, and after much searching, he found the eyelet and made his way out.

The Moon stood low in the western sky, with her pale hair around her, looking for him. "Well," she said, "you were gone a whole night. Is the garden fair?"

The moth told her that it was. He described the manner of it, the plants and fruits, the lights and fragrances, and the animals which inhabited it.

The Moon was envious. "I wish I might see this also," she said.

The Moon sat in her twilight pavilion under the western horizon, thinking about how she might trick the Sun.

Their quarrel was many thousands of years old. They had forgotten what they had quarreled over, but neither would unbend to the other.

At length she made a plan. "I shall not traverse the sky tonight, but leave the earth in darkness. Wrapped in a black mantle I will go into the east. The moth found a way into the garden, and so will I. Is the Moon less wise than a moth?"

When the Sun rode west in his blaze of glory, the Moon had moved her pavilion into the east. When the final torches of the Sun's procession vanished, the stars came out with mirrors and bells. They called to the Moon to join them, but the Moon had other business. She wrapped herself in her black mantle and stepped down the night until she came against a vast encircling wall. Higher than heaven it seemed, without beginning or end.

The Moon searched awhile, and then she stood awhile in thought. "Perhaps it is not so after all," said the Moon. "I am no wiser than the moth. Indeed, I am less wise."

After a time, she heard the sound of water. Turning from the great wall she found a range of hills, and there a cave. She passed into the cave and in it was a stream bed and a stream flowing away under the ground.

The Moon spoke to the stream in its own language.

"Where are you going?" asked the Moon.

"Into the Sun's garden, where all is gold and glad."

"May I go with you?"

"It is forbidden," said the stream.

"Why?"

"You are the Moon, with whom he has had words."

"No," said the Moon, "you are mistaken. I am only the light of seven silver cities quenched by a cloud far away." When she denied herself, the Moon felt a pang, but she was resolute.

The stream believed her. It permitted her to lie down upon it and bore her with it under the ground, and under the mighty wall, into the garden.

Here the stream bed was laid with shining jacinth and jasper. The Moon rose from the water, and looked about. Soon she walked through the garden, its high places and its hollows. She touched the golden fruit on the trees and it rang like gongs, she beheld the fiery beasts playing on the lawns. She was filled with jealousy and admiration. As she walked, the flowers in the grass turned silver. She was reflected in three pools, to the east, the west, and the south of the garden.

Eventually the night began to fade. The Moon went to the stream which constantly entered the garden.

"No," said the stream. "I brought you but I will not return you hence."

"Alas," said the Moon.

She hurried to the wall, seeking a way out as she had sought a way in. She grew anxious, for the first torches were alight in the eastern sky. Finally she perceived the little eyelet by which the moth had escaped the garden. The Moon waned, making herself slender as an awl. But when she lay down to pass through the eyelet, she discovered the web of a spider had been spun there, all golden with the Sun-strength of the garden—and the Moon could not break it.

The Moon was angry and afraid. In the east she saw the burning incenses and firecrackers of the Sun's procession. Resuming her usual form and size, the Moon ran to a vast tree hung with foliage. Into this she climbed, and hid herself under the leaves.

Then the Sun came over the horizon. He rode a tiger of cinnabar. Scarves of yellow and rose unfolded from the beams that danced in his following; the banners were loud as the noise of trumpets.

As he passed, he looked down into his garden. His light was so colossal it blinded even him. He did not see the drifts of silver in the grass, or the paleness smoldering there under the boughs of a tall tree. He reflected his glory into the three pools where the Moon had been reflected, and rode on, well pleased.

When the Sun was gone, the Moon tried many things to get out of the garden. She called her half brothers, the lunar winds, but they would only shake the trees, and when the golden fruit fell, they sported with it—they were very young. And she called the nightbirds that worshiped her as a goddess, the nightingale who has bells in her throat, and the owl with his glimmering temple windows for eyes. But the birds, though they had somehow got through the wall, were half asleep and could find no egress suitable for the Moon, and they chirruped and whirred and mourned and yawned, and stared, and were sent away abashed. It was now almost night again, and the sky moonless.

Some upstart star, thought the Moon, *will take my honors. She will strain herself to shine more brightly, and say she is the Moon, and the earth will forget me.* Then the Moon wept, and her tears made pearls about the trees, which slowly turned to rubies in the sunset.

Presently there came a sound that caused the Moon's tears to dry in horror. It was the note of a great key turning in a large lock somewhere in the wall. Then a solar wind rushed through the garden, twanging the blades of the grass and ruffling the fur of the fierce beasts there. It was the Sun's messenger, and the Sun himself came close behind, blazing in a mantle of dark red.

"Ah, how beautiful my garden is," declared the Sun possessively, "more beautiful than ever before. But what is this?" he added, as his own radiance lit the ruby-pearls upon the grass. "Come now," said the Sun, parting the branches of the tree, "who is hiding there?"

"It is I," whispered the Moon.

"Is it you? Who are you?"

The Moon started. *He does not remember me,* she thought. *Well, it has been an eon or two since we met. And he has always dazzled himself.* And wrapping her own mantle closely about her, she descended and stood before the Sun, very timidly.

"I am," said the Moon, "an especially brilliant star. So brilliant the Moon was envious, and she sent me from her court. I came here by mischance, and could not find a way out again. Will you let me from your garden?"

"Stay," said the Sun. "You are very fair. I can see quite easily how the Moon, that pallid hag, would be jealous."

"Can you indeed?" said the Moon, and she seethed in her mantle. "Nevertheless I have duties to perform in the nocturnal sky."

"Stay with me only this one night," said the Sun,

winningly. "Then, when I myself must leave to light the
sky, you may go before me. I have long had a scheme to
choose of all the stars one of the loveliest, who should then
be my herald in the east. Perhaps I shall choose you."

"How generous you are, how you flatter me," said
the Moon. And she hid her looks, which might have splintered glass, in her mantle.

But the Sun vowed he would not let her go until morning, so the Moon stayed with him, perforce, and pretended
to be dazzled by him also, and it came to be that she was.
For as they strolled through the marvelous garden, he
showed her the most fragrant of its flowers, and the best of
its fruits he plucked for her. And his hands, which guided
her, were warm. When they were weary, they reclined
upon the blissful turf, and the Sun dallied with the Moon,
and the Moon said to herself, *Since I make out I am a
mere star, I must permit this.* And the Sun charmed her,
despite the old resentments. She softened to him. So much
so indeed, that when the torches and trumpets of his eager
retinue drew near to call him forth to dawn, the Moon was
rather regretful. Yet, as he was departing, she waxed
vexed again. So she snatched surreptitiously a throbbing stone
from a waterfall and a burning flower from the grass. And at
the last she cut off by stealth a lock from the Sun's flaming
mane, with a little silver knife, as he embraced her in
farewell.

Then the Sun let her out of his garden, and away the
Moon fled up the sky, all in disarray, her mantle slipping
from her white shoulders and her hair fluttering about her.
She ran across heaven and did not stop until she reached
her pavilion, and here she fell down in a faint of griev-
ance, pleasure, and shame.

The Moon brooded. She became thin, less luminous,
more pale. She thought, *I will pay him out, for his fine
garden, for my humiliation. That he thought me a star
only, and dallied with me. But most of all because I
permitted it.*

Then the Moon took the flower and the stone from the
Sun's garden, and the lock of hair from the Sun's own
mane, and she made magic. When she was done, she wove

a robe for herself, and this robe shone so wonderfully, the stars who had come to her pavilion to visit her shrank back in surprise.

Now let him think me *a star,* thought the Moon, and she rose up the sky blindingly.

So fair and so glorious she shone that night that in the lands of men, the poets who had written *harsh bitter Moon* crossed out the line and wrote instead *O Moon of man's delight!* And those who wrote *old cold silver witch* changed it to *warm golden girl.* Truly, warm and bright as gold, the very sun of night, she was. Only the secret lovers did not bless her that evening, or thieves, who formerly had made her offerings.

But the Sun saw too, where he had his own red pavilion in the west. And mounting the black tiger he used for nighttime excursions, he rode furiously westward to follow her progress, and all the way he heard her praises. *It was she all this while in my garden,* he thought, in anger. *She I plucked fruit for, and pretended to think pretty. And she has stolen from me essentials of my light, and boasts to men and gods that it is only her own glaze that adorns her. Well, let her rule the sky, then. Till I have justice, they may manage as they can without me.*

And going back into his garden, the Sun slammed the gate.

When the procession of morning called upon him, the Sun sent them away alone, and it was a vague dreary dawn that day, and for many days after. But the Sun, in his garden, learned something to his advantage.

Now in those far-off times, the gods were young. They took an interest in all things. And when mankind began to complain at their altars that the Sun no longer smiled on the earth, and that therefore everlasting winter and barrenness overtook them, the gods heeded.

They sent to the Sun and asked him what he meant by his absence. The Sun replied that he had fallen sick, let the Moon oversee the day as well as the night, for she burned so magnificently, surely it would be no bother to her. (The Moon, when she heard this, blanched, and even her finery could not disguise it.) The gods sent again to the Sun, and summoned him into the upper tiers of the sky, where they looked down on him: He had come muffled in a storm cloud.

"It is this way," said the Sun. "Someone entered my garden and stole from me a part of my essence, the soul of my light. I am weakened and dismayed. Correct the matter, and I will resume my office."

"Who stole from you?" inquired the gods. (Even then, they would tend to speak in concert.)

"I do not know," said the Sun, "but I guess." And he told how he had found one in the garden who assured him she was a star, and he had been attentive to her, but next the Moon had appeared in glory, while he sickened.

Then the gods sent for the Moon. She came, veiled in mist, and trembling much.

"Did you enter the Sun's garden?"

"I?" said the Moon, astounded to be asked.

"Did you steal from the Sun?"

"I?" said the Moon.

"What proof," said the gods to the Sun, "do you have that ever she entered the garden? For if she denies both things and is found guilty of one, then guilty she must be of the other also."

Then the Sun grinned and the Moon shuddered.

"Only come with me there," said the Sun, "and you will see."

So the gods descended into the garden of the Sun, and walked about there, and the earth echoed at each footfall of theirs among the great-leaved trees and by the gleaming waters.

Night entered presently, and in the dark all glowed most entertainingly, and to the water's edges came the orange beasts to drink, while the topaz fishes leapt. Then through the glades by the waters rang female voices, and next there advanced dancingly three lovely young feminine forms. They were white as the ashes of lilies, and their long pale hair hung around them; they wore garlands of yellow flowers, and amber necklaces and anklets, and these were all their clothing.

"As I lay here in my illness," said the Sun, "I saw these three rise up from the pools of my garden and run about here, and when I spoke to them they came to me lovingly and respectfully, showing no fear, and calling me their father.''

''Who then is their mother?'' asked the gods.

''You must ask them,'' said the Sun virtuously.

The gods did so. And running happily to the Moon, the three called her ''Mother'' at once.

And the Moon blushed red as a sunrise.

For it had been this way. She had reflected in the three pools of the garden, east, west, south, and the powers of the garden, which could imbue even a spider's web, had retained that reflection, and imbued it, and later the Sun reflected there too. . . . And later still there had been some dalliance, which had brought all symbolically together.

''They are daughters to be proud of,'' said the Sun. ''One shall light my way in the morning; she shall be the Morning Star. And another, who is a little darker, she shall walk behind me at sunset to close the doors of the west—and she shall be the Evening Star. But the fairest of them I will keep by me at all times, for there is not yet any situation vacant that is good enough for her, though there may come an age when that may happen.''

But the Moon covered her face and said, ''All is proved against me. I was peevish and dishonest and have done wrong. For he would not let me in the garden, and he did not even, finding me there, remember who I was. And, worst of all, I loved him again, as once long ago, and could not remember our quarrel.''

Then the Sun, hearing that, went to the Moon and kissed her.

''I had no right to shut you out. You are my beloved, and only the distance that is always between us made us enemies.''

However, the gods pronounced judgment for all that, for they were not invited lightly into any affair.

The Moon they allowed to keep her gorgeous robe, and even to wear it, but not often. And they decreed that she must hereafter endlessly alter her shape in the heavens, shrinking and enlarging and shrinking, as she had done when she tried to get out of the garden by stealth, in order that men recollect she was inconstant, the lady of secret

lust, and thieves. But this they added, that since the Moon
and Sun were reconciled with each other, and only distance had made them enemies, at particular times they
might meet, there in the sky, before the gaze of mankind
and all the world, and that at these infrequent meetings the
Moon should stand before the Sun as he kissed her (which
undoubtedly he would do), so that his beauteous and great
light would be dulled. And so they reprimanded the Moon's
sulky deception and the Sun's vainglorious pride.

As for the two chosen daughters, they came to be the
Morning and Evening Stars, and they greet their mother
joyfully when they see her in heaven. But the third daughter is still waiting for her appointment. For the garden, it
passed from Being as such wonders did in the maturing of
the world.

But the Sun and the Moon have stayed close friends,
and so we have seen them to be. For it was the privilege of
men, by this midday shadow, to know that the lovers had
embraced each other over men's heads. That darkness was
only their kiss.

Now who could be churlish enough to be afraid of that?

And even as Dathanja closed the story, the moon swam
from the sun, and the light of day shone out again, and the
birds sang, and the hippopotami frisked in the river.

5

THE SUN, having displayed his kingly face again,
rode westward and vanished.

The crowd upon the river bank arose and also went
away, pointing, with intimate irony, to the evening star, as

she walked sedately after her father, to shut the doors of a yellow sunset.

The priest and the child turned toward their house. The child, who had been very silent since the passing of the shadow, said to him at last, "If the sun can be a darkness, cannot darkness be a sun?"

Dathanja said, "It would depend upon the form of the darkness. It would depend on many things."

"Most youthful Father," said the child, "it is not possible for me ever to thank you for your goodness to me, nor did you do it to be thanked. But I have sat at your feet and listened. I have learned. And the whole earth has spoken to me. Also, my own heart. Such excellent teachers I have had. And when the shadow left the earth, the shadow that was on me, this too drew away. Here I am. No longer Sovaz, or Azhriaz. No longer Soveh, your child."

The crepuscule had come. The land was blue, and the river, and in her eyes the blueness of every dusk the world had known. And in his that regarded her, every black night which followed.

"I am glad for you," he said.

"For the sake of that gladness, for a little while," she said, "let us remain as we have been. For each grows up, as you have told me. But the moon, changing her shape, is still the moon, and just so with love."

So he took her hand, as he had done in her three-year childhood, and they walked together along the river bank where the lotuses still burgeoned, to the house.

Not a lamp was lighted there, not even in the upper room, which was also noiseless.

"He has argued with the mirror again," said the girl, and she and Dathanja burst out laughing. In the midst of the laughter they held each other close, and he said to her, "We should not laugh at him," and they laughed, and she said, "No, we should not," and they laughed more. "Oh little girl, I rejoice you are yourself at last." "Am I myself? Who is she? But I think no longer am I another's, not even yours, my kinsman, my kind lord, who cared for me." "What now? You will leave me now?" he said. "And you," said she, "will be pleased to be left. To your work, and your princess who gives you *shoes*—" "Oh little girl, how do you know that?" "Oh dear friend, my father-brother, the whole land knows. Even the frogs talk about it. 'What did he with her *then*?' they ask. And the grasshoppers tell them." At that they laughed all over again. And flirtatiously, by sorcery, they each of them lit the lamps of the lower room, so the flames winked up out of the darkness like spring flowers. And then they lit the fire on the hearth, blew it out, lit it, and they were both children, she and he, who had lived and died and lived, each in their own fashion, a girl of seventeen whose years amounted to almost half a century, a man perhaps in his twenty-fifth year, who had known whole centuries intact, and numberless.

"Let us," repeated the girl, "not speak for a time of parting. Though you have wintered in this region, yet you are and will be again a wanderer. And I—I must seek my life under every stone, upon each pinnacle, within the shade and shine of the earth, and elsewhere. . . . But not yet. We have the last days of winter still. And I will be a dutiful daughter-sister to you. I will be a girl of the village and the town, and cook your food and mend your clothes, set flowers by your pillow, and sing to you. If in return you tell me still your stories, and hold me in your arms as you have held me, asking nothing but the love of a child."

"Here are all the lizards and frogs, waiting by the rain-jar, to be let in," said he. "Shall I allow them to come to my hearth, when they have been gossiping all this while with the grasshoppers concerning myself and the princess?"

"Shame them by overlooking their faults."

So the assembly of frogs, and other creatures of the bank, were permitted the warmth of the fire.

Then, by the firelight under the lamps, the man and woman ate a rustic supper, augmented by two pitchers of wine ensorceled out of the vaults of a nearby potentate.

And later they slept, in their allotted separate places, which were close enough together. Neither experienced desire for the other. It had not been their fate to be lovers, though to love.

Dathanja dreamed that he was seated on a hillside with a maiden whose hair was the color of apricots. They spoke and laughed together, while she fed wildfowl of the air, and slender reptiles from under rocks, out of her hands. And later they lay, he and she, in the blazing grass, in love. Below, on a plain beside a lake of clear water, unicorns were dancing, white and rose and gold. Somewhere a bell rang from a distant temple's tower, and leaves sighed as they opened.

And Zhirek, as Simmu relaxed her clasp upon him, and he his own of her, kissed her flame of hair and said to her, "Have you punished me enough, have you been sufficiently revenged on me?"

"You yourself punished yourself, and avenged me. And such things are, anyway, a silliness."

"The priests are liars?" asked Zhirek.

"Yes. All but one."

And soon they joined in love again, in love of love. And at that time, love was enough.

But the Vazdru Goddess-girl, Sovaz-Azhriaz-Soveh, she dreamed this:

There was a blue mountain above a green valley. Buildings grew up in the valley, the stalks of towers. There was a temple, blooming from the mountainside, row upon row of pillars, and the stairways of roofs ascending. Aromatic smokes traveled from its courts, straight as ruled lines in the sublime summer air.

But high up, near the mountain's summit, was a small shrine made of blue marble, so like the sky it might be missed altogether. Here an old priestess dwelled, and very old she was. "Three centuries she has seen out," the pilgrims said to the dreaming girl, as she climbed the path with them. "But she is tired now. Tired by all her wandering. She is a healer and teacher, and a prophetess. Decades she has resided here. Kings come to her to explain their visions. Queens come and ask that their destiny be told them, or the meaning of portents. And though she is ancient, this woman, as one of the great snakes that dwell in the mountain's core, yet she can make herself to seem a young girl, satin-skinned and fleet as a deer. Why," they added to the dreamer, "have you sought her out?"

"I would have her explain a dream to me," the dreamer said.

And then she was within the mountaintop that lay behind the shrine. Enormous columns rose, glossy as milk, and vapors from the cavern's throat, some perfumed and some acrid. An elderly woman, all wizened and bent, a crone, sat on a ledge, and she caressed the diamond-shaped head of a serpent, which head alone was the length of a man's foot.

"Do not trouble about the snake," she said, in a voice like a dry old leaf, so faint, yet audible as is a tiny noise within the ear.

"Snakes I have never feared," said the dreamer, and going near, she stroked the snake also. And looked up into the priestess's face and into such blue, blue eyes, her own were filled by tears.

"What is your name?" said the girl to the crone.

"It is Atmeh."

"Why did they name you that?"

"None named me but myself. In the land where I was reborn, and where I was a child, I had another name. But in the language of that country my name, which meant a petal of the fire, had another meaning, which was *spark of life*, and the word for this, in that tongue, was Atmeh. Thus, when I set out to find myself, I took that name to be my own. Ah, young girl, pretty dreamer," said the ancient priestess, "one day we shall meet, you and I. Go now, and find your life."

And Azhrarn's daughter woke up, there in the house by the brown river shore. She looked at once at her companion, as he slept, seeing his beauty and his youth, his age, his sorrow, and the recompense of knowledge—all that upon his slumbering face.

She would not have woken him, yet she yearned to tell him of her dream.

But even as she sat there undecided, the house door rushed inward with a terrific crash—and woke the entire world, it seemed.

6

IT HAD SWUM for miles, and years. Beneath the sea, in the long depths under the dark green hills, whose crowns were islands, and on the surface also, under the blister of sun and glister of moon. Tall ships had sighted it, and called after it, thinking to effect a rescue. Or they had avoided it, supposing it to be what once it had been. And the huge fish of the aqueous abysses had tried to detain it, or fish-girls with cool green lips and eyes like stars that had drowned. But on and on it swam, indifferent, determined. And sometimes even it went in circles, searching and not finding. And sometimes it crawled through subterranean channels. And sometimes it rested, whole hours at a stretch, before it crawled or swam on again. So at last it reached the mouth of a river, and swam up that. The waters altered from the tones of ocean to a tawny glass, now and then blackening with night. Rime lay over the river, where enormous bladders floated with closed-up eyes. At length the swimmer broke from the water among the ice-cold stems of lotuses, and so came to a house, and flung wide the door.

And there it stood, the body of Tavir, a prince of Tirzom Jum, spangled with wet, and with the seaweed still upon its shoulder.

The body of Tavir had not decayed, not in three years and more. Perhaps the cataclysm—chaos, which touched even angels—had done something to the fibers of a corpse that lay so close to the shock. Or else, its link to the immortal magician had preserved the discarded flesh.

To the girl and the man Tavir's body gave no attention, though both were sorcerers, and greater than that.

It prowled across the floor to the stair, and up it went, and giving there the second door, that of the upper room, a mighty shove, strode into chamber of the mage.

Tavrosharak had been seated at his table (pilfered from a king's library and laid with books and curios obtained in the same spot). He had been long silent, but now he leapt up, oversetting some bizarre unuseful experiment, so holes were burned in the table's wood, and in the very atmosphere.

"Pay heed," said Tavir's body.

"I will," said Tavrosharak, although he made a pass or two and uttered a mantra or three that should have rid him of the apparition, and failed.

"I am no ghost," said the body. "I am the whole skin, and the physical soul—the *ego* of Tavir. You lured me to you, sensing your liberty would shortly come, and claimed back the spirit-soul out of me. But I had lived. I had been a mage, like you. And I am young, as you—when you acquired your immortality—no longer were. Now," said Tavir's body, "Simmurad is no more. It is destroyed, for the fire ran through it, and then a fearsome fiery wave that ran the other way. Where fire and unmatter met in water, a red sun was born, that dashed away. And I was galvanized to pursue it, awhile. But then, my mind awoke in me, and I remembered you. So I sought out you instead. And here I am before you."

"What do you want?" quavered the sage-mage, still flapping about in efforts to effect some spell of riddance, ineffectually.

"A soul," said the body. "Yours, *mine*. That which I had."

"And what of me?" howled Tavrosharak.

"What of you? Look at the life you have given our soul, shut up day and night, dabbling and dithering, hating all men. What will you learn in here but what a fool you are? Come," said Tavir, black, beautiful, a lord of the sea, shining green of hair and eye, "come, dear soul, back to the one who truly values you. See in me what you will gain. And consider what you have lost, with him."

"Stay, dear soul," gabbled Tavrosharak. "I will mend my ways. We will go out and change men into stones and stones into sheep, and overturn the whole earth—"

"Come, dear soul," coaxed Tavir, "and we will enjoy the loveliness of the world, and try to repair the pain of it. We will found a city under the sea where the ocean peoples shall live at peace together. All the teaching of the priest Dathanja, which the one who traps you has overheard—and dismissed—but which you have pondered on, all that we will try, and bring to bear upon our future life together."

The mage-sage sat abruptly down in his chair. He gave a grunt, and from his parted lips spun flame. It was a soft fire, barely visible. But Tavir opened wide his arms to receive it.

"There is," said Tavir presently, "a goddess in this house, and the teacher, who has such skill. But also this body I have now will not live forever. I must be swift. No distraction. And so—farewell without greeting—"

And Tavir spoke his own mantra for a disappearance, soul-possessed and so a magician once more. And was gone.

Meanwhile, the body of Tavrosharak, soul-empty, sat hard as coral in the chair, and it muttered: "How am I to work upon occult science with such a disturbance?" And it called a whirlwind in at the window simply to berate it. For the immortal flesh of the sage had kept much of its mage-craft, even soulless, and did so still, and, too, its irritated personality, that needed no soul to fuel it. So there it sat, and would sit for centuries, grumbling and complaining, studying and disparaging the books, quarreling with itself in the mirror, and performing feats of annoying sorcery.

And the cattle herders going under the window three hundred years hence, when trees had rooted through the floor and roof of the house, and the shores of the river widened almost to the door, would still say in propitiating voices to it, "Pray do us no harm, Uncle."

7

THE WINTER, who had lain hard upon the earth so long, pressing her down, having his will with her, left her suddenly with only a chilly kiss, and mounting his branch-bare chariot, he stormed away.

Pale gleaming days, like zircon drops, came to the earth, and clothed her in filmy yellows and wild greens. To the brown land they came also, bringing robes of a denser dye, setting fire to flowers, sprinkling the fields with whispering fringes. On the trees the heavy leaves sprang out. The hippopotami washed off their mud and fought each other in the river. The elephants, breaking their tethers, screamed and stamped among the hills by night.

The prince's daughter, the princess, cried in her painted bed. "Now he will leave me." But it seemed he would not, yet, though he did not promise her all time.

The girl who had been Dathanja's daughter walked on the shore, and took the last winter lotuses for a garland. Against her throat, in a little silver cage, a mote of amethyst constricted their color. (Even chaos, toucher of angels, had not been able to melt that gem. Or had avoided doing so.) Its influence had been with her then and since, for good, for ill. And she had had her days of madness, surely, simple and a child?

A white ibis stalked among the stems. It bowed as it passed her, and uttered a weird cry. *Atmeh*.

For the earth knew the name she had chosen for herself, the name which meant hereabouts Flame, or Flame of Life.

One other too, maybe, knew of her rebirth and her naming.

And she looked with more than sight across the brown river, away toward the land's boundaries. The snow had dissolved from the mountains where they rose, afloat like jeweled ships in the sky. Beneath, on one single hill, one dot of asphodel snow. The Malukhim, unfolding his wings.

It might have been he had hibernated, or even flown to some warmer clime. Or he had only sat out the interim. Who could divine what retributive angels did in the cold months, the will of the gods being so loose upon them?

Dathanja had left the house and stood before the door-post. Atmeh went to him. "It is," she said, "today that I will go from here."

"Yes, it is today."

They looked at each other.

She took up his hand and kissed it.

"Wise healer," she said, "gentle priest. We may never meet again."

"One day, far off, maybe we shall."

"Will you know me then?"

"Do we not," he said, "always remember, through all our several lives, old friends and former kindred, however we, or they, are altered?" He held her to him, and stroked her hair, long, black, demoniac. "There is the angel," he said.

"I shall meet him. The gods are conscious, surely, I am no longer a god."

"You do not know for sure your road," he said. "But you will find it."

"So I shall. Dear love," she said, "farewell."

"Farewell," he said. "Dear love."

Then moving from him in the rays of the early sun, Atmeh went along the bank and left the house behind her.

The hippos paused in their jousting to see her go. The white ibis raised their ebony heads. All the winter lotuses crumbled away to smoke.

But for Dathanja, his face was not to be read, nor the dark eyes of it. He watched, or seemed to watch her, for some while. But then he turned to the tree at the top of the bank.

The little crowd which was already there saw him approaching, and cried out to him thankfully. He smiled at them, at each group of features, each healthy or diseased body, for in every one there burned the flame of life, in all of them, and in him. And in the girl, even if by another mode, in the manner of immortals, that flame yet burned. They were, near or far, all one. All things were one. All men were gods. And love was enough.

Atmeh walked toward the mountains. She walked as a lovely human girl would do, gracefully, through the contact of her soles with the ground. Before the mountains she would reach the hill, there, westward, where the Malukhim opened and shut his wings.

She had, the girl, the woman, all her memory. Yet she had been reborn into childhood, and known it, then left it—lacking only the growing pains of an adolescence. The world was therefore very fascinating to her, known and new, seen equally at dawn and at noon. By this means she had come to recognize the helpful power, the actual lesson of birth, death, and rebirth. It seemed to her that her soul had itself lived bodily, often, before it had been summoned to the child in Dunizel's womb. For though Azhrarn believed he had invented true life, could even he do so? The humblest peasant could create a child, and so could the least sensible of men. Azhrarn, too, formed a fleshly case, though his method had not been the same (the carnal act being art and pleasure to demons, but never procreative). Nevertheless, could he, any more than the peasant or random lackwit, who by a spillage of semen got life on a woman, create the soul itself? By the variation of the lives—and deaths—Atmeh had clearly undergone in this existence, she had detected the others that had made and unmade her, in the past. And now an immortal, the question came to her, was there not more to be learned through a diversity of lives, through the confusion of genders, temperaments, creeds, wishes—through the very and natural *un*knowing of the infant, through the continuous *re*-learning even of the same lesson—for was it not, in point of fact, on each occasion learned in a different way?

And thinking these thoughts, she traveled through the

brown land, day by day, sleeping by night at the edges of the budding fields, or under some spreading tree at the roadside. Supposing her a wandering holy woman, goatherds gave her milk from their flocks. She did not require sustenance, yet accepted it. Sometimes, when it was needful, she performed acts of healing or mending, as she had seen Dathanja do, and rather in his character, with some uncomplex paraphernalia to offset marvel.

After a palmful of days (how many fit inside a palm, a woman's palm—seven then), she came to the feet of the hills, baked as cakes in the morning light, and behind stood the mountains westward. But between the two, Ebriel, awaiting her, and with sword drawn—for she saw its glitter like one glaring sliver of ice the winter had left behind.

So she climbed toward the angel. She climbed through midday, and all one afternoon, and when the sun was westering, she came over a ridge, and there the angel was, with the sun behind him like a ball of gold. He showed black on the brightness, and this struck her—again—how dark might become light, since pallor could be black as ink.

"Ebriel," said Atmeh. (She knew his name. There was little she could not know of the earth, and its adjacent environs.) "Ebriel, look at me, and consider me. I do not challenge heaven, now. If ever I did. Say then what must be between us."

The angel did not reply, not by word, nor any action.

Now, she had been tended by Eshva. And that unspeaking speech of theirs was still second to her nature. It is not properly said—which in itself is a sort of pun—how the unspeaking speech was spoken, or heard. It was not exactly a mind-language, telepathic. Nor entirely corporeal, though the breath, the eyes, and movements of the hands, limbs, and torso, even of the hair, contributed. A language possessed of symbolism, certainly. Whatever it was, and however exercised, the inspiration came to Atmeh to employ it with the angel. And so she spoke to him again, by this tongue. She said, "You have heard my words, and you have read me clear as still water. But we cannot stand

here forever, you and I. Nor go on as we have done, flying
and flown after, hesitating and always overlooked.''

"Forever," said the angel. "What is that but the eternal
state of all things? Why should we not?''

And he too used the Eshva speech, or an approximation
of it, which seemed also natural to him.

"Your masters are the gods," said Atmeh.

"That is so."

"What do the gods instruct you to do?"

"I have their instruction. The first and only motivation
given me, as to my brothers."

"The gods, if they still concern themselves, which I
suspect they do not, realize I am no longer any nuisance to
them.''

"That has no place in the scheme of me, or of my
being.''

It was true. Automaton that he had remained, this Ebriel,
his first command was the sum of him. He had cast down
a city and a worlddom because of it. And here the very
cause of the command confronted him.

"But," said Atmeh, "I have been left unmolested by
you."

"You slept," said the angel. His eyes burned out of the
silhouette of him, each a savage topaz, and each not like
the eyes of an eagle—but like the eagle itself. "Now you
waken, and come here, as is right, that we may meet in
combat. And so, at your awakening, I perceived you
would.''

"To fight is an emblem," said Atmeh. "Must you have
it, Sun-Born? *Must* you?"

"Behold. The sword is from the scabbard," he said.
"When I have sheathed it, the matter will be done. Until
that hour, then.''

"I am an immortal," she said. "And you, I think. We
may transmute, but not perish.''

"All lives are so. It has been discussed before. Such
things do not obviate our combat.''

"Impoverished Ebriel," said Atmeh, with the flash of
dark and anger in her eyes, or perhaps just the last flash of
the sinking sun, "you are only a fool.''

As the evening moved over the hill to meet the coal-blue

wall of the mountains, it found two warriors there. An angel, the sun-holding citrines of his breastplate, golden hair and sword. And Atmeh become Sovaz again, or Azhriaz, in mail the color of the mountain's face, night hair, sword of metal like a pale twilight. And the evening glimmered across them, then passed on. But they stayed, and they fought.

How they fought.

It was related that, from a hundred miles off, men saw the ignition of those blows a quarter of the way up the night sky. It was related, that when the swords smote each other, an arc of brilliance tore out. And sometimes the hill itself was struck, or the air, and lava burst from the one and boiling steam from the second. And then again the sword of each of them might strike home into the body of the opponent. At this, the atmosphere itself must have caught its breath with agony. But they, one an elemental thing, the other scarcely less, agonized or otherwise, healed in an instant, or did not need medicine. It was like the former fight in many ways, that between Azhrarn and Melqar, save for the mutual woundings, but then these two were younger. As with that former conflict, it is nearly useless to describe it. It was inexplicable, it was an affront to every mortal warrior who ever dueled. An emblem, as she said.

Midnight passed over the hill in the wake of evening and mere night.

Atmeh fell back, and leaned on her sword. Though she might fight until daybreak, all day till sunset, all night till dawn (forever, as he had said), yet she allowed herself to be weary, almost to sink with weariness—of the soul if not the body.

"If you would rest," said Ebriel, in the Eshva speech, "do so."

"Fool," said Atmeh, aloud, in the voice of Azhriaz, "resting and toiling till time's end. *Fool*. And I a fool to permit this." Then she dropped down on the earth, her eyes shut. Her soul was so weary it had drained her body.

The angel stood nearby, to guard her if the need arose. She was valuable to him. She was his reason, after all, for existence.

But presently, as if she had inhaled strength from the hill, Atmeh opened her eyes again. She lay and looked up at the angel in the starlight.

"Ebriel, bargain with me. There is some kinship between us; we both have sunfire in our veins. Now if I can strike you three times, and not myself be smitten, before the sun returns—the sun who is directly father and mother to you, and indirectly a grandparent to me—if I can do that, will you grant me a boon?"

Ebriel regarded his adversary. His eyes grew peculiarly lambent, as though he had come to love her. Of course, they were sworn foes; perhaps he had.

"Since we shall contend forever, it is reasonable that we should be courteous, and play such games as you submit. Smite me three times unsmitten before sunrise, and your boon I will grant, provided it is in my scope."

"Oh, believe it," said Atmeh, and she smiled, for she had heard—at long last—a fallible trace of earthliness in his choice of phrase.

The strife on the hill then changed its tone, seeing it now had a purpose.

As a combatant, Atmeh was capricious, cunning, and swift. Perfect coordination and vision were hers—which in themselves made her a peerless swordswoman. The adroitness may have been inherent in her, for the Vazdru sorcererprinces were sorcerous also in many types of martial skill. And perhaps, in the years of her bored goddesshood, she had had herself, for diversion, trained by her war captains in the crafts of affray public or personal. Yet she did not engage in this fight with a format either female or masculine. Her attitude was not human. Neither, of course, was that of the Malukhim—which doubtless would have slain a human swordsman, and one of uncommon cleverness, inside seven seconds.

Three hours of darkness were unspent.

In the first hour, a crescent bow of moon, having cast its quiver of light, went down, and as it did so, Atmeh came close to the Malukhim, and lowered her sword.

As Ebriel's moon-outshining blade leaped toward her heart, Atmeh said, "You are beautiful, Sun-Created," in the voice of Azhriaz, and Ebriel's stroke was missed—in surprise it would appear: Who would think to say or be so bold as to say such words to an angel? And as he missed the stroke, the blade of the demoness clove through his right arm (not at all wounding it), and she said, *"One."*

The angel drew away. He stared at her, the white eagle of heaven.

They fought the rest of the hour, then, and by her competence she did not let him touch her. But in the second hour before dawn, she spoke again to him, in the voice of Sovaz. "If you were only a man, Ebriel, there is a way you might overcome me. There is a way you might pierce me, and kill me too, for a little while. Do you know of this way?"

"Do not attempt to trick me again," said the angel. His wings opened like towering fans, and Atmeh sprang beneath his sword and clipped the left wing a glancing blow.

"Two," said Atmeh. "You trick yourself. I know your kind does not lie down in love. Nor loves in any other posture. Save for this."

Then they battled like two hawks that have fallen from the sky, like two lynxes above meat. They battled like a man and a woman finally, in that old battle each sex knows, yet without the flavor of desire.

And three times, despite her finesse, the angel almost struck her, negating her double assault upon him. Twice, chance saved her, small things—a rock that turned her foot (she who never stumbled) and flung her from the zone of the stroke, or a sudden gust of shale from the hill which, tossed against his sword, deflected it. (Chance? Her Uncle Kheshmet?) But one time she herself spun up in the air to escape, and did Ebriel forget wingless things might also fly?

In the east, the night wore thin.

Abruptly the girl drooped, her body, the slim cruel arm, and the weapon of blue metal. "Enough," she said. "Enough."

Ebriel in his turn let down his sword.

"Let me rest," said Atmeh, in the voice of the child Soveh. And she sank to the earth and closed her eyes once more. Her body lay boneless as her long hair. There seemed no vitality in her.

Ebriel stood for a space, looking at her. Then, lifting his eyes, he gazed toward the east, where the first magnificence began. And in that moment, Atmeh cast herself upward, fast as lightning, and she came against him and thrust her sword all its length into him, through the very heart of him, if he had had one. And next minute the sun rose and showed each of their incredible faces, and lit their amazing eyes.

"Beloved," said Atmeh, "demons are not to be trusted. And mortals, neither. And I am both. *Three*, Ebriel. I have won. You owe me my boon." And she kissed his mouth, briefly, in the way a bird alights upon a bough where it knows it may not linger.

But Ebriel laughed. He *laughed*. Aloud, and beautifully. He said to her: "I award it you, then. What must I do?"

Atmeh said, "We will construct a truce. During this, we will go together and seek your two brothers. Yabael, the Sword of Blood, the Second-Scorched, torment of the ocean. Melqar, the third out of the sun, the Sword of Snow, he that the Prince of Demons strove with."

"To this I agree," said Ebriel.

And now he *spoke*, aloud, as a man does, and Atmeh smiled again.

There rose up the sky then, with the unjealous sun, the Sun-Created on his wings and the demon-created, wingless, in a cloud of hair.

They knew where to seek Yabael. They could know almost anything. (Though that also may have been true of mankind, and yet may be true.) Thus over the mountain peaks they went, and down the lands beyond where the earth smelled pungent as a spicery, and so from sugar to salt, and to the cup brim of the sea. And here they plunged, and descended from azure to green ember, and from that to dimness. There they found a niche in a mighty cliff and stood waiting, breathing the water, yet circumspect, since the oceans' laws were different.

Perhaps a mile below the cliff, a tall city of the sea people lay on the sand, built of shells. Its skies were doved by white whales, that mysteriously sang an endless song, which, by magic alone, under the water, could be heard.

Soon one of these marvelous pale beings came drifting

from the city where their music was prized above the captured gold of men. It came to the niche and gazed in at Atmeh and the angel. Its eyes were small for the size of it, yet huge by any other gauge, and sapphire-blue.

"Travelers," said the whale, or rather, it sang these words to them, and politely in a language of earth, that they might understand it better, "as I see you hear me, and as I see you breathe in ocean, I conclude you are great in magery. But do not go out of the cliff for a while. Shortly, a comet of the sea will journey by. This obliterates whatever comes in its path."

"White Lord, we thank you," said Atmeh, singing, Vazdru that she was, a song to complement his own. "What of the city there, and of your own people?"

"A magic protects the city, of which our singing is an ingredient." And having told her this, the whale swam back again among the others, and resumed his portion of the endless song.

Perhaps one twelfth of an hour later, a vast bloody glow diffused in the sea, and a fearsome noise that was no noise, but the cliff thrummed and rumbled at it, and from the plains beneath spouts of sand sheered up. It moved so quickly, the comet, there was slight warning of its imminence. It came all at once on the stages of its flight, and suddenly it came now on this one. Everything was drowned in redness, and rocked and griped to its roots, and through the sea came a burning fiery sword, shapeless yet awful, and with a lashing tail of flame. This then, Yabael.

Whatever ability the second of the Malukhim had had to reason—it was gone, as shape was gone. Chaos had blended with Yabael, that compendium of ether and sun, sparking the complementary sprinkle of chaos already in his atoms. And Yabael became a savage little sun that hunted the water for prey it did not remember—and in the event raced by that very prey, Atmeh, and by Ebriel, its kin, and by the city, whose towers rippled—and away on the circling, blind chase.

As the fires died, the water softened from scarlet to silver, the whales sang on. The shell metropolis stood.

Atmeh looked into the face of Ebriel. It told her nothing. She spoke, by the Eshva means.

"Yabael is the first lesson I offer you. It is possible even for the Malukhim to alter, or for change to be forced on them. And, too, it is possible for the Malukhim to continue in a hopeless task, which, like the stricken tree, will bear no fruit."

Ebriel's face told her nothing, but his eyes burned with the fire of the comet, red within gold.

"You cannot follow him, beloved. You cannot change as he has done. Come. Up to the world again."

Up to the world they sprang. And the seas parted about them as though every princess of the waters had flung the contents of her jewel casket at the sun.

They could discover almost anything: They discovered where to seek Melqar. Nevertheless, this discovery was not so easy as the first, for while Yabael's comet raged, the substance of Melqar had grown vastly quiet.

Melqar, last from the solar melting pot, Melqar the sun of midsummer dawning. He that fought with the Demon. He that had, for a time, vanquished the Demon. He that had, finding Azhrarn also a light in the sunrise, let Azhrarn go down into the earth and the dark. Or was beguiled into doing so, in certain stories. Or did so for reasons less and more obscure. Melqar who stole the voice of Azhrarn to speak with. Melqar who, when the fight was done, stood on a tower of Az-Nennafir with sightless-seeming orichalc eyes, and sheared the City through with a blade of whiteness let from his hand itself. But what then?

When Azhrarn lay in the Underearth, what of the angel who caused it? And when Azhrarn, salvaged by the fire of his garden, which might be of the essence of his own immortal fire, when Azhrarn retrieved his power, threw down his enemy and made him a lover again—where was Melqar then?

They covered now a notable distance, Atmeh and Ebriel, beating through the sky. The sun entered the west and vanished. The roof above went black and the moon—herself wingless yet traversing air—crossed heaven. The stars bloomed in their parks, which were only visible at night (for the stars did *not* move, as they had in Dathanja's parable). Through the dark, as the day, the angel and the demoness flew on. And when day came back, flew still.

For though either of them might have reached any earthly place instantly, in an eye's blink, the psychic shrouding about Melqar did not allow this. It demanded of them a slowness, an attempt. There must be arrival rather than mere advent.

No source describes the route. They tell of days and nights, sun, moon, stars, and distance. No road or geographic clue. Well, then. One cannot presume too much.

It was a high place, inevitably. It was a mountain in the middle of a waste or desert, which maybe, centuries before, had been the bed of an enormous lake or landlocked sea. Where the water had gone who could say, but gone it was, and only the mountain poured statically skyward.

Atmeh and Ebriel put down upon the mountain, just below the summit, and climbed to a platform that lay out under the sunlight like an altar table.

At the center of this platform, which was neither long nor wide, there glowed a kind of mound of faintly honey-colored crystal. But it was not that at all. It had been made from heat and cooling and the ethereal breath that flowed against the mountain's thin atmosphere, out of a creature which reclined there, and which had always breathed, or which had learned to breathe.

Under the shining quartz, Melqar. He slept deeply, he slept a sort of death. His excellence, in sleep, dazzled through the mound and seared the eyes. His eyes were shut. The extraordinary wings lay beneath and by him, framing him in the muscular feathers of gigantic swans. His right hand rested across his breast and gripped lightly yet completely, even unconscious, a sword of snow. It had formed from the light he had wielded, or from his own unusual flesh. The sword was Melqar, Melqar the sword. Yet, he slept.

"Is he waiting, perhaps?" said Atmeh. "For the orders of the gods. For something as crucial. For the end of earth."

Ebriel gazed upon the last of his kindred. Ebriel's face told nothing. Then his eyes half-shuttered themselves.

"Your second lesson is, as was the first," said Atmeh, "that the Malukhim may change. And they may pursue fruitlessness. And they may achieve nothing but a race, or a slumber. But the third lesson is also here, Ebriel, child of the sun. He does not start up, does he, this one, to fight with me? He grips the sword, yet does not lift it against me." And she struck the quartz three blows. "Wake and do battle with me!" But Melqar only slept in the sheen of the sun through honey crystal. He did not stir. "Ebriel," said Atmeh, in the voice of Atmeh. "The gods forget and that is all they do. Men forget, yet men remember even in forgetfulness. I am half demon, and immortal. I will tell you how I mean to proceed. I shall seek to lose my immortality, that fabulous gift for which men have murdered one another. I will strive to be only mortal. For now I know too much to learn the rest. And the rest I must learn, for it is so much more than all I know. It is my mother's blood which understands this. My quest, Ebriel, is not to be a goddess, or a demon. But to be a human thing which lives, and dies—and is reborn. To slough my immortality—will be to gain it. To search for true life, Ebriel, that is my hope, to find my soul. Therefore, make peace with me."

Ebriel turned from the contemplation of his brother. He opened his eyes wide and looked at Atmeh.

He saw a lovely girl, dressed in a blue garment belted with a cord of silvery metal, her black hair falling about her, and in her face the absurdity and joy of what she had said.

And Ebriel, for heaven was dumb and deaf and high above, raised his bright sword, and broke it in two pieces, and threw them away into the dead lake. But where they entered the earth, glittering waters bubbled up, and flowers came out like small suns, to look about them with their purple eyes.

Ebriel flew up into the sky, beating his wings against the lowest floor of the Upperearth, and he changed himself into an eagle then, and the sunlight hid him.

Atmeh walked down the mountain.

She walked over the bare tiles of the waste which soon might fill with water and flowers.

She walked some while, and then she made sorcery. A beast soared to the ground. It was the winged lion of her past, or another that was its twin, blue-maned and philosophical of face. "Dear friend," said Atmeh, "do you know me?" The lion bowed and licked her hand. Then she mounted it, for she was tired at last. And they, too, flew away.

PART
TWO   *Uncle Death*

1

ON THE SHORE of a sea stood a deserted temple.

Those that came there, and infrequently some did come to that place, descended a stairway of hills. The beach was of fine pumice, which glinted. The sole thing that stood up on it was the temple, whose domes were like a collection of beehives. Beyond, the sea surged with curious tides. From a distance it looked merely peculiar. But getting closer, you saw it was an ocean of cloud which foamed and creamily ran in and out on the shore. From some subterranean vent these mists poured up, or were now and then sucked down. On occasion, the tide was so far out that a hard bare pastry of rock might be seen, into which heat and moisture had formed the loose pumice.

Late in the day, under a pomegranate sky, a traveler moved along the beach and entered an arch before the temple. Under that vault, carved with maidens, camels, iris flowers, and dragon-winged bats, hung a bell of black bronze. The traveler rang the bell, which clanged.

But the clangor died away along the shore, and was forgotten there. The sea of cloud smoked. The sky deepened, and a star appeared.

Unanswered, but with no show either of disappointment or impatience, the traveler seated him- or herself (mantled, booted, it might be a youth or a woman) under the arch, and leaned upon a big stone bat there.

Presently the bat spoke.

"What do you seek?"

"One," said the traveler, in a female voice most musical, "who reputedly abides in this spot. A sorceress, that in these lands they call Kiras."

"Just so," said the bat. "Pray do not lean upon my belly. From time to time I become fleshly, and fly by night and feed. My stomach is now full of digesting mangoes and plums. You will, besides, find my left wing more comfortable." (The traveler obliged the bat. The wing was not more comfortable, but for graciousness' sake, she made no comment on the fact.) "For Kiras, she is here and I am her slave. She bids me inquire what business you have with her."

"The same that all have who search her out. You are her slave, she is another's, and that other the slave of one I wish to visit."

"Tush," said the bat, "Kiras is not a slave. She serves, and she that Kiras serves, serves also, yet *she* is more a familiar and consort than a servant, to that One you refer to. Who, in any case, is not visitable. I must warn you, everyone will take umbrage at your description."

"Unfortunate," said the traveler. And she gave the bat an affable tap. It fell from the arch and became fleshly alive, and chittered with relief at the transformation. In a short while, seemingly unremembering its task as interrogator, it zoomed, burping, into the twilight.

Shutters flashed open in a dome of the temple.

"Who," squawked a woman's voice, "rashly tampers with my creatures?"

"Invite me in," said the traveler. "You shall learn."

"Oh, some arrogant sorceress, is it?" cried the raucous one at the window. "Let you be instructed. I am twice your age, and am a paragon of my art. Besides, I boast a powerful connection."

"Well, well," said the traveler. "How pleasant for you all that must be. You need have no fear, then, to unfasten your gates to me."

"Overbearing brat that you are, can you not even penetrate one little door?"

"So be it," said the traveler.

And standing up, she walked toward the dome where the window gaped. As she did this, the very temple wall itself, with all its carvings exclaiming aloud in shocked surprise, flew wide.

Kiras, the paragon, withdrew. The traveler passed up the avenue and in by the wall, which closed at her back.

The temple was in foxy darkness. It whispered, perhaps only with the discussions of the carved creatures therein.

Great spiders, large and brachial as copper chandeliers, hung in luminescent webs from the roof, and stared at the traveler from a multitude of cool intelligent eyes.

"Greetings, sisters," said the traveler politely, and the spiders, who did not imagine themselves associates of Kiras, bowed. Moving each her eight furry arms subtly, they spun more light upon their looms.

But just then Kiras entered, bringing light with her.

Seven unsupported torches of red fire roared about her, to reveal she was dressed in snakes, which hissed, and that her headdress was the spiny skull of some monster dug out from the shore, but set with jewels for feminine vanity. In age, she was some twenty years. But her eyes were eldritch, and her voice uncommonly *loud*.

"Upstart!" began screaming she, for she was used to sorts of reverence. "On your knees! If you will not respect me, then you must my lady, from whose name my own is adapted."

The traveler put off her hood, and her black hair cascaded around her, and to the floor indeed. Demurely she kneeled.

The witch Kiras took note of the cascade, for such quantities of hair often denoted some superhuman power or cleverness. She nonetheless screeched, "Now say who you are."

"My name is Atmeh. I have a weird kinship with your mistress's master. He is by way of being an un-uncle of mine, my father being something of an un-cousin of his."

Kiras was now truly taken aback. But she squalled out:

"If you have fathers and uncles who are Lords of Darkness, why approach any of them through an intermediary?"

"To observe all proper forms," replied Atmeh, without

rancor. "My uncle, the kingly Uhlume, has never formally made my acquaintance. It is a fact, I might find a means to go instantly into his presence. But I choose to knock."

"It is all lies, that," quoth Kiras, who though she served the wily and the wonderful, was herself neither. "Take *this* for your sauce—"

And pointing toward Atmeh, Kiras produced a swarm of gigantic stinging hornets, which tore upon the suppliant.

Atmeh arose, and opening her hands, she gathered the hornets in a silver net. And the hornets were golden flowers, whose perfume filled the temple.

Then Kiras (a stupid girl, and no mistaking it) clapped her palms noisily together, and up from the paving there billowed a hideous beast, the precursor, maybe, of her headgear. It pawed the floor and rushed upon Atmeh.

But Atmeh sang a single note, and the beast became a swath of silk, which draped her in becoming folds.

Kiras now backed a step. But even so she raised her arm to try again, and in that moment Atmeh seemed to grow impatient. She spoke a word, and all Kiras's magic left her. There she stood, garbed in snakes and skull, and unable to summon a solitary mote of dust. Then Kiras lamented from fright and humiliation.

"You shall have your toys again," said Atmeh, "but for now, I have left you only one ability, to call your lady, Kassafeh."

"She will not heed me," cacophonously sobbed Kiras, on the paving herself now. "She is *his* courtesan, she is *his* very *wife*— She may be busy."

"Oblige me," said Atmeh, "by attempting it."

And she altered the snakes of the witch's dress to birds— and with much singing they all, every one, flew rejoicingly away and left her, naked and afraid, under her monster skull.

It was beyond doubt that, at this era, Death's methods had been revised. No longer, as in the legends, would he deal quite directly with humankind—or if he did, it was done most secretly. Gone the days, and nights, it would seem, when men saw him stride by them along the highways, and thanked their gods at the escape. And gone the days of bargaining, when, for access to some emperor's tomb, or in order to meet the reanimate form of one deceased, mortals sold a thousand years of their time, postmortem, to King Uhlume. Some odd happenings had gone on in the Innerearth, which was, or had been, his kingdom. There was a Queen Death also ruling down there, men said, Naras, that certain death-obsessive races worshiped. But for Kassafeh, who had been the handmaiden of Death, she had grown dearer and more dear to him. And the tale ran now that Death did not dwell below the earth, but somewhere upon it, in an unnormal house on wheels belonging to his beloved, or else in some best-avoided fastness—fashions change. Even in mythology.

Yet there remained such as Kiras, who were claimed to be in service, by turn, to Kassafeh, and thus some path for macabre commerce was left open.

As the blue-mantled traveler, Soul-Flame, Atmeh, had said, she might have found ingress to Uhlume's retreat, wherever it was, and burst in on him, but she chose good manners. Thereafter, though, she did not waste too wide a while on Kiras's utter lack.

Soon enough then, Kiras was in a closet of the temple one side of a lopped pillar, and Atmeh the other, and between them on the pillar-drum, a little wheel of yellowed bone upon a stand of iron. Kiras had struck the wheel and it spun, around and around, on and on. Minutes whirled away upon it, and hours.

Night had come and cloaked the temple. Later the moon bathed it, and the carvings splashed themselves over with the moonlight, the nymphs philandered with each other, and the camels munched the iris flowers—which bit them back. (And still the wheel spun, and Kiras sat one side of it and Atmeh the other.) Then the red forests of morning blossomed. The sun galloped up heaven. The temple carvings kept still. "We are stone," they told the sun. "We cannot move." The cloud lake boiled and purled under a heliotrope sky. (And the wheel spun. Atmeh sat like a stone girl off the temple wall. But Kiras muttered loudly as a yell: "See, she does not hear. See, see, no one attends.") In the afternoon all the birds delivered from Kiras's dress ran races in the ether, or began to build nests on the roofs. "We are still snakes," they told the temple, and they stretched and wriggled their long necks. "We shall lay eggs—what else does a snake do?" But the temple no more believed the birds than the sun believed the temple carvings who said they never moved—for if the sun now and then met the moon, she perhaps informed him of what went on by night. (And the wheel spun.) Then the sun set. Under a nectarine sky, far out on the cloud sea, one golden cloud appeared in the air. *And the wheel stopped spinning.*

The golden cloud drifted in and indoors, and came to rest between the two women in the temple closet. The cloud grew itself to be a woman, shawled in a golden veil. Only her eyes were visible. First they were dark, then pale and feral.

Kiras obeised herself. But the apparition of Kassafeh the Changeable-Eyed regarded only Atmeh.

"In the past," said the apparition, well tutored now, it would seem, "I did not care for your kind."

"I am also half mortal, rather in the manner of yourself," said Atmeh. "And besides, once also you hated Lord Death."

The apparition's eyes turned black, then violet.

"I did not come here to talk of myself," said she. "Your problem?"

"There is a hidden thing I would learn. Since it concerns mortal death, Death may know the answer. Therefore, I would attend him."

"He will allow it," said Kassafeh, or Kassafeh's image. "He has entrusted me to tell you so. He will meet you below, in the old place, his kingdom at the world's core. Do you know your way?"

"I am also half demon, *not* in your manner," said Atmeh. "While, in most things, there is more than one way. Which will offend him the least, please him the most?"

"Pleasure and offense are small items to such as he. But I believe it might satisfy him if you should go down to him as your demon self. For that is what you would be shot of, is it not, your immortal part, the very thing which lends you any claim on him?"

"Oh, Kassafeh," said Atmeh, "you are an immortal. That is your road. Do not begrudge me mine because it is unalike."

Then Kassafeh closed her eyes—upon the lids of which were painted eyes of gold that changed to green—and she dissolved.

Atmeh got up, and looked upon Kiras, who lay along the floor.

"Be kinder, Kiras. Recollect, for every seventy travelers that seek you, and that you distress, there may come another like myself. Yet not so temperate as I. On the understanding you will remember my warning, I restore to you your arts."

Kiras spoke softly then.

"I will remember."

And when Atmeh had left her, Kiras constructed a robe of crystals for herself, and walked like a dancer. But later, when the birds laid their eggs, she stole some, and these hatched snakes. . . .

2

WHAT WAS it, of course, but mere politeness when calling on a relative, to journey in family resemblance and name?

She had called down from the hills her mount, the winged lion with the philosopher's face. Then rode upon it to some spot deep or high. And there she drew upon herself the persona of Azhriaz, and she stamped her foot—or some say she pulled up a tall gray weed which grew there—and the earth cracked, it parted. And again mounting the lion, she spoke to it, and bound it by safeguards, and even by a garland of her own hair.

Then like a flung spear they descended.

Down, down, through galleries of rock and soil, through veins of water, mineral arteries, and the grass roots of all the world. Down, down, through a shadow and a sheen, through a sluggish cold lava flow which might have been a deadly languorous river—and which was—down, down, through the last strands of ordinary matter, bursting the final links with day or time or the mundanely beating heart of life—

And made landfall as a spear would, hitting firm upon a surface ground, in Innerearth, the sphere of mortal death—if only in ignorant parlance.

Innerearth was the way it always was and had always been. Nothing new, or seldom, was ever said of its general landscaping. There is sometimes virtue in repetition.

Atmeh-Azhriaz stood upon a plain, and about the plain were rolling hills with, here and there, another plain beyond, and on the left hand a range of cliffs. The color of this land was gray; the plain was a desert of gray dust, the cliffs were lead, and the hills stone, and where their shadows fell they were black. Above, the sky of Innerearth was dull white and might be described also as comfortless—though none of the prospect was remotely cozy. No sun or moon or stars were lit here. The sky did not change, only occasionally a cloud blew over it like a handful of cinders. And though, through the deaf blankness, there sometimes sounded thundering wind, it had barely the strength to push these clouds before it.

Now, the winged lion, whatever it actually was, remained a creation of the earth above, and so it was a sort of inverted ghost in the deathland. It cast no shadow, and its step could disturb none of the gray mosses or dull pebbles underfoot. It seemed, too, disinclined to fly, as if it doubted the miserable sky could keep it up, and certainly there were no air currents sturdy enough to fill its wings.

Atmeh spoke soothingly to the lion, and it set about a walk, she riding its back, cross-legged between the folded wings. And she, being what she was, cast a shadow, as the cliffs and hills did, long, slender, and pitch-black upon the ground.

They walked a long while. The sky did not alter; there was no specific time.

They roamed between the cliff shades, and over the stony hills, and by a sky-white river on whose edges grew petrified poppy husks, depressingly gray as all the rest.

But eventually, having followed the river a whileless while, there began to be visible on the horizon a bank of dark cloud, which was not cloud at all, nor stone, nor shadow. But a forest, and of full-blown trees.

Illusion was previously rife down here. It had been the key and the clue to survival for those living corpses who were the guests of Lord Death. From thin air might be constructed anything. Yet to one such as Atmeh it was amply evident that neither illusion, delusion, nor delirium of any kind had made the forest. It had seeded. It had matured. It *lived*.

Lion and lady entered the trees.

There were black pines, whose quills bore the faintest blush of blueness, cedars denser black, but vaguely bloomed with viridian. Silver-gilt and prone to clink, yet they were cones that hung on the boughs or littered the ground, where a dark moss grew that budded swarthily.

Among the live thickets too were stirrings. Birds showed themselves that did not fly, but stalked along the branches. They were like ravens, but their beaks were flushed, their eyes prisms. And where the trees thinned, you came on pools of sea-green water—and from the basins pairs of leopards were drinking, in coats of black spotted by broken rings of gold. They raised their canine masks at the lion, which growled, then lowered them to drink again. In their ears were precious drops the color of the water. And once a peacock crossed the forest floor before the rider and her mount, with eyes of polished turquoise in his tail. They were the immortal animals of Simmurad, maybe. Had Uhlume not presented them to Naras, when he razed the city?

The trees soon divulged a road of grape-dusk marble, which spilled into a valley beyond. Pylons towered by the road, obelisks of smooth translucent black, and on either side, and throughout the valley, such standing stones arose, some in groups, others isolate, and between and around

twisted marble avenues. The valley otherwise was all lawn,
a turf of blackest green, like ivy. Black mansions clustered
about on it, where the pylons did not. It might be a town of
the dead. At the valley's farther end, up under the mindless sky, was a sable palace with inky columns braceleted
by gold, and slashed in lizardine windows and windows
salamander. Albino poplars ranked like white feathers by
the walls. There were gardens blotted by scarlet plants,
and trees whose fruit looked poisonous. Before the high
portico a three-legged stand of silver held a bowl of fire,
which streamed up smut, ceaselessly and seemingly without purpose.

In the stories, Death's domicile had been a simple
affair. But in the stories of Naras, neither had her palace
been this way. For she recreated the substance of her
earthly life here, or had meant to, they said. Possibly the
essential nature of Innerearth had corrupted her work. Or
had she grown enamored of the new state over the old?

Naras had outstayed her thousand years, so much was
positive. Naras, Queen Death—what was the modest title
Narasen of Merh, to that?

Atmeh paused above the valley. A tributary of the
blanched river ran before the palace, and the palace
reflected in it, and the fire-smut the windows, the poplars.
Nothing moved about the house, nor in the town. If all the
prior guests had departed, no more had been garnered.

Atmeh urged the lion on, down the marble road.

As they passed, not a grass blade shifted.

At the river, Atmeh dismounted. She tethered the lion by
sorcery to the limb of a venomous damson tree. As she
walked on alone, the insolent fruits of these trees fell into
her very hands, to tempt her, but she only let them go. She
crossed the river by walking on the water, and when she
did so, two or three of the poplars bowed down to her. The
liquid itself smoldered at her footsteps. Conversely, the
smoking fire at the door went out.

Ebony inlaid with ivory, the doors. They swung inward,
and Atmeh entered the silent hall of her un-uncle, King
Uhlume, Master of the Dead, one of the Lords of Darkness.

Yes, there would seem to have been a compromise. The
hall was this way: Grim stone hung with the pelts of things

which could not die (somehow), banners from wars unfought (surely?), burnished weapons, carpets and draperies that delicate fingers of earth had woven and embroidered, their dyes oddly altered, their patterns changeable—

The floor, like the doors, was inlaid with ivory, but this was the internal scaffolding of men and beasts and fishes, tibias, ribs, pelvises, craniums, the last with gems in their eyes.

Between pillars girdled gold, the court of Death, men and women young and antique together, posed to gaze at the one who now came in—but through the bodies of these courtiers, as through the floor, you might see—not to a skeleton, but to an emptiness. They were phantoms, these lingerers. Souls and flesh, both were gone, and the psychic residue had worn thin as old gloves.

However, at the hall's far end, a quarter of a mile perhaps from the door, rose two mighty chairs of whitest bone. Bone-white hounds lay at their carven feet, and black hounds, and one hound that was pastel blue.

In one chair sat a woman, and in the other a man. She wore a gown the color milk would be, if it were blue. Her skin was black as black would be, if black were blue. Her eyes were lighter blue, but that was the whites of them, and at their centers shrilled infernos of yellow. On her grape-purple hair—like the marbles and windows—was a queen's diadem, and like the pillars she was ringed by gold, save her right hand, which was as much a skeleton as anything sunk in the floor. This then, Naras, Queen Death.

But in the other chair was a man of the blackest skin, the whitest hair, clad in white and unjeweled. His eyes were two tears, two openings into bright fog, two nothingnesses—

"Lordly Uncle," said Atmeh, "I extend my homage."

"Despite your misapprehension of our relationship," said Uhlume, "you are well-mannered. You did not learn it from the Vazdru."

"No," said Atmeh. And she bowed (another slender poplar), in parentheses as it were, to Naras. But Naras only glared.

"What do you want?" said Death.

"Has no one told you, lordly un-Uncle-who-is-not? I
have confessed freely. I would become one of your subjects."

The Lord Uhlume, King Death, or alternately King
Uhlume, Lord Death, rested his black chin upon his black
hand, and looked upon her beautifully and with an icy
endless majesty. (In the other chair, Naras snapped her
bone fingers, once. When she did so, every one of the
hunting dogs disappeared, save for the hound of chilliest
blue. This dog, a bitch, she fondled. But that was all she
did.)

"You are the daughter of Azhrarn," said Death at
length. "And his demon blood it is which has made you an
immortal. This is within the present order of things. You
are no concern of mine."

"You are Death. Tell me how I may learn to die."

"Why do you yearn to?" said Death, leaning yet his
sculpted chin upon his ringless hand.

"To liberate my soul from my body. That my spirit may
inhabit many lives and be lessoned in these, and so join
the adventure all human souls have as their right."

"Men do not consider in this way," said Uhlume.
"Men shun bodily death with terror, and envy those who
do not perish."

"That is only the safeguard of forgetfulness. Enhance
your reputation by it," said Atmeh. "Make me mortal and
perishable. Greater even than your overthrow of Simmu.
Immortality's Thief—called also, sometimes, Death's
Master—to bring down a demon's child to the clay."

"You are hungry for endings."

"Not at all," said Atmeh, with a very melodious laugh.
"I shall live long. I shall learn much, even as I am. But it
is not enough. Metamorphosis is necessary. Will you grant
the favor?"

"Atmeh-Azhriaz," said Death, "it is not within my
jurisdiction."

"You refuse then."

"I do not," said Death, Lord of Darkness, potentate of
earth's core, "have the power to do so."

Then Atmeh turned to Naras.

"Lady," said Atmeh, "do you suppose he lies?"

It was, apparently, the part of Naras now to laugh. She

did so. The laugh, nearly inaudible, had a frozen heat in it. Then she spoke in a low voice that was, one might say, of the tonal value of her hair.

"You mention metamorphosis. Here is one. There has been a truce between us, he and I. We do not exchange chit-chat, but as you note, we present ourselves as joint rulers of this muck heap. And in the world, they tell often now of me. Death, they say, *she* walks on the battlefield. Death, they say, I met *her* in the marketplace. Behold," said Naras, stooping forward a little, "I might have left this stony midden centuries ago, to partake of that adventure you hanker for, that savage flight of souls through witless birth-and-death and birth-and-death-and-birth. But I was cheated of the life I valued, my life as Narasen. And now I have assumed it here, and here I will live it and queen it, till sated—which shall not be for a while yet. As for him, this one, this uncrowned Master of Death, you will find he has lost interest in grave matters. He skirts the plague ships and the war zones, he rests on silken beds, not all inanimate, avoiding tombs. Is that not so, O black vulture?"

Uhlume glanced at her. Then his eyes returned to Atmeh. Now, they were like opals. They had sight and might be seen. There were, most oddly, dreams of color in them. Changeable. (Like Kassafeh's?)

"It is so," he said.

Atmeh looked at Death.

"You say you will not or cannot aid me. But you yourself—"

"No more," said Uhlume, gently. "You perceive, if I abdicate, I leave a worthy and practiced successor behind me."

Now, it was a bizarre conversation, this, if it is to be credited (be sure, it is credited). But there is this to be assessed. If the state of death were only interim, and men, spiritually eternal, never died save in the flesh, Death, even his symbol, had ultimately no function. Why should he not, bored and wearied by those deadly millennia, take up other pursuits?

"Then, Uncle," said Atmeh, "I will wish you joy of your new *life*. And go elsewhere to seek mine."

But Uhlume stretched out his shapely hand, and Atmeh, an immortal still, was able to take his hand in conscientious farewell. A mortal, naturally, would have died of it instantly.

Atmeh therefore vacated the hall of the palace of Queen Death, where Uhlume had thought fit to receive her. And as the phantoms of Uhlume's long-departed courtiers fluttered about her, Atmeh brushed them off like cobwebs.

No sooner was she outside under the bleak sky than something came bodily yelping and rushing after her. It was the blue hound. It ran to Atmeh, and ingratiatingly panted. Then it cried in a young girl's voice: "Do not abandon me, O mistress of astonishments—deliverance!"

"Can it be?" said Atmeh, questioningly.

"I am Lylas," whined the bitch-hound, "once an enchantress, now ignominiously bound and *kenneled* here by that *woman*, who, for all my pains on her behalf, continually ensorcels me into this image, to tickle her sadistic whim."

"From what I have heard of you," said Atmeh, "might that not be just?"

"Like all great ones," snapped the hound, "you are a dolt. Too feebleminded in your pride to see that if you were to help me, I might be of use to you. I might tell you the answer to your riddle. For I am cunning Lylas still, I am winsome and witty and pretty and *myself*."

"I commiserate, but will promise you no help. For yours to me, you have already given it immeasurably—for by your very words I discover some answer does exist, which I had come to doubt."

At that Lylas leapt and pawed at Atmeh's skirt, and licked her wrists, until the lion, still detained at the damson tree, growled and beat its wings.

"Let me give you all the answer! It is such an easy task. There are mirrors here which show everything of the world, what passes there, who does what. Sometimes I glimpse in them, and I am so astute, learn much in a second." So whimpered poor Lylas, dropping away. "Let me be useful. Then reward me."

Atmeh laid her hand upon the blue bitch's anxious brow.

"I can allow neither. Your path is not mine. Your punishments and rewards not mine to render."

"Cruel foulness," said Lylas, trying now, regardless of the lion, to take off Atmeh's fingers, and unable. "Your filthy sun-damned race were tricksters ever. And you are mad besides. Be accursed with them, all madmen and demons." And hurrying to the silver tripod, where the fire had begun to smoke again, Lylas boyishly lifted her leg against it. She had always been something of a slut. This attended to, she loped back indoors to fawn upon her tormentor, Naras.

But Atmeh, having untied the lion, remained to walk the empty town of the dead, in thought.

She hesitated at last on a garden slope where poppies flamed, and after a little, she plucked one. For she had heard there was an answer to the riddle of immortality's ending, that the task was easy, and she—mad.

3

SHE COULD know almost anything, Atmeh, but not all. Her very quarrel with her condition was that she knew too much to learn as the innocent may, or the infant, or the sagacious one who sees he is a fool. Yet, by some law of the earth's, or the gods', when they had bothered to make them, the library of a sorceress's mind, or a demon's, lacked here and there a vital volume. The way to rebirth she must find out.

But for the other business, it was child's play.

One evening therefore, as the stars were coming out, there entered an impoverished little village between some hills a starry maiden riding on a lion with wings.

"Look! Look!" outcried the populace of the village. "It is the king's youngest wife."

"Or perhaps it is a demon," ventured a few of the poorest and silliest inhabitants, and were immediately ridiculed and put to merciless scorn.

Atmeh rode down the street of the village, between the sad huts. A sick dog lay by the muddy well. It had assisted the village in hunting, but now it ailed they had decided it must be killed and cut up for its meat—but no one had yet had the heart to do it. Atmeh made a graceful pass above the dog with her white hands. The dog sprang barking to its feet. It was strong and healthy, and would live for a hundred years.

"A sorceress," said the villagers, as one, and came toward her warily.

But Atmeh spoke a word or two to the village, its stones and mud bricks, and the well, and the fields beyond. To the yards she spoke, where the pots were stacked, and to the spaceful larders, and the orchards, and the three goats, and the very air. Once she had turned cheeses to jewels to content Azhrarn. She knew better now. Every store overflowed, every field wildly burgeoned, every flaw and hole was sealed, new shirts, new roofs, new shoes . . . or, that is to say, the old ones, as they had been, before years of wear wore them. The goats were friskily getting under the billy, and the billy obligingly filling each with baby goat inside the hour. The well had water sweet as wine. The jars of sour wine indoors were fit for the king, and too good for him, indeed. While in the air hung a fragrance and a balm. It would come to be, in the rescued dog's twenty-fifth year, that this place would be famous in the region for its curative properties, and sufficiently prosperous it had lent money to the king's sons, so that—in the dog's thirty-fifth year—a man of the village would himself be made the king.

For now, when the village had done congratulating itself, it applied to Atmeh. Why had she performed this kindness?

"You also," said Atmeh, "unasked, and with no suspicion of return, have done a kindness to a stranger, a kinsman of mine."

Wondering, the villagers looked at each other.

"There has only been one stranger, saving yourself, since my granddam's time. An insane mad lunatic, who is in a desperate mad insane state in the ruined cot up the hill. It could not be of him you speak."

But it was, of course, of him.

They had come on him seven seasons before, or longer, for their method of telling time was somewhat inventive. The goatherd who drove the village's herd of three goats— soon to be increased to thirty—had been terrified on the hills by a sudden howling and a lumbering shape which accompanied it. Even as the herder turned to run, the horror stumbled and fell down, slavering and cawing and kicking its legs at heaven. Then it lapsed. It lay as if dead. And the goatherd inquisitively went to see.

The felled thing looked to be a man of eighty years, skinny and wasted, his head and face quite lost in matted hair representing all colors and all earthly dirts. Naked he was, and by this nakedness, the goatherd beheld that his life had not been tranquil. Many dreadful acts had been performed against him, beatings and whippings, and impalings by pikes, and even there seemed to have been attempts to hang him, to brand him, to put out his eyes and lop his ears, and to deprive him of his manhood. These forays, while they had left fearful scars, he had somehow survived intact. (And it had seemed later on, to the women of the village, that in his youth the maniac, for such he proved to be, was not uncomely.) Yet the madness, and the raving that was on him always while he had the strength for it—they did not abate. There was no means, in the village, to try to set him right. This they saw from the start, as they did with their own who sickened. The first day, the goatherd went to fetch his brothers, and when they returned, they met the madman on the track, revitalized, yodeling and jumping and rending himself, while gnashing his broken fangs. But once more, his failing vigor could not hold up the paroxysm indefinitely. Soon he crashed down again. They bore him to the empty cot. Here presently they shackled him, for fear of what he did to himself when able, and might also do to them.

So, he became the village's property.

When he was quieter, or unconscious, they would clean his hurts and cover him with straw and their own ragged quilts. If he roused, and would let them, they spooned broth into his writhing mouth. There was a girl of the village who had a sweet voice, and she would go to the cot and sing to him, and it soothed him, the madman, to hear her. And in the spring, she took white blossom and laid it by his face, and in the summer she brought him roses with the thorns removed, so he would not harm himself, he who had torn out his own hair and clawed his skin— "She is a little touched herself," the village said. "She understands him." But then a famine came to the village, which meant that instead of each man having nothing, he then had less than nothing. And in that time, the girl died. That night, under the crisp mockery of the stars, the madman rolled in his chains and made a noise so unhuman, so desolate, the entire village thought it should itself be driven mad.

"And since then," they said, "he has been dying. Dying in great anguish. His energy is exhausted, for even when he screams now, no sound comes from his throat, and when he rolls and kicks, only the cot shakes a fraction, where before boulders would plunge downhill. Yet, though he dies, he cannot die. This we see. He struggles to throw himself in at Death's door, but some portion of him will not allow it. Or cannot. So they say the immortals are, who never die, if such even exist."

Then they conducted the beautiful maiden up the hill to the ruined cot.

"Here," said the village men, and opened the door.

The maiden thanked them civilly, and sent them away.

In the village street below, the women brought the winged lion bowls of milk and honey, and the children braided violets in its mane. There was to be a feast out of the full larders. As they lit the lamps and torches, and took from chests old instruments of music to string and oil them, they did not glance toward the ruin. "He is in her hands," they said.

Atmeh had sealed the cot by her magic. It was out of

time, out of the world. Perhaps it was only her heart, and not her magic, which had done this.

There was no light in the cot, yet there was light, fragile as starshine. It seemed to stream from Atmeh, from her garments and her hair, and, softer, brighter, from her eyes. She stood and watched the wrecked creature, tied by iron and wrapped in quilts. It was awake, and looked at her. It did not cry out, or attempt to, but its huge starting eyes, whites bloody and irises pinched away to nothing, strained upward into her own that were so clean and beautiful.

Lylas had said to her: *You are mad*. And from the positioning of the phrase, its coincidence with those other phrases concerning the riddle's answer, Atmeh extracted her cue. Fate was on her side. That being so, scarcely anything would be random. And because she had sloughed all the former angers, spites, resentments, dashed the dregs of bitterness away, Atmeh saw clearly to the earth's ends, and so found, and at the proper hour, the means, and also—nearly incidentally—the lover of her dawn.

Had he been parted from her? Even split into the grains and fragments of insanity, somehow had he not been with her still? Lotuses opening, that offered jewelry dice, petals that flew and kissed, water flowers that bloomed in winter frosts . . . he had loved her in her mother's womb, they said, crazy Chuz, Prince Madness.

And now, lying on the straw, in the last deluded delirium, under Azhrarn's curse, dying grossly as Azhrarn had decreed—yet immortal in the essence of himself, unable quite to die—thus, Chuz, finally. The hill trembled in its sheath of grass, to have such a circumstance taking place upon it. The stars above crackled in their dry dews, having no choice but to look down on this.

She did not say to him: "Do you know me?" He did not. He did.

And she did not say, "You deserted me. You preferred suffering's game to the music of love." He had. He had not.

She said, "Beloved." And she laid her hand upon the warped and raddled, hairy, bestial face. And when the bloodshot eyes closed at her caress, she offered in her turn her flower to him. It was the poppy she had plucked in

Death's garden. Its petals dripped, like the purest blood, upon his eyelids, his lips, and breast. All pain it took from him at once, this scattering of the flower. That was the secret of the poppy, which even to this day it has not been able to keep.

For the pod of the flower had been despoiled, the fruit of it. Atmeh and night together had drawn from it a tiny vial of bitterest juice. Like all the fruits of Death's garden, this too was poison. And this she offered to her lover.

"You have done all he asked of you. It is accomplished, and it is over. You have paid in full for a crime of which you were not guilty, as I shall hear you tell me, too, from your own lips, in the future. Drink now. Here is life."

But at the last, and despite everything, as she set the vial to his mouth, her hand shook. She could not help herself. And a drop of the drink spilled on the quilts and it wrote a symbol there of the demon tongue, probably an insignificant one—but it was enough. Azhrarn's bane apparently had an energy of its own, and outlived both the intention and the settled debt. Recollecting his allotted labor, the madman reared in his chains. He nudged the vial from him—it soared up in the air—and a hand caught it. Not the hand of Atmeh, but one she had clasped not long ago, black as a raven's back; blacker.

Uhlume stood within the cot, tall enough his head nearly brushed the rafters. He said nothing to her, but going by the girl, he bent to the struggling madman.

When the creature saw him, which it quickly did, the fight left it. Even madmen heard legends. Even madmen knew of Lord Death. It was excuse enough.

And when Death offered the vial, and in the vial the blood of the poppy which Death's own blood had made, the madman craned and stretched to meet it. Thirstily, greedily, he gulped the liquor down.

For a moment his eyes were only cloudy. They were glad, seeing in their blindness all the vistas sight denied. Then, as a clockwork stops, he died.

"I stole from you," murmured Atmeh. "Did I do wrong?" She hung her head, and her tears fell. "You have forgiven me." If she spoke to Chuz or to Uhlume, none will say.

But it was Uhlume who brushed away her tears with the edge of his white sleeve.

"There will be a night," he said, "when I shall come to you and offer you another drink and from another cup. But you will drink it."

"Thank you for your courtesy in that," she said. "But will you, then, be Death?"

"It may be I shall not. But still, for you, I will perform the office."

"The wheat grows," she said, "and is cut down. And again the wheat grows. Yours was a heavy task. But if you are only the chrysalis, lord, what will the butterfly be?"

"Ask that of all things. Nor exempt your father."

Then Atmeh laughed, like a child—for she would ever be a child, much as, *when* a child, she had seemed also ancient decades beyond her span. And like a child she embraced Uhlume, and Uhlume—he suffered it. And they say he smiled, but who can be sure, for even the skull grins cheerfully as if it knew something the flesh did not.

Yet so they parted, the niece and her uncle, for a couple of hundred years.

After their parting, Atmeh performed a very ordinary mortal deed. She bathed the body of the madman, and poured over it spices and perfumes. She laid the limbs straight, and combed the hair, and shaved the face. And when all was done, she brought to the body, by sorcery, the clothing of a great prince, the silks, the gems, and dressed it in them.

And there he lay at last, dead Oloru, or the replicate of Oloru, rather aged and emaciated, yet still a handsome man, even a king, it would seem, who had fallen on hard times.

And over this body, in its splendor, the village was afterward to puzzle, for like a petrified substance already long dead, it never decayed, but remained firm and wholesome. Therefore they built a tomb above it, with a window of crystal in the side. Those that came to take the curative air of the village would also stare in at the wonder of this cadaver.

"What can it mean?" they asked. "What can it portend?"

For it was, and is, often that way, with instances which mean and portend nothing.

But Atmeh had left the body at once, when she was done with tending it. She passed through the village feast unseen, and calling the winged lion, rode over the night sky.

They flew high up, near to the starfields, and below, the world unrolled its carpets of seas and shores, forests and mountains.

"I rule none of it," called Atmeh to heaven. "Listen to me, you peerless soulless gods, I rule nothing and no one, and soon, soon I will outshine you, for I will be a mortal. And one day, as you never can, I and mine shall inherit the earth."

PART THREE

The Lotus

1

WANDERERS there had always been. From the choicest city to the direst hovel, they were a likelihood, if not always welcome. Nor so much remarked, unless they sold wares, or knew scandal, or were sorcerers, or caused death. Atmeh then, a beautiful girl accompanied by a large lionlike dog—which some, but not all, claimed had wings—traveled quietly. It was true some also said this girl performed healings, and others declared they had been told of those who had found a dish filled with pearls when they had only given her a dish of milk. Others remembered she had told stories which children and the aged liked to hear. Still others recommended, "Do not get on her wrong side." But not many had been inclined to do that. Those who did were unsuccessful in any case. For example, rich landowners who chased itinerants off their estates with

dogs discovered their dogs would only adore this one. In
places, persons entreated her to stay, for no reason but that
the look of her lifted their spirits. Yet she never remained
anywhere for long. In her diligent practice for humanness
and mortality, she would eat and drink, she would learn
weaving and the care of plants by simple means, and she
would take up and rock in her arms this baby or that, the
rich woman's infant wrapped in velvet, the naked one
raised from the warm ashes of the fireside in some cave
where the poor subsisted. And these children did well, as
if those slim arms, fine hands, had imparted to them
something rare. Yet now and then, despite all that, there
were those thought they saw the young girl flying about in
the evening sky on her dog. And now and then too, the
many men who fell in love with her came asking for her as
their lady, or their wife, and these, gently, she put aside,
though to a handful she granted her favors, but only in a
woman's way: She shielded them from demon lovemaking, for they must be content with mortal women after,
and she too, one day, content to be such women herself.

In this manner, time moved on, and late summer came,
a great glassy heat, into the land where Atmeh wandered
with her dog-lion beside her.

On a rosy afternoon, as Atmeh walked along a dusty
path, a child of, perhaps, seven years appeared before her,
a boy raggedly dressed and clumsy of feature, but with
hair of rose-gold like the sky. On either side the hills went
up and rills of water glittered down, but ahead the way ran
flat and broad with nothing on it but dust, and light, from
which the child seemed to have been formed.

"Luminous mistress," said the boy, bowing to the earth,
"there lies before you, three miles distant, a humble village. Do you journey there?"

"Perhaps," said Atmeh.

"My master," said the boy, "who has heard of you, for
you are famed, trusts you will pause in this village. He
may then elect to meet you there. In token of which he
sends you this."

And the child came to her and offered her a single tiny
seed.

Atmeh accepted the seed.

"And may I pat your dog?" asked the boy.

Atmeh assented. So he patted the lion with the partial illusion of dog upon it. (And the lion wagged its tail.) Then the boy vanished, becoming only dust, or light. But the seed lay hard and still in Atmeh's palm.

Atmeh continued along the path, and after three miles came to a gap in the hills and the village. It was a small one, but prosperous, well used to travelers, but kindly careful of them. It welcomed Atmeh in, and as the dusk fell, spread out a banquet, under the stars which hung overhead thick as grapes on a vine.

And it seemed the village knew that here was a witch, for it prompted her eagerly to perform feats. So she did such things as might be pleasant, and which were the stock in trade of what they thought her, doubling and trebling the quantities of food, turning water to wine, causing lights to burn in midair, and strange visions to dance and to foretell interesting happenings.

But of the one who had said he might meet her in that village, the boy's master, she saw no sign. And presently, when she looked for the tiny seed, it had crumbled into nothingness, less substantial even than dust, or light.

Next day Atmeh left the village. She climbed up a steep hill, the dog-lion trotting at her side.

As the afternoon was drawing out toward sunfall, Atmeh came upon a grove of wild orange trees beside a pool. And by the pool stood a youth, about thirteen years, waiting for her it seemed. He was of a staid appearance, but well dressed, like a merchant's son, yet his hair was his only jewel, a lustrous rosy blond.

"Iridescent mistress," said this youth to Atmeh, bowing to the earth, "there lies before you, three miles distant, a proud town. Do you journey there?"

"I wonder if I do," said Atmeh.

"My master," said the youth, "who has heard of you, for you are illustrious, trusts you will linger in this town. He may then elect to meet you there. In token of which he sends you this."

And the youth came to her, and offered her a single pale bud on a single slight stem.

"I looked for your master last night," said Atmeh.

But she accepted the bud.

"And may I pat your animal?" asked the youth. "Which is not a dog at all."

Atmeh assented, so he patted the lion, which had less than usual of the disguise of a dog upon it—and which purred. Then the youth vanished, becoming, it seemed, another of the orange trees. But the bud lay warm and still in Atmeh's palm.

Atmeh continued along the slope, and in something less than three miles, she crossed the brow of the hill and saw the town below. It was indeed a proud one, and let her in only after some interrogation, though the sun was by now sinking.

As the dark came, Atmeh entered the marketplace, where the storytellers had put up their awnings and sat under their colored lamps. Here the girls of the night also sat, in rows, beneath bold torches, with copper rings in their ears and cornflowers in their hair. Atmeh took a seat not far off, upon the ground, but she lit no light for herself, though a light did seem to be there, where she was. A man quickly approached and asked her if she was a whore or a fortune-teller or a teller of tales. "None of these," said Atmeh, "yet we are of a brotherhood and a sisterhood. For we deal in magic, all these, and I."

"How is a whore to be magic?" scoffed the man.

"Go lie with one, and you will see," said Atmeh.

At this, the girls under the torches became interested in Atmeh in an amiable way—before they had suspected a rival, and some had been plotting to push her off.

Gradually then, the night-walkers of the town came to sit about Atmeh on the ground, the stones of which were yet warm from the day's oven. The people debated and discussed matters with her, and sometimes they fell silent, and she told them stories that were not stories, and gave them news of their fortunes without divination, and seduced them quite, without lying down in their arms. What she said was amusing, too, and comforting. She spoke the truths which are forgotten, but which all men know in their hearts. These, being given them again, were like long-lost friends that they embraced gladly, if only for one short minute. "A man may say to himself," said Atmeh, "why should I trouble to do anything that is useful or compassionate for half an hour, when in another hour's half I shall go back to my former selfish, cruel ways? But there is all the more reason for him, then, to do good when he can. Ten years of evil do not cancel a single moment of gentleness or a solitary profound thought.''

Then a prostitute said to Atmeh, ''But what of such as we, who sin day and night?''

''What you do,'' said Atmeh, ''is not a sin, unless you think it so. And then it is. For who can say they do anything wrong by giving joy to another? And is it less noble to ask money for joy than to ask money for oil or silk or spice? But if you think always, *Oh how I sin,* and so despise yourself, you lessen and wound mind and heart, and there is no worse crime on earth than to sour the sweetness in yourself. For the sweetness comes from the soul, which no act of the body ever can, at the last, corrupt.''

As she spoke and discoursed, however, Atmeh became aware that someone, a mantled shadowy figure, sat far out at the edge of the large crowd that had gathered. And now and then he partly raised his head, and it seemed to her that under the hood his hair was like the sheerest gold. But he never addressed her, or came near, and finally the night waned. In the first ray of sunlight, Atmeh looked for him, that recalcitrant figure, and he was nowhere to be seen. As for the bud on the stem, it had crumbled into air.

That day Atmeh left the town. She walked through a valley thick with new wheat, and the lion flirted with the grain and played with her, just like a dog, certainly.

Beyond the valley there opened a wide paved road. No sooner had Atmeh alighted on it than a young man stood at her side, of perhaps three and twenty years, well favored, and clad like a prince, though his fair hair was his greatest glory.

''What now?'' inquired Atmeh, walking on.

''O mistress blinding-bright,'' replied the young man, bowing to the earth, then falling into step with her, ''there lies before you, three miles distant, an arrogant city. Do you journey there?''

''Not at all,'' said Atmeh, but she laughed.

"That is a shame," said the young man, laughing also, "for my master—"

"Who has heard of me," said Atmeh, "for I am famed and illustrious—"

"And also you are blessed and revered everywhere," embellished the young man, "and therefore my master—"

"Trusts I will pause, linger, hesitate, and delay in this city," said Atmeh. "That he may then elect to meet with me there. Or not. Or he may arrive and not exchange a word or look with me. Or he may arrive and greet me, and next abscond. Woe and despair," said Atmeh, and she laughed again. "In token of which," she added, "what?"

"This," said the young man, and he held out to her a lotus of the palest clearest honey amber, or a stem of damson-colored quartz.

Atmeh took the lotus. It had a fragrance; the sunshine lay in it like a fish of flame within an orb of fire.

Then Atmeh wept, only for a moment, but her tears fell into the heart of the flower—and the amber and the amethyst were gemmed by sapphires.

"You may," said Atmeh to the young man, "pat this lion."

The young man did so. The lion kissed him fondly.

"I will tell my master," said the young man, "that you accept his gift. And that I was kissed. If not by you."

And he was gone, into utter nothing—but the lotus gleamed and refracted in Atmeh's hand, and its perfume filled the day.

It was something more than three miles to the city, but Atmeh came to it at length as the sun was westering. Its towers and tiers rose up in the gold-leaf air—but Atmeh had seen many cities, and ruled over one that had been to cities as a year is to a day.

Yet this city was grand, and arrogant as the messenger had promised.

So, to get in, Atmeh, who might have put on herself the presence and adornments of an empress—if not a goddess, from consideration of the gods' thin hides—and stormed the gates by her glamour, Atmeh turned herself into a dove, and the winged lion into a winged lion as small as a dove.

And together they flitted in over the mighty battlements whereon were done in enamels just such doves and lions with wings, but each of these was the size of an elephant.

As the sun set and laved the sprawling city, its temples, its palaces, and its warren of slums, Atmeh the dove sat upon a high cornice and gazed about her. Honey and amber was the light, and damson the aftercolor that soaked upward from the east.

She flew down to the steps of a temple. Here, by day, there was a market. Now the commerce ceased, and brazen bells boomed out from above, summoning men to honor heaven. In the shadow of a painted column, Atmeh transformed herself again into a girl, and the lion resumed its size. None of the worshipers noticed this, as they hurried up the stair, on their way to plead with and bribe the marble images they thought were holy and might be persuaded to listen. Nor did they feel compelled to turn aside and ask this female figure, subtly clothed in blue, her dog at her feet, to help them instead.

It grew dark under the temple's heavy brow, and the sky filled with purple and stars. And then a man came walking up the stair, also cloaked in purple, with stars upon and in the folds of it. He reached the column, and casting off his hood, leaned down toward the woman there. And he regarded her. Somewhere a lamp was lit in the portico above, or else some other light had found their faces.

"It was not so very great a while," he said. "Do you remember me?"

"You? Who can you be?" she said. And she raised her face and her arms to him, and he, taking hold of her, drew her up. Any who saw them then might have been startled by their beauty, and by something more about them, beautiful also. But none saw them, only the paintings on the column, and the birds that nested under the temple roof, and the flame in the lamp there, and all the stars of the sky.

"Say my name," he said.

"Oloru," she said.

"No, that is not my name."

"Perhaps you are like another," she said, "a prince. But they say he is also ugly—"

"Never with you," he said. "How could anything be ugly, in your company? That one, half hideous, half deformed, when he approaches you, he grows handsome. Even his eyes, both of them, are golden. Look, do you see?"

She whispered his name. Only he heard it. His face was matchless either side, as all his body was (and the stars on his mantle were stars—not jabs of cutting broken glass). He also smiled. *Chuz,* she had whispered.

"But you are called Atmeh," he said. "How you have changed. Where are the tricks you worked on mankind? The lands are littered with those you have healed, and those who teach as you taught them, these philosophies of the undying mortal soul."

"Let us not talk of that. Tell me rather how it is I met you three times over disguised on my road, and why you teased me, appearing and disappearing, referring to yourself as 'master.' "

"I have served my term for Azhrarn the Marvelous," said Chuz, laconically. "Am I not therefore again my own master?"

"None to rule you now."

"Save only you."

They drew yet closer then, and their mouths touched as the mouths of lovers will.

They had been parted five or six decades, half a century, a little more—not long. But at their kiss, curious events took place. The birds started from the roofs and began to sing, as if to greet the dawn. And the bells rang in the temple top with no one at their ropes. And elsewhere mirrors turned to icicles, or melted, emerald necklaces were frogs—

"What is this madness?" the citizens exclaimed. "Some enemy is playing a joke."

And others, looking up from their high avenues and roof pavilions, pointed and said, "Now what is that? Some huge bird, or a bit of blown washing—"

"It is," said a child, "a man and a woman seated on a velvet carpet, and a lion flies beside them."

"Nonsense," its elders told the child.

And in the temple top one of the bronze bells whirled

off in a shower of fireworks, and roses rained, and all the unlit lamps were kindled.

"Some noble is holding a feast," said the elders.

How mundane life was. Only another evening, like all the rest. For even so soon the world was growing skeptical, and sensible, and sound, and blind.

But not for them, this dark of experience and reason. Unreasonably he and she, on the cloud of a carpet, magicians up in the air, lovers least reasonable of all—the world a garden through which they passed. Through which they might pass forever. Or not, as they chose.

2

THEY JOURNEYED then awhile together, or they left off rambling and made their home, now in a cottage, now in a mansion. They were wandering entertainers, musicians and story-makers, they were a lord and his courtesan, a queen and her warlord, or they were two cats, one black, one yellow, two birds of the sky, two lights that shimmered over marshes and woods by night. And there are the tales, too, of a black-haired man and a blond girl, for both were now shape-changers. . . .

And a year and a day, or one long elemental day that was a mortal year, this they spent together. They asked very little of each other, except to change stones into gold, to walk through walls for amusement—small things. If the gods noticed them at this date is not recorded, and probably they did not. And if any other paid them attention, he did not provide evidence of it. Azhrarn, the instigator of their woes, he had slept then woken, and his waking was more of a sleep than the sleep. Mortals were nothing to him. And of similar worth such royalty as Lords of Darkness. There had come to exist a saying in those times: *He does not look at us.* Those that said it hardly knew what they meant. But demonkind knew, and came up on the world like the moon, and toyed with them all the more for it.

But for the lovers, they were happy. Happy even after a mortal fashion, for they too understood their idyl could not last beyond its season. This was the bitterness of joy, that it must end, or else grow stale. Dunizel herself had written as much, in the desert shrine of Bhelsheved.

So, then, a scene may be pictured. A day like many others, gilded. A meadow curded with flowers, mountains along the sky's blue hem, far away yet visible, like the foreshadow of parting.

Atmeh is, on this day, a king's youngest, loveliest daughter. Eye-blue her dress, flowers in her hair. At her throat a collar of electrum set itself with a strangely wrought flower, amber, amethyst (which, they moot, may have been made for one Lord of Darkness by the Drin-folk of another). Before Atmeh stands a bold winged lion, looking as if it had stepped directly from the enamelwork upon some mighty city gate—whereas in fact such enamels have been inspired by sights of such animals as the lion.

The lion purrs as Atmeh sings in its ear. Then Atmeh claps her hands, and with a flaunt of great pinions, the lion tips itself up into the ether, soars, becomes a tiny daylight star, and is gone.

Atmeh sits down upon the earth to plait a garland of yellow flowers.

A tree nearby opens, and lets out Chuz, a poetic warrior captain mailed and purple-fringed. But the sword in the scabbard at his side is a mauve-eyed serpent waiting only to be drawn to terrify bystanders.

Chuz kneels by Atmeh. He is so handsome, so unlike himself as legends have him to be, you are not entirely sure it is not, after all, Oloru come back again. Yet he is certainly too fabulous for Oloru. Too absolute. Mortals never have this look, of flashing fire made cool and everlasting.

"Where have you sent your lion?" Chuz asked, as the girl set upon his golden hair the golden garland.

"Where it wishes. We have said farewell."

Chuz reclined. He lay down, and his head rested upon her lap. He looked up at her. No mortal woman, with such a lover by her, could have said farewell in turn to him. Atmeh was not yet mortal.

"Tell me," she said, as she gazed down upon him, "what I desire to be told."

"And what is that?"

"You know it."

"And did you," he said, "facilitate my return to you, only in order to get from me the information?"

Atmeh gazed upon him.

"Oh, tell me," she said.

"That you may grow old and die, and this exquisite skin, this hair, these bones, your eyes that are the sun twice over if the sun became the sky—that all this may decay, end, feed soil, and slugs. For that? My reward for telling you, to see you ruined as your mother was?"

"You did not," said Atmeh, "slay my mother. That I know. I knew when I forgot to hate her. When I loved her again, then I knew. But not how it came to be."

"I will tell you that," he said. "If you wish."

"Be wary," said Atmeh, "for if you do tell me that, you confirm the means to my own mortality. You note, I am already aware of it."

They had dressed as humans. Like two humans they rested together in the meadow, mountains about, heaven above, and earth below.

But how did he describe for her the death of her mother and his portion of it, and his guiltlessness—when for that guilty crime Azhrarn had insisted Chuz be punished? Not in words, surely. In a glance. By a method of silent speech even the Vazdru and the Eshva had not coined. Those that came after, however, had only words, nor now the words of the flat earth. Be patient, be attentive, the storyteller cries. Never more needful, these virtues, than now.

In the era of Bhelsheved, it had happened Azhrarn's blood had spilled in the desert there, three drops. Chuz had come on them, or sought them, and taken them up and

hidden them. Out of motives of mischief or admiration or
vindictiveness or all of these, and yet other promptings.
For if the intellect of such as Azhrarn is awkward to
gauge, how much more alien the brain of Madness.

But there is also this. By removing those three polished
obsidian drops of unearthly ichor, Chuz kept them from
the grasp and plots of men.

Now presently Chuz stood on the lake of Bhelsheved,
and offered to Dunizel, in a courtly way, an amethyst die,
which Azhrarn refused on her behalf. And after that, the
die, one of a pair of dice, maybe, had been found by an
insane sect who worshiped stones. And then the die—
acclaimed as a radiant stone—was put into a leather bag
about an old man's neck, and venerated as a god. But
presently again, when Dunizel had been brought out before
the angry people as the harlot of demons, and they debated
on how to execute her, and if they dared, Chuz had tried to
retrieve the amethyst. A scuffle ensued. Dice, pebbles,
and other objects dashed from the robe of Chuz. A shout
went up that stones were being thrown at the accursed
woman, and so other stones were thrown, with lethal
intent. Under Azhrarn's protections, nothing harmed her
until, along with all the debris, someone chanced to pick
up and cast at her one of the drops of Azhrarn's blood.
And that being the only item which could pierce his safeguards on her, it killed her outright.

Finally, when the child—Azhriaz—was alone in the
fane, Chuz appeared again and proffered her, infant that
she was, the amethyst, the very clue, it seemed, to her
mother's murder. And Azhriaz did not accept the jewel.
Not until Azhrarn had had his revenge on Chuz, not till
she was a woman and alone, did Dunizel's daughter take
the amethyst from that lotus in the swamps by the river
delta. And then ever after she wore it in a little cage of
silver at her throat.

She had begun to guess, or knew all of it. Chuz told her
freshly, and for the first, in the silent incomprehensible
speech, or by a glance, or by nothing save his agreement
that she learn.

Perhaps he had cared for Dunizel, or for Azhrarn. Perhaps he had been proud, and not liked mankind to get

power over a fellow prince. Or it had been just the madman's pernickety wish for tidiness. Chuz, finding them, kept safe the drops of blood. He stored them *inside the die of amethyst*. It was an eccentric jest, then, to offer Azhrarn's own property to Azhrarn, through Azhrarn's lover, and to be refused, spurned, put off. Then, as the storm gathered over Bhelsheved, Chuz, madly forcing the issue, bringing down the roof on Azhrarn's schemes, even mistrusting himself (well advised), gave the fateful jewel away. He gave it to the stone-worshiping madmen, his subjects. And the old man stowed the amethyst in a leather bag, from which he never would have allowed it to be taken for any base use. But, oh, Fate—if not Kheshmet, his essence, the happenstance from which Kheshmet had evolved. Prior to the jewel, the old philosopher had kept in his leather bag an amulet of gold. Gold, that was inimical to the demons, and to demon tissue.

The echo, the ghost of the gold, in such naked proximity, worked upon the drops of Vazdru blood. They began to move inside the die, to seek an exit. And Chuz, sensing that, in turn tried to regain the amethyst, and was unable. By the moment the die was scattered with other objects in the fray, a single demoniac drop had broken free from its prison. A nameless hand seized it, and flung it for a pebble. It did the very thing Chuz had not meant it to. And Dunizel, though not the soul of Dunizel, perished.

Two drops of blood remained inside the die. They had stayed there, and were there to this minute, protected by silver, about the neck of Azhrarn's daughter.

"By which you confirm," said Atmeh now, "that they are also the means to my death. As with my mother. That power laboring against itself, diamond cutting diamond. If I absorb that immortal energy changed to black stone, it will wear away *my* immortality. I will live long, and grow old at length, and finish. And thus I shall be free."

"But as you also know," said Chuz, "I sealed the amethyst. Only my will can give those drops of death to you."

"Or," she said, "the mere action of gold."

And she raised the collar of electrum with the lotus set in it. Under that, in the hollow of her throat, lay a golden acorn on a chain of gold. The gold had silvered; she had worn it some while.

"The die is here, within the gold. I believe it has already completed its task. But I was always half mortal. It was necessary to me, to learn from you and from no one and nothing else, that you did not kill my mother."

"Throw the bauble away," said Chuz. "Perhaps I lied."

"Azhrarn warred with you for a deed of which you were blameless. I too must be given my right to savage foolishness, the glory of self-denial."

And Atmeh tapped the acorn. It cracked in bits. Into her palm sprinkled brilliant lavender dust, all that was left of the die, ground between the struggle of the gold and two drops of ichor. These last appeared too in Atmeh's palm, black and boiling, sudden as meteors. Her hand flew to her lips. She took those drops of death within her mouth, on her tongue. She swallowed them.

Chuz sprang to his feet. Like a young man whose wife or sister has abruptly eaten poison.

All around, the birds had stopped singing. The flowers wilted. A shadow masked the sun.

"It is done," said Atmeh, looking up at him. She said it quietly, with compassion. "Now I shall live."

Prince Madness stood staring at her.

"You are Dunizel," he said. "She betrayed *him* with death. Now you do it to me."

"Did you not say to me, once, there is all time for us to meet again? And there is this life yet. With me, it has not been a piercing weapon cast—it will be mild, and slow. I shall live a few days longer, some hundreds of years."

"You will be a hag," said Chuz. His face was pale and serious. "You will die. You will come back to the earth in disguise, beautiless, ugly, diseased, witless, a woman or a man. Unrecognizable. This you wanted? To see my shoulder turned to you? To see the foul side of me, and that hand which sends men shrieking to the mind's brink?"

"Chuz," she said,"are you not the symbol of everything —the fair and the vile, together? And you, the dealer in lunacy, a pitying father, a rescuer, the kind physician who binds the bruises of life. The spirit of poets, and prophets, the lord of frenzies, religions, music, magic,

love, and wine. You are the master of the key to the inner
mystery. You are the breaker of chains. I am your subject,
my lord, as I am your lover. Always. And you will know
me, till the last star blooms and fades. You will know me
beyond the ending of the earth.''

Then Chuz kneeled once more beside her. Like two
humans, they clung together, and the cloud left the sun
and showed them there. The flowers lifted their heads. The
birds exchanged their singing gossip. What was the world
but passing things? What is it now?

''What will you do, Atmeh, as a woman?''

''What I have learned to do. But I shall love you
always.''

''Love is everywhere,'' said Chuz gently, stroking her
hair, ''and the death of love. And time, which is built of
the histories of death and love. Death and time I had
always conceded, and acknowledged. And now I see plainly
what love is. Not in you, pretty, mortal child. But in my
arms that comfort you for wounding me, in my hands
which soothe you for it, in my words which say to you, in
despite of me, Do whatever you must. This lesson I will
not remember. Nor shall I ever forget.''

And Chuz lowered his eyes, his matchless eyes. He,
magnificent, a Lord of Darkness, held in his arms now a
mortal woman. As Azhrarn had discovered, that was like
clasping the tides of the sea, the winds of heaven. How
massively the mountains stand, while low to the ground
the sand blows. The sand blows on and on. And then there
are no mountains, none at all, the sand has kissed and
whispered them away. And still, the sand blows on.

EPILOGUE   *Three Handsome Sons*

MANY THOUSANDS had come to consult the seeress, over the years. She was kind, and partial, but most significant, she was clever. She sat inside a shrine of sky-blue marble, far back in the throat of it, where the vapors rose out of the mountain. Perhaps these vapors were conducive to prophecy. Huge serpents dwelled, or had come to dwell, in the mountain, and these were the attendants of the seeress, smooth pythons and patterned anacondas. They did no harm, except sometimes to scare the unwary. It seemed the seeress-priestess had an affinity with snakes.

How old she was, the woman. Some said two centuries, or three. Others said she was a young girl of exceptional acumen, who had given herself the appearance of age in order not to tempt or anger gods and men. Certainly she had been in that place a very great time, for grandfathers and grandmothers remembered that their own grandsires had related how *their* grandsires spoke of her.

She had previously traveled the world, to its four corners. To its deeps, its elevations. Even under the sea, they said, she had gone. And it seemed she had married, or been loved, also, but this was normally only murmured of: She was beyond weddings and couchings now. Now she was here, a blown grain of sand come to rest.

A city ripened in the valley under the mountain. A temple blossomed from the mountain's side. When strangers stayed there, they asked, "To which of the gods is this fine temple dedicated?" But the temple was not dedicated to the gods. It was dedicated to man. And man was

worshiped there. In all his stages—as a seed within a
womb, as a baby, and as an infant. As a female and a male
child next, then as youth and maiden, woman and man,
father and mother, stoop-back and crone. And in the inner
cloisters mankind was shown in beauty, or ugliness, as
prince and beggar, as the leper and the strong, being
crippled or upright. One found icons of the artisan and the
warrior, the scholar and the slave, the king, the priest, the
sage. And, cut from polished stone, effigies of the enraged
and drunken, the mad, the stupid, the sly, the genius, the
artist, the murderer, the savior, the innocent. All these,
and more. And chiseled in the pillars here and there, or in
the marble of the floor, these words:

REMEMBER THIS: ALL THESE YOU MAY HAVE BEEN,
                    OR MAY BE.
REMEMBER THIS: IN EACH AND ALL
                    THERE BURNS THE FLAME.

They said she had made the temple, or inspired it, the
ancient seeress of the snakes.

Or perhaps she had only chanced upon the temple, and
been prompted to remain.

Or some said she dreamed it, and her dream laid the
foundation, but she was then a child in a distant land.

Whatever the truth, it was to the old woman they went,
the pilgrims, for consolation, after they had worshiped their
own image in the halls below.

The sun had set; there was nothing new in that.

The stars came out and crowned the mountain. Nothing
new in that, either.

The moon sailed up in the east. This had happened
before.

Down in the valley, where the poplars grew along the
road leading to and from the city, there came a tapping
sound. *Tap-tap, tap-tap*. The cattle had been driven home.
The travelers had found their lodgings. The troupes of
players, the journeymen—all these had made their camps
in the grassy meadows, under trees. And the native citizens were indoors. *Tap-tap*. Even the brigands did not

lie in wait upon that thoroughfare, out of respect for the temple in which they too, and their hungers, were represented. *Tap tap-tap*. Who could it be, making along the nighttime road, where the moon cast the shadows of the poplars down in stripes? Along the road, toward the temple, steady and intent. *Tap*.

After dark, the temple too was dark; only a lamp hung here and there. But one lamp was on the outer porch above the gate, and a young priest would sit there, to watch through the night, to look at the stars, to think, and in case someone might have some need or trouble.

He saw then, the young man before the Temple of Man, a hunched inky figure, formless as a blot upon the air, inching up onto the slope of the mountain like a black snail. And it leaned upon a staff and it tapped with the staff. And for some reason, the hair shivered on the priest's scalp. He stood and watched the tapping snail crawling up the slope, around the turns and curves of the mountain, all the while getting nearer. The priest shuddered and was amazed. He said to himself, *There have been night visitors before. True, it is not quite canny. But there is nothing bad in it, surely. Besides, I never saw one of them, and now I shall. And besides again, whatever it is, I am human and will live forever. Even if a dragon comes and tears me in pieces, the fire of my life it cannot quench. Let me be easy therefore, and brave.*

Finally the black being had tapped all the way to the temple gate.

There it raised its head, and the lamplight showed a seamed face, and lizard-lidded eyes. An old, old man, nearly old as the seeress, maybe.

"Good evening, sir," said the young priest, mastering himself with difficulty, for to the sense of fear had now been added a curious awe. But the old man nodded, and leaned on his staff. From under his hood strayed charcoal locks. One gnarled hand gripped the staff's neck, but the fingers of the other tapped on, upon the staff's head, which was in the shape of black dog, long in the muzzle, pointed in the ears, with two black jewels for eyes. Just so were the eyes of the ancient, also, when he widened them at the priest, black and brilliant. In like manner, the eyes of the seeress had stayed bright in her ravaged face. *For sure, this is another of her kindred*, thought the priest. And he trembled.

"I am informed," said the old man, "there is a prophetess here. Atmeh, she is named."

Then the priest sighed. The voice of the old man was so beautiful, so full of music and power, yet so full of darkness, too. The very sound of it swept through the young man, like water through a channel, like a drug through the veins.

"Just so," stammered the priest, "you will be welcome to go in, doubtless. As are the rest of her family."

"Her family?" said the old man. "Who might they be?"

"Well, she is aged, aged as trees and hills, sir. But it would seem, late in life—or through some magical means—she bore three sons, and by three different fathers—three kings, they say. But I have never seen them—" And the priest grew silent, faintly ashamed to have disclosed so much, and to one who presumably knew it already.

But the old man pondered. He said, "You must tell me more of this."

And it seemed to the young priest that very definitely, he had no choice in the matter.

So, he told the story, as he had often heard it, from those who had witnessed the priestess's three night callers. They did not, it appeared, ever arrive together. Nor were they at all alike.

Except that each was handsome, and each was rich—what could it be but that, in her extensive life, Atmeh had conceived and borne them? And that their fathers were kings, who could doubt it from their wealth and their demeanor? Apparently they thought it best to travel incognito here, and steal up the mountain alone, to pay their respects to their mother.

One wore clothes the color of a sunset, orange and gold, and his skin was brown as a nut. He was the most dutiful son, and had stopped by the most often. Sometimes even he was early, and several pilgrims had beheld him in the westering light, sitting on a rock at the wayside. And these declared he was then dressed as a beggar, the further to mask his regal person. The second son was less dutiful and had not been seen so frequently. He was blond of hair and complexion, wore magenta and diamonds, and his beauty upset the evening birds, who would begin to bleat like sheep. (And there were other things when he was about—doors opening in unexpected directions, milk fermenting to alcohol, the hair of girls plaiting itself.) An odd one, the second son. The third son, he wore pure white raiment, and patently he had been fathered by a lord of the black races. In the beginning he had never once called on his mother, being the least dutiful of the three. Yet, in recent months, he was noted often. "He is trying to make it up to her," they said.

The old man in black, when he had heard this recital, gave a laugh. It was melodious, but not good to hear, somehow. "And I," he then said. "What do you suppose I am? The lady's father, perhaps?"

"No, honored sir," said the priest, "since you are not old enough."

"Nevertheless," said the old man, "I will go in."

"Nevertheless," said the priest, "I am not inclined to prevent you."

At that, the old man drew close to the young one, and putting out his elderly claw, he touched the priest upon the breast, once. This touch was gentle as a kiss, yet from it such a rush of ecstasy ran through his body that the priest fell to the earth. And reaching sightlessly, he caught the hem of the black mantle to his lips. "Oh supreme master, you are surely a god, a loving god, you warm me like wine, like love itself. The sun by night—you are that sun—" But there seemed under his mouth and fingers only a fierce beating like colossal wings—

Coming back to himself, the priest gazed around him.

No one was by. The gate was shut. The lamp burned placidly, and all the motionless stars.

"Did I dream it?"

The night wind, browsing in the grasses, answered *Yes*.

"Yes," agreed the young man. "A dream."

The priestess-seeress was sitting within the shrine. By day, it was the color of the sky, but by night pale, like a smoky moon. Inside the shrine, the vapors floated and the pillars stood still, both substances with a liquid glimmering on them. Between, on a ledge, was Atmeh.

Her robe was blue and fresh in the light of the little dishes of oil which burned there. Yet she was bent nearly double, she had shrunk and withered, her skin to parchment, her hair to gauze. Only her eyes blazed on, as if the flame of life itself directly kindled them. They were keen, her eyes. A snake, which if it had stood up on its tail would have knocked the high roof with its skull, lay about Atmeh like a coil of costly rope, its head quiescent on her lap. Atmeh said now to the snake, "See, beloved. Here is one you must bow down to. Or he may change you into a cat."

The snake obediently looked, then, where Atmeh looked—into the shadows—and lifting itself, the snake let itself down again to the floor in a fluid obeisance. That done, it swam away across the shrine, and twined itself about a pillar, seeming to sleep, open-eyed in the fashion of its race.

A man walked from the shadows then. He was marvelously handsome, with hair that shone like blue-black fire, and clothed in all the magnificence of night. If any from the temple, or the city, any pilgrims or passersby had seen him, they would have exclaimed: "Why, we had supposed the seeress had three handsome sons, but here is a fourth!"

But there again, the faces of the three sons formerly noted had had a similarity of expression. They were enigmatic, perhaps, but benign. What expression did this fourth prince convey, so pale, so black of hair, in his mantle of black that seemed to hold the light of a thousand black-blue lightnings? Expressionless, this one, yet surely not benign.

"Lord of lords," said Atmeh, firmly, softly, "pardon me if I do not, as the serpent did, render you the correct homage. But it is a mortal failing, this stiffness. My spirit bows down to you, even if my frame may not. Will that do?"

"*Mortal*," he said. "There you are."

Atmeh replied, "And here also are you, my father."

Azhrarn's face assumed an expression then. It was one

of blasting contempt, or repugnance. But, after a pause, he spoke to her again.

"The Drin," he said, "take pride in their ugliness, for beside the unsurpassable glamour of the Vazdru and the Eshva, what is there left for them but to be hideous—a paltry comeliness would not suffice. The Drin, nevertheless, convey their rejected beauties by what they make, and everything they make, from the most complex artifact to a tiny pin, everything is exquisite. Yet when a Drin makes anything that fails to please him, which—to his mind—is imperfect, he destroys it instantly. It is a habit indeed with all demonkind to eradicate a fault. And you," said Azhrarn, the Prince of Demons, "you, who were made by me, from sable shade and clear nocturnal light, you, carried in the flawless vessel of Dunizel—I regard you now. To this abjection you have brought yourself. What should I do, confronted by that fact?"

"My death is near," said Atmeh. "You need only wait."

"Yes, he will have told you so, that third 'son' of yours, Uhlume. He is readying a tender stony cup for you. But the end I might present you with would bring you pain, I think."

"If that is your wish," said Atmeh, "to cause me to die in agony, then do it. I will not struggle or deny you."

Azhrarn's face altered. It was not friendlier, only different. He said, "With such words, your mother came to me, at the first."

"She loved you from the first."

"Love," he said. "Why pretend you have invented it?"

"Was I not," she said, "a demon, once? And did not the demons invent love?"

"Not the love you mean."

"Are not all loves secretly the same? A hundred flowers sprung from a single root. The body's love will teach the spirit how to love. The spasm of the body's carnal pleasure, forgetting all things but ecstasy itself, teaches the body to remember the ecstasy of the soul, forgetting all but itself, the moments of oneness, and freedom. The love a man feels only for one other in all the world will teach him, at length, love of all others, of all the world. A cry of joy, whatever its cause, is the one true memory of those wonders the flesh has banished. A cry of love is always a cry of *love*."

Then Azhrarn's face truly and utterly altered. He looked at her, and though he was the dark incarnate, yet darkness fell away from him.

"Little girl," he said, "I would have killed you seven times over, each death a death more vile. Humanity is my plaything no longer, only a toy for those that are mine under the earth. But you, you are *her* child. You are hers. You are Dunizel. Not mine. Never mine. Though I made you to be my curse upon the world. Though I made you to be myself. You are Dunizel, that I loved, Dunizel who was the moon and sun together. Your mother's daughter. I could no more hurt you than I would tear the stars from the sky."

Then Atmeh got to her feet, old and bowed and withered in her robe of sunny blue, and she went down to him, across the floor, peculiarly graceful, as a crumpled dying leaf has grace. When she stood by him, Azhrarn kneeled before her on the ground. He bowed his head, and she set her hands upon it, upon that midnight ocean of hair, that case of ivory bone beneath that held the firmament of his brain.

"Dear Father," said the crone, "do not weep."

He said, "That is the bane on me. I cannot."

"Each word you have spoken," she said, "was a tear."

She was so bowed and shrunken that even as he knelt, his head might lie upon her sunken breast. He laid it there, and so she held him, the aged mother with her fourth handsome son, and she sang to him then, as the Vazdru sang—for some mysteries had never been lost to her.

The substance of her song they do not tell.

Who does not know?